LINDSAY BUROKER

STAR KINGDOM

SHIP OF RUIN

BOOK TWO

Ship of Ruin

Star Kingdom, Book 2

by Lindsay Buroker

CHAPTER 1

PROFESSOR CASMIR DABROWSKI BANGED HIS TOE ON THE lip of the hatchway as he stepped into navigation. He was surprised at the size of the research vessel they were approaching, the display showing its cylindrical length and three large rings, all spinning to create artificial gravity as it orbited the frozen mooof Skadi. The Machu Picchu, its identification transmitter said.

"Morning, Casmir," Captain Bonita "Laser" Lopez said from the pilot's pod, the seat cupping her like an egg. "We're less than a half hour away now."

"How did you know it was me?"

"Nobody else trips going through the hatchways."

"They're not uniform. The lip on the hatchway going into the lounge is at least a centimeter higher, and there isn't one at all when you walk into my cabin. In engineering, it's like stepping up into a bathtub."

"Facts that do not negate my statement."

Casmir, not in the mood to explain that his strabismus impaired his depth perception, pointed at the ship ahead of them. "Have they responded to your attempts to comm them yet?"

"No."

Casmir could think of a lot of reasons a research vessel wouldn't respond to their comms. Unfortunately, none of them were good.

"They're not answering the Kingdom warships, either, if that makes you feel less rejected," Bonita said.

"I wasn't feeling rejected. Not for *that*. Give me a minute, and I can come up with a list that applies to life in general."

"You and me both, kid."

Casmir patted her on the shoulder.

He couldn't say that the bounty-hunter-and-smuggler Bonita Lopez reminded him of his loving and supportive physical-therapist mother, beyond their shared lack of interest in coloring their gray hair, but he felt a kinship toward Bonita since she'd helped him escape from Tenebris Rache and his nefarious band of pirate-mercenaries. Actually, the pirate-mercenaries were probably run-of-the-mill. *Rache* was nefarious. And apparently, Casmir's identical twin. A full day later, the revelation was still mind-boggling.

He wished he could talk to his mother about it, not that his adoptive mother would have any knowledge of Rache. She hadn't known where *Casmir* had come from, beyond whatever the placement agency in Zamek had told her, the agency that had disappeared when he'd been little. Still, he found himself missing Shabbat dinners with his parents and spilling the details of his life to them. He hadn't dared answer their messages these past weeks, other than a brief note to say he was fine, off-planet, and that he would explain it all when he got home. He was too worried that crushers would show up on their doorstep if whoever wanted him dead learned how close he still was with them.

"Remember those three Kingdom warships that were heading out to Saga to check on the destroyed refineries?" Bonita waved to the scanner display. "Two of them are still on course."

"I don't suppose the third decided the mission was boring and turned for home."

"It's veered off and is on course for the same research vessel you've talked *me* into visiting." Bonita gave him a frank look over her shoulder. "Perhaps this would be a good time to remind you that we didn't leave Forseti Station under the best of circumstances and may be wanted by the Kingdom Guard."

"I haven't forgotten." Casmir had personally disabled the station's torpedoes so the *Stellar Dragon* could escape. "How far away is that warship?"

"We'll get there a good ten hours before them, which gives us some time to figure out if anyone on the research vessel is left alive."

Casmir stared at her. "Why wouldn't they be *alive*?"

"You tell me. What else could explain their comm silence?"

"I assumed they didn't want to talk to us because we're... dubious."

Bonita snorted. "Maybe."

That, however, wouldn't explain why the researchers weren't speaking with the warship. Casmir rubbed his shaggy hair, contemplating the conundrum and wondering if Laser Lopez could wield trimmers. Kim had already told him that bacteriologists who'd endured eight years of higher education did not cut hair.

"Should we dock with their ship and go see if they're all right?" Casmir asked. "Maybe they need help."

"How would you give it? By fixing their robot vacuums?"

"I do have a few more skills than that."

"Medical skills?"

"Well, no." Casmir almost pointed out that Kim had medical skills, but she was a researcher, not a doctor. She made customized strains of bacteria; she didn't bandage owies.

"I know you were thinking of asking for a ride with those guys," Bonita said, "but we might want to abort this. If the crew is gone or dead, the Kingdom Fleet may think we're on an illegal salvage mission and give chase when we try to leave. Or they could simply comm the Kingdom ships guarding the gate to tell them not to let us through. I'm afraid the *Dragon* doesn't have a slydar-coated hull. But if we leave now, while the Kingdom ships are preoccupied with Rache's destruction of those refineries…"

Casmir blew out a slow breath. "I need to stay in the system and figure out who wants me dead. And then convince them *not* to want that."

"And remind me how visiting this research ship orbiting a moon in the armpit end of your system is going to convince anyone of anything?"

"It's not, but Kim's mother is missing, and we believe she was last seen in a video recorded on that very moon by archaeologists from that ship. She's my friend, and I have to help her."

Casmir also hoped the research ship would give him and Kim sanctuary. Bonita had burned some bridges and wanted to leave the system, so he didn't expect her to stay longer than it took to drop them off.

"Kim's mother, formerly a person and now a person's brain inside an android monkey."

"Technically, there was a transfer of memory and consciousness. No actual brain matter is inserted into the computer chips and circuits. That would be messy."

"Whatever," Bonita said. "How much trouble can she truly be in? Androids are fairly indestructible."

"Fairly." The crushers could disassemble one quickly enough, though Casmir didn't have a reason to suspect the archaeological mission had anything to do with the person or organization that kept sending the killer robots after him. "But she hasn't responded to Kim's network messages, just as this ship hasn't responded to our comm attempts."

"If she was last seen on the moon, can't we skip visiting this ship and go straight down there?"

"We can if you find an ancient wreck down there for us to investigate." Casmir had looked earlier and knew nothing showed up on the scanners.

Bonita shook her head. "If there's a ship, it's probably buried under a glacier. I can only imagine how a team of archaeologists found it to start with."

"The answer could be on the *Machu Picchu*."

"Think you could find it in ten hours before the warship arrives and arrests us for snooping?"

"That would be ideal." Casmir's nerves tangled like wires stored in a junk drawer as he glanced at the scanner display. He'd been cavalier about the warships when he first talked Bonita into taking them to the research vessel, but at the time, he'd been certain they would head straight after Rache and ignore her little freighter. He didn't want to get Bonita in trouble. *More* trouble. "Has that warship commed us?"

"No."

"Do you mind if we comm them?"

Bonita peered over the side of her pod at him. "Do I need to remind you that the Kingdom authorities know we fled Forseti Station with a bioweapon in the hold? And that they have no way to know that Captain Rache took it from us and that he may or may not be in possession of it now?"

"No, I have an excellent memory." Casmir smiled, though Rache was the last thing he wanted to think about. He pointedly hadn't asked if the mercenary shuttle, which had left the destroyed refinery shortly after they had, was still heading in the same direction as they were. "But in order to ensure the Kingdom doesn't think we're scavenging that ship, I can have a chat with the captain."

"Captains don't chat with fugitives. You'll be lucky to get the sub-lieutenant in charge of pots and pans in the mess."

"Just comm them, please. Let's find out now if I can schmooze them into working with us. Otherwise, you can drop Kim, Zee, and me off and head out of the system. I know you were interested in the gate mystery and possibly capitalizing on it to make some money, but there must be less-dangerous gigs."

"Trust me, I've been thinking about that. Fine. I'm contacting them and requesting a *chat*."

"How are you going to get them to believe we don't have the bioweapon and never wanted it in the first place?" Kim asked quietly.

Casmir jumped. "I didn't hear you back there."

"That's because she doesn't trip over the hatchway," Bonita said.

Kim ignored her and merely focused on Casmir, raising her eyebrows in inquiry.

Remember that message I left in the torpedo launchers that we sabotaged? he asked, switching to chip-to-chip communication, since he hadn't told Bonita about that attempt to save his own ass. To be fair, she'd been trying to collect his bounty then.

Yes. But what are the odds they believed it? The station tech who found it, if it was found, may have erased it without informing anyone.

Casmir shrugged. *I'm going to volunteer for truth drugs. That's probably the only way to clear our names.*

Eslevoamytal, the drug the military uses for interrogations, has an eighty-five percent efficacy rate. Some people can beat it, so juries are instructed not to base their verdicts entirely on testimony given under its influence.

Are you sure? It always seems to work wonderfully in the police procedurals.

She gave him the flat look the comment deserved.

"They're accepting our comm," Bonita said. "Get ready to schmooze."

Casmir faced the display as the view of the *Machu Picchu* minimized, replaced by a man in a blue military galaxy suit with gold trim. It was the captain, not a pot-scrubber, and Casmir recognized him. Given how few interactions he'd ever had with Fleet officers, that surprised him, and not in a good way. His left eye blinked three times in his habitual nervous tic.

"Casmir Dabrowski," the captain said coolly. "It really is you. I recognize the eye."

Casmir cleared his throat. "I'm so glad it made an impression on you, Sora Ishii. Though I was hoping you'd remember me more for my ability to annihilate your robots with my robots."

"It's *Captain* Ishii, and I remember you getting lucky *once*. I remember you crying a lot more often than that."

"Then it's *Professor* Dabrowski, or Scholar if you prefer the general academic title for someone with an advanced degree, and I was lucky in *all* of our encounters but the last. And for the record, those were victory tears." Casmir grew aware of Kim and Bonita gaping at him, but he couldn't keep from adding, "That's why they were accompanied by whooping."

Ishii's eyes narrowed.

"If this is how you schmooze people, Casmir," Bonita whispered, "you're not doing it right."

"The original Yiddish definition of that word conveys only that it's an intimate chat," he murmured while wondering if Ishii's bridge officers were also gaping at their captain in puzzlement at the odd conversation. The video pickup only focused on his face.

"I understand you've turned criminal of late, Professor," Ishii said. "Upset by the paltriness of your university pay?"

Casmir took a deep breath, worried Kim was right and that the message he'd left on Forseti Station hadn't been seen by anyone in authority. Or if it had been seen, it had been ignored.

"Actually, no. A pair of crushers appeared at the university, tried to kill me, and a knight warned me to flee the planet. The entire system, actually. Since then, all I've been doing is trying to stay alive and figure out what's going on. I'd love to tell you about it." Casmir worried Ishii would turn him down, deeming his confession too lowly to bother obtaining—it was true this was more a matter for the Kingdom Guard than the military. Hoping to pique his interest, Casmir added, "I also have some intelligence on Captain Rache that you may find useful. He blew up a couple of refineries, you may have noticed."

Kim stirred behind him, but Casmir kept his attention on the display.

Ishii's face hadn't been warm before, but now it turned to ice. "You'll tell me everything you know. From the brig of my Great Raptor 7 warship." His chin came up, as if he were bragging. Maybe he was. Letting Casmir know he'd gotten a toy far snazzier than the robots they'd made at camp that summer?

"The brig wouldn't be my first choice for a tête-à-tête, but I volunteer to answer any questions you have while under the influence of one of your truth drugs. I'm eager to clear my name." Casmir smiled as warmly as he could, hoping that twenty-odd years and a lot of growing up would keep Ishii from holding a grudge.

Any questions? Kim's text scrolled down his contact. *Such as that you and Rache apparently share faces? And all of your DNA?*

Casmir kept his smile locked in place, though alarm charged through his veins at the reminder. He hadn't forgotten about that, but it hadn't occurred to him that it might come up. Which it should have, since he'd just volunteered to share information on Rache's recent activities.

"I'm sure you are," Ishii said, his dark eyes closing to slits. Suspicious slits. "We'll be there soon. If you want me to look favorably upon your transgressions, present and past, you'll stay away from that research vessel. Is that freighter's captain present?"

Casmir looked to Bonita, silently asking if she wanted to admit to being present.

"Captain Laser Lopez here," she said.

Ishii snorted. "Laser, right. Listen, Lopez. That research vessel has just been declared off limits due to a medical quarantine. You will not dock with it and will not go aboard. If you do, we will blow up your ship and everyone on it, as will be our right per Kingdom Military Command Procedures, Chapter 12, Quarantines, Section 3, Failure to Comply. Do you understand?"

He was speaking to Bonita, but his icy gaze remained locked on Casmir.

Casmir didn't allow himself to squirm under it. Or believe that Ishii truly wanted to kill him. He *did* allow himself to realize that twenty-odd years might not have been long enough for memories of harsh emotions from rivalries to fade.

"We're not to dock with the research vessel," Bonita said. "Got it, Captain."

She made a circle with her finger and thumb that likely referenced one of Ishii's orifices in an uncomplimentary way, but she kept her hand out of sight under the console.

The comm closed, Ishii's face disappearing, and the view of the research vessel returned. The *quarantined* research vessel. Or so Ishii claimed. Was he lying or exaggerating the truth to make Casmir and his allies too fearful to visit it before the warship arrived?

"Transgressions present *and* past?" Kim asked. "What did that refer to?"

"Robotics camp." Casmir clasped his hands behind his back. "When we were ten, we spent a summer doing weekly battles with new robots we constructed and perfected during the days leading up to the competitions. Robot Wars, we called them. I loved it. We competed as teams. He was the leader of his team, and I was the leader of mine, so we sniped back and forth a lot. My team's robot won every week except for one—he's the one who got lucky that last week—and I suspected him or someone on his team of cheating, because we saw afterward that ours had been damaged, inside the casing where it couldn't have been an accident. He always accused *me* of cheating."

"I assume you didn't," Kim said.

"No, of course not, but thank you for assuming that. He's noble, from a rich family, and he was a snot at that age. Maybe he still is."

Bonita leaned forward in her pod and dropped her face in her palm. "Robot Wars. Of all the military officers in the Kingdom Fleet, I get one with a grudge against my passenger, due to *Robot Wars*."

A hum vibrated through the deck, and Casmir felt the shift in gravity as the *Stellar Dragon* increased its deceleration.

"Wait." He lifted a hand. "Don't stop."

"We can't dock now," Bonita said. "I'm not giving that smug ass a reason to fire on us."

"We won't dock, but there must be a way we can still check out that ship before they get here. What if Kim's mother is on there? As a droid, she wouldn't show up on a life-detector scan. But if they're going to blow up the ship…"

Casmir looked over his shoulder and met Kim's grave eyes.

"They said they'd blow *us* up," Bonita said, "not the research ship."

"If they're willing to blow us up for docking with a quarantined ship, I'm betting they already have orders to blow *it* up. If it truly is quarantined." Casmir shrugged. "It's possible he was trying to scare us, but I wouldn't think a Kingdom ship captain would lie in front of his crew, and it looked like he was on the bridge, didn't it?"

"It did," Bonita said.

"You may be correct, Casmir," Viggo, the ship's computer and a previous owner who'd uploaded his consciousness into the *Dragon*, said. "I just read the chapter on quarantines that the captain quoted, and the military has the right to destroy both military and civilian vessels suspected of a virus outbreak if the crew and passengers are believed to be deceased. I am currently reading no life forms over there."

"Wait, what virus?" Bonita lifted both hands. "This can't have anything to do with the bioweapon we had. We didn't come by here. Even if those vials and Rache somehow made it off that refinery, he hasn't had time to get over here either."

Casmir spread his hands. "I don't know. That's why we should investigate. Or send someone impervious to viruses to investigate."

"Zee?" Kim asked.

"Zee." Casmir nodded. "He's capable of recording what he sees. We can send him over without docking and disobeying Ishii, and he can come back before anyone even notices him. We'll run him through the *Dragon's* decontamination chamber just in case."

Kim closed her eyes and nodded slightly. Casmir doubted she'd wanted to ask anyone to get into trouble on her behalf, but she had to be worried that her mother might be over there—and in danger of being blown up. And then there was the mystery of where the rest of the crew had gone. What was going on out here, in the armpit of the system, as Bonita had called it?

"*Me parece una mala idea*," Bonita grumbled as she adjusted their speed again. "I should know better than to listen to passengers."

"Even delightful passengers who fix your ship's robot vacuums?" Casmir asked.

"Especially them."

CHAPTER 2

DR. YAS PESHLAKAI SAT SHOULDER TO SHOULDER WITH Chief Jess Khonsari in the middle row of one of the *Fedallah's* two combat shuttles. A harness belted him in, but he felt the g-forces shift as Rache switched from accelerating to decelerating toward Saga's icy moon, Skadi. Or maybe he was targeting the escaped smuggler ship and his quirky twin that nobody else knew about. Or even the research vessel orbiting the moon. Rache hadn't said anything of their plans or their destination, just that he needed his doctor along.

Apparently, he also needed two giant cyborg mercenaries and his assassin along. The hulking men in their combat armor took up the back row of seats. The man named Chaplain was Rache's size, barely over five and a half feet tall, and sat on Yas's other side, also in full combat armor, save for his helmet.

Yas hadn't seen the man in sickbay yet and didn't know if he had any cybernetic implants, but he barely looked human, with tattoos swirling and throbbing as they danced across his face with every movement. When he opened his mouth, sharpened metal teeth glinted where human ones should have been.

Jess's gloved fingers tapped restlessly on her thigh. Yas wondered when she'd taken her last dose of the trylochanix she'd stolen from sickbay. Knowing she was likely addicted to the potent painkiller and antidepressant had only disturbed him on moral and humanitarian levels when they had been on the *Fedallah*, a large warship with numerous engineers and numerous failsafes; now that Jess was likely the only one here who knew how to fix mechanical issues, he wished he'd spoken to her about her problem earlier.

Yas shook his head. With a murderer on one side, a drug addict on the other, and a bunch of gun-stroking meatheads behind him, he had little confidence in his ability to survive the near future. Whatever it would entail.

"Captain," Yas said, since none of the others had addressed their putative leader during the first half of the trip, "will you be briefing us before we reach our destination? Or telling us what our destination *is*?"

Rache looked over his shoulder, his hair covered and his face masked, as usual.

Yas did not point out that he knew what the man looked like now, in part because he doubted anyone else in the shuttle did, and in part because it was possible he didn't truly know. He'd seen Rache's twin brother, Casmir Dabrowski, but Rache might be hiding some disfigurement that had nothing to do with genetics. The mystery around Rache's origins puzzled Yas. The fact that he had some Odinese robotics professor for a twin brother didn't seem that significant. Especially since they apparently hadn't been raised together and hadn't known of each other's existence until recently.

Was it the fact that the brother was from Odin? Because it implied *Rache* was from Odin? Or at least the Kingdom? That wasn't surprising. Rache had a Kingdom accent, so Yas suspected his origins were common knowledge. What Odin had done to kindle such hatred in him was another story. Yas could only guess.

"With luck," Rache said, "we're going to retrieve something before that research vessel sends a team down to get it or that warship gets here and sends soldiers down to get it."

"That circuit board thing?" Yas asked before considering if Rache would be irritated that he'd hinted of the video they had watched together. "Aren't we assuming they already pulled it up? And it's what they were killed for?"

Jess eyed him curiously.

"That particular piece I'm sure they took. But I'm guessing there's a lot more down there." Rache tapped the control console, and the display shifted from the frosty white moon to an image of the monkey-droid holding up her find. He zoomed in until the screen filled with just the circuit board. Then it zoomed out, far out, and a great circular shape filled a dark background.

Yas had no trouble recognizing that. It was one of the twelve stationary wormhole gates that linked the Twelve Systems humanity had colonized two thousand years earlier.

"Shit," Jess said. "Is that a piece of one of the gates?"

"A piece of *a* gate," Rache said. "Probably. We're only going by the video. Videos can be faked. But I suspect this one was not."

Yas made a strangled noise. Yes, probably not, given that he'd pulled the chip containing it out of a capsule in a man's colon. The engineer clearly hadn't wanted the information to fall into the wrong hands. Such as Rache's?

Yas grimaced, not wanting to see that. He'd promised to serve as the mercenary's ship doctor for five years, in exchange for Rache saving his life, but he hadn't promised his loyalty beyond that.

"That first picture looked like it was taken in a ship," Jess said. "Is there a wreck down there, sir? A very old wreck?"

"We're going to find out. The *Fedallah* needs extensive repairs and to hide from the Kingdom warships while it undergoes them. It'll be four or five days before it can leave the system. I'm giving us that much time to find the wreck and anything valuable it might contain."

"I didn't know treasure hunting was one of your hobbies, Captain," Yas said, keeping his tone polite.

As much as he didn't want to bow and scrape before the man, he'd fallen into addressing him in the same respectful manner that his mercenaries did. It seemed safest. Rache always had an air of danger around him, like an old-fashioned stick of dynamite ready to explode if mishandled. Someday, when he did snap, Yas didn't want to be standing next to him.

Back home, Yas had been a respected surgeon and toxicologist. Until he'd been framed for murder. Here, he was… not nothing, but certainly nobody with resources and friends to stand up for him. It was depressing to admit, but all he had was Rache.

"I'll do much to keep King Jager from getting ahold of the gate technology," Rache said. "The Kingdom is *not* going to duplicate the gates, build new routes to new systems, and colonize and spread their antiquated beliefs and prejudices to the rest of the galaxy. Nor will they turn it into a weapon to be used against people in other systems. They have enough weapons already."

"Nobody knows who made the gates or how to replicate the technology, right?" Yas whispered to Jess. As a doctor, he wasn't the most up-to-date person when it came to space-travel technology.

"That's right, Doc," she replied, not bothering to whisper. "Some people think it was aliens that have been hiding ever since humans have had telescopes strong enough to see other planets." She lifted her hands, fingers curling like claws, as if to emulate some evil predatory aliens—or maybe boogeymen from children's closets. "Others think humans were the ones to make and place the gates before sending out the colony ships, and that we've since lost the technology. Disassembling the existing gates to try to better understand them is strictly forbidden since if we broke something, we'd be cutting off an entire system from the other eleven. It's possible that breaking one could even bring down the entire network."

"But if we had a spare…"

"We might be able to reverse-engineer it and finally learn the technology. There's no known physics, such as we understand it, that would allow for wormholes. And yet…" Jess waved a hand toward the stars. "Three weeks ago, we were in System Hind, ten thousand light years away."

Jess leaned forward in her seat and tapped a display built into the hull beside her. "Sir, how are we going to find the wreck? Nothing shows up on the scanners except for a couple of crashed robotic explorers that look as dusty and old as the Kingdom's beliefs."

"I've got a search algorithm crosschecking publicly available references to the moon with the existing maps of Skadi, looking for trenches and fissures in the icy surface large enough to hide a ship. It's compiling a list of some likely spots to check first. If there are too many for us to search quickly, we'll try the research ship in orbit. The *Machu Picchu*, its ident transmitter says."

"If they're the ones who originally sent that team to the surface, it seems like they must know where the wreck is." Yas didn't want to recommend Rache go interrogate people, but he was a little surprised the mercenary hadn't opted for that from the start.

"If they're alive, I'm sure they do."

If they're alive. Yas remembered the mysteriously dead team on the refinery. Did Rache believe the crew of the research vessel had suffered the same malady? Was that why he wanted to avoid it?

"You think the people we found dead on the refinery originally came from there?" Yas asked.

"They were in a short-range shuttle. It had to come from somewhere, and I don't see any other research vessels in the area."

"Probably because there are other less inhospitable and boring places in the system to research," Jess suggested.

Chaplain watched the exchange but said nothing. The grunts might as well have been sleeping for all the input they gave.

"If we find this wrecked ship on the moon," Yas said slowly, "we could still have to deal with whatever killed those researchers."

Rache glanced back. "Do you deem that likely?"

Yas hesitated. He had never identified a pathogen or poison or anything else under the microscope. He'd only seen the cellular damage itself. Damage that had killed all of those people within days. But had it originated at their dig site? Or was it that they'd found something important, and someone else had killed them in a creative way so they could take the secret for themselves without anyone linking the murders to them?

"It's two hundred degrees below zero on the surface of Skadi," Rache added, "and there's never been any life discovered there."

"I agree it's unlikely that there's a virus or bacterium down there," Yas said.

"It looks like your two prisoners are heading to the research ship, Captain," Jess said, tapping the scanner display.

"I know," Rache said.

"I admit, sir, I thought we were going after them when you ordered us all to the shuttle." Jess waved toward the big armed men in the back row and at Chaplain. "To pay them back for all that damage the ship took before we got out of there."

Chaplain flashed a fang-filled grin. Someone in the back cracked his knuckles. The grunts were awake, after all.

"It crossed my mind," Rache said.

His tone wasn't as icy as it got when he talked about the Kingdom. Yas didn't know if Sato and Dabrowski had been responsible for the premature explosions on the refinery—he hadn't been there—or if the crew of the smuggler ship had handled that as part of a rescue attempt, but he'd witnessed Rache grow irked before at his own mistakes. He seemed more inclined to blame himself than whoever had bested him, whether smuggler captain or robot sentry. Which again made Yas wonder how the Kingdom had gotten so deeply under his skin. Whatever it was, it couldn't be something that Rache considered at least partially his fault.

"We'll capture them and interrogate them if we need to," Rache said. "That's a Kingdom research vessel, and the dead on the team hiding in the refinery were Kingdom engineers and archaeologists. And like I said, I'm *not* letting the Kingdom claim the secrets of the gate for itself."

Kim caught herself clenching a fist as she stood at Casmir's shoulder in navigation, watching the video footage transmitted back to them from the crusher he'd made and dubbed Zee.

The six-and-a-half-foot tar-colored and nearly indestructible robot existed as a liquid or a solid, depending on its needs, and was currently in humanoid form. It—*he*, Casmir always called it—had timed the spin of the research vessel, sprung from the *Dragon's* airlock chamber, arrowed hundreds of meters over to the other ship, and forced open a hatch to gain access. He had done it in less than thirty seconds, fast enough that the Kingdom warship, still some eight hours away, may not have noticed.

On the video, the empty corridors of the *Machu Picchu* passed quickly, the crusher running instead of walking, the ship's spin gravity making it easy. Zee reached the bridge—and the first body.

Kim's shoulders slumped. She'd had a niggling suspicion they would find everyone dead.

Was this the captain or first mate? Whoever it was had died on the deck next to a command chair. The woman wore a galaxy suit with the helmet on.

"I was afraid of that," Casmir whispered. "I wasn't being rejected earlier. They weren't answering the comm because they're dead." He rubbed his face. "Maybe there *is* a deadly virus."

He looked at Kim.

She could only shrug. "You should have asked Rache more questions when you were chatting with him."

"I was distracted by his doctor shoving a giant needle in my jugular to take a blood sample."

Bonita looked back at him, and he fell silent, waving a dismissive hand.

Casmir had told Kim all about his new knowledge of the twin brother he'd never known he had, but she didn't think he'd told the captain or her assistant, Qin. Who wanted to admit to sharing identical DNA with an infamous pirate loathed by the entire Kingdom?

The crusher walked around the bridge, recording everything.

Kim didn't see any other bodies. "You'd think there would be more people up there if they all died at their duty stations."

"Maybe they died in their bunks," Bonita said. "Or puking out their guts in the lav." She slanted Kim a hard look.

Kim refused to feel bad that she'd infected her with a virus, not when Bonita had been in the middle of enacting her plan to hand Casmir over to Rache for two-hundred-thousand crowns.

"Zee, please check the computer banks for logs and to see if the *Machu Picchu* has shuttles that were launched." Casmir glanced at Kim. "Also keep your eye out for a monkey-shaped droid."

The crusher was capable of speech, but it complied without comment. The robots seemed designed to be silent killers rather than conversationalists. Kim hadn't known the things could speak at all until Casmir created Zee, and he had introduced himself.

She noticed something as Zee walked near the command chair again. "That dead woman is wearing an oxygen tank. Isn't the life support working on the ship?"

"Ah?" Casmir held up a finger as he checked something—he was linked to the crusher through his embedded chip. "Zee shows the temperature is a pleasant twenty degrees Celsius over there, with the air set to the same mix as in Odin's atmosphere. Environmental controls appear to be working fine."

"So, for some reason, she was relying on independent oxygen." Kim grimaced, afraid the virus scenario looked more and more likely. But why hadn't that woman's galaxy suit protected her? Had she donned it too late? Kim hadn't noticed any damage that would have allowed an airborne pathogen to penetrate the self-contained suit.

"The ship's computers are protected by passwords and require retina scans," Zee said. "I am unable to gain access."

"Right." Casmir didn't sound surprised. "Head to the shuttle bay and do a manual check to see if they were launched. And then check sickbay and engineering to see if anything is amiss. I guess we'll do a check of crew quarters last if there's time." He met Kim's eyes. "I don't suppose your mother is the type to keep a diary."

"She has a computer brain, so she remembers everything she sees."

"I guess that's a no."

"I don't even know if she ever did." Kim shrugged. "She's my mother, but… she had me delivered in an artificial womb after she—her human body—died. And she handed me over to my father for care when I was young. She visited regularly, but I honestly don't know her well. My father says I'm like her, or like she was when she was human, but—"

She shrugged again. She was here, trying to find her mother out of a familial sense of obligation, not because she felt great love for the woman. She wasn't sure she'd ever loved anyone. She never felt completely comfortable around her father and half-brothers even though she usually saw them every week. That, she also did out of a sense of obligation. And because it pleased her father when she came to workouts at the dojo. She'd long suspected that part of her was broken, the part that felt love and other strong human emotions. Sometimes, she felt like the one in an android body.

"Odd," Casmir murmured.

For a confused second, Kim thought he'd read her thoughts somehow, but he waved at the video. The crusher was striding through engineering, where there weren't any alarms showing, and everything appeared to be operating within normal parameters.

"There haven't been any other bodies," he added. "It's a big ship. You'd expect…" He paused, accessing the network. "For that model, it looks like a crew of thirty or forty is typical, and then it can hold hundreds of research scientists and their equipment. There are levels and levels of laboratories devoted to the various sciences. Zee passed a bunch of them on the way to engineering, and I didn't see any bodies."

Kim focused on the display, not admitting that her thoughts had wandered and she hadn't noticed. "At least one team went to the moon, we know."

"Days ago, yes. It would have to have been days ago. I wonder where Rache got the footage that you liberated."

"I am unable to access the systems in engineering," Zee said. "I will check the shuttle bay next."

"Good," Casmir said. "Thank you, Zee."

"You're the only one I've met who says please and thank-you to robots," Bonita told him, drumming her fingers on the control console and watching the warship approach on the scanner display.

"I doubt that's true," Casmir said.

"He also apologizes to the furniture at home." Kim tried a smile, though she wasn't in the mood, and it was a half-hearted attempt at a joke.

"I try not to make enemies of humans, robots, or furnishings."

"Just fellow students in robotics camps?" Kim couldn't believe they'd run into the one person in the Kingdom Fleet that knew Casmir—and didn't like him. She vowed to stand next to him and watch out for him in that interrogation.

"I hadn't yet fully developed my life policies at ten," Casmir said.

"One shuttle has been launched," Zee announced from the threshold of the bay, "and three remain docked."

"Captain Laser," Casmir said, "now that we're closer, can you search the moon to see if there's any sign of that shuttle?"

"Checking." Bonita smiled slightly.

Maybe she was pleased that Casmir had agreed to use her nickname.

"I don't suppose there's anything in that bay that would suggest where the shuttle went?" Casmir asked.

"Negative," Zee said.

"Doesn't anybody leave handwritten diaries around?"

"I was not programmed with instructions for journaling," Zee stated.

"We can try adding that code in the future." Casmir smiled faintly, but he looked tense. He also kept glancing at the approaching warship. "Check sickbay next, please, Zee."

The crusher jogged off again.

"That may be ugly," Kim said quietly.

"You think that's where all the bodies of the missing crew will be?" Casmir asked. "All except the one person who stayed to die on the bridge?"

"That would be my guess."

The crusher strode into sickbay. There were a couple of bodies under sheets but not as many as Kim expected. The crusher strode deeper into what turned out to be a facility full of laboratories as well as patient-care areas. He came to a large well-lit room in the back, sectioned off with a thick Glasnax wall. Several bodies lay on temporary cots while others sprawled on the deck. They weren't in galaxy suits but instead wore a mishmash of civilian clothing and what had to be ship's uniforms.

A big sign on the transparent wall read: *Quarantine Chamber.*

"There's your dead crew," Bonita said.

As the crusher stopped in front of the locked Glasnax door, one of the "bodies" sat up and stared at it. A woman. She poked someone beside her, and other people sat up.

"Or not so dead," Bonita said as Casmir gaped.

A few of the people rose to their feet, frowning and pointing at the crusher. One pulled out a stunner. They were speaking, but the crusher either wasn't recording audio, or the quarantine wall was soundproof.

"Are they sick?" Casmir asked. "Or protecting themselves from those who were sick on their ship?"

Kim shook her head. There wasn't any way to know without speaking with them.

"Can you have Zee ask them questions?" she asked.

"They don't show up on my scans," Bonita said, running a new one. "I mean, it's hard to pick out individuals under any circumstances, but from this close, I ought to be able to read their body heat. Viggo's scanners are fairly sensitive."

"Correction," Viggo said. "My scanners are exquisite. They were upgraded less than five years ago."

"Maybe the quarantine chamber insulates them," Casmir said. "Sickbay is already right in the center of the ship, according to the schematic I pulled up."

"That could be," Bonita said.

"Say hello to them, Zee," Casmir said.

"Hello," Zee announced, his voice coming over the link without trouble. "I am a Z-6000, programmed to protect Kim Sato and Casmir Dabrowski."

"Why does he always say my name first when he does his intro?" Kim asked.

Casmir gave her a lopsided smile. "I prioritized you."

That was sweet, and she appreciated it, but the other way around would have been more logical. "You do know I'm more likely to survive a fight than you are, right?"

The smile turned into a grin. "I have no doubt. But your work is more likely to change the world—the systems—for the better than mine. If I had to pick, I'd rather you make it."

Kim swallowed a lump of emotion. She should have hugged him, but she'd never been that comfortable with physical contact, even with old friends. There was a part of her that sometimes wished she had romantic feelings for him, but aside from vaguely admiring the agile interplay of muscles of men at the dojo now and then, she'd never been attracted to anyone. She doubted she was capable of such feelings. They were wrapped up with love, and as she'd just been thinking, she hadn't ever experienced that.

"You're a good man, Casmir," she managed to say.

His grin widened, and he gave her a quick bow before returning his focus to the camera display. "A good man who can't hear what those people are saying."

Fortunately, she'd never gotten the sense that he harbored some secret romantic feelings for her. He was the best friend she'd ever had, and she would hate for anything to get in the way of that.

"It doesn't look like they heard the crusher's proclamation," Bonita said.

"Is there a speaker somewhere?" Kim asked. "There must be a way to communicate with those people."

"It might be easier to go over there in person." Casmir waved at them. They'd all stood up—at least thirty of them—and backed to the far wall. A couple more stunners appeared, and they pointed nervously at Zee.

Kim wondered if they'd seen the news from Odin about the crushers destroying the university parking garage and killing a knight. Even if they hadn't, Casmir's robots looked like pure evil. She would also find one alarming if it appeared out of nowhere on her ship.

"If there's a virus, that's not a good idea," Kim said.

"If there's a warship planning to blow them up, it's *definitely* not a good idea." Bonita glanced again at the approaching vessel.

Casmir frowned. "If Viggo's exquisite scanners can't detect those people on board from right next door, then the warship won't have sensed them either. If they have orders to destroy that ship…"

"We better comm them again and let them know there are people alive there," Kim said.

"Or we could rescue everyone and bring them back here to safety." Casmir's eyes glinted with enthusiasm for this heroic notion.

Kim was starting to miss the days when he'd been too space sick to leave his bunk.

"Virus," Kim said.

"Warship," Bonita said.

Casmir sighed. "Right. Those are definitely problems. Captain, will you comm Ishii, please?"

"Only if you promise to let someone else do the talking and robotics camp doesn't come up."

Indignation flashed in Casmir's eyes, but he bowed again, this time in acquiescence. "Kim might be a better choice to explain a quarantine situation."

"Or any situation," Bonita muttered, looking at her.

Maybe she also longed for the days when Casmir had been space sick.

"I'll do my best." Kim waved to the comm panel.

A moment later, a face appeared on the display. It wasn't the dyspeptic captain. Kim didn't know if that was good or not. She was fairly certain the lone star on the young man's galaxy suit denoted him as an ensign.

"I'm Kim Sato," she announced, not bothering with pleasantries. "A medical researcher on Odin. Look up my credentials. I have them. We haven't docked with the research vessel, but we're close enough to read that there are people aboard. If you truly were intending to nuke the ship, I suggest you don't, as you would be murdering thirty civilian scientists."

The ensign had the grace to wince and appear alarmed. That was good. Kim would have been disturbed if it turned out the military knew there were people on board and planned to destroy the ship regardless.

"I'm willing to volunteer myself to go over and assess the situation as a medical researcher if your captain wishes it," Kim added, not reacting when Casmir looked sharply at her. "Viruses aren't my area of specialization, but I have experience dealing with deleterious bacteria and quarantine situations."

"I'll tell him," the ensign said, and a hold screen with a logo featuring the warship came up.

"Kim," Casmir said, his voice distressed. "Zee can't protect you from microbes."

"A design flaw?"

"I should have equipped him with laser eyes that could sterilize a ship."

Kim clasped her hands behind her back and waited for the captain's response. She didn't *want* to put herself into a quarantine situation, but the thought of unqualified people handling it—or murdering innocent civilians to *avoid* handling it—sent chills through her. If the warship had been sent out to deal with Rache, she feared it would not have the specialized medical personnel required for this task. She hoped she was wrong. Maybe it would turn out that the captain had known about the quarantine situation from the beginning and had a team of experienced experts.

"What *is* your area of specialization?" Bonita asked her. "You had that virus along that made Qin and me sick enough to feel like we were going to die."

"I happened to be delivering some virus specimens for a friend at work when all this started," Kim said. "I specialize in bacteria that have, or can be made to have, a symbiotic and mutually beneficial relationship with humans."

Bonita's forehead creased as she parsed that. "And that involves quarantine situations?"

"Not my work specifically, though I do sometimes start with antagonist strains of bacteria with desirable attributes and alter them, but some of my colleagues work with viruses, so I have familiarity with procedures. Further, since our facility is well-outfitted for dealing with biological hazards, we occasionally get surprise deliveries that the government wants us to neutralize. Everyone on our campus has training to handle those instances."

"Huh."

The hold screen disappeared, and Captain Ishii's charming face appeared. He scowled briefly at Casmir before focusing on Kim.

"I was told everyone on that ship is dead and that it simply needed to be checked for evidence and then destroyed," Ishii said without preamble.

Evidence? Of a virus? Or did they know about the piece of a gate that was found? Presumably, the archaeology team had been keeping someone up-to-date back on Odin. Had that someone been speaking to the government?

"We're not reading anyone alive on there now," the captain added, squinting.

"Approximately thirty people are in a quarantine room in sickbay," Kim said. "We believe it may be insulated enough that scanners can't pick up their signatures."

"How did *you* pick them up?"

Kim opened her mouth to suggest it was because their ship was closer—she didn't want the captain to have a reason to punish Bonita or take shots at the *Dragon*—but Casmir spoke first.

"I sent a robot over," he said, then shrugged at Kim. "It was going to come out sooner or later when they question me."

Ishii ground his teeth. "To look for top-secret military intel?"

Kim decided the captain definitely knew about the gate piece. And didn't want anyone else to know.

"To look for Kim's mother," Casmir said. "If you have the roster of the scientists that were on that ship, an Erin Kelsey-Sato should be on the list. She's missing."

"I'm sure a lot of those scientists are missing. As in dead."

"I'm positive a virus didn't get her," Casmir said.

The hold screen came up again.

"Sorry," Casmir told Kim. "I don't know if you wanted them to know, but I think we're going to have to be very honest with the military if we don't want to end up in prison. The authorities have gotten some odd notions about us lately."

Bonita snorted.

"It's fine," Kim said. "I don't disagree."

Ishii's face returned. "She was on the roster, yes. Retrieve your robot, Dabrowski. Send any footage it recorded, and then destroy your copy of that footage. If you don't, we'll find out about it."

"Uh, all right." Casmir looked like he was trying to sound puzzled, but Kim knew he followed right along. The military didn't want them to have footage that contained clues about what the archaeologists had found.

"I will speak with my chief medical officer," Ishii said, "and get back with you on your offer, Scholar Sato. In the meantime, stay the hell off that ship and get your captain to back away from it." He looked at someone off to the side of the vid pickup. "If they don't move at least ten klicks away, shoot them as soon as they're in range."

A woman's emotionless "Yes, sir" was audible.

"Ishii, out."

"Get your robot back here, Casmir," Bonita said. "I'm not delaying. They'll be in firing range soon. They could send a long-range missile any time."

Bonita grumbled under her breath, and Kim had a feeling she regretted not leaving the system right after they'd escaped the refinery.

Kim closed her eyes. She just wanted to make sure her mother was safe, make sure people were done trying to kill Casmir, and go back to her work on Odin.

After seeing that video, she had sent numerous messages to her mother, but they'd all gone unanswered. She hated the idea of having to tell her father that she had been destroyed and lost forever. Even though her parents had been divorced by the time her mother contracted the bacterial infection that had done in her human body, Kim knew her father still cared about her. Maybe even loved her. He'd always been the one with the romantic streak, and Kim didn't think it was possible for him not to care about someone he knew. More than once, she'd wondered why that trait hadn't been passed along to her.

CHAPTER 3

YOU'RE GOING BY YOURSELF?" QIN STOOD IN COMBAT armor with her big Brockinger anti-tank gun slung over her back on a strap and a helmet tucked under her arm. The pointed ears poking up through her thick black hair rotated slightly.

Casmir raised his eyebrows as Qin looked Kim up and down, pursing her lips and shaking her head. The three of them were in the cargo hold, waiting for the warship's shuttle to arrive and pick up Kim to take her to the research vessel. Ishii, or more likely his chief medical officer, had accepted her offer of assistance. Casmir wasn't sure whether he was afraid for her or envious. Maybe both. She got to go explore a ship full of mysteries but also a ship full of something that had driven the crew into quarantine.

Meanwhile, he was waiting for another shuttle that would supposedly pick him up and deliver him to the warship where he would be greeted by an interrogation specialist with the appropriate drugs. When he'd volunteered to be questioned, he'd imagined being on the neutral ground of the research ship, or even here on the *Dragon*.

"You don't even have your little sticks anymore," Qin added.

"My bokken weren't really weapons anyway," Kim said. "I was carrying them home from the dojo when this all started. I would like them back someday. They have sentimental value." She looked at Casmir.

As if he had any way to contact Rache and request their belongings back. After all the damage they'd caused to Rache's ship during their mad escape from the exploding refinery, Casmir feared his newly discovered twin brother would kill him the first chance he got.

"I'll be sure to let him know you'd like them back if I get the opportunity," Casmir said, though he was relieved the mercenary shuttle had headed down to the surface rather than chasing down the *Dragon*. The last he'd seen, it had disappeared from the scanners. He wondered if Rache already knew where the wreck was.

"I could go with you," Qin offered Kim. "I bet the captain would let me be your bodyguard."

"She may need you to be *her* bodyguard," Kim said.

A valid point. Ishii hadn't mentioned the bioweapon, but Casmir had a hard time believing he hadn't been briefed, even if it had been the Kingdom Guard handling security on Forseti Station, not the military. Maybe Ishii had been distracted by memories of robotics camp.

"You think so?" Qin sounded hopeful. "Do you think they'll force-board us? Do you think they have any knights?"

A clang reverberated through the ship, and a light on the airlock control panel flashed, indicating the Fleet shuttle had hooked onto them.

"Knights are rare," Casmir said, bemused by the nineteen-year-old super soldier's interest in the topic. Admittedly, they were the stuff of legend and fairy tale, having existed since the Kingdom's founding, and highly romanticized. "And they're closer to secret agents than soldiers. It would be surprising to find one on a random Fleet warship."

"Oh." Qin scuffed her boot on the deck.

"Besides," Casmir said, hoping to distract her as Kim headed to the airlock hatch, "if one was there and force-boarded the *Dragon,* you'd have to fight him."

"That would be all right. I'm curious about their legendary fighting prowess."

Casmir tried not to think about the knight who'd given his life battling two crushers in order to buy him time to escape the university campus back home. "I thought you were curious about, uhm, romantic things."

"I just think knights sound terribly chivalrous and would treat a girl right. I don't have many delusions about how romance works." She sniffed.

The hatch swung open, and two soldiers in blue combat armor walked out, one aiming a rifle around the cargo hold, one stopping in front of Kim. He looked her up and down, then handed her a bright yellow suit. It was bigger than her galaxy suit, which was on loan from Bonita, and a hood draped the helmet. Casmir recognized it as a hazmat suit, a higher level of protection than what Kim wore now, and his stomach flip-flopped, his concern rearing up again. It worried him that she was going somewhere that she might need that—he had been incredibly naive when he'd been thinking of going over there himself— but he was relieved that the military intended to treat her right, not like some criminal to be sacrificed.

"You can put it on in our shuttle Scholar Sato," the soldier said politely and led her into the airlock.

The second soldier was gaping at Qin, who had her helmet off, revealing that she wasn't quite human. He kept his rifle pointed at the deck, but he backed warily into the airlock with the others, his heel bumping the lip of the hatchway. Casmir almost joked that he *wasn't* the only one who tripped on those things, but Bonita wasn't there to hear it. And he wasn't in the mood for jokes.

As the hatch swung shut, Kim sent him a message that appeared on his contact display. *Wish me luck.*

Of course, Casmir replied. *And shalom, my friend.*

What's the literal translation of that? Deep peace? That may be a stretch to find on a ship full of dead and quarantined people.

Hence my wish that you find it anyway.

"They're departing," Bonita said over the comm, "and the second shuttle is pulling in right after them. I feel like a gas station here."

"Just hope they don't ask where you got your last fill-up," Casmir said.

"That's the truth."

Qin gave him a concerned look as he walked to the airlock hatch. "Do *you* need a bodyguard?"

Either he looked like he was going to pass out, or she really wanted to see a knight.

"Very likely, but I'm going to do my best not to mention you or the captain, in the hope they'll forget about our actions on Forseti. It'll be hard not to mention you if you're along."

"I can stay quiet and keep my helmet on."

"They'd take your gun away, and you wouldn't be happy." He gave her armored sleeve a thump. "Thank you for offering, though. I'm glad you're not irritated with me for, uhm, sort of tricking you into telling me about the bounty."

She studied the deck as the airlock light flashed again. "I was just upset at having to choose loyalties. I knew we weren't... that it wasn't right, but—"

"I know. You don't have to explain anything to me. I've never been in the military, but I know that loyalty is important there."

"I think it's important everywhere, isn't it?" Qin cocked her head. "You said you lead a robotics team. Are they not loyal to you?"

"Well, nobody's stabbed me between my shoulder blades and tried to patent one of my inventions behind my back, but civilians are a little harder to wrangle. You have to convince them that they really want to do what you need them to do. That it's good for them. And rewarding."

"Sounds like a lot of work."

"It is." He grinned, but then the hatch opened and four armed and armored men stomped out, and he sobered quickly.

Zee strode up behind him, and Casmir realized he hadn't given him a command to stay on the *Dragon*. The crusher might assume he needed to come to protect him. Casmir looked wishfully over his shoulder, especially since he had a feeling he might *need* some protection. Kim had only garnered two armed soldiers, after all. And they'd brought her fancy clothes. He got four rifles pointed at his chest and no proffers of gifts.

Zee stomped in front of him, and the soldiers almost fired.

"It's all right," Casmir blurted, raising his hands. "He's—" He was on the verge of saying not coming, but he realized two things. First, he might be able to get away with bringing Zee. Second, Bonita didn't truly have a reason to stick around, beyond a vague notion of profiting from finding the gate, and she might prefer it if there was nothing keeping her from making a getaway. "He's my personal assistant robot," Casmir finished. "He has the footage that Captain Ishii asked for."

Casmir also had the footage copied onto his chip, but no need to mention that.

The soldiers exchanged dubious looks, and he was sure they were muttering to each other over their helmet comms.

"Ishii said he wants the footage wiped after he sees it," Casmir added. "The only way to do that is to bring Zee along."

"*Captain* Ishii," one of the men growled, looking like he wanted to point his rifle at Casmir's chest again.

Alas, Zee was big enough and broad enough to do an effective job of blocking the soldiers.

"I'm not in the military," Casmir pointed out. "Not only am I not required to call him by his rank, but I could whisper his nickname from robotics camp into your ears."

One ordered, "Get in the airlock," without humor as another sidled close and whispered, "I'll give you twenty crowns for that information."

"You can keep the crowns if you slip me a wrench, a magnet, and a piece of gum after your captain throws me in the brig."

"Because... you can use them to escape?"

"Nah, that's silly. But magnets are entertaining, and gum helps keep the saliva flowing if you're deprived of water."

Three out of the four soldiers snorted. They weren't exactly guffaws of laughter, but at least their rifles weren't pointing at Casmir or Zee now.

"What about the wrench?"

"Ssh, don't waste his time," another said as the lock cycled. "I want to know the captain's nickname. And when did you know him? Did he really go to robotics camp? That's *so* dorky." He snickered and poked Casmir in the arm. "If you tell us, I'll bring you a cupcake when you get thrown in the brig."

"I'm pretending I'm not hearing any of this," the grumpy soldier muttered as they walked through the tube toward the shuttle.

"Oh, like you don't want to know, Sergeant."

"He *did* go to robotics camp," Casmir said. "We were ten, and his nickname was Queenie, because win or lose, he couldn't get through a chess game without sacrificing his queen."

"*Queenie?*" one of the men blurted with a giggle as the hatch to their shuttle opened.

Casmir came face to face with Captain Ishii. A scowling Captain Ishii. The giggle cut off as if the man had been garroted.

"Ah, hello, Sora," Casmir said. "I didn't realize you would come to pick me up personally."

"Clearly." Ishii folded his arms over his chest, which might have been intimidating if he'd been any taller than Casmir, but they were the same below-average height. "I see your growth spurt wasn't any more impressive than mine," Ishii growled.

"There was a spurt? I think I slept through mine."

"I bet. What is *that*, Dabrowski?" Ishii pointed at Zee, who was looming impressively at Casmir's shoulder.

"*That* is one of the robot monsters that killed Friedrich," someone said from one of the shuttle's seats.

Casmir recognized his telltale armor and purple cloak as the man lurched to his feet and reached for the weapon hanging at his belt, thick brown hair swinging around his shoulders.

"No, this is one I made." Casmir held up a hand and stepped in front of Zee. He would trust the crusher to handle himself against the soldiers in armor, but the knight's pertundo and its mysterious piercing and cutting technology might seriously damage Zee. "To protect me from the ones that attacked Sir Friedrich. Did you know him? He tried to give me a message, but there wasn't enough time for it all. I don't suppose you…"

Casmir trailed off because the knight was glowering at him as much as he was at Zee. He was young but didn't look naive. He had angular features made more pronounced by a short beard and mustache and looked to be twice Casmir's weight—all in muscle.

"Want to question you?" the knight finished his sentence with an eyebrow quirk. "Yes, I do. And so does the captain."

Ishii nodded once, a pleased glint in his eyes.

"Will drugs be involved?" Casmir asked, wondering if he was truly going to get a chance to clear his name, or if these men would devise a way to cause him to incriminate himself further. Ishii had been a clever ten-year-old, and Casmir didn't imagine that had changed much. Maybe he had been naive in volunteering to come to the military, but what choice did he have? He wanted to go home, and he hadn't had any luck figuring out who was after him yet. He couldn't flee forever, not if he wanted his life back, his work and his projects and his friends and his parents.

His adoptive parents, yes, but he'd never known any others, and they had always loved and supported him. His father's birthday was coming up, and Casmir and his uncles always got him gag gifts, much to his mother's horror. She always gave him something respectful and proper. Casmir was convinced his father preferred the goofy things, including the ambulatory soap dispenser he'd made that dispensed soap everywhere except into one's hands. Casmir had never missed his father's birthday, and he didn't want to start now.

"Oh yes," Ishii said. "Several kinds of drugs, I should think."

"Goodie," Casmir murmured as the shuttle departed, heading for the ominous black spear of a warship. He tried not to think about Kim's admonition that the truth drugs might knock his brain cells out of alignment or how he would look convulsing on the deck at Ishii's feet.

Yas stared at the display as the shuttle settled onto hard snow, deep inside a dim canyon full of spikes of ice that appeared to be natural formations. If not for the headlights, he wouldn't have seen the frosty metal structure almost entirely buried in the side of a glacier in front of them. Since Skadi was one of the farthest bodies from the sun in the solar system, little sun reached it, especially down here. Yas wasn't sure how deep the canyon was, but they had descended a long time before reaching the bottom. A thousand meters? Two? At least.

"I can't believe you found it, Captain," Jess blurted, unbuckling her straps.

Rache looked over his shoulder from the pilot's seat, though of course, his expression wasn't visible through his mask.

"I mean, I figured you would," Jess amended, "but not on only the fourth try."

Was that all it had been? Yas's butt was numb, and he felt like they'd been flying forever. He'd dozed off more than once, and his stomach growled.

But Rache didn't suggest anyone partake in a leisurely lunch. He stood, tapping his chest control so that his helmet snapped over his head, and grabbed an oxygen tank from a rack on the wall.

"Check your suits," he said, talking over Yas's and Jess's heads to the combat men in the rows behind them, "and take a look around. Scans don't show any life forms, but they also can't penetrate the metal in the hull of that ship." Rache waved at the buried structure.

A ship? It could have been anything under all that ice.

"There could still be archaeologists in there," Rache added. "Or the people who killed the archaeologists."

"Do we shoot to kill, Captain?" Chaplain patted his rifle lovingly.

"Defend yourselves with deadly force if necessary," Rache said, "but try to take someone alive if we meet a team. I have more questions than answers, at this juncture."

Yas wasn't sure whether or not to be glad he wasn't the only one.

"Dr. Peshlakai, Chief Khonsari," Rache said, grabbing a rifle out of the armory cabinet, "stay here for now. If there's a need, I'll call you in once we've secured the ruin."

"Gladly," Yas said, as Jess made a noise of protest.

"Captain, is that an ancient Earth ship?" she asked. "Don't you think I'd be more useful in there than Chaplain and Chains?"

Chaplain hadn't put his helmet up yet, and he flashed his metal fangs at her.

Jess was too focused on Rache to notice.

"We'll secure it first, Chief," Rache said firmly but not as coolly as he might have to someone else who questioned him. "Then you can come in and rub your hands on the engines."

"You know how to get a girl excited, Captain."

"Disgusting," one of the men muttered.

"I can get girls excited too," one said more forlornly.

Yas barely heard them. He was gaping at Jess, surprised and a little distressed that she would flirt with Rache. Did he ever flirt back? Something about that notion was alarming.

Rache didn't acknowledge the comment.

"Put your helmets up," he told the men, then reached for the hatch controls. "We'll leave the shuttle running, but it's cold enough out there to freeze your ears off in seconds."

Yas complied even though he wasn't going outside and the comment probably wasn't for him. The men exited into an airlock chamber before stepping out onto the frozen moon. The display showed frosty bullets of snow skidding sideways through the forest of stalagmite-like ice formations. In their black combat armor, the men were imposing figures striding toward the wreck, but the moon itself seemed far more forbidding and dangerous.

Yas was tempted to ask Jess if she'd ever had a relationship with Rache, but that was definitely none of his business. Instead, he eyed the navigation control panel while realizing this was the first time he'd been left alone—mostly alone—with a means of escaping the mercenaries.

"Can you fly a shuttle?" he asked Jess casually, though his heart rate sped up, beats thundering through his body, at the mere thought of slipping away.

Unfortunately, they couldn't leave without stranding Rache and his fighters down here. Yas didn't want to do that—if Rache escaped, he'd likely come after Yas and kill him in the most horrific manner—but he couldn't help but think about how badly he wanted to go home, clear his name, and get his old life back. A life where he'd been respected and had helped good people, not thugs and murderers.

"Well enough to get one in and out of the repair bay," Jess said.

"Well enough to get it out of a canyon and to a station somewhere?"

Jess gave Yas a frank look. "First off, no, these shuttles don't have the range to get far. Second, of all the men in the Twelve Systems you might betray without repercussions, Rache would not go on that list. He saved your ass, Doctor. And you agreed to his five years. I was there, remember? You almost spilled my coffee when you collapsed at our feet."

Yas closed his eyes, the memories of terror still hot and fresh in his mind. "I remember, but I didn't know who he was when I agreed to that. It's like working for the devil. You hear how cavalierly he said it was all right to kill any archaeologists they might find in there? Oh, except one that he wants kept alive for questioning. I was desperate and didn't have time to think."

"You want out of that deal, then reason with him and try to make a bargain. Don't screw him over, or it'll be the last thing you do."

Yas dropped his head into his palm. "I know. But *would* he be reasonable? I always feel like I'm on thin ice with him. And you said he likes me." Yas laughed shortly.

"Nah, I said he told the men not to kill you. Could just be that doctors are useful."

"Thanks. I think."

"I don't think he likes anyone, but the only time I've seen him be *illogical* is when he's pursuing his revenge. He's a little mad when it comes to the Kingdom and Jager."

"No kidding. You have any idea why?"

"Nope. Like I said, he doesn't talk to the crew." Jess hopped to her feet and headed past the tiny mess and lavatory and into the engine compartment. "I better earn my pay and run a maintenance check on the shuttle while we wait."

"Is that why you're here? The pay?" Yas followed her partway back and poked into a cabinet for a ready-meal. "Or did you also make a deal with the devil out of desperation?"

"I'll admit my head wasn't in the best place when I joined," Jess said, "and it still isn't all of the time."

Yas wondered if, since they were alone together, he should bring up her relationship with trylochanix. Maybe offer to help her wean herself off it and find some less addictive alternatives.

"I actually hired Rache," she went on. "That's how we first met. I was recovering from some injuries…"

"The injuries that resulted in you having more than a few cybernetic bits and a brain that's half circuitry?"

Jess leaned out the door and grimaced at him, and he wished he'd asked more delicately. The mercenaries were all so blunt and cavalier about everything that it seemed the way to broach things with them.

"Yes. Star Strider terrorists attacked our hab in System Geryon when I was home visiting my family. My brother and parents were miners—almost everyone that lives in Shiva Habitat is—working on pulling ore out of Pushya, and admittedly not worrying too much about defacing the planet. It's an ugly hunk of rock. It's not like we were destroying life or even a ruggedly appealing landscape. Anyway, some politics and arguing and negotiations had been going on, but I'd been out on the soccer tour, where I was playing professionally at the time, so I wasn't that aware of how bad things had gotten. I happened to be home for a visit when the Strider terrorists decided they were tired of negotiating and wanted to make a statement. Because they were upset that humanity was mining planets, they blew a hole the size of a moon in the side of our hab. My parents and my brother didn't make it. I almost didn't make it either. Some doctor recognized me and figured I'd have the money to pay for surgery, I guess, since he'd seen me play and knew I had sponsors and the like. He did all this." She waved at her eyes and lifted her cybernetic hand. "Then gave me the bill afterward."

"Did you pay?"

"I paid. For that and for my brother's and my parents' funeral." Jess disappeared back into the engineering compartment, and a few clanks and thunks sounded. "I knew I'd never play on the tour again, since it's skins only, nobody with implants, and the implants weren't such that I could have been competitive on the teched tour. Not that I wanted to play anymore after that anyway. I took what money I had left and hired Rache to kill the terrorists that had masterminded the bombing."

"Did he?"

"Yes. He understands the revenge game very well."

Yas kept himself from making a snide comment. He'd never expected her or any of the mercenaries to bare their souls to him, and he didn't want her to regret it. Besides, his dissent was with Rache, not her.

"We talked a few times during the process," Jess went on, "and when he learned I'd graduated with honors from an engineering program before going into soccer full time, he offered me a job. Had I been in a different frame of mind, I probably would have said no, but as strange as it seems, I'd hired a criminal to kill people without giving them a trial, so I was a criminal myself at that point. And with my family all gone… I had nowhere else to go."

A few more clanks sounded.

Yas didn't know what to say. "I'm sorry," he murmured, though it was inadequate.

"I know you don't think much of Rache or the men," Jess said, "but they've become a family of sorts for me. And even if Rache doesn't let anyone get close, and I can't claim that we're buddies, I know he'd have my back if I needed it."

"Does that mean you and he haven't, ah, had more than coffee?" Yas almost smacked himself as soon as the words came out. Why was he worrying about that? Because he wanted to ask Jess for more than coffee himself? That wouldn't be appropriate, not when she was essentially a patient. A patient with a problem that he needed to help her address. On a professional level.

"Rache doesn't have more than coffee with anyone, as far as I know." Jess joined him in the mess and pulled out a ready-meal for herself. "But if you're interested in him, I can try to put in a good word for you." She winked.

Yas coughed and dropped his ready-meal. "Er, no, thank you." He picked it up and tore open the wrapper. "It did cross my mind that if I served him for the five years he asked for, he might be willing to help me find those who killed President Bakas and framed me. I go back and forth on whether to ask him about that or to try to escape and handle it on my own. I'm afraid that if I wait five years, it'll be too late to find the tracks."

"So don't wait. You could do like I did. Offer to hire him."

"How much did that cost?" Yas opened a pouch labeled *Masala Vat Lamb Cubes Stew,* the contents warming in his hand from the internal heater.

"In my case, I paid him a hundred thousand Union dollars."

"That's a lot more than I have access to right now. My banking chip was cut off within days of me disappearing from Tiamat Station. My parents… I don't want to go to them and ask for help hiring mercenaries. I haven't even contacted them since I was framed. I didn't want to get them in trouble."

Nor was Yas sure they would help. His father, in particular, who had political aspirations, might be doing his best to distance himself from his supposedly criminal son.

"Noble, but they're probably worried about you and would like a message." She pointed a fork with noodles dangling from the tines at him. "Don't assume your parents will just be alive and well the next time you get around to visiting them."

Given the story she'd shared, he couldn't argue with that.

"Maybe Rache would take less for that," she said. "An investigation, followed by an assassination, wouldn't take his whole ship. Ask him about it."

Yas didn't want people assassinated. He just wanted justice. And to have his name cleared. Could he truly hire criminals to do that? What was the alternative? That those who had killed the president would never be brought to justice? And that he would be a fugitive for the rest of his life?

The comm beeped.

"I need you inside, Doctor," Rache said. "Suit up. I'll meet you at the hole in the side of the wreck."

"What about me, Captain?" Jess asked. "I'll be bereft without Dr. Yas's delightful company."

"His what?"

"Delightful company. Has he not delighted you before, Captain? He asked me questions about myself and listened when I answered. That doesn't happen often with mercs. I practically felt wooed."

Yas dropped his face into his hand, not surprised when Rache didn't respond to that.

"Stay there," Rache finally said, "and watch for other ships. We're not the only ones who know about this wreck."

"Yes, sir."

Yas grabbed an oxygen tank while wondering what Rache had found that required a doctor's presence. Last time, it had been a body. He had a feeling he couldn't hope for anything better this time.

CHAPTER 4

KIM STOOD QUIETLY ON THE SHUTTLE, GRIPPING A handhold as her feet floated in microgravity, and wondering what it said about her that she was more worried for Casmir than herself. She was simply going to deal with what she assumed was a potentially horrific and extremely contagious bacteria or virus. So, stuff she dealt with semi-occasionally at work. *He* was heading into what could turn into a full-fledged interrogation by a high-ranking Fleet officer who clearly didn't like him.

A few weeks ago, she wouldn't have worried about either of them being in the hands of the Kingdom military, but that had been before those bungling oafs at Forseti Station had somehow come to believe that she and Casmir were assisting Bonita in smuggling that bioweapon. It had also been before some unknown entity had started sending crushers to assassinate Casmir. And before she'd known he was, at least according to Rache's doctor, the genetic twin of a man hated and loathed by the Kingdom. She worried that connection, if it became widely known, could get Casmir into trouble simply because of shared DNA.

"Scholar Kim Sato?" a woman asked, floating into view.

She was with a man, both in yellow hazmat suits, and they gripped nearby handholds as the shuttle sailed closer to the research vessel. They had been in the back when Kim first boarded. The man, his broad face visible through his faceplate, settled closer to Kim than she would have preferred, and she wrestled with the urge to push back to the next handhold.

"Yes," Kim said, nodding to the woman.

"I'm the *Osprey's* chief medical officer, Dr. Sikou," she said, bowing awkwardly in the nonexistent gravity, "and this is our surgeon, Dr. Angelico. I'm familiar with your work. I've inoculated a number of our crew with your radiation-consuming bacteria. Our ship is part of Phase II testing."

Kim returned the bow and groped for an appropriate response. *Thank you* wasn't right. *Good?* For some reason, she always felt awkward when she met people who knew about her or her work.

"I hope it's going well," Kim settled on. She then felt compelled to add, "The radiation-eating bacteria have been the work of many people on my team," lest it seem she was allowing Sikou to give her too much credit.

"Yes, extremely so. The crew members have reported evidence of some of the beneficial side effects mentioned in the literature. I wish we had time to discuss it, but..." Sikou looked toward the two pilots guiding them toward the same airlock on the *Machu Picchu* that Casmir's crusher had used earlier to board.

"I haven't heard of you," Dr. Angelico said, thrusting a gloved hand toward Kim, "but I look forward to making your acquaintance." He grinned and winked.

Kim hesitated, then returned the handshake, trying not to show her reluctance at such familiarity among strangers. She might have grown up in the mixed-culture capital and be used to greetings that ranged from bows to hugs and from handshakes to high fives, but touching always felt uncomfortably intimate to her. At least the gloves kept her from feeling callouses or hand sweat. Unfortunately, the man held the grip longer than she would have liked, and she was the one to break eye contact, though he continued to look at her through her faceplate.

"You have experience with outbreaks?" Sikou asked.

Kim thought about the last time she'd been in a positive-pressure hazmat suit, when the Kingdom Guard had swung by the lab in a panic, bringing a package some terrorists had delivered along with blackmail demands. Typically, military specialists handled problems like that, but her corporation's lab had been much closer than the nearest base with proper facilities. She'd been brought in as an advisor and had ended up with a nice consulting fee that had covered the cost of paying for an editor for her fantasy trilogy. She snorted softly at the memory, still amused that some terrorist's attempt to infect King Jager with a designer disease had ended up financing her hobby.

"Yes, some," was all she said, not wanting to explain everything.

"Good. Angelico and I have had the basic training courses, but we're far more often called upon to remove bullets and repair damage from DEW-Tek bolts. " Sikou waved to a couple of hulking figures that appeared more like robots than people, since they wore combat armor under their hazmat suits. "The captain sent a couple of marines in case there's any physical danger we need to worry about."

Kim almost mentioned that Casmir's crusher hadn't found any danger, but what kind of bandit—human or robot—would leap out and pick a fight with Zee? She truly had no idea what to expect and looked forward to speaking with the people in quarantine. Had they placed themselves in there? Or been thrust in by someone else?

Gravity returned with a lurch as the shuttle latched onto the research ship, and Kim felt a twinge of vertigo as they started rotating along with the vessel, the stars outside appearing to move past the portholes.

As soon as the marines ran out and assured them there wasn't any immediate danger, the rest of the group hurried into the *Machu Picchu*, where the interior was aligned so that the spin gravity pushed them toward the deck instead of a random wall.

"We don't know what to expect, I admit," Sikou said, walking beside Kim. "A few days ago, Headquarters got a message from this ship's captain, speaking about the archaeological find of the century and also a mysterious illness that a team may have brought back from a wreck on the moon. Our warship, along with two others, had just been dispatched to address a threat, the pirate Rache blowing up first one and then the second of Saga's refineries. Run-of-the-mill stuff for us. But as we were en route, we received an update that the crew on this ship was sick." Sikou waved to the walls of the ship. "Our original orders were to divert and give assistance. That later changed to blow up the ship. We were told it had been confirmed at that point that there weren't any survivors. We were also supposed to blow up the wreck on the surface, but we don't even know where it is. Our scanners couldn't pick it up."

"Ours didn't either." Kim wondered if Captain Lopez had taken off or would stick around. Given how quickly the situation had escalated, the military might not appreciate a civilian lurking nearby.

"Then your ship commed ours, saying there were survivors on board. The captain was livid that you'd disobeyed his orders to avoid the ship."

"He told us not to dock. We didn't. My friend sent a robot over to look around."

"Right, but it's a quarantined ship. Nothing should have been sent, certainly not by civilians."

"The captain," Dr. Angelico added from behind them, "was going to blow you up just to be sure you couldn't spread whatever this is around the system. Your presence, Scholar Sato, and Sikou vouching for you, was the only reason he didn't."

Kim wasn't that surprised by the statement and didn't argue against the notion. If her mother hadn't been missing, she would have waved away Casmir's curiosity and argued to avoid the *Machu Picchu*.

The marines led the way deeper into the ship, asking the computer for directions a couple of times—it was a large vessel with numerous levels. They passed a couple of bodies that Zee had missed earlier. Kim shook her head grimly. She had been afraid more than that bridge officer would be found dead.

"Can we get one of these to autopsy?" Kim asked the big men, though they seemed more inclined to hurry past them.

The marines hesitated. "You want us to pick them up?"

One wiped a gloved hand on his suit, as if he already worried he'd caught something.

"Maybe there's a hov-gurney somewhere," Kim suggested. "Or we can find some medical androids willing to do the job."

"I'll get one," one of the men said with a grunt and hefted a body over his shoulder.

Kim glimpsed a woman's features through the faceplate, her hair fallen into her eyes. She looked like she was sleeping rather than dead. Perhaps thinking the same thing, Dr. Sikou pulled out a scanner for a quick check, then shook her head.

"I don't think anyone here has been dead for that long," she murmured.

They reached sickbay, and Kim headed straight for the quarantine room that Zee had found. The people who'd been sleeping before must have been expecting more company. Most of them stood, facing Kim and the newcomers. One pointed to a comm panel on the wall. It hadn't shown up in Zee's video, but Kim had been certain it would be there, and she nodded and activated it. She glanced toward Sikou, wondering if she would want to take charge and do the introductions, but she and Angelico were instructing the marine to lay out the body on an exam table.

The people inside the quarantine room watched with grim expressions. Interestingly, they weren't wearing galaxy suits or any kind of hazmat suits. They were clad in a mix of civilian clothing, styles typical of Odin.

"I'm Kim Sato, a medical researcher," she said into the speaker, "and these are doctors from the Kingdom warship *Osprey*. They received some of the crew's comm messages about an illness, but we need to be updated on everything so we can help you. Have you been afflicted?" Kim tried to poke what appeared to be a Glasnax quarantine wall and was surprised when her gloves met resistance before touching the wall.

"As far as we know, we haven't," a man inside said. "The team that went down to the moon warned us as they were flying back up to the ship that they were experiencing some anomalous health readings. They didn't think it was a virus, or that they could have possibly encountered something living on Skadi, but the captain decided to quarantine nonessential personnel and only leave out the crew necessary to run the ship. Nobody's come down here in two days." The man looked at the body on the table, then swallowed and licked his lips. "Is that… Is everybody who was left out dead? We know some pirates came by and took advantage, and that most of the original team launched another shuttle, trying to lure them away from the *Machu Picchu*."

Pirates? Kim would have scratched her head if she hadn't been wearing a helmet. She never had gotten the story of how Rache had come to have that video.

"We haven't had an update for days," the man continued, "so we don't know what's going on. We've been stuck here, hoping someone would come by." He raised his eyebrows hopefully.

"Are you all civilians? Researchers?" Sikou asked, coming over.

Angelico was removing the dead woman's suit to begin performing an autopsy.

"Yes," the man said as others nodded. There were thirty-two people inside. "We have a mix of scientists, civilian engineers, and archaeologists. I'm Erden Ayik, archaeologist. I specialize in underwater and under-ice investigations. I was supposed to go down to the moon with the original team, but I had a cold. Who knew that would save my life?" He laughed, but it had a hysterical edge to it.

"Was an Erin Kelsey-Sato on your ship?" Kim asked.

"Yes, she went down with the original team, and she stayed down there, from what I was told, since she couldn't be infected with anything. Wait, what did you say your name is? Sato? Are you related?"

"She's my mother."

Sikou gave Kim a sharp look. Maybe nobody had given her that detail. Kim had a feeling there were a lot of details that weren't being shared around.

"So, she might still be down on the moon?" Hope blossomed in Kim's chest. She hadn't realized she'd already been bracing herself for the worst when it came to her mother, fearing she'd have to deliver the news to her father that she was truly gone this time. "I've tried sending her a number of messages, but she hasn't responded. Is there network access on Skadi?"

"Technically, there should be some delayed access from the Saga satellite, but we had trouble comming back and forth with our team after they landed. They may have been down in one of the fissures in the ice."

"Dr. Sikou." Angelico waved her over.

"You'll find a great deal of cellular damage," Ayik said, "and nothing to account for it. Our ship's doctor was trying to figure out the problem before she disappeared—succumbed, we fear. She thought some intense radiation at first, and that's why our engineering friend, David—" he waved to someone in the back of the group who waved back, "—rigged a magnetic field around the quarantine chamber, in case the team had accidentally brought something radioactive back on the ship, but that never made sense. First off, our people should have had equipment to detect radiation, and it's not like anyone would be stupid enough to bring a radioactive artifact on board, and second, the way people died is similar to but not the same as getting an intense burst of cosmic radiation. It's more like their natural aging process was ratcheted way up, and their bodies didn't have a shot at repairing it."

"Thank you for the input," Sikou said. "We'll try to find your doctor's records and start up where he left off."

"We may want to rig a magnetic field around sickbay if we can," Kim suggested. "Since these people are inside of one, and they're alive. I'm skeptical that the Glasnax alone is protecting them, since we've now encountered numerous crew who died in full and, at least at first glance, un-breached galaxy suits."

"It may just be that they—" Sikou pointed at the quarantined scientists, "—never came in contact with the—whatever it is. Ayik, you said your people got in there before the team returned?"

"Yes. And we haven't left in case…" He waved at the sickbay, or maybe the air in sickbay and the ship as a whole.

"A good idea," Sikou said. "I'm going to suggest you stay in there until we're able to ensure there's no threat out here. But don't worry. We're on it, and the labs here look state-of-the-art. There's equipment for everything from specimen analysis, incubation, biosafety, and research and development. There's even a cryonics chamber. We should have everything we need to solve this problem."

Kim didn't point out that the *Machu Picchu*'s doctor, who'd had access to everything here, hadn't managed to do so.

Sickbay on the warship reminded Casmir more of a vault than a hospital. It was located in the center of the great vessel, with no portholes and pale gray walls that matched the pale gray ceiling and complemented the dark gray deck. There weren't any entertainment displays, bookcases, or holo-games. He imagined patients got better as quickly as possible so they could escape.

He wasn't sure whether to be encouraged or disturbed that his interrogation was going to take place in sickbay rather than the brig. He had a lot fewer bad associations with jails.

It wasn't that he'd ever received poor care in a hospital, just that there had been so many trips in his youth. Countless tests related to his seizures, the eye surgery, instances of anaphylactic shock from allergies, broken bones from his woeful attempts to participate in sports. All those childhood visits should have inured him to the hospital experience, but he'd always had a gift for mentally torturing himself with worry. Even as an adult, every time he went for a simple doctor's visit, he was certain someone would confirm his suspicions that his inevitable and painful death was close at hand.

A male nurse saluted sharply when the captain and the knight came in, the man's face as serious as a dagger to the heart. A female nurse winked at the knight and saluted her captain with a saucy jutting of her hip. Ishii's lips pressed together at this slight irreverence. Casmir promptly liked her. She was pretty, with glistening ringlets of black hair that made him want to tug at one to see if it bounced. Other things, he could already tell, bounced nicely.

The presence of the captain, the knight, and two guards flanking Casmir quelled any urge to flirt. He clasped his hands behind his back and waited for instructions.

He didn't see any doctors and wondered if they had all gone over to the research ship to help Kim. Or maybe this procedure was simply so basic that a doctor didn't need to stand by. He hoped so.

"We're questioning this man, Lieutenant Adjei," Ishii said. "Prepare a dose of eslevoamytal."

"Yes, sir." The female nurse—Adjei—smiled at Casmir. "Are you on any medications? I need to make sure nothing in your system could interact with the eslevoamytal."

Flustered by the smile, which was even more intriguing than the hair, he stumbled over his words. "No. I mean, yes. Er, I was, but they're probably out of my system now. A pirate stole my meds." His eye blinked and watered, and he wiped it. "Even the antihistamine," he added, hoping allergies might explain his tics.

"A pirate? Unfortunate. Do you have any known allergies or reactions to drugs?"

"Do you want a list?"

Her lower lip drooped—in surprise?

"The only drug I'm deathly allergic to is the seizure medication ethosuximide," Casmir said. "Found that out the hard way. Also, you can kill me with cashews and pomegranates. Though I'd prefer it if you didn't. I'm doing my best to stay alive this month."

Ishii made a disgusted noise. "There aren't cashews in the truth drug. Sit there."

He gripped Casmir's arm and propelled him to a chair locked to the deck. He swiveled it so it faced the room.

If Zee had witnessed the rough handling, he might have attacked, but Casmir had ordered him to wait in the corridor. That wouldn't, he hoped, prove a mistake.

As soon as Casmir sat, Adjei came over with a jet injector full of a dubious fluid that looked like it should be used to clean drains rather than inserted into someone's vein.

"Efficient," Casmir murmured.

"We strive for that on the *Osprey*. Will you tug down your suit top, or do I need to get the burly men to do it?" She waved at his sleeves and gloves.

Casmir resisted the urge to be stupid and ask if *she* would remove his suit for him. Besides, she kept stealing glances at the knight, who was tall, handsome, muscular, and probably starred in women's fantasies on a nightly basis.

The knight didn't seem aware of her glances. He'd pulled out a physical book from who knew where under his cloak and was reading.

"I'm here to cooperate." Casmir flashed back to Rache's doctor drawing his blood from his neck, and he unfastened the top of his suit. He caught the captain glowering at him and realized it would be a good idea to attempt to befriend Ishii rather than continuing to pick at old scabs. That might have been easier if Ishii hadn't heard him sharing his childhood nickname with his men. "I'll answer anything you need to know, Captain. By the way, I know we were busy sniping at each other earlier, but the *Osprey* is really impressive. Congratulations on the command. Have you had it long?"

Ishii gazed flintily at him. As much as Casmir wanted to dislike him and assume his noble blood had gotten him the command, that was probably only partially true. Casmir didn't interact often with members of the military, but even he knew thirty-two was young to have a ship like this and the responsibility that went with it.

"You said it was a Great Raptor 7, right?" Casmir went on, having found success enticing sullen colleagues into talking by bringing up their passions. Ishii *had* to be proud of his ship and know all about it. "Two fusion reactors for redundancy, and what, twenty or thirty DEW turrets, ten torpedo bays, and six railguns? Crew complement of over five hundred?"

"Six hundred," Ishii said grudgingly. "We have a company of marines too."

"You must have been sent to hunt down Rache." Casmir doubted platoons of marines would be sent along to deal with a quarantined civilian ship. That suggested the *Osprey* had only recently been diverted, as he'd suspected.

"I'm surprised a roboticist knows anything about spaceships," Ishii said. "Or would be out here at all. I seem to remember you puking on a children's ride once. The Teacup, I believe it was called." His eyes glinted with pleasure at this memory.

Nurse Adjei was focused on his bare forearm, finding just the right spot for her injector, and only twitched an eyebrow at the comment. Casmir wondered if it was too late to crawl under the desk next to the chair.

"I have a colleague who collects model spaceships of all kinds," Casmir said. "He educates me on the attributes of everything in his collection whenever we have lunch together." Which was more often than Casmir might have opted for, but the rest of the faculty tended to avoid Kovacs. He didn't have an off switch, as Simon always said.

The jet injector hissed as the drug entered his bloodstream.

The nurse paused, a frown creasing her brow. "You're not on anti-nausea medication, right now, are you?"

A twinge of worry went through him at her reaction and the possibility that he *did* still have some in his system. The *Dragon* had plenty of non-prescription stuff in its little sickbay, but he didn't think he'd taken any since his capture. His body had finally somewhat acclimated to the variable gravity of the ships he'd been on.

"Not for a couple of days," Casmir said. "The gravity on your ship here is actually quite delightful." He smiled at Ishii, having no problem making the statement sincere.

"Uh huh." Ishii looked at the knight. "Do you want him first?"

The knight, whose name hadn't been mentioned yet, put a finger in his book to mark his spot and extended a hand toward Casmir. "Go ahead. Establish whether he's done anything criminal or not, as that will affect what I divulge to him."

Casmir studied him with fresh curiosity, trying to decipher the statement—was it possible this was another knight who'd been sent to warn him of something? Before he could get far in his musings, Ishii distracted him by leaning forward and dropping his hands onto the armrests of the chair.

"This would be more intimidating if you were taller," Casmir informed him.

Ishii's eyes closed to slits.

Casmir hadn't meant to resort to insults. Was that the drug already affecting him?

"Did you know about the bioweapon when you boarded the *Stellar Dragon*?" Ishii asked, getting right to business.

"No. And neither did the captain. She thought she was smuggling weapons, I gathered. The guns and cannons kind, not the terrible disease-in-a-vial kind." An uncomfortable warm sensation plucked at the back of Casmir's throat. God, he wasn't having an allergic reaction to the drug, was he? "She's a bounty hunter, but she's run up against some hard times, so she started smuggling stuff. Except for when she tried to collect a bounty on *me*. Did you know Tenebris Rache—"

"Stop," Ishii said.

Casmir complied, glad for the command since he'd been burbling. He'd hoped to avoid the subject of Rache, at least the part where they were twin brothers.

"Did Kim Sato know about the bioweapon when you boarded?" Ishii asked.

"No, she didn't even want to come along." Casmir moaned. "It's my fault that she's here. Those crushers came after me, and that knight told me to flee the planet because someone wanted me dead, and I was afraid they'd interrogate everybody who knew me in order to find me, so I told Kim she had to leave home. She's my roommate, you know. She was buying me celebratory wine because my prototype bird flew. Isn't that nice? People don't always get her, because she prefers work or being alone to social gatherings most of the time, but she doesn't dislike people. They just make her uncomfortable in large numbers. She thinks I'm all right though. Most of the time. Do you know the story about how we almost didn't become roommates?"

"Stop." Ishii sighed and looked at the knight in exasperation.

Was this not going as expected? Casmir had no basis for comparison, but he hoped Ishii hurried this along. He'd imagined this would be like consuming alcohol—something that tended to leave him awful at lying—but it was definitely a drug. Sweat beaded on his forehead, his heart pounded in his chest, and his throat was itching in earnest. Should he tell the nurse he needed some allergy medicine? Or was he simply having a panic attack? It wasn't as if *those* never happened...

Ishii snapped his fingers in front of Casmir's face, and Casmir realized he'd missed some more questions.

"Did you cheat at robotics camp?" Ishii asked.

Casmir wasn't sure if it was a test question or something for calibration. He couldn't imagine Ishii cared after all these years, but he heard himself answering promptly, as if his mind was detached from his body, and he listened from somewhere else in the room.

"No, you did," he said with unfeigned distress. "Or someone on your team did. Rocky—that was our final robot—you remember? Rocky was sabotaged before the battle. We didn't realize it until afterward, but he was missing..." Damn, why was his throat so tight? And was he breathing heavily or was that Ishii? Someone definitely was. He was so hot. "Someone took a piece out of the high-torque servo—he was walking kaput. Like me. I can't—uh, nurse? I think I need..." He was wheezing. That was definitely him. He patted Ishii's arm urgently. "Epinephrine, please."

He had to be polite with nurses and doctors. Reasonable and logical. His mother had told him that once. He couldn't be afraid all the time or talk about minor issues, or they would think he was a hypochondriac.

"Sir," the nurse said from somewhere far away. "Back up, please."

"What the hell is wrong with him?" Ishii stepped back and squinted at Casmir's face. "Are those hives?"

The nurse approached with a jet injector. Was that an antagonist? Or more of the truth drug?

Casmir shook his head violently, abruptly afraid of the latter. They would kill him.

"Sir, he's—"

The world disappeared from his awareness, and Casmir didn't hear anything else.

CHAPTER 5

"THIS WAY, DOCTOR," RACHE SAID, WAITING IN THE shadowy interior of the buried wreck.

Yas didn't know when it had crashed, but it looked to have been embedded in the glacier filling one end of the canyon for a long time. Maybe the glacier had shifted and revealed some of the ship only recently. He didn't know anything about this moon, other than the ridiculously frigid temperature his helmet display reported, but he assumed Skadi had some kind of tectonic activity in its core, something that had created its varied terrain features.

"Nobody's had their suits or helmets off," Rache said, apropos of nothing, as far as Yas could tell.

He led the way into the wreck, through shadowy holds and corridors, the walls more akin to circuit boards than the panels or smooth surfaces that humans would typically cover things with. Yas paused and touched one of the exposed surfaces, shivering even though he couldn't feel the extreme cold through his gloves.

"I would assume not," Yas said, eyeing the environmental stats displayed in his helmet. "It's rather lacking in oxygen out there. And nippy."

"The temperature is the least of our concerns."

Rache led him into a cavernous space filled with… Yas wasn't sure. Giant empty molds? Then he spotted a couple of bodies, and he forgot to wonder what had been in them.

They wore yellow and brown galaxy suits that had frosted over, so they weren't Rache's men. Were they part of that original archaeology team? For scientists, they had an unlikely number of rifles and pistols strapped to their suits. How long had they been there?

"Am I here to look at the bodies?" Yas asked quietly.

"Take a blood sample. See if they had the same thing that killed those scientists on the refinery."

"Do you think they're part of that team that got left behind? Guards, maybe?" Yas waved at the rifles.

"No."

He waited to see if Rache would explain further, but he only jerked a hand toward the bodies. "Do you have something in there to cut open their suits and get their blood?"

Blood that would be as frozen as they were. But that shouldn't matter much. He could still test them for the cellular damage that had killed the others.

"Yes." Yas patted his medical kit.

"See if you can identify them too. I'm guessing they're not from this system."

Yas wasn't either, so he wasn't sure about the significance of that, but he said, "Yes, sir."

"After you get that, you better take samples from the rest of the men too."

Yas looked sharply at him.

"Chains and Getton both independently reported feeling off. I've got Chaplain running scans of everything to check for radiation or any strange energy readings. Nothing so far."

"We've been down here for less than two hours," Yas said. "Even if there was a pathogen that they had somehow contracted through their suits—I deem that highly unlikely—they shouldn't have symptoms of anything yet."

"Test everyone, anyway."

"Yes, sir."

Rache walked over to join Chaplain. The other men must have been exploring elsewhere, deeper in the wreck. Dark conduit-lined corridors—or maybe access tubes?—headed away from the bay.

Rache and Chaplain pointed at the huge molds while holding a private discussion. Chaplain gestured with his hand scanner and shook his head. Each of the molds was wider across than a person, and whatever had lain inside had stretched thirty or forty feet in height and a dozen feet in thickness. Had they been empty for centuries? Or only recently cleared out? It was hard to imagine anyone in a shuttle coming down and taking even one of the large pieces, much less hundreds.

After some final orders to Chaplain, who jogged off deeper into the ship, Rache headed back toward the exit.

"Where are you going, sir?" Yas asked, a little alarmed at being left alone in the strange place, especially when he didn't yet know what had killed the two armed men on the ground.

"To look for signs that something larger than a shuttle filled with archaeologists landed here recently," Rache said without looking back.

He sounded irked. Because someone had cleared out the place first? What did he think had been in the molds? Pieces of a gate? An *entire* gate?

"Take those blood samples, Doctor," Rache said.

"Yes, sir," Yas murmured and set to work.

He took his samples as quickly as possible and returned to the shuttle, setting up a small lab in the mess area. Over the next couple of hours, he analyzed specimens and had Rache's grunts report to him for blood draws.

By the time Rache returned from his search of the area, Yas had some results. Alarming results. His bloodwork was normal—he'd tested himself first—and so was Chief Khonsari's. But Chaplain and the four fighters were showing the first signs of abnormal cellular damage, the same as Yas had seen in the dead scientists from the refinery.

"We have a problem," he said slowly, staring grimly and numbly at the microscope as Rache walked up.

"We've been affected?"

"Not everybody, not yet, but it may be only a matter of time." Yas stepped aside and waved for Rache to peer through the microscope and see.

"Is there a way to reverse it?"

"I don't even know what's causing it. I definitely suggest leaving."

"Not yet," Rache said. "I didn't find signs of another ship having landed, certainly not one large enough to remove those gate pieces, if they were there to start with. I've got the men searching deeper in the labyrinth of the wreck. It's huge, and maybe it's possible the pieces were moved somewhere else in the ship. If they've simply been gone for a long time, it may be possible to find more of the circuit boards like that monkey droid held."

"Sir, I think staying here is a very bad idea."

"Noted. We won't stay long." Rache leaned back from the microscope. "Just long enough to complete the search. Meanwhile, if you can figure out how to give us immunity from whatever is causing this, and how to reverse the damage, that would be ideal."

Yas made a choking sound. "I'm sure it would, but I can't do that with the contents of my medkit. At the least, I'd need a fully stocked lab of—"

"There's more medical equipment secured in those cabinets." Rache waved to a storage area opposite the little mess.

Frowning, Yas opened a couple of cabinets. There was a lot of equipment, far more than would have been typical on a combat shuttle.

"You knew," Yas whispered, unable to keep the accusation out of his voice. "You knew this was a possibility, that we'd be infected."

"Of course I knew it was possible. I didn't think it *likely* that a pathogen originated down here, but…" Rache twitched his shoulders. "I deemed the possibility of acquiring pieces of a gate worth the risk. This find could change the course of human development and the development of the entire galaxy. And whoever holds and controls that technology would be able to direct those changes."

"*Worth the risk?*" Yas couldn't keep his voice from rising in disbelief. "You decided that for all of us?"

"It's my prerogative as the commander of the *Fedallah* to make decisions on behalf of my crew every day, Doctor. Stop wasting time, and research how to stop this damage to the cells while we continue to search the ship."

"I don't know how to *do* that," Yas said.

Rache had already been turning away, but he turned back to stare at Yas.

"I'm a surgeon. Occasionally a toxicologist. Whatever is affecting people—killing them—isn't a drug or a poison. I checked. I don't know *what* it is. If it's a pathogen, which I saw no sign of in any of the blood samples, I don't know how it's being transferred. I already investigated all this when I did the autopsy on the dead archaeologist. I didn't know then, in the lab on your ship, and I'm not going to figure it out in some dinky field lab set up in the *kitchen*." Yas flung a dismissive hand at the tiny mess area.

Rache wasn't moving, didn't seem to be breathing or blinking at all behind that mask. Yas licked his lips. Had he pushed the man too far? He'd been ready to ask him for a favor after talking to Jess, but what kind of bastard would do this? Risk his own crew's lives, and for what? Empty molds that may or may not have ever held pieces to a wormhole gate?

"You should have kept the bacteriologist," Yas added. "Why'd you send her to the damn refinery if you knew you were coming here and might end up infected with something?"

"In hindsight, that was a mistake," Rache said quietly. "I didn't know what to expect from the bioweapon."

Yas hadn't even known there had *been* a bioweapon. Did Rache keep anyone in his crew in the loop?

"You think she would be better qualified than you to solve this?" Rache asked.

"I *know* she would be. I mean, from what I saw of her record, she's not a virologist, but this is far closer to her realm than mine."

"Very well, Doctor." Rache opened a channel to speak with the whole team. "Chaplain, Chains, come with me. We're taking a short trip. Chief Khonsari, join the rest of the men in the wreck and see if you can help them find some interesting technology while we're gone."

"Yes, sir," numerous people said.

Yas, however, blurted, "Wait. Where are you going? You can't just leave Jess and the others down there. And are you leaving me too? I can't even get a network signal down here. If something happens to you, we'll all be marooned." Marooned until they ran out of air and died, which wouldn't take very damn long…

"Then pray nothing happens to us." Rache headed toward the pilot's seat. "I'm going to bring you help."

Yas stared at his back, realizing he'd just condemned that bacteriologist to being kidnapped. Again.

Kim leaned over the microscope while the computer analyzed blood samples the team had taken from four different bodies. All manner of results came up for bacteria and viruses that were typical human companions and usually lay dormant, occasionally rearing up to cause some illness during times of stress. She didn't see anything that would explain what they were seeing. As Ayik had said, these people had died of intense cellular damage, which had caused multiple systems to shut down.

Every sample she looked at was filled with massive clumps of misfolded proteins, the kind of thing that happened over time in degenerative diseases and could be caused by age, mutations, and environmental stressors. Acute radiation poisoning was the only thing she could imagine causing such an abrupt response, but she'd had Dr. Angelico check the ship for excess radiation, and she'd checked the bodies and the galaxy suits the crew had been wearing when they'd died. Nothing out of the ordinary. Nor did the bodies have any of the outward signs of acute ionizing radiation poisoning, such as bruises, bleeding, and hair loss. On the cellular level, the damage was more akin to what one might expect to develop over time from slow doses of non-ionizing radiation. But these people had all died in days.

Kim leaned back and rubbed her lower back. Her head throbbed, reminding her it had been a long time since her last cup—make that squishy bulb—of coffee.

She craved espresso shots from The Roasting Tree on campus back home. She could imagine the rich velvety coffee caressing her tongue, making her feel alert and alive as it warmed her throat. God, she missed her life. As it was, she would probably have to find some caffeinated booster in sickbay so she wouldn't have to deal with withdrawal symptoms while she was trying to work. She couldn't keep herself from giving the microscope a disgusted sneer.

"How's it going, Kim?" Angelico ambled into the lab she had claimed and leaned an elbow against the counter.

She hadn't invited him to use her first name and bristled inwardly at the familiarity, but she reminded herself social conventions did not matter now. "I'm aching for a good cup of coffee, and I'm ninety-nine percent sure we're not dealing with a viral or bacterial infection."

She wished they *were* because that would have been far more in her wheelhouse than this. Not only was she mystified as to what was causing this; she wasn't sure how to stop or reverse the damage. Might some of the proven anti-aging therapies out there help? And if so, would this research ship have any of the equipment necessary? People typically went to specialized medical spas for treatments.

"Coffee," Angelico said. "There's an addiction if I ever met one. You should wean yourself off it. Why rely on exogenous substances to feel normal?"

"Because they taste good. Can I help you with something?"

"Sikou wants a blood sample from you. She's taking them from everyone on the team to see if we've been infected. Or, if you're right, I guess it would be *affected*?"

Kim wondered why he used Sikou's last name and presumed to use her first name. Then she wondered why it bothered her.

"I'll go see her in a minute," Kim said.

She'd thought of testing herself earlier, as soon as she'd realized that her hazmat suit wasn't likely to do anything to stop this, but a part of her didn't want to know. It would be easier to do research and think clearly if she wasn't worrying about her own impending death.

All she'd wanted when she'd asked Casmir and the others to head this way was to find her mother. How had she gotten herself tangled up in all this?

"I'll let her know." Angelico stepped closer and rested a hand on her shoulder. "If you *do* like coffee, there's this place on the Odin Orbital Station with all these pools and waterfalls and trees that serves all manner of fancy drinks. You can sit and have a great view of the planet while you imbibe your chosen poison. They've got great green smoothies too—those are my stardust. Super healthy, you know. We should go have a drink sometime after we survive all this. Take in the views, chat about work. Or recreation." He smiled and squeezed her shoulder.

She stared at him in disbelief. Was he *hitting* on her while there were corpses in the other room and they were trying to keep more people from dying? *Why?* He couldn't even have a good idea of what she looked like through her suit and faceplate.

"After this, I'm looking forward to enjoying the views of Odin *from* Odin. Thanks."

He chuckled. "Maybe you'll give me a chance to change your mind later." He patted her on the shoulder, letting his hand linger for intolerable seconds, then winked and ambled back out.

Kim decided that was a good excuse to step into the lab's little sanitation room so she could thoroughly decontaminate before doing a quick blood draw. She may have scrubbed her shoulder more than necessary.

When she was done, she checked her blood herself, trying for her usual calm detachment as the test ran. It was just another blood sample. No reason for the moon rocks of dread weighing down her stomach.

Relief flowed through her veins when her blood didn't show any more than normal signs of aging, at least not yet. Was it possible that only people who went down to the wreck were affected?

No, according to Ayik, the crew members who'd died here on the ship hadn't gone down there. They were the ones Angelico had used for his autopsies. Kim wondered if they had all had contact with the returning team. Unless she went over all of the ship's internal camera footage for the last week, that would be hard to discern. The only people left living on the *Machu Picchu* had been locked up in quarantine when that team returned to the ship.

"Scholar Sato?" Sikou said from the doorway to the lab. "Did Dr. Angelico—"

"Yes, I just tested my blood." Kim waved to the display. "It's negative, so far. I can send you the results."

"Good. The people inside the quarantine still read as normal too. As does our team. Let's hope that continues." Sikou frowned and looked toward the exit to sickbay, then held up a finger and left.

Kim followed her out to the corridor and looked in the same direction. She hadn't heard anything, but noticed the marine who'd stationed himself at the door was gone.

An alarm wailed, and red lights flashed.

"Security is compromised," the ship announced in a female voice. "Weapons fire is taking place in the corridors. Security, dispatch a team to sickbay."

If the entire crew was in quarantine or dead, there was no security team to be dispatched.

Sikou cursed and stepped back into the lab, waving Kim to go with her.

"Roark, report," Sikou said.

A boom sounded, and the deck shivered.

"Was that an explosive?" Kim looked around for something she might use as a weapon. Unfortunately, she didn't see anything deadlier than small scissors and scalpels. Both would be useless against combat armor.

"Roark," Sikou shouted this time. "Report!"

Two men in black combat armor charged into sickbay. Shit. Those weren't Kingdom Fleet colors.

Another explosion reverberated through the walls, much closer this time. Shards flew, and Kim glimpsed a blue-armored man skidding across the deck outside, arms flailing, a blackened hole yawning in the chest of his armor. That was one of the marines. He struck the wall and didn't get up.

One of the black-armored intruders sprang through the doorway and into her lab. Sikou scurried out of the way, pressing her back to the counter. The intruder didn't seem to notice her. He lunged for Kim.

She sprang to the side, but he moved faster than should have been possible, and he caught her shoulder, a steel grip latching onto her suit. She cried out in anger and slammed a palm strike into his side. It hurt her hand far more than it hurt him through that armor, but she hardly cared. She struck again, trying to knock him back so she could twist away and flee into the bowels of the ship.

But he didn't let go. He hoisted her over his shoulder and strode out of the lab.

She twisted enough to slam her elbow into the back of her captor's helmet, but she didn't get so much as a surprised grunt. The arm wrapped around her tightened, and she could barely breathe. Her captor strode through the deserted corridors, passing charred and warped bulkheads.

"I don't know what you think you're doing," Kim gritted out, reluctantly accepting that her martial-arts training was worthless on someone protected by combat armor, "but everyone on this ship is afflicted with some killer disease that can pass through galaxy suits and combat armor. You're an idiot for coming here."

"Really," came her captor's dry reply.

It was a familiar dry reply, though it took her a moment to place the voice. It almost sounded like Casmir. Casmir with a more cultured Kingdom accent.

Kim groaned. "I was hoping I'd never see you again."

"How distressing for my ego." Rache set her down in front of an airlock hatch but kept his hand around her neck, the pressure of his grip all too noticeable through her hazmat suit. A normal human might not have been able to hurt her through it, since it was as strong as the material used in galaxy suits, but he wasn't normal. "Any chance you'd like to come along voluntarily, so I don't feel like an ass for kidnapping you?"

"You're asking me this with your hand around my neck?" she asked in disbelief, her fingers curling into fists. She wished she knew one vulnerable spot on that armor, as she would gladly risk herself for a chance to send him flying. "After you just killed the marines sent along to protect us?"

"I suppose my timing could be better."

"You *are* an idiot. I don't know how that could be possible, all things considered, but it's as clear as Glasnax."

"An idiot who needs a doctor to help his men down at the wreck."

The wreck? The wreck where her mother had last been seen? She did want to go down and look for her, but not before she found a solution to their medical mystery and not with some murdering pirate.

A second man in black armor jogged up. "Nobody's coming after us, Captain. Made sure of it."

"Good." Rache waved him through the open hatch into a shuttle. "Scholar Sato?"

"I'm not volunteering, if that's what you're asking."

"Unfortunate." He lifted her and spun her toward the shuttle.

Furious at the manhandling, even if her suit protected her from injury, she twisted in the air, coiled her legs, and slammed a side kick into his chest. She knew it wouldn't hurt him, but she trusted that he needed her alive, and it felt good to protest. Childish, but good.

"She's feisty for a doctor," one of Rache's men commented.

There were two of them in the shuttle, each carrying weapons that looked more like cannons than guns. They'd probably been designed to take down aircraft. Or men in combat armor.

SHIP OF RUIN

Kim shook her head bleakly as Rache, unbothered by her mighty kick, strapped her into one of the two front seats. She wondered if Dr. Sikou or anybody else who'd come over with her was left alive. Not certain where she was going or how long she would have reception, she thought about sending Casmir a short message, but she knew he would worry.

CHAPTER 6

CASMIR WOKE UP WITH A POUNDING HEADACHE AND stared up at a gray ceiling, confused. Where was he? He wanted to be home, with his mother taking care of him, but unfortunately, awareness returned quickly, and he remembered where he was. And that he'd had an allergic reaction to the drug he'd so wisely volunteered to take, and broken into a wheezing hive-speckled mess in front of the cute nurse. How lovely.

The nurse's concerned face came into view, and she touched his shoulder. "How do you feel?"

"Alive," he croaked. His throat hurt, but at least it wasn't swelling shut anymore.

"That's good. You scared me." She smiled quickly, but the worry didn't fade from her eyes. "Doctors Sikou and Angelico are over on the other ship, and I didn't know… I mean, I've administered epinephrine and diphenhydramine for allergic reactions, of course, but then you had a seizure."

"Yeah." Casmir patted her arm, wondering what it said that he needed to comfort her. Just that he was used to his life, and she wasn't, he supposed. "Like I said, Rache took my meds."

"You should have told me that you're prone to seizures."

"You didn't ask. And I wanted the drug to work, so I could clear my name. It's been a very confusing month, and I think the authorities are, unfortunately, even more confused than I am. Uhm, you don't, by chance, have some rivogabine in here, do you? I can print off my prescription for you if you need it." He made a vague gesture toward his embedded chip.

"I'll check the inventory, but people with seizure disorders aren't allowed into the military, so I'm not sure…"

"Yes, I have a whole list of stuff that ensured I wasn't going to enlist when I turned eighteen. It's fortunate I was far more interested in building things to do my fighting for me than flinging myself out on the front lines."

Ishii walked into view and frowned down at Casmir.

Casmir decided that statement had sounded rather cowardly, even if it was true. Oh, well. He'd given up on trying to impress the nurse as soon as he broke out in hives, and Ishii, who seemed fixated on the antics of ten-year-old Casmir, wasn't responding well to his overtures of friendship.

"You really didn't cheat at robotics camp?" Ishii asked.

Casmir almost laughed. "Has this really been bothering you all these years?"

"No. I hadn't thought about it until you showed up on my display, but it may have checkered my belief that you could be involved in something criminal now."

Casmir closed his eyes, weariness making his lids heavy. He wasn't sure how long he'd been knocked out, but he suspected it had been longer than typical for a seizure. He probably had an impressive cocktail of drugs swimming through his bloodstream.

"I did disable the weapons on Forseti Station," Casmir said, compelled to honesty. He didn't know if it was the aftereffects of the drug, or if he just needed to confess. "So we could get away, but only because Captain Lopez promised me that bounty hunters would be after me, and I needed to get off the station. I already knew the crushers were after me. I don't suppose you people know who sent those?"

"We people?"

"The military. I've assumed the government isn't after me, for several reasons, including that the crushers were stolen from the military research lab instead of merely checked out."

"I don't know. Sir Asger might. He arrived only a few days ago, docking his shuttle in a bay here and giving me travel orders from Royal Intelligence signed by the commander and the queen. Neither he nor the orders said what he wants here—I *thought* he'd been assigned to assist with capturing Rache—but he was awfully interested in collecting you." Ishii raised his eyebrows. "What are you involved in, Dabrowski?"

"I really don't know, but I was on the design team that invented the crushers." Casmir lifted his head. "Uhm, is Zee still in the corridor?"

"Looming and collecting dust, yes."

Casmir refrained from mentioning that Viggo's vacuums would have kept that from happening and that Ishii's fancy warship might have a substandard cleaning system.

"From what I've learned about the crushers from a brief chat with Asger, I'm relieved you ordered him to stay out there."

"Yeah." Casmir shivered as he imagined dying on the deck as Zee hurled the nurses around and kept them from helping him.

"I'll send Asger in to talk to you now." Ishii walked toward the door.

Casmir was curious about what the knight would say, but he wished he could sleep for twelve hours before anyone else questioned him. When Asger and his purple cloak swept into view, Casmir struggled to get his brain into order.

"You look like hell." Asger had walked in with his book. He lifted his cloak and made the tome disappear into some pocket.

Casmir wouldn't have guessed cloaks *had* pockets, but they weren't a garment he ever shopped for, so who knew?

"Thanks. You look like the guy on the posters plastered around the capital to perpetuate the legend of knights and convince kids with a smidgen of noble blood to apply for the program."

"Actually, I'm on the bodybuilding posters, promising dazzling delight to all who come to my shows." He posed, flexing his biceps. He wore his gray liquid armor, but that didn't keep the size of his arms from being apparent.

"Bodybuilding?" Casmir asked, surprised by this turn toward the whimsical.

"You haven't seen any of my shows? What about the calendar? No? That's disappointing."

"I wouldn't have guessed knights were allowed to engage in, uh, spectator sports."

Asger shrugged. "It's something I got into as a teenager. A little modeling but mostly bodybuilding in competitions. I got an agent and was doing shows all around the continent while I was still a squire, and he talked my commander into letting me continue, as long as we didn't use my knighthood as a selling point. I'm pretty good at filling the seats based on my own merits."

"Merits?" Casmir wasn't sure if he was confused because his mind was a postictal, drug-addled mess or because this wasn't even vaguely the conversation he'd expected to have with the knight. Maybe both.

Asger did the pose, showing off the biceps again. His blue eyes glinted with mischief or humor, maybe both, and Casmir hoped that meant the man didn't take himself too seriously.

"Of course," Casmir said. "*Merits*. I see now."

"If you were female, you would have noticed them right away."

"Undoubtedly true."

Casmir decided his new knight acquaintance was younger than he'd realized. Early twenties. It crossed his mind that this might be a suitable knight to introduce to Qin, merits and arrogance aside. Someone that age might be less likely to hold the old biases tight to his chest. Casmir wondered if he could set them up for a coffee date. Or a sparring date. He wasn't entirely clear about what Qin wanted to do with a knight, beyond meeting one.

"How much did Sir Friedrich tell you?" Asger asked, thankfully switching topics.

"Hardly *anything*. The crushers showed up, and he jumped out the window to fight them, to give me time to get away."

"You know he's dead." Asger's eyes narrowed, and Casmir remembered that he'd lied about that when he left his message on Forseti. Did Asger know?

"I suspected, yes. I saw some of the footage from a parking-garage camera."

"Our… employer sent him to help you, to get you to safety. She sent *me* to try to find out who stole the crushers and wants you dead. I followed two of the crushers to Forseti Station and then got bogged down in the mess you left there."

"Sorry. I—did you say *she*?" Casmir's breath caught. "Do you mean—Sir Friedrich said my *mother* sent him to deliver the message to get off the planet."

"Mother? That would be a rather surprising turn of events. Friedrich was my senior and actually lived at the castle, so he might have known more, but…" Asger squinted at Casmir, then shook his head. "I don't see it. Not even vaguely. Unless he didn't mean in a biological sense."

Casmir felt a twinge of disappointment, even though it didn't sound like Asger knew much for certain. As much as he loved his adoptive family, he'd gotten his hopes up at the idea of potentially meeting the woman who had given birth to him. Or at least commingled her genetic material with someone else's to have him created and birthed in an artificial womb.

"Are you talking about…" Casmir bit his lip. "*Who* are you talking about?"

Asger hesitated.

"It's not the queen, is it?" Casmir couldn't imagine why the queen would care about him, but Ishii had said she'd signed Asger's orders personally. Did that make her his employer?

Asger glanced over his shoulder. The nurses were gone, and so was Ishii.

"I asked that this not be recorded," Asger said, "but…" He shrugged and looked at Casmir.

A text message scrolled down Casmir's contact: *Messaging rights requested from Sir William Asger. Accept or deny?*

Accept, Casmir thought promptly.

The queen was the one to assign me this task, yes. And to tell Friedrich to help you get off-planet and—she hoped—out of danger. I don't know if the king knows anything about any of this. They have a close and amicable relationship, as far as I know, but they monitor different parts of the government and often work on different things.

Was Casmir a *thing*? And if so, why?

Aware of Asger watching him, Casmir nodded slightly, trying not to react much to the news, in case they *were* monitored. Did this silence mean Asger didn't know if he could trust Ishii? Or was all this supposed to be kept secret for some reason? Casmir's mouth went dry at the idea that the queen not only knew who he was, but might know more about who he was than he did.

I've only had modest luck with my part of the assignment, Asger continued, *but there's a terrorist outfit back on Odin—the Royal Intelligencers haven't yet been able to find their main base of operations—and I'm beginning to suspect they may be involved.*

Terrorists want me dead? Any idea why?

I don't know. It's more that there are clues linking them to the stolen crushers than anything obviously pertinent to you. Asger squinted at him. *You'll have to pardon me, but… you're not what I expected. I'm a little flummoxed as to why someone would consider you a threat.*

Yeah, you and me both.

Given that the knight had so far only seen him go into anaphylactic shock and have a seizure, Casmir could understand why he was underwhelmed.

Asger's forehead creased. Maybe it wasn't the response he'd wanted.

The terrorist organization—they call themselves the Black Stars— is working against Jager and his desires to expand again into other systems. They've struck both at home, near Zamek and the castle, and abroad. If they want you dead, it must be because they believe you have some value to Jager and his plans.

I've never met King Jager. Or the queen. Or anyone in the royal family. They don't slum at Zamek University that often.

It must have to do with your work.

Casmir shrugged helplessly. *Any input I had in the crusher project ended a year ago. I don't even know who the team lead for the robotics division of the military research lab is right now.*

He wondered what Asger would think if Casmir asked him to leave. He truly could use some rest, but now that he had the name of the group that had stolen the crushers and might have sent them against him, he wanted to scour the network for information on them. Black Stars. Maybe he could find something that had eluded Asger.

Did you travel outside of the system at all when you worked for the military research lab? Asger asked. *Do any work that could have caused grudges? Right now, the Kingdom is getting blamed for some things perpetrated by various organizations out there that want change. Numerous prominent habitat and world leaders like President Bakas have been assassinated in the last six months. It's true that Jager wants to bring more systems back into the Kingdom and is vehement about condemning the freaks of nature out there and what humanity is turning itself into, but I doubt he's behind those assassinations. The Senate would never approve of anything even hinting of that. Someone may be using us as scapegoats.* Asger rubbed his short beard, continuing to consider Casmir as he transmitted his words. *If you were out there, maybe someone is using* you *as a scapegoat.*

Casmir shrugged. *This is my first time off Odin. Before last month, I'd never even left my continent.*

Huh. Maybe it's not what you've done then, but something they think you will do. Asger waved toward the corridor, perhaps indicating Zee.

Uh, unless someone's scientists have mastered time travel, I don't see how anyone could know what I'll do. I certainly have no plans to create any more killer robots. I turned down a big bonus when the military asked me to continue research and development for them. I prefer being poor and being able to sleep at night. Casmir didn't want to downplay his worth or importance so much that the knight would grow disgusted and abandon him, but he found everything revealed thus far puzzling. *All I do now is teach and work on medical robots. Occasionally, robotic flight on the side. None of that should drive fear into the hearts of terrorists or any enemies of the Kingdom.*

Regardless, the latest I got from the queen is that she wants me to protect you. It doesn't matter if I understand why. Though I am pleased that it doesn't look like you've turned criminal. That would have created complications of loyalty and morality for me.

Casmir was bemused that his garbled answers to Ishii's questions had somehow proved his innocence, but he was happy if that meant no more Kingdom Guard officers would try to arrest him. He was less happy about Asger's promise of protection. The last knight who'd tried to protect him had gotten himself killed, and that made Casmir very uncomfortable. It was like he'd failed a test before he'd even realized he was taking one. He would prefer to rely only on Zee. He didn't want to lose Zee, either, but that would be less devastating than a human being.

The sickbay door hissed, and Ishii walked back in.

"We have two problems," Ishii told Asger, ignoring Casmir.

"New ones or old ones?" Asger asked.

"New. The Kingdom ships that guard the gate are under attack from an unidentified cargo vessel—what *appears* to be a cargo vessel but has massive shielding, a huge arsenal of weapons, and stealth technology. There's speculation that it's something even greater than a slydar hull, but someone may simply be making excuses to explain why they haven't taken it down." Ishii clenched his jaw. "It almost slipped past our people, but they've got the gate blockaded sufficiently right now and are keeping it in the system. But at great cost. They've requested backup. The *Goshawk* and the *Kestrel*—the two other warships we were traveling with—have left the refinery investigation and search for Rache's ship, and are heading over, but we've also been commanded to set course for the gate to help."

"That seems like overkill for one ship, no matter how high tech," Asger said.

"I wasn't given many details—" Ishii grimaced, sounding frustrated at that, "—but I read between the lines that the cargo ship may have used its stealth to sneak into the system and steal something important. Something we're going to be in trouble over if it gets out."

Casmir frowned down at his blanket and mulled over whether that could have to do with the missing archaeologists and the piece of gate they'd discovered.

"What's the other news you mentioned?" Asger asked.

Ishii finally turned his attention to Casmir, and a twinge of dread drove out his other thoughts. Before Ishii spoke, Casmir knew it would be bad news.

"The other news is that Kim Sato was kidnapped."

"What?" Casmir lurched into a sitting position, not caring that his headache intensified, as if someone was hammering his skull with a mallet. "How?"

He almost asked *who,* but somehow, he already knew. His dread curdled in his stomach.

"A combat shuttle sneaked up to the *Machu Picchu* from the moon, and a raid team shot the marines I sent over and snatched her away before anyone commed us. My medical officers are injured and the marines are dead." Ishii's eyes turned molten with anger.

"I'm sorry you lost men." And Casmir was, but he couldn't keep from blurting, "Where was she taken? Do we know?"

"The shuttle was heading back toward the moon before it disappeared from our scanners." Ishii frowned at Asger. "I'm irritated at all the mysterious tech that's shown up this week. Why are we behind? Don't we have intelligence officers—and knights—stationed all over the Twelve Systems so we won't be surprised like this?"

Asger sighed. "Just because you're surprised doesn't mean Royal Intelligence doesn't know about new developments."

"We have to get her." Casmir barely heard their conversation. He swung his legs over the side of the bed, wondering why and when someone had put him in a loathsome hospital gown, and teetered as soon as his feet touched down. Unfortunately, he didn't think he could blame the gravity. "It's Rache. It's got to be."

Asger gripped his arm to keep him from tipping over. "What do you mean it's Rache? You think he's on the moon?"

"I think he's kidnapped my best friend."

"Why would he want a bacteriologist?"

"Why did he want *me*? I don't know." Casmir looked around. Clothing. Where was his clothing? And his borrowed galaxy suit? He needed to be dressed to rescue Kim.

Ishii scratched his cheek. "We didn't get to that part of the interrogation, did we? Why *did* he kidnap you? And what happened to the bioweapon?" He glanced at Asger.

Asger only shrugged. "We've been trying to get a spy onto Rache's ship for years, but he's talented at ferreting them out. It's unfortunate that the female assassin didn't succeed. We'd thought…" He waved a dismissive hand. "That was years ago, and we're certain she's dead now."

Ishii seemed to find the answer more frustrating than enlightening, and he turned back to Casmir.

Casmir spotted his suit draped over a chair and clawed on the lower half, again with Asger keeping him from falling over. His weary limbs were even more lacking in coordination than usual.

"He didn't kidnap me," Casmir said, sensing he'd have to explain what he could in order to get Ishii's help. "He put a bounty out for me, and I don't know why." He was glad he had the excuse of focusing on dressing to avoid looking Ishii in the eyes. He didn't know if curiosity about their blood was the only reason Rache had wanted him, but it was the only one he knew, and he didn't want to admit that link to anyone. "Maybe the same reason the people who stole the crushers sent them after me. Whatever that is."

Casmir didn't buy Asger's reasoning that he might one day invent something important that would help the Kingdom. Who could possibly know that?

"As for the bioweapon," he continued, guessing that concerned the men more than his bounty, "I'm crossing my fingers that it blew up along with the refinery. The case holding it was open and in the middle of a firefight when Kim and I escaped. There were explosives everywhere. Captain Lopez and her co-pilot helped set them off and get us out, apparently feeling guilty about handing me over to such a notorious pirate. If the bioweapon didn't blow up, then Rache has it." Casmir tugged his suit over his shoulders and fastened the seam. "I was hoping *Rache* blew up, but then a shuttle appeared behind us. We thought it was chasing us, but it headed to the moon instead of to the research vessel. Rache must want what's down there. Maybe he got himself infected with whatever has people quarantined on the research vessel." Casmir looked at them. "Damn, that must be it. Why else would he need Kim?"

"What could possibly be down there that's making people get sick and die?" Ishii asked.

"I don't know. All I know is that the archaeologists found a gate fragment down there. At the least."

Ishii's eyebrows shot up.

"You don't know about that?" Casmir looked back and forth between them.

Did Asger seem less surprised? It was hard to tell.

"I assumed the archaeologists reported all their findings to the government when they asked for help," Casmir added.

Ishii frowned, looking perplexed.

"I'm aware that they reported finding what *might* be a gate," Asger admitted. "It's in pieces down there, or it was."

"How do you know more than I do?" Ishii asked in exasperation. "Isn't *he* your mission?" He thrust a finger toward Casmir.

"It seems so." Asger contemplated Casmir as if he believed someone had made a mistake in sending him out to protect a lowly civilian roboticist.

"Why wouldn't Fleet have told me about all this?" Ishii demanded. "I understand need-to-know, but they sent me to blow up a ship with quarantined survivors on it. Do they truly fear a virus or are they covering up that we may have found a gate? And how much trouble am I going to get in because I *didn't* blow it up?"

Asger lifted his hands in a gesture that wasn't successful at placating. "I don't know much more than you do. It's possible the Fleet higher-ups don't know anything about this at all, that it went straight to Royal Intelligence and the king and queen. That's a civilian research ship, after all."

"Is that what that teched-up cargo ship stole?" Ishii flung a hand toward the wall. "A spare *gate*?"

"I doubt anyone found an entire gate," Asger said. "The report mentioned pieces…"

"I bet Rache knows more than both of you combined. Maybe that cargo ship is full of his friends or employers." Casmir tugged on his boots. "If we get Rache, we can get Kim back, *and* you can interrogate him about all he knows. I'll cheer you on as you do it."

As soon as the last words came out, he wondered if they were true. If they got Rache's mask off, everyone would see the unsubtle resemblance, and everyone would know they were related. Would that land him back in trouble again? Guilt-by-association? Or guilt-by-blood, more accurately. Casmir snorted, wondering if Rache would have an allergic reaction to interrogation drugs.

"Dabrowski," Ishii said, "we have orders to go to the gate and stop that cargo ship from leaving the system."

"If they have gate bits in their hold, that seems like a good idea." Fully dressed, Casmir stood on his own and faced them.

He was ready to go get Kim, but he needed a shuttle. That was the only way off the ship and the only way to catch up with Rache. Except, ugh, he needed a pilot too. Casmir's poor depth perception would have gotten him laughed out of flight school if he'd ever applied.

"But you need to leave behind a strike team and a shuttle, Captain. And I need to be on it. We can't leave Kim with that man."

Asger frowned. "You don't even know that's who has her. Or why he would want her."

"Like I said, it's got to be for the same reason you wanted her. Nobody else out here has any experience with horrific bacteria that kill people." Casmir had no idea yet if that was what they were dealing with, but he didn't much care. He just knew he had to rescue his friend.

He didn't like the way Ishii and Asger were exchanging long looks.

"Just leave me with a shuttle and some men, Captain. Sora. Please." Casmir spread an imploring hand. "I promise not to tell anyone else your childhood nickname."

Ishii scowled, not looking amused.

"And I won't complain if you tell everyone you know about my Teacup experiences. Please."

"I have orders, Dabrowski. We've already left orbit."

"*What?*"

Casmir lunged to grab him, but Ishii stepped back and evaded the grasp easily.

"Asger, calm him down or put him in the brig until he calms down on his own," Ishii said. "I'd say to drug him, but I don't need him convulsing on the deck again."

"Wait, Sora—"

"*Captain* Ishii," he said and stalked toward the door.

As Ishii strode out, Casmir glimpsed Zee's shoulder, the crusher in the precise spot where Casmir had told him to wait hours earlier. He almost, in a fit of stupidity, ordered Zee to stop Ishii, to force him to give Casmir a shuttle and a pilot, but even Zee couldn't plow through a crew of six hundred, including a hundred marines in combat armor.

Casmir slumped into the chair, utter defeat making him far more fatigued than the drugs had.

"I'm sorry, Casmir," Asger said quietly. "As much as Rache hates the Kingdom, he doesn't usually target civilians. If she cooperates, maybe he'll let her live."

"I've known Kim for seven years." Casmir dropped his head between his knees and gripped the back of his neck with both hands. "If there's one thing she doesn't do, it's give in to the demands of bullies."

CHAPTER 7

YAS HADN'T FOUND ANYTHING ENLIGHTENING, AT LEAST IN regard to the medical problem, in the strange derelict, and he rushed outside as soon as the shuttle returned, descending slowly into the narrow canyon. It landed in the same icy spot, lights brightening the forest of frozen stalagmites. The sun had set, its meager light fading from the moon.

Yas strode toward the shuttle and waited for the hatch to open. Long moments passed, and he stepped back, wondering if some Kingdom soldiers might have killed Rache and taken it. What would he do if angry marines leaped out, pointing rifles at his chest?

When the hatch finally opened, interior light slashing out into the night, nobody at all stepped out.

"Come help your new colleague set up the lab, Dr. Peshlakai," Rache's dry voice came over the comm.

Yas grimaced and walked into the shuttle, expecting to find a hapless woman tied to a chair. He found Kim Sato in a bright yellow hazmat suit leaning against the navigation console with Rache next to her in his black armor. She wasn't tied and didn't hold any weapons, but the way her arms were folded over her chest made her attitude clear. When her dark gaze landed on Yas, he read accusation in her angry eyes.

Yas turned to close the hatch—and avoid her eyes. He wished he dared say he wasn't with Rache, that he was also a prisoner. But that wasn't strictly true. He'd agreed to this, and he had, however inadvertently, been responsible for Rache bringing her down here.

Rache pointed toward the back of the passenger area, to the mess-turned-laboratory where Yas had been working before. Yas sighed and headed back to pull out the medical equipment. Maybe he could apologize to Scholar Sato when Rache wasn't glaring at them both.

Rache reached for her, as if to force her to follow, but she jerked her arm away before he touched her. Chin up, she strode down the aisle toward the lab.

"I brought as much medical equipment from the *Fedallah* as I thought would be useful and that would fit," Rache said.

Even if they'd had all the equipment in the warship's sickbay, Yas, who'd done an inventory and knew what was there, doubted it would have been sufficient for their purposes.

Judging by the way Kim stopped and stared at the counter and the contents of the cabinets, she was unimpressed. Or perhaps in shock.

"Have you contracted the disease yet, Doctor?" Rache asked.

"I'm showing signs of cellular damage, yes. I retested everyone down here less than an hour ago, and everybody is now. We should retest you."

"I've been away from the moon and the wreck."

Kim spoke for the first time. "Numerous crew members from the research vessel who never came down here died—according to the quarantined people who remain unaffected. I was in the middle of determining if person-to-person contact caused it, whether something in the air did, or if they brought back something from the wreck that caused the people on board to be afflicted. By the way, I'd like to *see* the wreck at some point to see if it spurs any ideas. I was on the verge of going over internal video footage of the research ship to try to learn exactly what happened and how this spreads."

"Does this mean you're agreeing to work on this now?" Rache asked.

She shot him a hard look. "I was working on it *before*. You didn't need to drag me down to this frozen hell." Judging by the way she waved at the mess station, she might have been referring to her new work area more than the moon. "I had a state-of-the-art lab up there. I'd be hard-pressed to find evidence of the common cold here."

"I'll be happy to give you a tour of the wreck personally," Rache said.

"What an honor."

"This is Dr. Peshlakai." Rache waved at Yas. "He will assist you as needed."

Yas grimaced, hoping Rache wouldn't say he'd been the one to request Kim for the team. That hadn't been his intent when he'd brought her up.

Kim gazed at him with dark impassive eyes. It was his first time meeting her—he'd seen the roboticist, Casmir Dabrowski, when they'd been on board but not Kim Sato—and Yas wished the circumstances weren't so dire. He would have been curious to ask her about her work.

"Yas Peshlakai?" she asked.

"Yes," he said, surprised a Kingdom medical researcher had heard of him.

"I took a toxicology class at the university," she said. "I remember reading some of your papers and being surprised that you weren't much older than I was and had publications in a prestigious journal."

"It was something I got into at a young age." He felt wary with her but warmed a little at the recognition.

"I wouldn't have expected to find you working for a mercenary." She must not have heard about his president's death.

Yas snorted. "I wouldn't have expected it either."

"My people currently have a limited amount of time to live," Rache said coolly. "How about you get to work and save the lengthy introductions for later?"

"Their—*our*—lives wouldn't be at stake if you hadn't insisted on coming here, Captain," Yas said, feeling bolstered by Kim's presence, though maybe that was foolish. Did he think having a woman around would keep Rache from killing him? If anything, Rache might see him as superfluous now.

"A risk worth taking," he said again, heading for the hatch and waving for his fighters to come outside with him. So he could return to searching the wreck?

As far as Yas knew, nothing had been found while he'd been gone.

"Don't forget to send us a sample of your blood, Captain," Yas said.

"I will when I've had more time down here to be infected." Rache opened the hatch and stalked out.

"I suppose there's no chance he'll be the first to die?" Kim leaned against the counter with her arms folded over her chest again.

Yas realized she hadn't agreed to help. What if she stood there, glowering at the equipment, and refusing to do anything? It would be hard to blame her, given that she'd just been kidnapped, but he knew he'd soon feel the effects of all that internal damage, so he wanted her assistance. No, he wanted her to take the lead and know what to do.

"Scholar Sato," he said, "I'm very sorry you were brought into this, but I hope you'll continue the work you started up there. As I told Rache, I'm afflicted, as is our engineer." He wondered if introducing her to another woman might make her more inclined to help. But Jess's mouth might not endear Kim, and it wasn't as if Yas could tell the story she'd shared with him in confidence. Even if it might evoke sympathy from an outsider. "It's also likely that you'll be afflicted now that you're down here."

Yas had been wearing a galaxy suit and breathing from his oxygen tank while he'd been outside, but he removed his helmet now. Kim, ensconced in the hazmat suit, eyed him through her faceplate. He doubted he had to tell her that it was unlikely any form of suit would protect her from the threat.

"How *did* you end up here, Dr. Peshlakai?" she asked.

"You can call me Yas, and it's a long story. Essentially, I was framed by someone who made it look like I killed my president. Rache helped me escape, but there was a catch."

"I bet."

"I agreed to work for him for five years. At the time, I was desperate and didn't know who he was."

"Finding out must have been delightful."

"I may have cried a little. In a masculine way, as befitting a man of my stature."

Kim snorted, but she turned around and waved at the microscope. "Show me what you've got so far."

Casmir paced in sickbay while Zee stood by the door, and Asger sat in a chair, his book open in his lap. Casmir didn't know how much attention he was paying to it, as he'd been on the same page for a while, but he did know the knight wouldn't let him go out the door. He'd already tried. Sort of. After a few steps in that direction, he'd scurried back, because Zee had stepped ominously forward to intercept Asger's attempt to intercept Casmir.

He hadn't wanted to start a battle between his two allies, even if Asger's support was somewhat academic and stifling at this point. At least he hadn't followed Ishii's suggestion to throw Casmir in the brig.

In the last hour, Casmir had sent a number of messages to Kim, but wherever she was, she wasn't responding. He hoped that meant she simply didn't have network access, not that she was unconscious—or worse. Either way, her silence worried him.

"Get some rest, Dabrowski," Asger said, perhaps annoyed by his pacing. He stuck a finger between the pages and waved the book in a motion that might have meant go-to-bed or I'm-close-to-beating-you-with-this. The title on the front read *Either/Or.* How appropriate. "You're not going anywhere except to the gate with the rest of us."

Casmir gritted his teeth, wondering where Bonita and Qin were. Had they taken off in the *Dragon* or were they still lurking in the area, waiting to see if any opportunities to make money from the gate discovery came their way? Maybe he should have asked Ishii to drop him off on Bonita's ship—if it was around. Requesting a shuttle had been too much. Why would Ishii give him one of his shuttles? Even if losing Kim would be tragic because of her contributions to medicine, she wasn't one of his officers, so he probably didn't feel obligated to protect her.

Not like Casmir. She was only out here because of him, damn it.

While he paced, he accessed the network and found a chip ident for the only Captain Bonita Laser Lopez listed in the directory. He'd never spoken chip-to-chip to her when he'd been on board, but she didn't wear glasses, so he assumed she had an implant and contact display.

He sent a request for approval and paced, hoping she wasn't sleeping or already in another system. Though if there was a small war going on at the gate, she would have a hard time leaving.

How's your interrogation going, Dabrowski? came her response.

I had an allergic reaction and a seizure, Laser. Please call me Casmir. Thank you.

So it's going well, eh?

Kim was kidnapped from the research ship. Casmir was relieved she'd responded quickly, but he didn't want to waste time chitchatting, not when the warship was taking him farther from Skadi Moon with every passing minute. *Are you and the* Dragon *still in the area?*

More or less. We're orbiting the moon on the opposite side from the research ship, mostly hoping the military forgets about us. Viggo is finishing the repairs that we started. They need to be done before we jump to another system, and...

You're still waiting for an opportunity to make money?

There was a long pause before a response came back.

I don't want you to think I'm a greedy, money-grubbing ratera, *Casmir, which wouldn't be surprising since I was willing to sell you, but I could really use a break. I don't have anything lined up, and because I was an idiot and sent that money back to Rache, who's probably dead...*

I don't think he's dead. I think he's the one who kidnapped Kim. And you didn't sell me. You tried to collect what was, presumably, a legally issued bounty. He was about to ask for a favor, so he didn't want her to think he held anything against her.

Why would he want Kim? Did he get himself infected with something vile when that bioweapon exploded?

Casmir hadn't considered that possibility, but if Rache had been infected by the bioweapon, he would have gone after Kim immediately. He wouldn't have taken a meandering route down to the moon first.

I think he got infected with whatever is in that wreck down there. The same as the archaeologists who visited. Casmir returned to pacing—he'd stopped and was staring blankly at the wall while he read his messages, and Asger was squinting suspiciously at him. Casmir kept his head down, studying the deck.

You think I should take the Dragon *down there and fire my railgun at him, his shuttle, and the wreck? See if I can blow them all up for real this time? There is a bounty on his head, FYI. I checked. The Kingdom government has issued one for almost a million.*

While I understand your desire to rid the systems of him and collect a bounty like that, I'd prefer you not attempt to obliterate him when Kim is standing next to him.

Ah, right. Sorry. What did you have in mind? I assume you didn't contact me just to catch up. You're not in the brig over there, are you? I would have assumed they had their cells shielded to prevent inbound and outbound messages, but you're probably crafty enough to get around that.

No, I'm in sickbay with a knight standing guard.

Ah, the seizure. Right.

Casmir thought about pointing out that the allergic reaction had been more alarming than the seizure, but it didn't matter. *Will you help me if I can get Captain Ishii to transfer me to your ship?*

Another long pause followed. He knew he was asking her to risk getting close to the military, who might have a grudge against her thanks to the Forseti Station mishap, and also to potentially confront Rache. It was a major request. What could he offer her—legitimately offer her—to make it worth her while?

To help her snatch a piece of the gate? His conscience wouldn't allow that, not when she might take it and sell it to the highest bidder. But maybe…

Laser, I know I'm asking you to put yourself in danger for me—for Kim—but in exchange, I'm willing to help you make some money. I'll either build something with my robotics skills that you can sell, or I'll help you brainstorm ideas. I'm good at talking people into giving me money.

Please, I've seen your wardrobe. That can't be true.

Let me correct that. I'm good at getting people to give money to my department for research. I've gotten grants for millions, Laser. Just this past winter, I talked BornTech into giving us four state-of-the-art robots worth a million crowns each so we could focus on programming and not have to worry about building our own from scratch. I'm the one who gets sent to all the fundraiser dinners.

Is that because you're such a gifted negotiator or because you're the least socially awkward person in your department?

It's possible I've spent too much time on your ship.

I guessed right, didn't I?

All right, let's talk patents. I have several that I've never tried to make any money from. They were a result of extra-credit projects. I know enough people in the industry that I'm sure I could find a buyer for some of them. I'm willing to sign them over to you and get you in touch with those people.

If they're worth so much, why haven't you sold them?

I don't have a ship I need to keep flying, and I live in faculty housing with a roommate. My salary has always been sufficient for my needs. Laser, time is of the essence here. Please say yes so I can switch over to negotiating with the captain. You have my word. Help me, and I'll help you.

I'm positive I'm going to regret this. Why am I agreeing to it?

Because you've missed me terribly since I left?

That can't possibly be it.

Because Viggo wants someone to repair his vacuums?

That's closer to the truth.

He grinned and sent her the information on the medical vending machine he'd patented a few years back. It scanned a user's injury and dispensed bandages of the appropriate size along with a small tube of Skinfill. He would have to do some poking around once he got home and life settled down, but he believed he was being honest and could find a corporation that would be interested in it.

"Sir Asger." Casmir stuck his hands into the pockets of his suit and faced the knight. "I'm guessing the captain placed you here to keep me out of trouble, such as wandering off and trying to hijack his ship and turn it back around."

"Actually, I'm here to protect you. I sincerely doubt Captain Ishii is worried about you hijacking his warship."

"Ah." Casmir decided to take that as a logical assumption based on the prowess he'd thus far displayed rather than a deliberate insult. "Would you be willing to escort me to his office? I have a proposition for him."

"If I deny your request and try to keep you here, would I have to fight your robot? It seems to be programmed to protect you."

"I am a Z-6000, programmed to protect Kim Sato and Casmir Dabrowski," the crusher announced in his flat monotone.

Sadness struck Casmir in the chest like a hammer. Kim wasn't there to be protected.

Why hadn't he sent Zee to the *Machu Picchu* with her? Rache and his mercenaries had gotten the best of the crusher before, but if it had been a small strike team, maybe Zee could have made the difference this time.

"Yes, quite," Asger murmured, eyeing the crusher.

He knew about Friedrich's death and had surely seen the footage of his fellow knight's demise. Casmir should be pleased Asger hadn't gone berserk and attacked Zee the instant he saw him.

"I don't want to start a fight," Casmir said. "I just want to—need to—talk to the captain."

Asger stood, his long purple cloak swirling about his calves. He stuck his book into that hidden pocket.

"I'm a guest on Ishii's ship, and Fleet orders are usually the same as the king's orders." Asger's tone turned dry. "I'm not helping you escape."

"What makes you think I want to do that?"

Aside from the joke he'd made about doing so, of course…

"The steam coming out of your ears as you were pacing. The last time I saw someone think so hard, his brain exploded from spontaneous combustion."

"Was that a joke?" Casmir asked, hoping to divert Asger's thoughts, since he was fairly close in his guess. "I didn't know knights were encouraged to have senses of humor."

"We're normal people."

"With terrifying weapons, deadly reputations, and cloaks."

"That last naturally being the thing that precludes humor."

"You never see a stand-up comedian in a cloak." Casmir extended a hand toward the door. "Will you come? Or not stop me if I go?"

"Oh, I'm coming. I'm keeping an eye on you. Much like your solid friend here. He's taller than the other ones. Did you build him?"

Did Asger look the faintest bit intrigued or even impressed? Maybe that was wishful thinking.

"Yes. I was tired of being picked on by crushers. And overzealous Kingdom Guards. I thought I should be prepared for the next would-be bully that came my way."

Asger arched his eyebrows.

Either thanks to sublime genetics or attentive grooming habits, they were as perfect-looking as his short beard, mustache, and shoulder-length hair, which fell in tidy waves to his broad shoulders. Casmir promptly felt silly admitting having had trouble with bullies to someone who'd probably never been picked on in his life.

Casmir stepped into the corridor, relieved there weren't any guards that he would have to navigate. "According to my model-loving friend, the bridge and the captain's office are this way, right?"

"You must pay more attention to his lunch lectures than most people."

For some reason, Casmir felt pleased that Asger had been paying attention to his blatherings to Ishii. Maybe this was a man he could work with. He already seemed better than the knight at Forseti Station.

Asger didn't object when Casmir led off with Zee taking the second position. Numerous uniformed crewmembers stared or lifted their hands, as if to object to these odd beings roaming their ship, but then Asger would step forward and nod. A nod from a knight was apparently enough to convince everyone that the ship was rotating as expected.

When Casmir reached Ishii's office, he paused outside to collect his thoughts and consider how this negotiation might go. What could he offer the captain of a top-of-the-line Kingdom warship? Ishii probably had everything he'd ever dreamed of and a few things he hadn't. What would be important to him? Successfully completing his mission, no doubt. Was there any way Casmir could help with that?

He grimaced, knowing he couldn't offer that without also delaying his retrieval attempt, but Ishii had already made it clear he wasn't going to lend Casmir a shuttle or divert from his route. But if Casmir could help Ishii, perhaps the captain would feel obligated to return that help afterward. Which would be extremely useful. It wasn't as if Casmir, Bonita, Qin, and the *Stellar Dragon* would be a match for Rache and all his mercenaries, especially if he'd already repaired his big warship. The *Fedallah* could already be stealthily lurking in the moon's orbit.

And, as much as Casmir hated the idea of leaving Kim with that psychopath, he doubted Rache would kill her. He ought to be willing to give her days to figure out their medical mystery, days during which she would be safe. Casmir worried he would hurt her, but he also trusted that Kim was incredibly capable and could probably deal with the man, at least for a few days. He prayed that reasoning was sound.

Casmir waved at the automatic announcer, and the door soon slid open.

"I thought I told you to put him in the brig," Ishii said—irritably, not jokingly. He sat at a desk facing the door and glowered at them.

Casmir glanced at Asger, the edge of his shoulder and telltale cloak just visible behind Zee.

Asger leaned further into Ishii's view. "He seemed wan and weak for that. I thought he might relapse."

Casmir rubbed his face. Maybe he ought to thank his medical issues for this unexpected help, especially if it was true, but he mostly wished they would cease to be a problem and everyone would forget about them.

"That would be unfortunate," Ishii grumbled, a tablet pen clenched in his fingers like the dagger he was possibly fantasizing about thrusting at Casmir. "What do you want, Dabrowski?"

"I would like to assist you in completing your mission."

"I'm sure."

"I don't want stolen gate technology leaving our system. If it was found here, it seems the Kingdom has the most legitimate claim on it."

"Yes, it does." Ishii squinted at him. Suspiciously.

Why did everyone squint suspiciously at him?

"I've already talked Captain Lopez of the *Stellar Dragon* into assisting us," Casmir said. "If you're willing to allow her to catch up and link to your ship, she'll take me on, and we'll be at your disposal to help with that cargo ship in creative and unexpected ways. We'll double the resources you can bring to the battle. We'll make sure the gate pieces aren't going anywhere before we head off to rescue Kim. Should you feel obligated to assist us in return, I wouldn't object, but I'll go after Rache myself, if I need to."

"Double the resources?" Ishii dropped his pen. "Are you claiming that freighter is equal to my warship?"

"No, I'm claiming that you have a mere *one* ship right now, and you could have *two* at your disposal. Captain Lopez is a capable pilot, and she has a very talented combat specialist on her crew."

"I have *hundreds* of combat specialists."

Casmir thought about mentioning that Qin was modded and perhaps more than a match for his marines, but she was only one person in the end. Besides, a Kingdom military officer wouldn't be impressed by a cat woman.

"Zee would also help." Casmir stepped aside and gestured to the imposing robot as he might a used scooter he was trying to sell.

"Well, that will just make all the difference in a space battle, won't it?"

"I think you're undervaluing how useful an outsider with permission to apply creative thinking to the problem could be to your efforts," Casmir said. "Did you know there have been numerous studies showing that radical innovation can often, when the chance is given, arise from people in different but analogous fields of study? It's because those people are pulling from different experiences and backgrounds, and they're not constrained by knowledge of the typical tactics and solutions in the original field."

"Do you think I'm an idiot, Dabrowski? You just want off my ship so you can go get your friend. Even if I thought your help would be as valuable as the drivel flying out of your mouth implies, there's no way you actually mean to give it."

Casmir had anticipated numerous objections and had responses ready, but he hadn't expected his word to be doubted. He promptly realized he should have. Just because none of his colleagues or superiors back home had reason to doubt his honesty didn't mean that would apply to someone he hadn't seen in more than twenty years.

"I wouldn't lie to you, Sora." Casmir gazed steadily into the eyes of his old nemesis, hoping to convey his earnestness. As much as he wanted to go right down and help Kim... if he promised to help at the gate, he would do that first. In whatever way possible. "We can fly in and comm them, try to distract them while your people plan thrilling military maneuvers."

"Put him in the brig, Asger," Ishii said. "I don't care if he collapses."

"Perhaps guest quarters would be sufficient?" Asger suggested.

"The brig. And the robot too. I don't want that thing to have free rein of my ship when Dabrowski is plotting ways to get off it. But if the genius boy can figure out a way to defeat our enemies from his cell, I'll happily help him recover his friend afterward." Ishii flicked a dismissive hand. "I have a command meeting with the other captains. Get out of here, all of you."

The door shut in Casmir's face.

"That didn't go as well as I'd hoped," Casmir admitted.

He wondered if he should feel heartened that Ishii had said he would assist with Kim if Casmir figured out a solution. The entire sentence had been laced with sarcasm, so he didn't know if he could truly put stock in it. But Ishii had made the statement in front of the knight. Maybe he would feel even more honor bound than usual to keep it. The problem was that Casmir had no idea how he could defeat an enemy ship while locked in the brig.

Asger gave him a pitying smile. Casmir shook his head bleakly. He didn't want to be pitied. He wanted to find a way to help Kim and help anyone who could help him help Kim.

CHAPTER 8

IM YAWNED FIERCELY AND CLUNKED HER GLOVED FINGERS against her faceplate when she instinctively reached up to rub moisture from her eyes. She should have been used to wearing a helmet after all this time in space, but she was tired and not surprised that her fingers had forgotten. She'd lost track of how long she'd been looking at blood samples and running analysis programs, but it had been well over an Odinese day and night since she'd slept.

Yas had helped her set up the equipment and briefed her about what he knew and what he suspected that Rache knew—apparently, surprise surprise, the captain wasn't forthcoming with his men. Now, Yas was sprawled out across a bank of seats while their various analyses ran.

Kim didn't blame him. There wasn't room at the tiny counter for both of them to poke around, nor was there much for them to do. She was running every blood test she could think of that the limited equipment could handle. So far, she could see the damage and see it advancing hour by hour, but she didn't know what was causing it or how to stop it. She kept coming back to radiation, or something close, but she'd dug up EMF and radiation meters, gone outside and pointed them at the exposed portion of the frost-covered metallic wreck, and gotten exactly the numbers she would have expected on a moon with no atmosphere to protect it from space.

She'd tried to double-check the data on the network but had been reminded, for the sixth or seventh time, that she didn't have access. She'd had it up on the *Machu Picchu,* but suspected the walls of the deep canyon put them in a dead spot. Now, she regretted that she hadn't sent a message to Casmir. She hadn't wanted to worry him, but he would worry, regardless, when he couldn't get in touch with her.

Assuming *he* had network access. She hoped he wasn't in as much trouble as she was. She could envision him in a brig cell, that grumpy captain with a grudge not having appreciated the answers to his questions.

The shuttle hatch opened, and Kim decided if it was Rache, she would ask him for that tour of the wreck. She wanted to take readings for radiation again from inside—it was possible the hull, however damaged, was blocking something—and see what exactly was in there. Inspiration, she hoped.

She wondered if her mother—or her damaged droid body—was in there somewhere. It had sounded like she'd stayed behind when the rest of the archaeology team left. So, where was she? Hiding? Disassembled somewhere?

Unfortunately, finding a cure had to be Kim's priority. On the research ship, her blood test had come back negative for any signs of cellular damage, but that had changed when she came down here. She'd tested herself an hour ago and confirmed she was also suffering now. How long until she started to feel the effects? Fatigue would be among the first symptoms, she suspected, but how would she know if that was from the damage or the lack of sleep?

She snorted and removed her helmet. Her eyes were watering, and she was tired of not being able to wipe them.

"Does that mean you've contracted it?" Rache asked, walking over.

"I don't think contracted is the applicable word, but yes. I'm starting to show signs of damage. But you knew that would happen, didn't you?" She frowned at him.

"I suspected. Everyone who came down here has contracted it." He lifted a shoulder and corrected himself. "Been affected by it."

"Thanks so much for dragging me into it."

"You were already researching it for the military."

"Somewhere with good labs and where I *wasn't* being affected." At least not in the hours she had been there. She supposed it was possible she would have eventually gotten ill, since the rest of the crew had.

He didn't have a comeback for that. Did he regret anything? Care about anyone? Who could tell when he hid his eyes?

Maybe she'd do the Twelve Systems a favor if she didn't find a cure and she let him die here. But that would mean sacrificing herself and the others who'd been affected. It would also mean failing to solve the problem, a thought that made her gnash her teeth.

She set her helmet down out of the way. "It's been clear from the beginning that the suits haven't done anything to protect anyone, hasn't it?"

"Yes. Why do you think that is?"

"Because it's not a virus or a bacterium that we can keep out. I'm guessing it's something akin to radiation, though I'm not getting any readings to verify that. Not from that wreck and not in people's blood. There's *definitely* DNA damage, which you'd expect, but there isn't any drop in red and white blood-cell counts, which there should be. It also doesn't make any sense that radiation exposure could be passed from person to person through contact, unless it was clinging to their suits, but damn it, we test for that every time someone comes in through an airlock. You get a nice shower if you're glowing like polonium."

"I ran scans inside the wreck and also didn't see signs of radiation, not higher than typical for the moon." Rache leaned against the hatchway jamb. "But I haven't seen the entire ship yet. There are miles and miles of corridors—well more like conduit tubes—back there in addition to the huge storage bays. And it's a maze. The layout is confusing. My men are still searching and mapping it. I expected something akin to the colony ships—though it's questionable whether our blueprints for those are accurate, since the colonists disassembled them for raw materials—but this isn't akin to… anything. It doesn't even seem like it was designed for humans."

Kim dug her fingers into the back of her shoulder, trying to soothe an ache from leaning over the microscope. "Another time, I'm sure I would find that interesting. But right now…"

"I understand. Where is Casmir?"

Kim blinked, surprised and then wary by the question. "Why do you care?"

"Believe it or not, I found myself wishing his robot was here to help with the search. It wouldn't have been afflicted with anything, I'm sure. I could use an army of those robots. But I gather his army is busy invading, oh, where was it? Stribog Station."

"What are you talking about?"

"The last I talked to my ship, they mentioned it. Stribog Station wanted to hire us to get rid of them if we were in the area. It seems Jager has a couple of ships there, trying to get a toehold in System Augeas." Rache's tone was icy with disapproval.

"I see." Kim wasn't sure if she believed Rache or if it mattered even if he was telling the truth. It didn't have anything to do with their current problem, and it would upset Casmir if he heard about it. Maybe she wouldn't tell him. "Casmir isn't in System Augeas and doesn't have anything to do with that."

"He made the crushers, didn't he?"

"When he worked for the military, he was always told his inventions would be used to defend Odin from outside aggressors, not to start a war, or whatever Jager is doing."

"Then he was naive," Rache said coolly.

"I guess he couldn't be the paragon of perfection that you are. By the way, you never gave me your blood sample." Kim looked at his faceplate, though she couldn't see anything through that stupid mask he wore. What a time to worry about his super villain costume. "I assume you're as affected as the rest of us, but I'd like to verify that."

He gazed back at her and didn't respond right away, then looked over to Dr. Peshlakai, who was snoring softly. None of his other men were in the shuttle. It made Kim a little uneasy to know she was essentially alone with this killer who had kidnapped her, but she told herself that he wanted a cure for himself and his men. He shouldn't pester her or do anything but assist her.

And there was a part of her that had a hard time believing he'd be a sexual deviant if he was related to Casmir. *More* than related to him. That was something she could confirm if she ended up being able to keep a sample of his blood. Not that it was anywhere near the top of her priority list right now.

"I see no reason why I wouldn't be affected," he finally said. "I've been here numerous hours now."

"I agree, but it's foolish not to gather all the data on hand. A blood test isn't going to tell me your real name, if that's what you care about. I haven't even got a network connection right now." She waved overhead, indicating the towering walls of the canyon. "If that's like other combat armor I've seen, you can have your suit take one and send me its analysis, but it would be better for me to have the sample itself so I can run tests." She pointed toward the vials she currently had being run for everything from vitamin deficiencies to who'd been vaccinated with what in their lifetimes.

Rache hesitated another moment, then removed his helmet and stepped toward her. He pushed up his hood enough to reveal his neck and flicked two fingers toward a syringe on the counter. "Go ahead."

"What, you want me to take it from your jugular?"

"It's a pain in the ass to take off the armor." He lifted his gauntleted hand. "Peshlakai has done it this way."

"Peshlakai is a medical doctor. I'm a researcher. My degrees are in microbiology and pharmaceutical bacteriology. I minored in literature. You don't want someone who takes blood draws once every five years sticking a needle in your neck. Though I'm sure many people fantasize about doing so."

She thought about pointing out that they could wake up Peshlakai, but Rache started taking off his chest and arm pieces and the gauntlets.

"Literature?" he asked.

"I needed electives, and I like books."

"Ah yes, you're a *Moby Dick* fan."

"I analyzed it for a class. I wouldn't say I signed up for the fandom." Kim grabbed the syringe, drummed the vial on her arm, and waited for him to finish undressing his top half.

"What books *do* you like?"

She couldn't keep from giving him an exasperated look. "This isn't a date at the coffee shop. You're my captor. I'm not discussing literature with you."

Though she would probably do it if it meant she was drinking coffee at the same time. *Good* coffee. It was almost embarrassing how much she missed it.

"Fair enough." Rache bowed an acknowledgment as he continued unfastening his gear.

He was right. It took several minutes just to remove the top half. Underneath it, he wore a thin black long-sleeve shirt that hugged his lean, muscular torso.

"You're really Casmir's twin?" Kim asked skeptically, then promptly grimaced, both because she wasn't sure how he would react to finding out that Casmir had told her, and because she didn't want him to misconstrue her comment as some kind of sexual interest.

"So Dr. Peshlakai's DNA test said." His tone was more amused than annoyed. "I don't usually get grimaces from women when I take off my armor."

"No? Given your occupational choice, I have a hard time believing you get hordes of voluptuous females flinging themselves at you in a sexual fervor."

He stared at her for a long moment, then laughed. "You're very blunt."

"I'm not good at editing words before they come out of my mouth." Kim waved for him to push up his sleeve. "Fortunately, nobody where I work cares, and my inability to schmooze people, as Casmir would say, rarely matters."

"I actually *do* get targeted by voluptuous females—more often than you might think. Females with low standards, clearly."

"Clearly." She waved at his sleeve again, finding it surreal that they were having this conversation. What a nut.

"I've learned to avoid them. Every now and then, there's an assassin in the mix."

"I'm shocked," she said.

She managed to catch herself before pointing out that he could hardly expect anything less when he'd decided to make himself King Jager's personal nemesis. He was still her captor, and it would be better to keep her mouth shut and avoid antagonizing him.

Not responding to her sarcasm, Rache finally pushed up his sleeve. "Now that you've told me how much experience you've had at this, I'm wondering if I should be concerned."

"A bruise from some spilled blood is the least of your concerns right now." She did the draw without trouble; the veins on his arms stood out and made it easy. "After I run this, can I get that tour of the wreck? I hate to admit it, but I'm stymied here. I'm hoping for some elucidation in there. Or to find something emitting a previously undiscovered relative of cosmic radiation."

Kim supposed that was a possibility. That they had discovered something *new*.

"I'm not aware that tests on the gates have shown that they do that." Rache started dressing again.

"Did you find any pieces of the gate in there?" Kim well remembered that video with her mother waving what Casmir had believed was a gate fragment, but she didn't bring it up, also remembering that she'd stolen the chip with the video on it from Rache.

Had he realized it yet? He'd probably been busy since then.

"Not yet." He sounded frustrated.

Kim divided his blood into smaller containers for the tests she would run and made a slide—she'd had no trouble seeing everyone else's cellular damage under the microscope.

"We believe we've found the molds that held a disassembled gate for transport, but someone cleared everything out. It's hard to tell if it was done thousands of years ago or last month. I'm hoping my team will come across a forgotten piece, so we'll at least get *something* out of this diversion, but I'm hypothesizing that someone else has been here since the original archaeology team came, and that they took everything valuable. It's possible they did something to cause this… not-a-disease."

Kim was skeptical that this was a manmade phenomenon, but all she said was, "What happens if we don't find a cure for it? Any chance you have a brilliant backup plan?"

"No. But I suppose I might, in a spurt of vengeance, fly to Odin and take a kamikaze run at Jager's castle. Unfortunately, I don't think I would live long enough to make the trip. People have been dying quickly from this."

"No kidding. I'd appreciate it if…" Kim grimaced, hating the idea of asking him for a favor. Of asking her *kidnapper* for a favor. "I have a father and brothers back on Odin. Friends and colleagues. I'd like to be able to get a message back to them. I guess if I could even send something to Casmir, he'd make sure they got it."

She swallowed, irritated at the lump welling in her throat at the thought of never seeing anyone again. Emotion wouldn't help anything, and she needed her mind calm and clear to work.

"You two are a couple?" Rache asked, his tone hard to read.

She fought down the urge to bristle and say it was none of his business, and why did he care anyway? Then it occurred to her that he might be curious about Casmir. Casmir had said that was at least one of the reasons he'd put the bounty out to collect him, at least according to Rache. Well, she wasn't going to answer questions about Casmir, not to this man. Who knew what his true motives were?

"Just good friends. We've been roommates for seven years." Kim slid his slide under the microscope and leaned in for a look.

"If we're not able to find a solution here, I'll fly you and the group back up to orbit. There will be reception for sending messages there."

She couldn't bring herself to thank him. He was the reason her life was in danger.

Rache tugged his helmet over his head. He'd never removed the mask and hood. She felt a twinge of disappointment, mostly because she wanted to know if he truly looked exactly like Casmir. Since she didn't have a blood sample from him along, or a DNA sequencer, she couldn't compare the two side by side to see if they matched.

But what she saw under the microscope made her forget all about that. "What the hell?"

She squinted, not trusting her eyes, and had the linked computer run a quick analysis.

"Something weird swimming in there?" Rache asked.

"You're not showing the same signs of cellular damage that everyone else is."

"Oh? Huh."

Casmir trailed Asger down several levels and through the corridors of the sprawling warship, not paying attention to their route or the stares of people they passed. He was trying to tell himself that Kim could take care of herself and that he'd done all he could, but he couldn't help but think of the *Stellar Dragon*, perhaps even now flying to catch up with the *Osprey*.

Because he'd asked Bonita to come get him. And now, he couldn't meet her for a transfer.

He needed to send her a message before he was tossed in the brig with cell walls that would muffle transmission, and let her know he wouldn't be joining her. But it was frustrating to admit defeat. If he could just get a ride over there, or convince someone to let the freighter attach to one of the airlocks...

But who besides the captain might be able to approve that? Some admiral back at Kingdom Fleet Headquarters? Casmir didn't know any admirals. All of his connections were in academia, and he couldn't think of any military officers on the board at Zamek University.

Asger slowed down, and Casmir stopped before bumping into him. Zee stopped behind him. There weren't any crewmembers in their current corridor to give curious looks to their odd party. Had they arrived at the brig?

As Casmir looked around, seeing a large doorway rather than a bank of cells, Asger turned to face him. And gaze thoughtfully at him. For several long moments. Casmir grew self-conscious and had the urge to comb his fingers through his hair. Or maybe his beard. He hadn't smeared hair removal gel on his jaw for several days and was bristly.

"If you were a woman looking at me for that long, I'd get my hopes up for a kiss," Casmir said.

Asger closed his eyes and shook his head slowly. "I can't believe I'm contemplating this."

"Er, it's not kissing, right? Because that woman thing is a requirement for me."

"I hope I'm right," Asger muttered and pressed his palm to a print reader beside the hatch, then leaned in for a retina scan. "He *should* have added me to the database since I'm parked in here," he muttered, seconds passing slowly. "I can't promise Ishii won't get an alert."

Abruptly intrigued, Casmir studied their surroundings again, looking for more clues as to where they were. *1A* was all the label by the door said. The corridor was wide here, the ceiling high, and he spotted a few insulated doors that might be for refrigerators or freezers farther down.

"Approved," a computer voice said. "Welcome back, Sir William Asger."

The door slid open, and Asger walked into a dim room. Lights came up, shining on two sleek shuttles resting on magnetic plating. One was a match for the blue-and-gold exterior paint of the *Osprey* and clearly belonged. The other was white with royal purple highlights, the color an exact match for Asger's cloak.

Hangar doors on the far side of the small bay offered an exit into space, and Casmir's stomach flip-flopped.

"Are we going somewhere?" he asked as Asger strode toward the second shuttle, a hatch in the side opening automatically.

102

LINDSAY BUROKER

"Not if you don't hurry up. Someone on the bridge will probably get an alert, since we're entering the captain's private bay, and Ishii can override the doors from up there."

Casmir convinced his weary limbs to jog to catch up. "This is your personal shuttlecraft?"

Being a knight came with more perks than he'd realized.

"It's one from the knights' ship stable back on Odin." Asger led the way inside and jumped into one of two piloting pods up front. His fingers were flying across the control panel before he sat down. An articulating arm with a chip interface swung toward his face, similar to the setup in the *Dragon*.

As soon as Casmir and Zee entered, the hatch swung shut, sealing them into the shuttle.

"Put your helmet on and pod up," Asger ordered. "Even if the bridge doesn't object, this is going to be a tricky takeoff. The warship left orbit a while ago and is accelerating for the gate." His voice lowered. "At a constant, I hope."

"How much piloting experience do knights get?" Casmir smiled, but he couldn't help but feel nervous as he sat in the pod next to Asger's and the intelligent insulation wrapped around him like a cocoon.

"Enough."

"Zee, sit in one of the pods, please," Casmir called to his silent robot friend. "Having you go flying across the shuttle and crash into us would be extremely painful. For us."

"I'll bet," Asger muttered, firing up the thrusters. "Let your friends know we're coming."

Casmir almost said that they should see if they survived the takeoff first, but for whatever reason, Asger was helping him. He had better keep his sarcastic thoughts to himself.

"Will do."

Asger looked over at him. Was Casmir supposed to add on a *sir* or a *my lord*? He thought *my lord* and *my lady* had fallen out of fashion over recent centuries, but he also didn't interact with the nobility often. Most of the qualifying people that he knew in academia acted like normal people, the main difference being that they lived on some centuries-old family estate in town or the countryside instead of faculty housing.

The shuttle-bay doors opened. An indicator flashed on the control panel.

Asger sighed and rotated the shuttle, so its nose pointed at the doors, before answering. "Yes, Captain?"

"Are you *going* somewhere, Asger?" Ishii's voice came over the speaker.

"For a jaunt to stretch my legs."

"My security officer reports that Dabrowski wasn't delivered to the brig. Don't tell me his legs need stretching too. It's not like they're going to get any longer."

"I know *he's* not poking fun at my height," Casmir whispered.

Asger didn't answer. He flew carefully around the other shuttle and toward the exit.

"Answer me, Asger," Ishii said.

"It's *Sir* Asger. And I'm not in your chain of command, Captain. I answer to the king and queen."

"I'm positive the king and queen don't want you to take a civilian roboticist off on some harebrained mission," Ishii said.

"Don't be so sure," Asger said.

The bay doors started closing.

Asger growled, and at some silent command he gave via his chip, the shuttle surged forward.

Casmir squinted his eyes shut, imagining them smashing into the doors. But the shuttle cleared them and shot out the back of the warship like a bullet. The *Osprey* continued on its course, and Asger turned them toward the bright blue dot of Saga, the planet far more distant than it had been the last time Casmir looked out a porthole.

"If you go get yourself in trouble with Rache," Ishii said, his voice glacial, "don't expect us to come bail you out. We have bigger problems."

"I'm certain you'll do whatever Fleet orders, Captain. Asger, out."

The comm light went out, and Casmir sagged in the pod.

"Your friends?" Asger brought up the scanner display to show ships in the area.

"It's the *Stellar Dragon*. I'm letting them know we'll meet them now." Casmir hurried and sent a message to Bonita, chagrined he hadn't already done that. "We're still going to the gate to help stop that cargo ship, right?"

Casmir looked at Asger, wishing he would override that plan, that for some reason he believed his employers would be more concerned about getting Kim back. But Asger nodded.

"Like you, I believe I can be more help out here in my own ship than standing uselessly on Ishii's bridge. And you…" Asger pinned him with an appraising look. "I'm not sure yet what you can do, but I'm hoping it's more than standing uselessly in a brig cell."

"I hope I can, too, but may I ask why you have any faith in me?" Casmir hated to admit it, but he understood why a Kingdom Fleet captain would believe a civilian robotics engineer next to useless in a combat situation. Wouldn't he feel the same way if a military officer came into his lab and offered to help assemble a robot?

That's not the vessel we thought you'd meet us in, Bonita's message scrolled down his contact while he waited for Asger to answer—if Asger intended to answer at all. *Qin wants me to ask if you're with a knight.*

I am. Casmir didn't say more, not when Asger had made that comment about freaks of nature. He had no idea how he would react to Qin's unique appearance and abilities.

Is he going to help us get Kim?

Not exactly. There's something else we have to do first.

I trust you'll explain that while you're telling me what this schematic you sent does.

I will.

Asger set a course to rendezvous with the *Dragon,* then gave Casmir another long, considering look. He opened his mouth, closed it, and shook his head at whatever thoughts were on his mind. He finally said, "The queen believes you are worth protecting. Even at great cost."

Casmir sank deeper in his pod, memories of Sir Friedrich returning to mind. Memories and guilt. What if he ended up getting Asger killed too?

Once the autopilot was engaged, Asger pulled out his book and propped his heels up on the navigation panel. He didn't seem inclined to talk further.

Casmir closed his eyes, knowing his body needed rest, but he doubted his mind would comply.

CHAPTER 9

KIM ALTERNATED BETWEEN STUDYING THE COMPUTER READOUTS ON the dozens of analyses of Rache's blood that she had going and studying *him*. For a while, he'd spoken to one of his fighters who'd come in to update him on the search, but he'd returned to the wreck, and Rache was back to leaning against the jamb next to the lab, waiting to give Kim the tour she had requested. But his blood had become her little mystery, and she wanted to figure it out. It might hold a clue that could save them all.

Every other person in his party, including her, was getting more and more damaged, and he seemed unaffected. No, not seemed. His bloodwork showed that he *was* unaffected.

Why? Kim didn't see anything abnormal in it. No nanobots roaming around repairing damage. His white blood-cell count was slightly higher than typical, but she'd seen that in people who got regular immune-system-enhancing shots.

"You've got cybernetic implants, right?" Kim asked.

"Yes, but so do many of my men who are affected."

"And you get immune-system enhancers?"

"Yes, but so does Chaplain. We go together whenever we pass Jotunheim Station." His tone turned dry. "While the other men visit the brothels and casinos."

Whenever Rache got dry, his voice reminded her of Casmir. Even though she wouldn't wish this illness on him, she wouldn't have minded having him down here. She had a feeling this was all tied in with that wreck, and someone with an engineering background might have some insight that she lacked. Maybe she could talk to Rache's engineer later.

She forced her wandering thoughts back on track. "Chaplain is one of the men here and affected, correct?"

"Correct."

"Damn, I wish I had some of Casmir's blood too. I'm curious if he shares your immunity. He's sort of the baseline you, right?"

Kim squinted at Rache, wishing he'd take off the mask. His sleeping doctor was the only other person in the shuttle, and it sounded like he already knew about Rache and Casmir.

"I see he swore himself to secrecy after our chat."

"We've been roommates for a long time. I know that he wears superhero underwear and uses Robot Remstar shampoo. Secrets are few."

"I don't know what to say to that."

"I'm fairly certain *he* doesn't know of anything unusual about himself or his genes. I don't suppose you, being perhaps more knowledgeable, would care to enlighten me."

"No."

"Nothing that could account for your apparent immunity?"

"We're not genetically engineered super humans, if that's what you're thinking."

"I've shared a bathroom with Casmir for seven years. I *know* he's not a super human."

"Since you said your relationship isn't romantic, I'll assume that's not a dig about the size of his reproductive organs."

"No. I just assume a modded super human would be capable of replacing the toilet paper after finishing off the roll."

"You think the geneticists code that in, eh?"

Kim made an exasperated noise and went back to the microscope and tests, scouring the data. The answer had to be here. It couldn't be a fluke that Rache was fine when every other single person was dying, their cells aging decades for every day.

The hatch opened, and the engineer came back inside, ice crystals dusting the shoulders of her black combat armor.

"Sir?"

"Back here, Chief," Rache said. "Any sign of parts of the gate?"

"No, Captain. We've been over about seventy-five percent of the ship at this point. We'll keep looking, but, uhm, is Dr. Yas sleeping?"

"The snoring suggests it."

"Shouldn't he be… It's Chains, sir. He's not looking too good. And I'm kind of…" The woman looked toward Kim and her makeshift lab, then lowered her voice. "I'm not sure how much longer we've got, Captain."

"Understood. Finish searching the ship, and then we'll get out of here if we find nothing."

"Back to the *Fedallah,* sir? Are the repairs complete?"

"Close to complete. I'll comm them when we have reception and get an update."

"Yes, sir." The woman saluted and left the shuttle.

"The archaeology team took whatever this illness is back up to their ship, and their crew is dead now," Kim said. "You might not want to—"

"I wasn't planning to."

Kim digested that. "Lying to the troops probably isn't good for morale."

"You have my blood, Scholar Sato. Find a solution." Rache headed toward the hatch.

Apparently, her tour was off the table.

"You and your muscles and enhancements aren't very good at people," Kim muttered, not expecting him to hear the comment or to care if he did.

Rache, his hand on the hatch, looked at her. She braced herself for a threat.

"What would *Casmir* do to entice you to work harder?" he asked.

"He would know I'm doing the best I can, but he'd definitely offer to help me if I helped him. I came here looking for my mother. I know you saw her in that video. If your people happen to run across any droid bodies, I'd appreciate it if you told me."

"They have not, but I will look myself," he said and walked out.

Casmir gave the *Stellar Dragon*'s airlock hatch a jaunty knock from the outside. Zee stood behind him in the connecting tube that Asger had extended. The outer hatch opened, and they stepped into the airlock chamber. Asger jogged up the tube and hopped in with them. He wore a helmet, and presumably his fancy knight armor doubled as a spacesuit, but the cloak still hung down his back.

"You don't need to stay and fly your ship?" Casmir had hoped to speak with Bonita and Qin without a stranger present, a stranger who might hurt Qin's feelings with some rant about modded humans.

"The automatic pilot and wireless interface are the best there is." Asger waved at his temple. "And I need to keep an eye on you. *Both* eyes."

"I hope that's not literal. I'm a little squeamish about being touched by organs."

Asger rested his hand on his pertundo, the telescoping handle retracted so it hung from a belt loop like a simple axe or mallet. Casmir hoped he didn't think he would need it on the *Dragon*.

A red light flashed, and Bonita's voice came through a speaker. "Just as a precaution, we're running the decon program."

"We haven't been over to the research ship since we were last here," Casmir said, "but if you feel you need to hose us off, that's understandable. There's a knight with me, so make sure the spray doesn't wrinkle his cloak."

Asger's eyebrows twitched upward. Casmir smiled innocently. He'd wanted to warn Bonita of his presence so she wouldn't have Qin answer the door, but he hoped Asger wouldn't think anything of the comment.

A fine mist sprayed them from multiple nozzles, and Casmir was glad he was still wandering around in the galaxy suit. When they were finally able to step inside, Bonita waited with no fewer than ten robot vacuums rolling around the deck next to her.

Casmir blinked. Had she brought them down for repairs? How much could they have been damaged in the last day?

The vacuums zipped toward him, and he fought the urge to spring back into the airlock hatch for protection. A boisterous song he didn't recognize played from speakers in the cargo hold, and the robots synchronized themselves as they flowed around and between Casmir's legs in something akin to an organized dance.

He looked to Bonita for an explanation.

She rolled her eyes. "Viggo missed you."

"The vacuums missed the one who repaired many of their faults," Viggo said. "They are expressing their gratitude."

"The *vacuums* aren't the ones who play that silly opera every time they clean."

"I've run tests. They perform more efficiently with music."

Bonita shook her head. "You're full of dung, Viggo."

"My internal sanitation systems ensure that's not possible."

Asger stepped out of the chamber warily as he eyed the exuberant robots zipping around Casmir. "That may be the oddest thing I've ever seen."

"You must not get off Odin much if that's true." Bonita frowned at him. Apparently, she didn't share Qin's fascination with knights. "You Casmir's keeper?"

"In a manner of speaking. I am *Sir* William Asger." He put some emphasis on the sir, as if to instruct her to use the honorific. He had better not hold his breath waiting for that. "Casmir, why does this woman think you need a keeper?"

"Well, she's met me."

As Zee strode out of the airlock chamber, the vacuums scattered, and the music stopped playing.

Asger focused on Bonita, his expression growing pensive. "You are Captain Bonita Lopez, a bounty hunter and smuggler?"

"Captain *Laser* Lopez, and I've retired from my brief stint with smuggling." She turned her frown on Casmir before aiming it back at the knight.

Casmir wanted to tell her that Asger had looked her up on his own, that he hadn't blabbed about her occupations. He hoped Asger wouldn't try to arrest her.

"She's also the pilot who's going to take us to the gate to help the Kingdom Fleet," Casmir said.

"Do we have to pay her?" Asger's lip curled as he looked down his nose at her.

There was a height difference of some eight or nine inches, but Casmir had a feeling he would have looked down his nose no matter what, and he glanced nervously about, hoping Qin was in her cabin. They would have to meet eventually, but maybe it could wait until Asger was settled in and less... stuffy.

He hadn't been that bad on the *Osprey*. It seemed smugglers and smuggling ships impinged on his knightly sense of morality.

"Casmir's already bribed me with useless schematics, though I do hope he's going to explain to me why we're now going to the gate instead of back to Skadi Moon to retrieve Kim." Bonita's gaze met his. "Didn't you say she'd been kidnapped? Is she still kidnapped?"

"Yes, and yes, but I promised to help Captain Ishii and the other Fleet captains with a problem—there's an extremely high-tech and weapons-laden cargo ship trying to bust its way out of the system with stolen goods. A couple of warships are blockading the gate, but they're having trouble taking the thieves down."

"And how are *you* going to help with that?" Bonita waved at him. "Are you even armed?"

"With my wits, yes."

"Dear God."

The vacuums, having recovered from their alarm at Zee's entry, buzzed in again. One ran over Casmir's foot. He wasn't sure if it was a programming mishap or if he had lint on his boot.

"I may also have a small robot army to call upon." Casmir waved at the vacuums. "And I left my tool satchel in the cabin here, so I can make things."

Asger considered the vacuums dubiously, then turned a more speculative eye on Zee. "Can you make more like *that*?"

"Not unless we go back to Forseti Station or Odin or somewhere with a huge manufacturing facility and all the materials and tools I would need." Casmir didn't mention how much it would cost to legally buy those materials, since he hadn't purchased the ones he'd used on Zee. He felt like more of a criminal than Bonita currently, even if he hadn't smuggled anything in his life.

"Too bad. An army of those *might* make a difference." Asger tapped an invisible button on his chest, and his helmet retracted. "But we'd still have to figure out a way to get them aboard the enemy ship. I suppose we should head to the gate and see if the Fleet even needs our help. They may have dealt with the problem themselves by now."

Casmir decided he should wish for that rather than for a chance to do something heroic that might cause Ishii to feel indebted to him so he would bring his big warship to help with Kim's retrieval. Besides, Bonita was right. He didn't have any weapons, and neither her freighter nor Asger's shuttle would be a match for a ship capable of giving multiple Kingdom warships a hard time.

"If I get all the way to the gate," Bonita said, heading across the cargo hold, "don't count on me wanting to stick around in this benighted system."

"*Benighted?*" Asger said with indignation.

"She might mean be-knighted," Casmir said, though he was sure all knights had heard the pun far too many times to find it amusing.

Asger ignored him. He was looking at something across the cargo hold, his eyes narrowing.

Bonita had paused to make a shooing motion with her hand. Casmir glimpsed Qin jerking her head out of sight—she'd been leaning around the corner.

Asger sucked in an alarmed breath. "What was *that?*"

"Not what, who," Casmir said. He had hoped to wait a while before introducing Qin, but they would have to get it out of the way now. Maybe Asger would be more reasonable than Casmir expected. "That is—"

Asger charged across the cargo hold, yanking his pertundo from its holder. He almost knocked Bonita over as he raced toward Qin.

"What the—" Bonita blurted, jerking her pistol from its holster. "Stop!" she cried, aiming at the back of Asger's head.

Bewildered, Casmir lunged toward her and knocked her arm up. The bolt fired into the ceiling as Asger sprang out of sight around the corner.

A *crack-thud* emanated from the corridor, and Qin loosed a bellow that sounded half shriek of alarm and half battle cry. The thuds and clashes of battle rolled into the cargo hold.

Bonita threw Casmir a scathing look, then charged toward the fray.

"Zee," Casmir yelled, "stop them. Don't let them hurt each other."

The crusher sprinted for the corridor, easily passing Bonita who ran with a limp, and sprang out of sight.

"And don't hurt either of them!" Casmir yelled, running after Zee.

What was going on? Why had Asger reacted so violently?

Casmir reached the corner at the same time as Bonita, who lunged around it, her pistol ready again.

"Don't you have a stunner?" Casmir yelled, trying to bump her arm to keep her from firing the deadly weapon at anyone.

Cracks and bangs and thumps continued to sound, but Zee's body blocked the view. Someone was backed halfway into the ladder well and fighting for his life. No, *her* life.

"Don't you?" Bonita snarled, pushing him aside.

No, he only had his wits, and they weren't doing any good.

Zee gripped Asger's shoulder and pulled him back and hefted him in the air. Asger hollered, swinging with his pertundo. The axe edge of the halberd slammed into the bulkhead, digging deep, blue branches of electricity flaring around the head. Zee only pulled him farther back. The weapon almost came out of Asger's grip, but he held on tightly and yanked it free.

The lights in the corridor flickered out, some electrical wire cut, but not before Casmir glimpsed a bewildered Qin crouching in a defensive posture, her fists up. She wasn't even armed?

"Explain yourself, knight." Casmir clenched a fist and glared at Asger.

Asger didn't hear him. He snarled, twisted in the air, and slammed a boot into Zee's torso, almost wrenching himself free. Zee's grip tightened on his shoulder, and he didn't let go. Asger drew his pertundo back to swing it at the crusher.

"No!" Casmir lunged forward, afraid the mysterious weapon would damage Zee.

The crusher was faster. He flung Asger away before the weapon could bite into his torso.

Asger twisted in the air, but he'd been thrown too hard and fast to manage to get his feet under him. He slammed into the deck, shoulder striking first. Qin lunged in from the opposite direction and snatched his halberd out of his grip.

"Stop!" Bonita yelled, waving her pistol.

"Everyone!" Casmir added.

Qin could have swung the weapon at Asger's head and taken advantage of him being down, but she only skittered back, holding it defensively in front of her. Asger leaped to his feet, eyes blazing, chest heaving as he faced her. He took a single step toward her, but Zee came in from behind him, moving so quickly Asger didn't have time to react. One robot arm wrapped around his body, pinning his arms to his sides, and Asger was hefted into the air again, his boots dangling above the deck.

"Hold him there, Zee." Casmir stepped past Bonita, trying to block her line of sight. She still looked like she wanted to shoot Asger. "Asger, did someone spill fizzop on your circuit board? What are you *doing*?"

"What is *that* doing on this ship?" Asger couldn't point with his arms pinned, but he jerked his chin at Qin. "That's one of the Drucker pirates' modified warrior freaks. They've killed hundreds. They've killed *knights*." He snarled, trying to buck free of Zee's grip again.

"No, that's Qin Liangyu, the captain's assistant." Casmir looked toward Qin, feeling responsible for the attack and groping for an apology.

To his surprise, her shoulders slumped, and she let her captured weapon droop to the deck.

"I'm sorry," she whispered, eyes downcast. "The captain said I shouldn't come out, that I should stay in my cabin. I was curious." She glanced at Asger, but the livid anger on his face made her flinch. "I'll stay out of the way." She leaned the weapon haft against the bulkhead and fled up the ladder.

The fury and indignation faded from Bonita's face, and she lowered her pistol.

"Is that where she came from?" Casmir had a hard time believing Qin as the killer Asger had described, but he did remember her alluding to pirates in her background.

Asger continued to stare at the ladder well, his face red, and all of his muscles tense.

"I'm not sure exactly." Bonita shrugged. "I know she came from— was, er, commissioned by, I guess—one of the pirate families, but I didn't ask for details about which one. She's smart, and she's an amazing fighter. She doesn't even care that I can't always pay her. She's a good kid." She glared at Asger, some of her anger returning.

Casmir held up a hand, silently promising he would find a way to create peace. As soon as he figured out how.

"Set him down, please, Zee." Casmir walked up to Asger's side, the corridor tight with the large knight and the even larger crusher filling the space.

Zee lowered Asger to the deck without releasing him.

"Get your thing off me, Dabrowski," Asger growled, finally looking at him.

"Zee will be happy to release you if you promise not to attack the crew again. Captain Lopez and *Qin*—" Casmir waved in the direction she'd gone, hoping to instill in Asger that she had a name, "—are on our side."

"That *creature* is not on my side."

"Well, she's on *my* side. And so is Zee. I think that means we've got you outnumbered."

Casmir walked over to pick up Asger's pertundo while he tried to think of something less antagonistic to say. He was irritated that Asger had attacked Qin and not being even vaguely diplomatic. Hadn't he prided himself in the past on being able to get enemies to work together? Admittedly, those had been engineers with clashing personalities, not warriors who'd watched friends die in battle.

Taking a deep breath, Casmir faced Asger and held out the weapon. "Which doesn't matter all that much to a knight, I suppose." He forced a smile. "Please agree not to attack anyone on the ship while we're here. I think it's very possible Qin isn't anyone you've faced before, but even if she is, we're all going to be working together for a few days. Qin and Laser have agreed to help the Kingdom with the gate problem, the same as I have. Even though they're not from our system. I think we should be gracious. You know, knightly. And chivalrous."

"Have your robot let me go," Asger said coolly.

"Will you give your word first that you won't attack Qin again?" Casmir gazed into the knight's icy blue eyes, hoping to find honor there under the anger. Maybe later, once tempers cooled, Casmir would ask what had happened—it sounded like Asger might have lost a friend, a good friend—but this wasn't the time.

Asger's shoulders flexed as he tried to escape the crusher without conceding anything. For good or ill, Casmir had made the robot well. Zee didn't budge.

"I will not attack her while I am on this ship and we are working toward a common goal," Asger said stiffly.

"Let him go, please, Zee," Casmir said.

Zee released Asger.

Asger stepped forward, toward Casmir and also toward the ladder. Casmir tensed, afraid he would have to shout an order for Zee to grab their new ally again, but Asger only snatched his halberd and jammed it into its holder.

"Where are my quarters?" Asger looked from Casmir to Bonita. "I would prefer to keep to myself during the journey to the gate."

"This way." Bonita shot a glare at Casmir as she walked past him. With her back to Asger, she mouthed, "Where are my quarters?" with a mocking face, then raised her voice and spat a stream of words in her native tongue.

Casmir had no idea what they meant, and Asger must not have either. He followed her up the ladder well without hesitation, and Casmir was soon alone in the corridor with Zee. A couple of the robot vacuums trundled in, cleaning the deck where the fight had occurred.

Casmir felt the need to apologize to both Qin and Bonita, but he would give them a little time to recover from the incident.

"Viggo?" Casmir asked. "Are you listening?"

"I'm always listening," the ship's computer replied.

Casmir decided not to find that creepy or alarming. "How far to the gate? And how soon can we head in that direction?"

"Approximately eleven hours. The knight's shuttle is detaching now. I shall ask Bonita if she is prepared to depart."

"I have a feeling she'll want to get this over with as quickly as possible," Casmir murmured.

"That is likely true."

"Let me know if I can repair or upgrade anything for you while I'm here." He was tired and should try to sleep while they traveled, but he didn't know if his brain would turn off.

"I will do so."

Casmir headed up to the cabin where he'd left his tool satchel but paused at the open hatchway to the lounge. It seemed strange to be back here without Kim. She would have already been running on one of the treadmills, he wagered.

Hoping he was doing the right thing, and hating that they were flying away from Skadi and Kim, Casmir turned into his cabin.

CHAPTER 10

YAS WOKE UP WITH A START, ALMOST FALLING out of the seat bank he was sprawled across. He clawed himself into an upright position, feeling dizzy, flushed, and more tired than when he'd gone to sleep. The disease, or whatever it was, was progressing.

He spotted Kim Sato studying data in the tiny lab and felt guilty that he'd left her to work while he'd slept for however long it had been. Had she made any progress?

Yas pushed himself to his feet, wobbling and gripping a seat back for support while he fought off a dizzy spell. Fear charged through his limbs, the fear that he might die down here in some forsaken frozen canyon thousands of light years from home. His parents would never know what had happened, never know that he'd had nothing to do with the president's death.

An unexpected sadness came over him at the realization that he didn't have anyone else except his parents who might lament his death. Shouldn't there have been a wife by now? Children? He'd always been busy with work and his goals, but deep down, he knew he'd used that as an excuse to explain his solitude. Even though he'd won respect from his peers, he had never been good at enticing women to appreciate his assets. *Him.*

President Bakas's words rang in his mind. *Perhaps your pomposity wasn't so lovable after all.* She'd barely known him, but she'd seen right into the heart of his problem. She'd been a good president, good with people. He regretted that he hadn't had an opportunity to find her killer. Her real killer.

He rubbed his face. His skin was warm and damp with sweat.

Needing a distraction from his thoughts, and a chance to be useful, Yas walked over to the makeshift lab. "Any progress, Scholar Sato? Is there anything I can do to help?"

"Do you know anything about Rache that I don't?" Kim asked without looking up from the computer display. Her voice was flat, hard to read.

"Probably not. He saved my life, so I suppose I should be grateful to him, but I'm mostly wondering if I'm going to survive this trip down here."

"Me too. *He's* not affected by whatever is killing the rest of us."

"No? Did he give you a blood sample?"

"Yes."

"Oh."

"I've been poring over it for hours," Kim said. "Right now, I'm running tests on antibodies to common illnesses because… I'm grasping at straws. Maybe it's just his enhanced immune system that's keeping him from being affected by this. But he said at least one of his men has had the same shots that he's had."

"Yeah. Most of the mercs are souped-up in one way or another." Yas thought of Jess and the story she'd shared. She was probably one of the few who hadn't altered herself to become a better killer. She'd had no other choice. He also regretted that she might die down here. "Let me know if there's anything I can do. I don't want to get in your way, but I'm afraid… I'm just afraid, Scholar Sato."

"Me too," she said quietly. "Call me Kim."

"I'm sorry that you're here. It's my fault."

Kim looked at him for the first time since he'd arisen. Her helmet was off, sitting on the counter, and numerous strands of hair had fallen free of her braid. She was on the plain side when compared to Jess's striking beauty, but he imagined she would be cute with a little make-up and a smile. Not that he should be worried about such things now. What was there to smile about?

"I told him you were more qualified for this work than I," Yas admitted, "so he decided to kidnap you."

"I see." Kim turned back to the computer displays. "I had access to a good lab up on the research ship. I'd much prefer to be working on this up there."

"I'm sorry." It sounded inane, and Yas knew it.

A soft ding sounded, and she shifted her attention to another display.

"That's interesting," she murmured, "but I fail to see what it would have to do with anything."

"What's that?" Yas stepped closer.

"It seems that the brave and virile mercenary Captain Rache was never inoculated against the Great Plague. Or, I should say, his ancestors never were."

"It's a hereditary vaccine, right? Everyone who received it… oh, about two hundred years ago should have passed it along to their children. Most doctors don't even check now to make sure it was administered. Back then, there were massive campaigns to make sure that everyone in the Twelve Systems was safe from the virus."

"That's right. So why doesn't Rache have immunity to that?"

"Because he was made in some scientist's laboratory instead of a woman's womb?" Yas smiled wanly.

Kim leaned her elbow on the counter and looked contemplatively at the wall. "I suppose that's possible, since even on Odin, artificial wombs are relatively common these days."

"You know I tested his DNA, right? And your friend's?"

Kim nodded. "I assumed you were the one. Did you find anything interesting? There's no DNA sequencer here."

"Mostly just that they were identical for the most part. Your friend didn't undergo gene-cleaning as a baby, and Rache did."

"That shouldn't have anything to do with vaccines. Rache has vaccine-induced antibodies to other typical childhood illnesses, Kingdom illnesses, that is. I checked. I've been desperate and checking everything. But as you pointed out, the Great Plague vaccine was hereditary. Technically, it wasn't a vaccine. It was a genetic modification to our DNA, specifically, the DNA in our mitochondria. A slight alteration that made them less appealing to a virus native to System Hind that, when humans encountered it, decided that our mitochondria were delicious. The virus spread so thoroughly and rapidly that the extinction of humankind was predicted."

Yas nodded, remembering reading about the Great Plague in his early years as a medical student.

"Even the Kingdom, which was as ravaged by the plague as anywhere else, couldn't object to the genetic tinkering, not when a few slight alterations proved effective at deterring the virus. By then, everyone was desperate for a solution." Kim tapped a pattern on the counter as she spoke, though she seemed unaware of doing it. "As far as I've read, there have never been any negative side effects from the mitochondrial changes. There's no reason someone would opt to change the DNA back on a baby born today. Or born thirty-two years ago. It would result in that person being susceptible to the plague virus, which doubtless still lurks in pockets out there."

Yas wiped sweat from his forehead. "It's an interesting find, but it doesn't really help with our problem, does it? Even if we could somehow snap our fingers and change every bit of our mitochondria to match Rache's, it couldn't possibly save us, right?"

"I don't see how, given that whatever is affecting us resembles radiation far more than bacteria or a virus, but I need to think about it. I feel like I'm missing something key." Kim covered a yawn, looking as tired as Yas felt, but she went back to drumming her fingers, working over the problem. "How could this cause Rache to be less susceptible to something like radiation?"

"You keep saying radiation. Is it possible this is some new radiation that we haven't encountered before and don't have a meter capable of registering?"

"That's what I've been wondering. If it originated with that wreck— that *ship* out there… who knows what star systems and empty space it sailed through before it arrived in our system? Maybe it encountered something deadly out there and is emitting it, and we're all standing around like idiots, sucking it up."

"Sounds like a good argument for leaving," Yas said, "but that's what those archaeologists did, and they still died."

"The team from the video?" Kim frowned at him.

"Yeah. We found them all dead on that refinery."

"Something else Rache didn't feel was important to share with me."

"I'm sorry. I should have realized you couldn't have known about that and told you earlier." Yas tilted his head. "Does knowing that help with anything?"

Kim closed her eyes. "I don't think so. If you got acute radiation poisoning, you could easily die a few days later, after you'd been removed from the exposure. Maybe that's what happened to them.

What's more puzzling is that people have died who weren't down here. The crew of the *Machu Picchu* is dead, maybe affected or contaminated somehow by the team that went back there before presumably leaving and ending up on that refinery."

"With someone chasing them. We saw that on one of the refinery cameras."

Kim opened her eyes and issued an exasperated noise, and he realized he hadn't told her about that either. Yas shrugged apologetically, now wishing he'd taken the time to carefully go over everything with her from the beginning. He'd already been feeling sick then and hadn't been at his best.

"I care less about that," Kim said. "I'm just trying to figure out why the crew died. Could it have been that circuit board? I suppose the team could have taken that with them back to the research ship. Yes, if they weren't aware that the wreck down here was oozing some… pseudo radiation, they might not have considered that piece of the gate or the ship or whatever to be dangerous. I mean, I'm sure they examined it with every scanner they had before taking it back…"

"But if it emits something we can't read, it wouldn't have been enough," Yas said.

"Right."

"Everyone up on the research ship died, then?"

"Not everyone. A bunch of the civilian researchers quarantined themselves in sickbay behind Glasnax—and a magnetic field."

"A magnetic field would protect against radiation as we know it."

"That may be the answer then, though…" She grimaced.

"That doesn't help those of us who've already been exposed," Yas finished.

"No."

"And it doesn't explain why Rache's mitochondria are making him immune."

"No. And I admit, we don't know if that's the reason he's thus far been immune. It's just an anomaly present in his blood that isn't present in anyone else's down here."

The hatch opened, and Rache and Jess walked in.

"Take a seat," Rache said. "We're going for a short ride."

Jess flopped down with a weary groan. By now, she had to be feeling as poorly as Yas.

"Find anything interesting in the wreck, Jess?" Yas asked.

She shook her helmeted head as Rache headed for the pilot's seat.

"I think we arrived too late, Doc," she said. "It looks like someone cleared out all the good stuff. There's not so much as a screw from a gate anywhere in there. Whoever it was, they may have had a spy in the archaeologists' camp. I don't think this wreck has been visible for that long. Some tectonic shift revealed it. I'm assuming that's why someone finally found it, even though archaeologists and treasure hunters have been searching for centuries."

Rache fired up the thrusters, and the shuttle rose into the night. He stayed in the canyon, lights playing over the forest of ice stalagmites ahead of them.

"If every piece of the gate is gone," Kim murmured, "what's emitting our pseudo radiation? The wreck itself?"

"It must be," Yas said. "Like you said, the ship probably traveled through something weird, and the whole thing is contaminated, including everything that was in it."

"Hm." Kim squinted at the back of Rache's head.

Still thinking about his quirky mitochondria?

"Maybe I should take that tour of the wreck now," Kim said. "I'd like to take some pictures before we go."

"You think we'll get to go soon?" Yas asked wistfully. He didn't want to die down here, but his fate was in Rache's hands.

Rache, who was focused on flying, ignored their conversation.

"It doesn't sound like he found what he was looking for," Kim said. "Not much point in staying now."

"True." Yas was about to raise his voice and ask Rache about that when the shuttle landed.

They had only gone a couple of miles. The canyon had widened slightly but appeared mostly the same, yet he opened the hatch, cycled the airlock, and trotted into the icy darkness outside.

"What did he find?" Yas wondered, watching the forward display.

Rache soon came into view of the running lights, jogging toward mounds of snow swept against one side of the canyon.

"Not what," Jess said. "Who. One of the original team of archaeologists, he said, though I was a little confused. He had me looking for metal on my hand scanner. Metal *outside* of the wreck, not in it."

"Metal?" Kim lifted her head.

Rache bent, digging something out of the snow, and Kim left the lab, her gaze locked to the display.

He withdrew the body of the monkey droid Yas had seen in the video. *Most* of it. He pulled a detached leg out next, and dug the dismembered head out of another pile of snow.

Yas caught a stricken expression on Kim's face before she jerked away, closing her eyes and bringing her fist to her mouth.

Yas didn't know the story of how her mother had come to be a loaded droid, but it must have involved the death of her corporeal body. He could only guess at what Kim was feeling and what it would be like to lose a parent not once but twice.

Casmir knocked softly on Qin's hatch. Bonita had disappeared into her own cabin to sleep while Viggo handled the flight to the gate, and he hadn't seen Asger since the incident with Qin. He did know the knight's shuttle was flying alongside the *Dragon,* matching its pace.

Casmir was a little surprised Asger hadn't insisted on returning to it and sleeping there, staying as far from Qin as possible. But it seemed he'd been serious when he'd said he needed to keep his eyes on Casmir. Even if that would be hard to do from inside his locked cabin. Maybe he felt that was close enough to keep Casmir from getting in trouble.

"He doesn't know me very well," Casmir muttered and stepped back.

Qin hadn't answered. She either didn't want to talk or was sleeping, something he'd only managed to do for a couple of hours himself. It hadn't helped that he'd dreamed of the attack in the corridor, but in the dream, Asger had succeeded in lopping off Qin's head. Her body had lain in blood on the deck, cat-like eyes staring accusingly up at Casmir.

The hatch opened as he was turning away. Qin stood with the lights dimmed behind her, her shoulders slumped, her six-plus feet of height barely seeming greater than Casmir's five-feet-seven. Her eyes weren't accusing, but moisture glistened on her cheeks.

Had she been crying? He promptly felt twice as bad for bringing Asger.

"I'm sorry." Casmir lifted an apologetic hand. "You were sleeping. I don't want to bother you. It can wait."

"I wasn't sleeping." She forced the briefest half smile he'd ever seen.

Right, she'd been *crying*.

"I came to apologize for bringing someone antagonistic on board," Casmir said. "I didn't have much choice since I was on my way to the brig, and he helped me avoid that fate, but I could have warned Captain Lopez sooner. Warned *you*." He extended an open hand toward her and met her eyes, hoping she would see his sincerity. "I wasn't expecting his reaction to be so strong. Combustible, you might say. I mean, I knew he was Kingdom and would probably share our prejudices toward people with genetic modifications, but that caught me off guard."

Casmir lowered his hand. He was curious about her past, and was tempted to ask if she'd truly worked for one of the pirate families, but it wasn't his business, and it shouldn't matter unless pirates were the ones attacking Kingdom ships at the gate. He doubted it. The pirate families ran small outfits, usually a single ship or a small fleet, and they didn't pick fights with military vessels. At least from what he'd heard in the news.

"Me too," Qin whispered, glancing toward the cabin Asger had been given. "I just wanted to see a knight. Viggo said he was here, and I'd been trying to see one for a while, to see if they're as brave and noble as they say in the vids and books." She dropped her gaze to Casmir's boots. "I know it's silly, but I guess I thought they'd be chivalrous even to me. In the stories, they're always protecting and rescuing ladies and risking their lives on their behalf. But it's not like I'm a lady. I'm a freak, like he said."

"Qin, you most certainly *are* a lady."

He resisted the urge to point out that she was quite beautiful to anyone who could see past the fact that her arms had fur instead of hair. Maybe she needed to hear that, but not from him. He was fairly certain she was younger than most of his students, despite the muscles and enhanced ability to kill, and he would feel weird saying anything that could be construed as flirting.

She looked up, her eyes wary. Almost as if she expected a blow and was prepared to flinch.

"And you're *not* a freak. I would know if you were. I can recognize my own kind, you know."

Her eyebrows rose with skepticism.

"It's true. You may not be able to tell from the handsome and suave gentleman I am now—" he wriggled his eyebrows, hoping to lift her spirits, "—but I've occasionally been ostracized. At school, at the synagogue, in sports—dear God, sports—I was that guy who didn't fit in. I may not have fur and pointed ears, but it seems to be part of human nature, or perhaps the nature of a crowd, to be able to home in on those who are more than a standard deviation or two from the norm. And make sure they never forget it."

"Yeah." She hung her head, looking so dejected that his heart ached.

That had been more honest than he'd intended, and he feared he'd only reinforced her feelings of chagrin and despair instead of helping. He reached out and rested a hand on her shoulder. "It's not your fault. And it's nothing wrong with *you*. And you really can't expect much from us backward Kingdom guys. We practically live in caves. Even my mild-mannered and scholarly father throws his head back and beats his chest with his fists when his favorite sports team scores goals."

"Well, *everybody* does that."

Casmir snorted but was glad she gave him a more sincere smile.

Once again, it faded quickly. "I didn't do what he said, Casmir. Maybe the others did, the older cohort. I don't know. I *did* fight for the Druckers—that's what they trained me to do from the day the scientists handed me over to them. They paid for me to be made, so it's not like I had a choice, especially when I was younger. But I'd never seen a knight before today, not in person. I've definitely never killed one."

"I believe you."

"*Good.*" She stepped from the safety of her hatchway and hugged him. Strongly.

He returned the hug, trying to react like a friend and not someone who was terrified she would snap his spine. He wasn't sure why his opinion mattered, but he was glad she seemed more at ease. He was tempted to promise her he'd help find her a nice open-minded knight if she stuck around in his system, but he feared that would be difficult to accomplish. He didn't know that many for starters, and he thought it might be challenging to find one who wasn't deeply indoctrinated in Kingdom beliefs. Perhaps some of his students would be a better match for her. If she ever ended up back on Odin. He'd recognized a few kindred spirits among them, young men who knew what it was like not to fit in.

Qin released him and stepped back, wiping her eyes.

"How old were you when—uhm?" He waved vaguely.

He hadn't intended to pry, but he wanted to know what bastard scientists made kids-to-order for criminals. They were probably too many light years away for him ever to have the power to do anything about it, but he liked to think he could start some network boycott or something. How much did it cost to have a tailored human being—or not quite entirely human being—made from scratch and raised?

"When they took delivery of me?" Qin asked. "Almost twelve. Old enough for training and for sex."

"For what?" he blurted.

She shrugged again. "I didn't care that much about that. They made us not-ugly enough that they could get their money's worth in bed as well as on the battlefield. I had seven sisters too, so the pirates' demands were kind of spread out. And then there was an older cohort that was delivered a couple of years before us. Not many of them are still alive. We all hated it there, even if some of us were quieter than the others and didn't complain much. Liangyu Two and Seven led a mutiny, though, and killed a lot of the pirates. Then they were killed themselves, and everyone who'd sided with them was punished or killed. There are a lot more Druckers than there were of us. You know them? It's a huge and powerful family. Hundreds of them, and they've got five ships now. It's not a good idea to cross them. That's why I used to wish…" Her eyes grew distant as her focus drifted toward Asger's cabin, and then to the deck again. "Never mind. It's silly."

"To be rescued by a knight?" he guessed.

"Maybe."

How disappointing it must have been for her to meet her dream man in real life and have him attack her and call her a freak. Casmir wiped moisture from his own eyes.

"I'm sorry, Qin. I'll let Asger know he mistook you for someone else. Maybe he'll be a little less of an ass."

She shook her head. "Thank you for caring, but don't worry about it. It was my stupid fantasy that was the problem. The galaxy is what it is."

"The galaxy, yes, but the human beings who live in it have the ability to change and be changed. I'd like to think there's hope that we can encourage people to change for the better."

"Thank you for caring," she said again and kissed him on the cheek before stepping back into her room and closing the hatch.

Casmir slumped against the wall, wondering when he'd shifted from being happy building robots to help a few people here and there to wishing he had the power to change the system—*all* of the systems. He'd enjoyed his life at the university and thought he was doing everything he'd dreamed of as a boy, but it had been a small life, hadn't it? Maybe when he solved his immediate problems—he refused to put an *if* in there—and could go back home, he would get involved in politics, try to get elected to one of the positions open to people who weren't of the nobility. Maybe he could at least help change the viewpoints of Kingdom subjects.

A hatch creaked open.

He looked up, half expecting Asger and already preparing words for him. But Bonita was the one to step out of her cabin.

She raised her eyebrows, doubtless wondering why Casmir was lurking in the corridor, but all she said was, "Good," and gestured toward the ladder leading up to navigation. "This is your problem. You'll want to see what's going on."

"I'm sure I will." Casmir followed her as she climbed the ladder, favoring one of her legs. "Which problem is it?"

"Viggo updated me on the gate." She plopped down into her pod in navigation.

The front display came to life, first showing a field of stars and then zooming in to the gate and two large warships placed to block access to it. They were almost side by side, but one listed a bit, and Casmir grimaced. Was that a strategy, pretending to look damaged, or was it genuinely damaged?

Smaller ships whipped around, almost like the robot vacuums had been doing around his feet earlier, firing at the large vessels. As they watched, one of the warships fired a huge weapon, one that resulted in a flash of white light. Two of the small vessels blew into pieces, but that didn't change anything. There had to be a hundred of them.

And what of the cargo ship? Casmir couldn't even see it. Ishii had mentioned stealth technology that might be beyond a slydar hull plating.

Was the enemy ship appearing and firing and then disappearing again? Continuing to battle until the Kingdom ships gave up and let it through the gate? Or until they'd been destroyed and had no choice but to let it through the gate?

If the cargo ship blew up the already-damaged warship, it could likely slip past the other one, depending on its size. Whatever that was. Casmir had no idea. The term *cargo ship* conjured notions of something big in his mind. The gates were all uniform in size, a couple of miles across, which seemed massive on paper, but theirs didn't look that large with the big warships in front of it.

"Those are the warships that were investigating Rache's mercenary actions." Lopez pointed at the vessels blocking the gate. "The regular ships that guard the gate are either missing, or they've been blown to pieces. If your friend Ishii's ship doesn't get there before *that* one is blown up or knocked out of the way—" she pointed to the listing vessel, "—then the enemy ship is going to escape before we get there."

"Are there any other Kingdom ships en route?"

"Two more warships heading toward the gate from Forseti Station, but it'll take them days to get there."

Another ship appeared on the display, and Casmir sucked in a breath. It was every bit as large as the Kingdom soldiers had described, spinning to create gravity for its crew, with turrets and railguns and weapons platforms he couldn't identify visible all over the rotating hull. The porcupines in the Zamek Zoo had fewer protrusions.

White-yellow light flashed, obscuring the gate and all the ships for long seconds, and then the ship disappeared again. A volley of missiles fired from the warships blasted toward the space it had occupied. The enemy ship's weapons—nukes?—arched toward the gate. The warships maneuvered, trying to shift out of the way, but Casmir realized the problem right away. They had to stay in front of the gate to keep it blockaded, so they were extremely limited in how far they could move.

A projectile slammed into the edge of one of the warships, and the hull seemed to shatter, shards flying in a thousand directions. Meanwhile, the missiles they had launched flew through empty space. They turned—were they heat-seeking?—but merely flew around, not finding a target. It was as if the enemy ship had shifted to another dimension. Casmir highly doubted that was happening, but it unnerved him that the experienced military captains were having trouble figuring it out.

"What a farce," Bonita said. "You really want us to get involved in that? One of those missiles flying around, not finding its real target, could find us, and we'd be dead." She snapped her fingers. "Like that."

"I wasn't planning to engage them in a firefight."

"What *were* you planning? Because I refuse to get close to that mess without a plan that ensures the *Dragon* won't be fired on."

"Understandable. Will you comm them for me?"

"Oh right, because it goes *so* well whenever you chat with the enemy."

"We might as well try. We might learn something if they answer, such as who they are. It didn't sound like the Fleet ships knew, at least not when I was over there. Did you get a shot of it when it appeared? Viggo, do you mind looking up that ship and trying to identify the model and what system it's out of?"

"I did scan it," Viggo said, "and I am looking for a match now."

"We can't comm them if they're invisible," Bonita said. "They're not showing up on the scanners any more than they are visually on the cameras."

"It looks like they have to appear to fire—or firing causes them to appear. I'll record a message that you can send the next time they pop up. And, Viggo, would you mind scanning for life on there when you get a chance? It would be nice to know how big the crew is."

Casmir thought of Asger's comment that an army of crushers might be useful if they could get them over there. As he'd admitted, there was no way he could build more crushers here, but if he and a team of elite fighters—specifically, Asger, Zee, and Qin—could somehow board that ship, maybe they could do something. Distract the bridge crew, at least, and give the warships time to home in on it.

He hadn't figured out *how* they would get aboard it yet. The Kingdom ships had squads and squads of combat marines, so if a forced boarding were achievable, they would have surely done it already.

He also wasn't sure why he was imagining himself leading that team. Not when he had the combat abilities of a slug. Maybe his subconscious was feeling frisky since it had been almost two days since he'd thrown up from space sickness.

"We're still too far away to scan for life," Viggo said, "but I can send a message once you prepare it."

"Your buddy is closer," Bonita said. "Maybe his people have done a scan and would share the results."

"My buddy? Is that Captain Ishii?"

"Do you have so many friends that you lose track of them?"

"Only the ones who threaten to throw me in the brig."

"Record your message so Viggo can send it," Bonita said. "If they can tell us to go away, we can save ourselves some time and turn around now."

"If I turned around every time someone told me to go away, I wouldn't have had a date to the Grad Night Dance when I was eighteen."

"I didn't know robots were that choosy." She waved impatiently at the comm panel.

"We know what kind of ship it is yet? From which system?"

"It is a modified Union-5 Cargo Hauler," Viggo said, "originally constructed in the Lunar-5 factory at Belt Station Etium. Greatly modified somewhere else. Some of its weapons are out of System Cerberus. Some are not listed yet in public records."

"Union? It was used in mining then?" Casmir groped for ways that might be helpful.

"To haul ore, maybe," Bonita said. "But not necessarily. The Union has a lot of power across multiple systems, with stakes in almost all of the asteroid belts out there. They have plenty of ships that are involved in trade and passenger transport, in addition to their mining fleets. But if that was originally an ore hauler, the Union princes *definitely* have the money to pay for modifications to ships. They have the money to buy planets and moons if they want."

"So they might want gate bits to make sure they're the ones to control the next evolution of humanity into the galaxy."

"Gate bits?" Bonita glanced at him. "Is that what they're carrying?"

"What they're *stealing* from our system, I gathered. Though I'm not sure if anyone is quite sure or if they're guessing."

Casmir questioned whether Royal Intelligence or Fleet Command had seen a version of the video Rache had gotten hold of, but it made sense that the archaeologists would have sent preliminary results home. Someone back there had to know what they'd found. And that someone else wanted it.

"If it's the Union," he mused, "do they just want to be first to install a new gate so they can stake out a place in the history books? Or do they already have a profit angle in mind?"

"If it's the Union, profit is more than an angle. Those people live and die by capitalist rule. You want to become a prince, you have to have the money to buy a private asteroid station, minions to serve you, and a harem."

"I didn't know harems were a requirement for rulers."

"It shows everyone how wealthy and important you are." Bonita sneered. "I wouldn't object to their methodology if there were any Union *princesses*. The princes always seem like misogynistic assholes."

Casmir thought about pointing out that a princess who could afford harems and private asteroid stations might not be a delightful person either, but he had little experience with the breed, either self-made or hereditarily appointed. The media always portrayed King Jager's twenty-something daughter, Princess Oku, as pretty but dim, using Kingdom resources to fly about the Twelve Systems, collecting flowers for her garden.

"Ready to record, Viggo?" Casmir leaned against the back of the co-pilot's pod.

"Ready."

"To the captain of the Union ship, my name is Professor Casmir Dabrowski from Zamek University on Odin. I am a mechanical engineer who's long studied the gates from afar and found them fascinating. I've won numerous awards, been published in dozens of journals and periodicals, and have an aptitude for deciphering engineering mysteries. I understand you're about to successfully leave this system with part or all of a previously undiscovered wormhole gate in your hold. I've been eager to leave the Kingdom for ages, and I'm willing to offer my services to the research and development team that you must certainly have waiting at home. I'm even willing to forgo pay, providing I receive an author byline on any papers published and credit for any discoveries made. Please let me know if I can transmit my résumé."

Bonita waited until he was done recording to let out a snort that echoed from the walls of the small navigation chamber.

"Careful. I think you blew your tonsils out through your nostrils." Casmir pointed at the deck. "Are those them?"

"Did you just offer to send your résumé to the enemy vessel trying to blow up your government's military warships?"

"Yes. I would send a message to the king to let him know it wasn't a sincere offer, since I am fond of Odin and my job in Zamek, but it's unlikely he reads mail from random subjects. I will inform Sir Asger, in case he has the capacity to pass messages along to His Majesty."

Bonita shook her head. "Was any of that true, or are you just hoping they don't decide to research you?"

"I *have* been published numerous times, and I *have* won awards." Just none that had anything to do with gates, an area about which he was completely ignorant. If someone from the enemy ship actually replied, he would have to take a crash course on astrophysics and wormhole theory. Or was it wormhole hypothesis? The last he'd heard, nobody understood how the gates worked, and the scientific community had no trouble labeling wormhole travel as impossible at the same time as they booked flights to other systems.

"Was the award for creating a robot girlfriend to take to that school dance?"

"No. Most recently, I was recognized for excellence in leadership in the robotics industry."

"Huh, maybe you *are* good at bamboozling people."

Casmir opened his mouth to object to her interpretation, but Viggo interrupted them.

"The enemy ship has made another reappearance."

Casmir grimaced, facing the display, though he feared they would only see more of the vessel getting the best of the Kingdom warships. He had zero experience with military maneuvers or spaceship battle tactics, but he decided right away that being on the defensive was awful. What was his backup plan if this didn't work? There was no way the *Dragon* could get close enough to force-board, not with the cargo ship appearing and reappearing and all manner of what looked like drone fighter ships whipping around to protect it.

After another round of exchanging fire—this time, the Kingdom warships clipped the enemy vessel before it disappeared—Viggo said, "I've sent your message, Casmir."

"Thank you, Viggo. I shall be eagerly waiting to see if they send a request for my résumé."

"Your résumé that says nothing about gates?" Bonita asked.

"Yes. Do you think I should spruce it up a bit, just in case?" He highly doubted anything would come of his attempt at a ruse, and if some Union miner asked for his résumé, he would be flabbergasted. Mostly, he was curious to hear what kind of response he *did* get. Surely, if he learned who they were dealing with, he could come up with a better plan than the one currently in effect: taking potshots at each other.

"I would," Bonita said.

CHAPTER 11

A S RACHE LED THE WAY FROM THE SHUTTLE to the wreck, Kim paused and looked up at the stars visible through the narrow slit of their canyon. She had queued a long letter to Casmir to go out whenever there was enough of a signal—she suspected that wouldn't be until Rache gave up on this place and flew the shuttle back up to orbit.

Her letter included wishes for her remains, messages to her family, what she'd learned—or hadn't learned—about the strange energy attacking their bodies, and that she'd found her mother's broken droid remains. It was possible Casmir or another engineer could repair her and get the droid powered back up again, but she wasn't working now. Kim had no idea if that was permanent or not. There had been damage to the head, aside from it being ripped from the body, which may have broken chips and circuits. All that her mother was might now be irretrievably lost.

Even though they had never been close, that filled her with a sense of bleakness and regret. She wished she'd had a chance to say goodbye, to have known her better before having to *say* goodbye.

"Scholar Sato?" Rache said from the hole in the side of the wreck that his team used as a door. "Are you coming?"

"Yes."

Kim forced her heavy legs to work. She could feel the affliction progressing and her weariness increasing. Dr. Peshlakai was sleeping again, and several of Rache's men had gone into the shuttle, peeled off their helmets, and collapsed on the seats or the deck. Only Rache remained unaffected.

She added that as a postscript to her letter to Casmir. That neither Rache nor his ancestors had received the Great Plague treatment and that he wasn't being affected by this cellular destruction, that maybe someone with more time could run experiments with mitochondria. If she'd had bacteria or viruses to work with, something she could have isolated, it would have been a simple matter to place them in solutions with both types of mitochondria and see if they preferred one over the other. But she had no way to capture whatever this was, not yet. Nor did it make sense to her that something akin to radiation would care one whit about a person's mitochondria.

She wished she had some of her radiation-eating bacteria with her to see if they might make a difference. It was possible they would be able to detect what human instruments couldn't. And if it was compatible, maybe they could even consume it.

But she didn't have them. She'd never planned to leave Odin, so she hadn't inoculated herself with them.

She wondered if Dr. Sikou had been inoculated with them. She'd mentioned the *Osprey* being in Phase II testing. If she had been, it might be possible to extract and isolate some of the bacteria from her body.

Kim had no idea if they would be useful against this threat, but it would be worth trying. She composed a quick message to Sikou, not surprised when all it did was sit in the queue with Casmir's, unable to go out until she had network access.

Rache shifted his weight, then stepped into the wreck. Kim ought to be arguing for them to go back to the research ship where she was far more likely to be able to find a solution. Instead, she followed Rache inside.

She wanted to take pictures to send to Casmir along with her letter, to hear what his thoughts were on the wreck. Rache's immunity nagged at the back of her mind, and she couldn't help but feel she was close to grasping the reason for it. And that in it, there might be something to help the rest of them.

"Just looking at the stars," she murmured to Rache when she caught up with him. "In case I don't get another chance." She didn't mention the messages saved in her chip, waiting to go out. "I cannot tell you how much I wish there was a coffee house here."

The idea that she might die without ever having had one last good cup of coffee distressed her almost as much as everything else.

"I admit," Rache said quietly, "when I decided to come down here, I thought at least some pieces of the gate would still be here. I also thought that if some killer virus lurked within the corridors of the wreck, I'd be as likely to die from it as anyone else."

"Does it not sit well with you that everyone around you will die while you live?" Kim had a hard time believing he truly cared.

"It doesn't, no. I've always known my choices would get me killed." He gestured toward the stars, maybe including his ship, wherever it had gone, named for a character from *Moby Dick*. "And those who signed on, well, they knew the job would likely get them killed eventually. They get good hazardous-duty pay. But you and Dr. Peshlakai…"

He didn't finish the thought, merely extending his hand toward the shadowy interior of the wreck.

"Did you also kidnap him?" Kim shone the flashlight built into her helmet around as she walked slowly into a strange, alien place full of harsh angles and exposed circuitry covered in layers of frost. There was a mathematical precision to those angles, and she thought that if she'd felt better, she might have stood there and picked out patterns.

"I saved his life, actually." As Rache walked at her side, he nodded toward a wide tube that led deeper into the ship—and deeper under the glacier. "He collapsed at my feet with his station's security chasing and shooting at him. Shooting to kill, oddly. That's not their *modus operandi* on Tiamat Station. I offered to help him if he would work for me for five years. I'd recently lost my previous surgeon. When he appeared, it seemed like fate, though it's a cruel fate that would place a hapless man in my path."

"You know and acknowledge that you're a villain?" She glanced at him. "But you choose that path anyway?"

"King *Jager* is the villain," Rache said, the frost crystals they walked on now lacing his tone. "If you haven't met him and aren't familiar with him enough to know that, consider yourself fortunate."

And naive, his unspoken words seemed to be.

"What did he do to you?" Her skin was flushed with fever, and sweat dribbled into her eyebrows.

"It's a long story."

"I guess I don't have time for that. Nobody except you does."

She'd put her helmet and oxygen tank back on to come outside, and already, the gear felt cumbersome, stifling. She wanted to be back home, reading in bed, feeling well, getting ready for work the next day. If fate did exist, her version was surely as cruel as Dr. Peshlakai's. She never should have been out here, wrapped up in this hell.

It was hard not to feel sorry for herself, but she berated herself in irritation when a sniffle slipped out. No doubt, the comm would pick it up, and Rache would know she was on the verge of tears. She didn't want him witnessing her weak moment.

He looked over at her as they continued, transitioning from the large outer chamber into a maze of tubes. "I would offer you a hug, but I think you'd find that particularly offensive coming from me. And hypocritical, since I brought you here."

Ugh, he *had* heard the sniffle. Damn it.

"Yes," she said. "I don't even encourage people I like to hug me."

They entered another open chamber, this one full of massive empty molds. Kim ordered her chip to take pictures of the walls, the ceiling, the deck, and the molds via her contact interface.

"We believe the gate was stored in here in sections," Rache said, walking among them. "A full gate, at least at one point. I'm not sure if it was all here when the archaeology team arrived, but I added up the dimensions of all the molds, all five hundred and twelve of them."

"And?" Kim looked around, curious about the gate even in her fevered haze, though she couldn't imagine what here would enlighten her when it came to fixing their health.

"There were almost exactly enough pieces to match the known dimensions of each of the gates in our gate network. There were two left over. I'm hypothesizing that this ship brought a couple of extras in case something broke in transport."

"Transport from where? Earth?"

"Possibly," Rache said. "Nobody has discovered an intelligent alien civilization yet—Odin is the only planet in the Twelve Systems that had higher-order animals, insects, and plants—but…"

"The gate technology is more advanced than we are *now,* two thousand and more years after humans came to the Twelve Systems. I know. I've heard the speculation. From my mother."

Kim leaned a hand against one of the molds, watching it to see if any mysterious waves of light crawled onto her glove. They did not. The cold seemed to emanate through the material, even though she knew that was unlikely. The galaxy suit adjusted to keep her body at the perfect temperature, fingers and toes included, but her brain felt hot. Her entire face did.

"I think we should get away from here," Kim said. "If whatever is wrong with us—with most of us—is exposure related, then maybe we'll buy ourselves a little more time."

"Any suggestion on where to go that might help?" he surprised her by asking. "I've been in contact with my ship off and on, and they're finishing up the repairs we can do outside of a shipyard. There's more lab equipment and space up there, but probably still not what you need."

What she needed. Did he still think she could master this somehow? Even if she figured out what was happening and how to stop it, the damage would still be there. Every hour here probably took five years off their lives.

"Judging by how quickly the archaeology team died," Rache added, "I doubt there's time to get anywhere with really good medical facilities."

"Your willingness to go must mean your men have finished searching the wreck and didn't find anything."

"Someone was here first. I wouldn't have guessed anyone could have cleared out so much so quickly." He waved to the empty molds, the *giant* empty molds. "But I think that whoever blew up the escape ship those archaeologists were in got the gate. Or however much of the gate was here."

Kim knew she was missing some information—what ship had been blown up when and by whom?—but she couldn't muster the energy to care. Her mother hadn't been on it. Her mother was back in the shuttle in pieces.

She wished she'd gotten another chance to speak to her before they both passed away, to ask her something she'd always wondered, why her mother had bothered having Kim when she'd had so little to do with Kim's upbringing. More than once, she'd wondered if she had disappointed her mother or not been what she'd expected, what she'd hoped for, and that had been the reason for the distance. Or had she simply realized motherhood didn't suit her?

Kim didn't think she'd ever wrapped up her own self-worth in her mother's approval, but... there were definitely things she would like to have known. She longed for the frank conversation they'd never had.

"I'll gather my men, and we'll head up to the *Fedallah*," Rache said. "Unless there's more of the wreck that you want to see?"

"The *Machu Picchu* would be better. It has excellent labs."

He gazed at her, and she expected him to object, to suspect duplicity.

"Very well," he said.

Kim nodded, pleased he hadn't argued. "I'll take a few more pictures and be ready to go back to the shuttle."

"Pictures? For what?" He sounded suspicious again. Was he still worried clues would get out and someone else would get to the gate first? Too late, buddy. Someone already had.

"Not what, whom." Kim was too tired for subterfuge. She waved to the walls. "It's computer-y. I thought it wouldn't hurt to get Casmir's opinion on the wreck, assuming I get somewhere with reception, so I can send the files."

"Ah."

Rache strode off without forbidding her to take the pictures or commenting further on it. She walked around and had her contact record some footage as well as take close-up shots of anything that looked interesting. Unique.

She wondered if she would still be alive when Casmir got the letter and files.

The Union ship hadn't responded yet. It had been two hours. Another hour, and the *Stellar Dragon* would be in firing range. Technically, they already were in firing range, but this far out, they could maneuver and get out of the way if the enemy sent nukes at them. Assuming they weren't heat-seeking nukes.

Casmir sat in the co-pilot's pod and alternated between nibbling on his fingernails and cracking his knuckles.

After one particularly loud crack, Bonita scowled over at him. "Why don't you take a nap? I'll let you know if they respond."

"Are you trying to get rid of me, Captain?"

"You just now noticed?" She shooed him toward the hatchway. "Don't you need to tell that uppity knight that you're not really out to get the Kingdom? Just because the enemy didn't answer your comm message doesn't mean the warships didn't notice it."

"Ah, good point."

Casmir pushed himself out of the pod and headed to Asger's hatch. He knocked and wasn't surprised when Asger promptly answered. It was hard to imagine anyone sleeping well knowing they were heading to a battleground.

"Come in," he called.

When Casmir opened the hatch, he found Asger in a pushup position on the deck. He sprang to his feet and stuck his head out to squint both directions down the corridor before stepping back and letting him in. What, had he been afraid Qin would be standing out there, ready to leap into his private space? Back on the *Osprey*, Casmir had been inclined to like Asger, since he'd helped him escape confinement, but his attitude toward Qin made Casmir wanted to punch him in the nose. Still, he shouldn't burn bridges—or knights—as they could be useful when trying to escape villains.

"Do you have a minute?" Casmir asked. "We're about an hour from the gate. I thought we should discuss our options."

"Do we have options?" Asger sat on the edge of his bunk.

A few wrinkles creased the blanket, but he clearly hadn't been under the covers. His book lay on the pillow.

"No. We need to make some."

"Ah."

"And I should warn you before someone else tells you that I offered to submit a résumé and work for the enemy if they would take me on board. I also expressed disgruntlement as a Kingdom subject, but I was actually quite enjoying my work and my life before all this started."

Asger gazed blandly at him, either thinking he was a loon or not knowing what he was talking about. Well, if he hadn't been sulking in his cabin, he could have been there for the genesis of that comm message.

"I thought someone who works for the king should know," Casmir added. "In case some overzealous communications officer on one of those warships recorded it to blackmail me later."

"What happens if someone on the enemy ship offers you a job?"

"The odds that they're here for job recruitment seem slim. I was just hoping someone would reply, and we could learn more about that ship and who's flying it and why. Also where they're taking their stolen cargo, in case we need to pursue them through the gate."

Asger grimaced and didn't deny the possibility. Maybe he was in communication with Ishii or someone else on the warship and had been keeping tabs on the battle.

A message alert came through on Casmir's chip, and it automatically downloaded a long letter and some large files. From Kim.

"She's alive." Casmir clenched his fist. "Kim's alive."

He started to smile, but as soon as he began reading her letter, grimness replaced relief.

"She's been afflicted with the… She's not calling it a disease. She says it's not bacterial or virological." His shoulders slumped. "And she doesn't think she has much time. She sent letters for me to send along to her family in case she doesn't get a chance to…"

His throat tightened, and he couldn't keep speaking. He tried to sit on Asger's bunk, but his focus was locked on the letter, and he missed the edge. He ended up on the deck, staring as the lines scrolled through his vision.

How long ago had she written this? She mentioned not being sure when it would go out due to limited reception because they were down in some canyon. He wiped his eyes. What if she'd already died?

There were three postscripts at the end of her message to him.

P.S. For some reason, this isn't afflicting Rache. You may be immune too. I found something interesting in his blood, though I'm not sure yet why or how it would convey immunity.

That confused him, but he read on, less concerned about himself now and definitely not concerned about Rache.

P.P.S. I found my mother… in pieces and inoperable. I don't want you to risk coming here, since everyone except Rache is deteriorating rapidly, but if you get the chance to collect her somehow and can repair her, I would appreciate it.

P.P.P.S. I went into the wreck and looked around. Rache believes someone got here first and stole the gate pieces that were in the hold. I'm sending a bunch of pictures and some footage I recorded, some of the molds, but more of the ship itself. Let me know what you think if you get this in time. Rache's people seemed more interested in searching it than in figuring out who sent it. It doesn't look like anything humans would build, so who did? If we figure that out, maybe it will help.

Casmir opened the attachments and watched her recordings. He'd gotten a sense of a dark, shadowy background before, in the video with the monkey droid—Erin Kelsey-Sato—waving a piece of gate around, but it hadn't focused on the walls or drives or anything in the ship. Now, he watched intently. Even though it didn't look like Kim had gotten back to engineering, it didn't take him long to form the opinion.

In case time was of the essence, he sent back a quick response. Later, he would go over the footage in more detail and send a longer reply.

Kim, I'm glad you're alive—please stay that way, as you know damn well how hard it is to find good roommates! Your pictures remind me a lot of images humans have taken from space of Verloren Moon, the one claimed by artificial intelligence and built out into one giant computer, as far as we know. Your mother might know more—I'm sorry her body is inoperable currently, and I will definitely try to fix her when we get back together, which will be soon—but I've always thought the theory that makes the most sense is that automated ships were sent from Earth to set up the gate network long before humans ever arrived in the Twelve Systems. If that's true, the archaeologists may have found one of the ships that didn't make it all the way for some reason. Or maybe it made it but had a spare gate, so its cargo wasn't used, and it simply landed on Skadi in case its gate was needed for backup in the future.

If that is what happened, those computerized ships would have traveled the long way to the Twelve Systems, and passed through who knows what strange places over the centuries. Is it possible they were equipped with a means to defend themselves if some previously unknown alien life tried to jump them and steal their cargo? And that the archaeologists triggered it somehow?

That's just a guess. My mind is on combat right now. It could also be that it simply flew through something strange and deadly to humans but not computers and is now contaminated. I'll do some research and send more information as soon as I have it.

I wish I could say I was on my way to help you right now, but I need to help the Kingdom warships keep what is very likely the stolen gate from getting out of the system.

Stay safe, my friend.

"Casmir?" Asger prodded his shoulder.

Casmir blinked, refocusing his eyes. Asger crouched in front of him.

"Are you all right?" he added.

"My best friend is dying," Casmir said, the words coming out raspy and broken. He was sitting on the deck, crumpled against the bunk, but he didn't care. "And I'm flying in the opposite direction when I should be back there helping."

Was Kim still down on the moon? With Rache? Or had they left after finding out the gate parts had been stolen?

"I'm sorry." Asger lowered his hand. "I spoke to Ishii earlier. He doesn't expect you to be able to do anything and said you'd just be in the way. I should jump in my shuttle and continue to the battle to assist in any way I can, but if you want to fly back to Skadi, I won't try to stop you."

Casmir dropped his face into his hand. A part of him wanted to run to navigation and tell Bonita to change course, but he'd told Ishii he would help, whether Ishii believed he could or not. And they were almost to the gate. Shouldn't he try to do something after they'd flown all this way?

Not that he wouldn't rather help Kim. Did he truly care which faction of humanity got hold of this new spare gate? Yes, it could change the face of the future, but it wouldn't likely change that much in his lifetime. And if Kim died—

A beep sounded, and Bonita's voice came over the comm. "Uh, Casmir?"

Her tone held a strange note.

Casmir pushed himself to his feet. "Yes?"

"You should come see this."

Casmir stepped into the corridor, pausing when Asger came out after him. He hoped Qin was sleeping in her cabin and that they wouldn't have another incident. He'd meant to address that issue when he knocked on Asger's door. Not that it seemed that important after reading Kim's message.

Casmir climbed the ladder and entered navigation, where a robot vacuum whirred along the deck. "What is it, Laser?"

"The last time the Union ship appeared, it launched that." Bonita pointed at the display.

They were close enough to the gate now, that Viggo didn't have to magnify the view much, and Casmir's stomach twisted with nerves as he saw the warships. The one that had been listing was now little more than a dead hulk floating in space. Shuttles ran between it and the other warship still defending the gate, and there was Ishii's *Osprey* stationed on the other side of it, also sending shuttles. To pick up the survivors?

Bonita wasn't pointing at the gate or the Kingdom ships but at a blue cylindrical shuttle speeding away from the scene. It was heading in their direction. Back toward the Kingdom planets and habitats?

"It launched a shuttle?" Casmir asked. "Is it an escape pod? Were they damaged, and they're sending their survivors?"

"The cargo ship continues to have the ability to maneuver, enter stealth mode, and fire weapons," Viggo said.

Bonita didn't answer, merely looking at Casmir as if he were missing something obvious.

"You think it's coming for us?" he asked.

It *was* coming toward them. *Straight* toward them? It was hard to tell without a top-down view of both ships.

"I think it's coming for *you*," Bonita said. "You're the one who offered to hire on."

"Uh, have they commed us?"

"Not yet."

A yellow light flared to life on the comm panel.

Bonita arched her eyebrows. "*Now* they have."

"Freighter *Stellar Dragon*," a bland unisex voice said. "Prepare to link ships and send over mechanical engineer Casmir Dabrowski."

Before Casmir could respond, the channel went dead.

"You may have just gotten the job you applied for," Bonita said.

"Uh," Casmir said again.

It was all he could come up with.

CHAPTER 12

A SOFT CHIME SOUNDED IN KIM'S MIND, LETTING HER know that her chip had found access and sent her files. She let out a relieved breath. She was sitting in the shuttle between Yas and the engineer, strapped in as Rache flew them out of the canyon and up toward orbit. Toward the *Machu Picchu,* Kim hoped.

"We going to die, Doc?" the engineer asked, her voice tired and defeated.

Yas didn't answer. Kim thought he might have nodded off again. The fighters were in the rows behind them and barely making any noise. One had been helped into his harness by his comrades, and Kim wouldn't be surprised if he died before the day was out.

"I'm hoping I can find something in one of the labs that can reverse our cellular damage," Kim said, responding when Yas did not.

"Is that possible?" the engineer asked. "I was meant to die a couple of years ago, when the rest of my family did, and somehow I survived. I always figured I'd been living on borrowed time since then, and there were times when I wasn't even sure I wanted to. But now that I'm looking death in the eye again…" She cleared her throat and glanced at Kim, seeming a little embarrassed.

Kim wouldn't have judged her. She understood perfectly.

"I'm Jess, by the way. I don't think anyone ever introduced us."

"Kim Sato. And as soon as the network access gets a little stronger, I'll do some searches. There are numerous proven anti-aging therapies out there. I'm hoping that something like that might work—and that the research ship has the appropriate equipment. The Kingdom doesn't embrace that technology as much as other systems since it strays into areas that most of the predominant religions find questionable."

"I sure wouldn't mind a room in the TamTam Medical Spa right now. A little massage, a little muscle stimulation, a little regenerating the crap out of my cells... I used to go there when I was an athlete. They have some stuff that works good."

Unfortunately, those medical spas were weeks away. Kim would have to find something on the *Machu Picchu* that could regenerate cells. She would also need to make sure any souvenirs the archaeology team had brought back were disposed of. *Something* had killed the crew, and there was little point in researching rejuvenation techniques if it was still up there, oozing death.

Not that she expected to find anything capable of doing that up there. It was a science research vessel, not a medical spa. The best she could hope for was—

She sucked in a breath as a thought bounced into her mind. Dr. Sikou had mentioned a cryonics lab. If the ship had the means of reviving frozen specimens, not just freezing them...

"That could be it," Kim whispered. "Cryonics by its very nature has to rebuild aged and frozen—i.e. *damaged*—cells from the inside out in order to revive a body."

"Enh?" Jess looked blearily over at her through bloodshot eyes.

"Just think hopeful thoughts." Kim nodded at her, unfastened her harness, and made her way up to the front to sit in the co-pilot's seat beside Rache.

"You came to keep me company?" he asked. "Thoughtful."

"I want to make sure you're planning to take us to the *Machu Picchu*," Kim said. "I need to do some research, but I have an idea that may work as long as we're no longer being exposed."

She thought of the quarantine area inside sickbay. If nothing else, she could ask the engineer who'd devised the magnetic field if he could extend it to include the cryonics lab. Assuming that lab had what she needed. If it didn't, they could all freeze themselves and order the ship to pilot them back to Odin where an advanced military facility could revive them. She shivered at the thought of essentially dying and being revived, but it would be better than simply dying. Forever.

Rache poked her shoulder.

"What?" She blinked at him. Had he spoken?

"I said I'll drop you off, but I can't stay. I need to rejoin my ship. They've alerted me to something that needs my attention."

"Your *crew* needs your attention." Kim waved behind her.

"It sounds like they need *your* attention. I'll drop you all off there."

Kim was tempted to object, but did she truly want him to stick around and breathe down the back of her neck while she worked? No, it would be better and more comfortable to be free of him. It just rankled that he would leave his dying people behind instead of staying to...

To do what? Hold their hands? She could hardly imagine him doing that.

Casmir would do that. He would give everybody hugs and make silly jokes to make them feel better.

She wished she'd hugged *him* before they'd parted ways. But as much as she hated to admit it, she was probably more like Rache. Stiff and aloof. Finding the idea of touch unappealing. She would rather throw herself into finding a solution than sit and hold someone's hand. Her brain knew how to work on solutions. It didn't know how to be... comforting. Sympathetic. Human.

She shook her head, irritated with her meandering thoughts. This was the time to focus on that solution-finding, not on her own deficiencies.

"Fine," she said, realizing Rache was watching her. "I'll do what I can."

He nodded. "Good."

As they flew higher, and more of the stars came into view, Casmir's response to her letter and files came in. Glad for the distraction, Kim read it promptly.

He thought that wreck had been a robot ship from Earth? And that the damage it was inflicting on people who came in contact with it might be an attack? Hm. Was it possible the gate pieces were booby-trapped to keep anyone—or anything—unapproved from taking them? That was one of his hypotheses. He also shared the same thought that she'd had, that the ship might have passed through something strange in space and carried it along with it.

Kim leaned back in the pod. Her helmet was off, and she brought her braid around to her face and rested it against her flushed skin while debating if Casmir's observations changed anything.

Did it matter if that ship had exuded some kind of defensive attack to keep people from getting the gate pieces? Would that even make sense? The existing gates that were anchored in space let humans go through them. Humans in ships, admittedly. There was no flesh-to-gate contact. But still, astronauts had gone out in suits to study them in situ. She'd never heard of them being afflicted with this accelerated aging.

She closed her eyes, feeling like she was close to grasping something, but it kept eluding her. Maybe because she was exhausted and her brain was turning to mush in her skull.

She looked at Rache, wondering if he would have any better insight. His brain ought to be fine. And in theory, as useful as Casmir's brain, though she had no idea what kind of education he had in there. He read books. But would that help with this?

"Casmir thinks that wreck was an automated ship sent from Earth to bring the gates here for installation—that one down there might have been a backup—and that when the archaeology team entered the structure, it decided they were unauthorized personnel and attacked. The archaeologists, and now us. Everyone except you, for whatever reason."

The *Machu Picchu* was visible on the forward display now, and their route shifted as he guided them toward an airlock hatch, but he glanced at her while piloting. "Did you ever figure out what's different about my blood?"

Oh, hadn't she told him? No, that long discussion about the plague had been with Yas.

"You—or your ancestors, I suppose—were never genetically altered to grant immunity from the Great Plague."

"That all happened about two hundred years ago, right? The Great Plague?" Rache nodded to himself. "That makes sense then."

Kim would have fallen out of the pod if not for its protective hug. "What makes sense?"

Rache guided them toward the airlock hatch. At first, she thought he was concentrating on piloting and couldn't answer. Eventually, she realized he didn't intend to answer.

"*Rache*," she whispered. "Why does it make sense that you weren't altered?"

A soft clank reverberated through the shuttle as they connected to the *Machu Picchu*.

Rache unfastened his harness, stood, and looked down at her. "I'm sure you'll figure it out when you're feeling better and your mind is clear. But to add my hypothesis to the one Casmir gave you, I'll posit that our blood is perhaps more authentically human than yours at this point in humanity's evolution. If those gates were intended for humans, maybe the built-in security of the ship or the gate itself didn't think the archaeologists quite qualified anymore. Or anyone else in this shuttle."

While Kim puzzled that over, Rache strode to the passenger seats. "Everybody up and out. Scholar Sato is going to fix you up."

The fevered fighters shuffled to the hatch without complaint.

Jess hesitated. "You're leaving us, Captain?"

"Yes," Rache said. "To make sure Jager doesn't get the gate. And to find out who *does* have it right now."

Kim wanted to wring his neck for a better explanation, but he wasn't paying any attention to her. He helped Yas, who was stumbling, to the hatch. Kim knew these people didn't have much time—they'd been down at the wreck longer than she and had received a greater dose—so her questioning of Rache would have to wait until the next time she saw him. Whenever that would be.

She went to the back of the shuttle where she'd secured the pieces of her mother's droid body and carefully gathered them up.

"Captain," Jess said, lingering inside, "should we meet up with you somewhere if Kim gets us healed up?"

"If you can," Rache said. "Let me know. I'll pick you up after I deal with the gate."

"Yes, sir."

Rache extended a hand for Kim to follow her out. "Do what you can, Scholar Sato."

"Please," Kim murmured, trailing after Jess and the others, her arms full. "What?"

She paused in the hatchway. "I'm admittedly not one for excess social verbosity, but even I like hearing a please and getting a thank-you occasionally, instead of being ordered around by a tyrant."

He gazed at her without comment.

Kim shook her head—it was like conversing with a wall.

"You definitely owe me a good cup of coffee if I figure out how to keep anyone else from dying," she told him in parting as she walked out.

She didn't expect an answer, but he gave her one.

"If you keep my men from dying, I'll have a crate of beans, a roaster, a grinder, and an espresso maker delivered to your door."

"Good. I'll hold you to that." Not that she had any intention of telling him where her door was. She would be delighted if she never saw him again.

"And I'll owe you a favor," he said so quietly she almost missed it.

Quality coffee would do. So long as she lived to appreciate it. She dearly missed sitting on her little patio during summer mornings, reading a recent publication, and sipping from a fresh cup of coffee while squirrels cavorted in the oak trees behind the house.

Rache's weary troops slumped down against a wall inside the airlock bay. Men who'd come less than two days earlier to kidnap her could now barely move. She thought about trying to arrange for them to be deposited in a cell, sans their armor, but she needed to see if anyone was even left alive here. If not, then it hardly mattered if criminals had free rein of the ship.

Kim found a safe spot to deposit the droid parts, then headed straight for sickbay and the quarantined area. With luck, those people had stayed put and were alive and well.

As she walked, Rache's words came back to her. *I'll posit that our blood is perhaps more authentically human than yours at this point in humanity's evolution.*

"Oh." She stumbled and gripped the closest wall. "*Oh.*"

Kim realized what Rache had meant—she and Casmir were going to have to have a chat about the impossibility of his mother still being alive—and that… none of it mattered as far as finding a treatment. She and the others were already afflicted—had stumbled across the robotic security system and failed its scan without ever knowing one was being done. Because their mitochondria—the DNA of their mitochondria—wasn't quite human anymore. It didn't matter now. She had to simply focus on healing everyone.

"Hello?" came an uncertain call from the general sickbay.

"It's Kim Sato," she called back, thinking she'd reached the quarantined people.

But Dr. Sikou stepped into view.

"Kim!" she blurted. "I got your message. How did you escape?"

Sikou rushed forward and gripped Kim's arms.

"It's a long story," Kim said, relieved to see her. "I'm pleased you're still alive. Have you had any progress with the pseudo radiation?"

"It sounds like you decided that's what it is too." Sikou nodded. "Some new radiation that we don't yet have a way to read and that doesn't react quite the same in the human body."

"That's my guess. Were you, by chance, inoculated with my bacteria during the *Osprey's* trials?"

"Dr. Angelico and I weren't, but the marines were, including the ones that accompanied us to this ship." Sikou grimaced. "They were killed in the attack, but we still have their bodies. When I got your message, I took samples and was able to isolate the bacteria. It was the proverbial needle-in-a-haystack situation, but they're fortunately quite distinctive, and the equipment and the computers here are excellent."

Kim nodded, disturbed that Rache's men had killed the marines, but she was glad Sikou had thought to check their bodies. The bacteria would have been able to stay alive for days after the deaths of the hosts. "Have you had time to run any tests yet?"

Kim checked the time stamp to see how much time had passed since her message to Sikou had gone out. It had been shortly after the shuttle had flown out of the canyon. It had taken a few hours for Rache to fly it up to orbit and catch up with the *Machu Picchu*, but even if Sikou had started her experiments right away, she might not have had time to do much.

"A few." Sikou hesitated. "When I introduced the bacteria to blood samples containing the damaged cells, they died rather quickly."

Kim stepped back, pulling her arms from Sikou's grip. "My bacteria *died?*"

"Apparently, they're as susceptible to this as anything else."

"They're extremely hardy. Very little kills them. Not even direct exposure to cosmic radiation."

Sikou spread her hands.

"This is definitely sounding like a weapon," Kim muttered. "But maybe I can learn something from how they died. Do you still have everything?"

"Yes. I was hoping you would make it back and that you could learn something useful. Er." Sikou looked down the corridor behind her. "Are

Rache and his men here? After they killed our marines, I'm not eager to see them again."

Kim shook her head. "I can imagine. Rache is obsessed with hurting King Jager, and he doesn't seem to care who lives or dies along the way."

Sikou reached toward her again. "Are *you* all right? I can't imagine being captured—being in that monster's grasp."

"The illness is more of a problem. I've got it now, and it'll kill me a lot faster than Rache would have."

"Angelico and I have it now too," Sikou admitted. "The quarantined people are still safe."

"You've been affected? Did you ever find a piece of the gate here?"

"The gate?" Sikou shook her head.

"We're going to have to go over the security camera footage and try to find the day the team came back on board," Kim said. "See if they were carrying anything. It was something I'd been on the verge of doing when Rache's people showed up. I also want to look at my bacteria to see what exactly happened to them. Oh, and I need someone to check the cryonics lab to determine if it's capable of reviving specimens."

Sikou looked daunted by the list, but she nodded. "We'll take care of that."

"Thank you. I know it's a lot, but we'll split it up. We don't have much time."

"I know," Sikou said. "I know that very well."

Kim nodded and strode straight for the lab she'd been working in before.

Casmir checked his suit and oxygen tank for the third time as he stood in front of the airlock hatch, waiting for the shuttle from the mysterious enemy cargo ship to dock. When he'd left navigation, it had been coming around, matching their speed, and extending a short tube.

He had a spare oxygen tank attached to the first, and he was already on the verge of hyperventilating as he wondered if he would have enough.

Viggo's scan of the shuttle hadn't shown any people on board—any heat signatures at all—or a breathable atmosphere. He crossed his fingers that the cargo ship had humans aboard and would have an amenable environment, but the idea of going off into the unknown with a limited supply of air made him worry. He hadn't forgotten his experience on the refinery, almost running out of air before he'd made it back to the *Dragon*.

"Are you ready to keep me alive, Zee?" he whispered to his silent companion.

The crusher loomed at his shoulder, needing neither tank nor suit to survive in space or anywhere else. Casmir envied him that. He wondered if he should update his will, however unofficially, before he left the *Dragon*, and leave Zee to one of his friends back home. Would the Kingdom even allow that? They might simply suck him up into the crusher army they'd already made.

"I am always prepared to protect and defend Kim Sato and Casmir Dabrowski," Zee stated.

The sad lump that hadn't quite left his throat after reading Kim's letter returned in full force.

"I'm glad," he whispered. "You've been a wonderful ally. I wish I'd had you around when I was a little boy. I bet you would have kept me from getting stomped so much by the kids in our tenement building." He smiled, imagining one scenario in particular where it would have been delightful to have the crusher step out into the hallway and hoist up one of the bigger kids who'd enjoyed picking on him.

"Stomping people is unacceptable behavior," Zee said.

"I agree completely. But I still have moments where I fantasize about it a little."

Something about being pushed around and chased and shot at these past weeks had memories of his childhood years rearing up far more often than usual. In the last decade, he'd gotten used to working with people like himself and having a modicum of respect from his peers and others at the university, a place where he'd largely fit in. Even the military research and development lab had been full of people more like him than not. It was depressing to realize that once he left those environments, he went back to being the scrawny kid who made an appealing target for the rest of the universe. Or at least some thugs with a grudge.

Metallic footfalls rang out on the cargo hold deck behind him. Asger walked up wearing his helmet and an oxygen tank strapped to his armored back, the cloak rucked up over it, making him look like a hunchback. A hunchback with a DEW-Tek rifle slung across his chest on a strap and his trademark pertundo in its holder on his belt.

Casmir had been prepared to go alone—this had been his harebrained idea—and hadn't asked for Asger to come, but he was relieved to have a true warrior along. Even if the shuttle was all automated, he fully expected to be greeted by bullies with rifles pointed at his chest when he stepped out of it.

"Trying to leave without me, Dabrowski?" Asger asked.

"It sounded like you'd given up on me being able to help."

"That was Ishii. I'm withholding judgment on you." Asger glanced toward the hatch. "I'm somewhat intrigued that you got us an invitation over there, even if we're likely walking into a trap."

Being the true knight that he was, he didn't sound daunted by the prospect.

Casmir didn't mention that the invitation hadn't included Asger.

A faint clang reverberated through the hatch—the shuttle securing its tube and clamping onto the *Dragon.*

"Also," Asger added, holding something out, "I forgot to give these to you earlier."

Casmir opened his gloved palm, and Asger dropped two bottles of pills and a jet injector into it. As he read the labels, he almost laughed. "You got my seizure medication for me? And what's this? Ah, motion sickness pills. And epinephrine. I hope nobody else sticks me with some drug I turn out to be allergic to, but thank you."

"The nurse brought them by while you were attempting to schmooze Ishii. It's possible the enemy ship will be overflowing with cashews and pomegranates."

"If that's true, the other systems are every bit as weird as they promised us in school."

"They are." Asger glanced over his shoulder. "Trust me."

Casmir hoped he wasn't thinking of Qin. Maybe once this was all over, he could get them in the same cabin together and figure out how to make Asger be the gentleman the legends said he ought to be. To *every* lady, not just Kingdom-appropriate ones.

"Thank you." Casmir held up the drugs, removed his helmet long enough to take one of the rivogabines, then found a sealed suit pocket for the rest of the medication. He had no idea how long this trip would take and didn't want to risk leaving them behind.

He wished Asger had thought to give them to him earlier, so his seizure medication would have had time to kick in. Unfortunately, it was meant to be taken twice daily as a preventative measure, and he had a feeling it would take a few days of uninterrupted doses before his brain righted itself, but he would take what he could get. Maybe he would be lucky, and nothing stressful would happen in the next few hours.

This time, he did laugh. It sounded maniacal in his ears. Once again, he felt he was on the verge of hyperventilating.

Asger eyed him. "Should I be concerned about you, or do drugs always make you weird?"

"I'm afraid it's not the drugs that make me weird." Casmir ordered his helmet back over his head and checked it three times.

"I'm coming too," Qin said from behind them. "The captain said I could. Actually, she said it was a good idea, that you'd definitely need my help, Casmir."

She walked toward them, her big Brockinger anti-tank weapon in her arms and a pistol and dagger on her armor's utility belt. Asger stiffened, his fingers twitching toward his halberd.

"Thank you, Qin." Casmir rested his hand on Asger's armored forearm and gave Zee a pointed look. "This isn't your fight, so I really appreciate your willingness to risk yourself. And I appreciate yours, too, Sir Asger."

Asger clenched his jaw, not giving any indication that he heard Casmir. At least he didn't try to draw his weapon.

"You stay out of my way, knight," Qin said, not taking her eyes off Asger, "and I'll stay out of yours."

She came up to stand at Casmir's side, next to Zee and opposite Asger. Casmir chose to think of himself as the glue that would bind this team together, rather than the little guy in the middle who would get smashed if they started trading punches.

Clangs sounded in the airlock hatch, and Asger turned stiffly to face whoever—whatever—was coming to get them.

"I meant that, Qin," Casmir said quietly. "I'm very thankful to you for coming and to Laser for allowing it." He wanted her to know that he wanted her here, even if Asger was as welcoming as a black hole.

Qin nudged him with an armored elbow. "She doesn't know what to do with that schematic, so she wants me to keep you alive."

"Naturally."

The hatch swung open. An unarmed android in unassuming brown overalls stood in the airlock chamber, his head bald, his face free of facial hair. One of his hands was composed of a complex toolset instead of human fingers.

"You are the mechanical engineer Casmir Dabrowski," the android said without preamble. "You will accompany me to the *Asteroid Hauler*."

"Yes," Casmir said. "I'm ready."

"You will come alone," the android added as he stepped forward.

"Oh, I can't do that. These are my assistants." Casmir gestured to Qin, Asger, and Zee. "She holds my wrench, he holds my toolbox, and Zee records my research notes."

"We are not unintelligent, Casmir Dabrowski," the android said. "You will not bring combatants along. You are being invited to perform work, not to assist the Kingdom warships in defeating us."

Perform work? Gods, did they expect him to know how to do something with the gate they'd picked up? He'd assumed that his ruse wouldn't work and that even if it did, they wouldn't expect him to do anything until after they'd finished their battle with the warships. That would have given him time to come up with something clever.

The android stepped aside, extending a hand for Casmir to enter the airlock tube even as he lifted the tool-filled one as a barrier to Qin and Asger. Interestingly, he didn't object to Zee.

"Look, friend," Casmir said. "I'm a little guy. I need assistants and bodyguards to survive in a realm of malevolent humans. Also to boost me up so I can reach things. If they don't come, *I* don't come."

Casmir lifted his chin. He also tried to catch Qin's and Asger's gazes. If one of them could grab the android and keep him busy, they could charge in and take the shuttlecraft. Whether they'd be able to fool anyone on the cargo ship and gain access to it, Casmir didn't know, but he wasn't stepping into the lion's den without help. All he had was a stunner, a spare oxygen tank, and his tool satchel.

They both seemed to catch his meaning, because they nodded behind their faceplates.

The android didn't answer right away. His head tilted as he presumably received some orders or advice from the ship.

Casmir wondered if one of the Fleet comm officers might trace those signals to their source and be able to track the enemy vessel and fire at the right spot. The last he'd seen, the warships were sending missiles into the expanse, hoping to get lucky.

"You may bring one warrior-assistant," the android said.

His willingness to negotiate made Casmir believe his superiors thought Casmir had some worth. He didn't know yet what they wanted him for, but for some reason, they did want him.

He folded his arms over his chest. "They all come, or I stay here. Actually, I leave this area completely. I have a friend in need of help farther back in the system."

Another long pause as the android communicated with whoever was over there.

Casmir sent a chip-to-chip message to Bonita. *Our android visitor is either having deep internal debates with himself, or he's communicating with his mother ship. Is it still invisible? Maybe Viggo can track its location through the signal and send it to the Fleet.*

It's still camouflaged somehow, yes, she replied, *but do you really want us sending its location to a bunch of frustrated warship officers with big guns? When you're about to board it?*

Well, we're still waiting to see if he's going to allow me to come over with all my large and heavily armed friends.

I'll see if we can trace it. Be careful, kid.

I'll try.

"You may bring your warrior-assistants," the android finally said, turning and leading the way down the tube.

"Thank you." Casmir waved for the others to go ahead, since he was the one with value, at least in the android's eyes. He doubted the android would do it, but he could envision a scenario where he flung the hatch shut after Casmir, disconnecting him from his allies.

They trooped onto the shuttle without incident and belted themselves into seats. The android also sat in one of the passenger seats, leaving the piloting station unmanned. The shuttle unclamped, drew in its tube, and headed toward a dark patch of nothing in the starry sky.

Casmir activated chip-to-chip communication with Asger. *Will you let Ishii know we're on this shuttle and not to fire at us?*

I've told him. He thinks we're idiots.

You too? Not just me?

He thinks you're an idiot for pretending you have a clue how to handle this and I'm an idiot for following you.

Are Fleet officers allowed to speak so bluntly to knights?

It depends on whether the officer has noble blood and a large warship at his command. And how much of a naive goof he considers the knight.

Casmir blinked at that last sentence. Asger was young, but Casmir wouldn't have expected anyone who'd passed the arduous knight training to be treated as anything less than an asset. He hoped Ishii hadn't formed that opinion because Asger had chosen to help *him*.

If you were chosen to work for the queen, I'm sure you've proven yourself many times already.

Asger looked at him for a moment, then flicked his fingers. It might have been in acknowledgment or dismissal. Casmir let the conversation rest.

As the shuttle sailed toward an indeterminate location down and to the left of the gate, Casmir looked up the make and model of the craft. It appeared very modern and new—if he hadn't been wearing a helmet, he fancied he would have smelled the newness of the recently installed carpet and upholstered seats—but it didn't look like a match to the cargo ship they had looked up.

The result that came back was that it was a combat drop shuttle popular in the contended System Augeas, which currently had numerous factions wrestling for control and launching guerrilla attacks at each other.

That made Casmir less certain that they were dealing with Union princes or miners at all. Maybe someone had simply been stealing ships, much as they had been stealing gates, and putting together the best force they could.

Casmir drummed his fingers on his thigh as minutes passed. His mind floated back to the postscripts in Kim's messages, especially that bit about how he might be immune to whatever was affecting the people who visited that wreck. Why would that be? And was it the wreck that was the problem or the gate pieces?

He realized with a start that they were traveling to the ship they believed had stolen the gate pieces. Its crew must have gone down to the wreck to retrieve them. Would they be sick too? If so, Casmir was the wrong person to help with that. He hoped that wasn't the reason they were bringing him in.

With those thoughts in mind, he was tempted to send Kim another message, but she hadn't responded to his first, so he feared the moon had rotated enough to take her out of satellite range. He prayed he wasn't about to get himself killed before they could talk again. The fact that he wasn't heading straight toward her as fast as possible to help her with Rache grated on him, and as the shuttle sailed closer to the gate, he couldn't help but wonder if he'd made a huge mistake. Was this even his fight? He cared what happened to the Kingdom and his friends back home, but how much difference would it make if some other government gained control of this new gate? He'd volunteered to help entirely because he'd hoped Ishii would then help him get Kim back from Rache.

"I never killed any knights," Qin announced, startling Casmir.

He was sitting between Qin and Asger, while Zee loomed behind him and watched the android.

"I've seen you before," Asger said coolly. "We fought at the Battle of Pirate Moon."

"I've never heard of such a battle, and I would remember if I'd fought knights before."

"Your... *people* may have called it something else. Do you deny being one of Drucker's creations?"

"I'm not a creation; I'm a person."

"Spawned in a test tube."

Qin's gloved fingers gripped her armored thighs, and Casmir had no trouble envisioning them forming into fists as she sprang across him to strangle Asger.

"Lots of lovely and impressively accomplished people have been spawned in test tubes," Casmir said. He wasn't in the mood to play conciliator now, but he realized he might have to if he wanted a cohesive team to walk onto the enemy vessel with him. "Even on Odin. Even before we had artificial wombs, there was assisted fertilization. My parents—adoptive parents, actually—tried quite a few different things before learning that my father had substandard sperm and they couldn't conceive even with the assistance of medical science. Uh, don't tell him I told you that, by the way. He's a little touchy on the subject. They fostered several children before me, and then officially adopted me when I was six. By then, they'd seen how delightful I am. It's possible I was also spawned in a test tube. I don't know my parents, so I can't ask."

Casmir smiled at Asger, hoping that his easy acceptance of Qin would make him feel that he should also accept her.

Asger glowered at him.

"I see you're fascinated by my story," Casmir said. "Perhaps we can discuss my family—and any other issues that might be of concern— further after we've completed this mission and there aren't strange androids watching on."

Asger issued something like a growl but faced forward and stopped talking. Qin's fingers remained tight on her thighs, but she also faced forward. Casmir was starting to miss his days of getting Simon and Asahi to work together. He'd known their weaknesses and how to bribe them to cooperate. He didn't know Qin or Asger as well yet, though he could envision a scenario where he sent candles shaped into mythological figures to Qin with a note saying they were from Asger.

The front display changed abruptly, and Casmir would have lurched from his seat if he hadn't been belted in. The massive blue hull of a ship bristling weapons appeared right in front of them, shuttle-bay doors already yawning open, revealing a well-lit interior.

Their android guide did not react. Still on autopilot, the shuttle flew through the bay doors.

White light flashed somewhere off to the side, brightening the display so much that Casmir lifted a hand protectively as his faceplate automatically dimmed.

Some force knocked against the shuttle. It lurched sideways, throwing Casmir against his harness. The craft jerked, scraping against the edge of one of the bay doors, and it tilted, then struck the deck. It skidded into the bay as red lights strobed.

Casmir flung his arm over his eyes, terrified of having another seizure.

"Not now," he whispered, "not now."

The shuttle struck a wall, and again, he was almost hurled from his seat. The harness digging into his chest stopped him, as did Zee gripping his shoulder. Somehow, the crusher defied physics and remained on his feet.

The lights in the bay went out, and the shuttle display also went dark. A few blue indicator lights flashed.

Casmir held his breath, not sure what to expect next. Had the Kingdom warships fired when the Union vessel appeared? As this shuttle was docking? He could feel gravity pressing down on him even though the shuttle wasn't moving. Had the big Union cargo ship been spinning before? He couldn't remember.

"You'd expect better piloting from a computer," Asger grumbled into the silence that fell.

The android rose. "We have arrived. I will take you to work, Casmir Dabrowski."

"Ah, good. Thank you." Casmir willed his hands to stop shaking so he could unfasten his harness.

"The ship must have gone back into stealth mode," Asger said. "Every time it reappears, our people fire at it. Which makes it the ideal place for us to be spending time."

Not wanting the android to hear, Casmir switched to a message for his response. *Just look for ways to disable it as we're taken… wherever we're going. You and Qin need to set aside your differences for now and work together. Maybe you can slip away while I'm doing… whatever they want me to do.*

Your vagueness is so reassuring.

I'm afraid it's all I've got.

The android waited by the now-open hatch. The lights flickered back on in the bay outside, revealing it to be devoid of other ships. Of course, they were all out battling the Fleet.

Casmir followed the android out of the shuttle, affirming that there was gravity, about half that of Odin, he guessed. Qin, Zee, and Asger followed as the android led them into the corridors of a ship with white-painted walls and arrows along the deck pointing to various important stations. The walls held plenty of signs and labels written in System Trade. *Engineering. Cargo Hold. Bridge.*

Casmir itched to go to the cargo hold and see if pieces of a giant gate were stored there, but the android followed the route to the bridge. They took a lift upward and stepped out onto the first deck that was modified from what Casmir would have considered the norm. He had a schematic of the ship pulled up so he could compare.

Tubes and cords ran along the walls, fastened by brackets that had been added after the ship left the factory. Machinery hummed somewhere up ahead, and the sound made Casmir realize he could hear. He glanced at the exterior stats displayed on the corner of his helmet's faceplate.

There was breathable air, and it was warm enough that he could have removed his suit, even a couple of degrees above what was considered room temperature back home.

The environment boded well for a human crew, but why hadn't anyone come to greet them?

The bridge doors slid open, revealing a greenish-blue light that seemed a strange choice. Numerous strange pods were fastened to the walls in between computer stations. Pods with green-lit liquid and naked human beings in them.

Asger cursed and snatched his pertundo from its holder. Casmir simply stared, trying to figure it out. There were twelve people, male and female, in the liquid-filled pods, with wires and tubes attached to their bodies and their heads. Their faces were a mixture of skin and some kind of grayish blue material. It might have been metal.

All of their eyes were closed. Panels next to the pods flashed ominous red warning lights.

"Ah," Qin said, stepping up beside Casmir.

"Ah?" Casmir felt bewildered, not enlightened. He'd seen something like this before in a news vid, a human hooked up to a computer in a pod while sleeping, but the man had been able to detach the cables, open the pod, and walk about. He hadn't been a permanent fixture in the thing.

"Astroshamans," Qin said. "They're basically just cyborgs, but they spend a lot of down-time linked to computers. They claim it's a superior state and how they find enlightenment. The Dakmook pirate family is all into it. I've met them at gatherings." She glanced warily at Asger. "Before I escaped." She waved at the closest pod. "I've seen this before. It's how they operate their ships. Linked directly into it. The tanks handle their biological needs and keep them in a somewhat suspended state while their minds are directly interfaced with the systems."

The deck shifted under Casmir's feet as a jolt struck the ship, sending him staggering. He caught himself on one of the pods and stared into a woman's face.

"I think we're visible again and being fired on." Asger looked toward the bridge display rather than the pods. The gate and one of the warships was visible, but only for a moment. Their cargo ship was making evasive maneuvers.

Was one of these pod people—astroshamans—navigating?

The android had waited by the doors as they looked around, but now he strode to Casmir.

"The handlers cannot be woken. You must fix this, Casmir Dabrowski."

"Uhm." Casmir looked from the woman's stationary face to the android's bland one, closed eyes to open eyes. "What exactly is the problem?"

His gaze drifted to the flashing red panel. An alarm indicated a systems failure. His stomach sank as he glanced to the woman's face again. He had a feeling these people weren't sleeping; they were dead. Did that mean computers were operating the ship?

"All of the bio-pods developed malfunctions within one day cycle of each other," the android said. "They report that the human inhabitants have died, but this is not possible. They were chosen for this mission because of their health and vitality. We are certain the bio-pods have developed an error, but we have not been able to fix the problem or wake our handlers. We are continuing the mission to the best of our abilities, but we must not risk gate travel while there is a threat to them. You must repair our handlers, Casmir Dabrowski. You work with robots; we saw this. You must have experience with human-computer interfaces. You were the only one in the area we could locate."

Casmir would have dropped his chin into his hand if he hadn't been wearing his helmet. He walked from one pod to the next, looking at the encapsulated people and the flashing alarm light. Systems failure. Systems failure.

Earlier, he'd worried the crew might be sick, but he should have realized that too much time had passed for that. These people must have visited the wreck before Rache arrived. Whatever had killed the archaeologists had also had time to kill them.

"Casmir?" Qin asked uncertainly from the doorway.

Several robots marched in, faceless constructs closer in appearance to his crusher than to the android. They had massive guns on the ends of their left arms. They spread out around the bridge and pointed those weapon arms at Casmir and his allies.

"You will repair our handlers, Casmir Dabrowski," the android stated again. "Or you will not be permitted to live. Kingdom subjects are enemies to the astroshamans, and you are now a threat to this ship."

"Are they as dead as they look?" Asger muttered, facing a pod.

With the android staring implacably at him, Casmir didn't answer aloud. Chip-to-chip, he messaged, *Yes.*

Asger looked around at all the robots pointing weapons at them, robots that appeared to be almost as indestructible as Zee. There were twelve of them. Twelve to match the twelve pods and the Twelve Systems? Or just twelve to ensure the ship's visitors were outnumbered three to one?

Are we as screwed as I think? Asger messaged.

Casmir looked bleakly at the dead people, the dead people that he couldn't bring back to life, no matter how badly the android wished it.

Yes.

CHAPTER 13

KIM LEANED BACK FROM THE DNA-EDITING COMPUTER AND dozen-odd petri dishes that were growing slightly different strains of her radiation-eating bacteria. When she'd looked at Dr. Sikou's results from her attempt to deploy them, she'd been encouraged rather than chagrined by their deaths. The bacteria had multiplied numerous times before dying, which suggested they'd not only been able to detect the pseudo radiation but that they'd fed off it. For some reason, they'd eventually been overwhelmed, but Kim had the resources to tinker. And that was exactly what she was doing.

Unfortunately, even bacteria took time to multiply, and she felt time bleeding past. Sweat dampened her brow, and even the intelligent weave of her galaxy suit couldn't seem to compensate for her feverish body's fluctuating temperatures. A part of her wanted to strip it off—to strip everything off. If she'd had some baggy pajamas to change into, she definitely would have.

A soft ding sounded to her left. She looked at the footage she had running on a different display, more than a dozen different ship's cameras that had recorded the corridors, bridge, engineering, and sickbay over the past week. She'd been trying to find the footage of the shuttle bay from when the original team of archaeologists had come aboard, but she hadn't had times or even dates, so it was tedious to go over it all. Finally, the program had spotted the human activity she'd been looking for. The airlock bay. That was where the team had come aboard.

She watched as the team walked out of a decontamination chamber. They wore galaxy suits and carried cases of tools and equipment and—

Her breath caught. There it was. A man walking with what looked like the same piece of circuit board that Kim had first seen in the video with her mother. It was secured in a clear insulated bag, but that wouldn't have done anything to block her pseudo radiation.

"Sync the footage from the other cameras," she ordered the computer, "and track that team as they walk through the ship."

All of the cameras showed footage with the same time stamp, and she watched the team progress through the ship, some splitting off to go to sickbay, others to the bridge, and others to their cabins. She stuck with the man carrying the circuit board. The two-thousand-year-old circuit board. Maybe she should think of it as an artifact.

The man carrying it removed his helmet, revealing sweat-dampened gray hair—had he been afflicted with symptoms at that point?—and stepped onto the bridge. He had a long chat with the bridge officer in the command chair. Kim remembered the lone body they'd found on the bridge and shuddered.

Another soft beep sounded as a different camera display alerted her to movement. It was one of Rache's marines, and it was happening now, not in the past.

Kim had decided against trying to drag them to a cell, especially when the computer had informed her that the *Machu Picchu* didn't have a brig, because she'd been too tired to contemplate finding a hover gurney and maneuvering the men onto it. They also hadn't been moving at the time. This one was on his knees, though, and looking around. Maybe he was sick and needed a place to throw up. Or maybe he was debating taking over the ship.

Kim commed the other two doctors, each working in different labs. "We have a problem."

"What's going on, Kim?" Dr. Sikou asked from the doorway a few seconds later.

Dr. Angelico also stood there, leaning heavily against the jamb.

"A couple of things," Kim said, only glancing at them as she divided her attention between the footage of the bridge—she had to figure out where that artifact ended up so she could get it off the ship—and the mercenaries. Most of them were still slumped down in the corridor. Dr. Peshlakai hadn't moved. "You said none of the Fleet marines survived the attack, right?"

Angelico grimaced. "Correct. I'm lucky those animals didn't rip my head off when they saw me."

Kim didn't point out that she'd glimpsed him hiding behind a lab station. It wasn't as if she could blame him for that. Being brave hadn't gotten her anything except kidnapped.

"You, Angelico, and I are the only ones who aren't in quarantine and are ambulatory," Sikou said. "Mostly ambulatory." She glanced at her comrade. "I told you we're showing signs of the cellular degeneration now too, right?"

"Yes. Because, unless I miss my guess, *that's* still here." Kim pointed to the artifact on the camera display. The archaeologist was still discussing it with the captain, but he'd laid it on a nearby console. "It's a small piece, but I'm assuming it also puts out the pseudo radiation. When I was kidnapped, I hadn't been exposed to enough here yet to show symptoms, but everything was accelerated down on the moon when I was in a shuttle parked right next to the wreck. I suspect anybody who's had contact with the wreck or any of the gate pieces will be in trouble. The more exposure, the worse it'll be."

"We should go find that then," Sikou said. "And get it off the ship."

"I will in a moment. I want to see if they moved it after their chat." Kim waved at the bridge. "What I need from you two is to visit the mercenaries and get them into a room we can secure." She pointed at the one who'd managed to get to his feet. "Also get them out of their armor, so we can stun them if needed."

"You want us to move a bunch of trained killers?" Angelico asked dubiously.

"Yes, please. I'll deal with that." Kim pointed at the artifact. "We've got to get it off the ship if anyone is going to have a chance at recovering."

"I'd rather deal with that than murderers," Angelico said.

"I wouldn't," Sikou said grimly.

"If they won't cooperate, maybe you can tell them you have a treatment and that they need to remove their armor to get it." Kim hated the idea of lying, but they couldn't risk someone getting an itch and deciding to take over the ship. "I'm hoping we'll have a genuine treatment soon. At the least, a way to clear the pseudo radiation out of the body."

Kim shifted her pointing finger to her strains of bacteria.

"Me too," Sikou murmured.

After they left, Kim ran the footage on fast forward. The artifact remained on the console for a long time, for more than one shift change. She had been on the bridge earlier and was positive it wasn't still there. The crew moved around it, never interacting with it, but she knew it was silently killing them, and she blinked away moisture in her eyes when she was forced to watch people showing signs of growing weaker. Some left. Some left and came back. The captain slumped in his chair for a long time, then stalked to the artifact. He glared at it and snatched it up.

Had he realized it was what was making them sick? He stalked off the bridge.

Kim was thankful for all the cameras on the ship, as she was able to follow him. He carried it down two decks and locked it in a vault in an engineering lab, maybe choosing that because it was far from sickbay.

"Time for a walk," she muttered, glancing at the mercenaries on the display before heading out.

Sikou and Angelico had reached them, Sikou waving a medical kit and holding up a jet injector. One full of a tranquilizer, Kim hoped.

Trusting them to handle Rache's men, Kim strode out of the lab.

She paused when she reached one of the dead marines—the body had been partially dragged into a lab so it wasn't in the walkway, but the combat armor would have made it onerously heavy to deal with. Kim knelt to pick up the rifle the marine had been holding as he battled the mercenaries. A part of her wanted to jettison Rache's men and let them die for their crimes, but she'd gathered that neither Jess nor Yas— especially Yas—was a killer or had wanted to kidnap her. She would do her best to save them. But if any of the others attacked her again…

She slung the rifle over her shoulder. She would deal with them without hesitation or remorse.

"Can you fix the pods and revive the handlers, Casmir Dabrowski?" the android asked, his wrists clasped behind his back.

Casmir had his toolkit open and a scanner out, pretending to contemplate the pods and the machinery linked to them as he bought time to think. "I'm attempting to diagnose the problem now. I'll let you know shortly."

The android accepted the answer without comment, but he hadn't given an order for all the robots on the bridge to stand down. Right now, several of their arm guns—more like cannons or grenade launchers than guns—were pointed at his back. Actually at Zee's chest, because he'd moved to stand behind Casmir to do his best to block any assault that might come.

Qin and Asger crouched nearby, their weapons in hand as they faced the robots. They kept glancing at Casmir, as if waiting for an order. Was he in charge of this strike team? A terrifying thought.

The only potential upside of the situation was that if everyone started firing, it might do damage to the computers, including the system that controlled the ship's stealth capacity. The cargo ship would be much easier for the Fleet warships to disable if it was visible.

Casmir had pulled up a schematic of the bridge, which had no mention of a stealth device, and decided it might be the large piece of jury-rigged equipment sticking out in front of a bank of computers on the side opposite from him. It was shiny and new, more so than the rest of the ship, and hummed and whirred, indicators flashing with activity.

"Are you the only one left in charge here, android friend?" Casmir suspected the armed robots had been programmed with security routines but not the ability for independent reasoning. "And do you have a name or designation?"

"I am Tork-57. I assist the handlers."

"Who's running the ship's attack and defense program? Are you trying to get through the gate as soon as possible, or waiting until the bridge crew is revived?"

Casmir downloaded everything he could find related to the ship as they spoke. Unfortunately, he didn't see any schematics on the network that matched what he'd chosen to dub the stealth generator. He couldn't even find a description of such technology to prove it existed. He *did* find the schematics for the astroshaman pods—apparently, they were standard interfaces for spacefaring followers of the religion—but with the people inside dead, there wasn't much point in examining them further.

"I will not answer your questions," Tork said. "You must be deemed an enemy and hostile until proven otherwise."

"Hostile? Me? I hardly think you have anything to worry about."

Tork glanced at Qin, Zee, and Asger and did not reply.

Through his chip, Casmir investigated the ship's local wireless networks. Not surprisingly, the pods, the main system computers, and security—did that include these robots, by chance?—were protected by passcodes, with some requiring retina and fingerprint scans as well. Even if he found materials, he doubted he could build a passcode cracker with Tork watching his every move. It would be easier to find a way to physically or virtually interrupt power to the systems.

What happens when he realizes those people are dead and you can't fix them? Asger asked in a message.

I'm not sure there's a way around fighting him—fighting all of them, Casmir replied. *I'm trying to figure out a way to interrupt power to the machine I believe is controlling the ship's stealth capabilities, at which point the Kingdom ships will start firing at us. Relentlessly. And at which point the robots and Tork will realize I'm working against them.*

You want the Fleet to fire at us while we're on the bridge?

I'm hoping that you, Qin, and Zee can best the robots, especially if they're distracted by an attack, and that we can take control and tell Ishii and the others to stand down. I'm hoping they're not going to try to obliterate the ship when the gate they want is in the hold.

Or so he hoped. Casmir hadn't been down there to look yet.

I'm ready, Asger said. *Get down and stay out of the way once the fighting begins. And don't have a seizure.*

I always suspected knights of having great wisdom. In some matters. Casmir kept himself from glancing at Qin and reminding Asger he was being an idiot in that regard.

In some, Asger agreed.

Casmir pushed back from the machinery by the pod he'd been poking into and started toward an electrical panel on the opposite side of the bridge. A couple of the robots shifted their aim to follow him. Zee hurried to do his best to block their access.

"Explain your actions, Casmir Dabrowski," Tork said.

"Oh, sorry." Casmir waved nonchalantly and pointed. "I need to get into that panel over there."

"That is an electrical panel. Electricity is flowing to the pods. That is not the problem."

"I think there may be voltage fluctuations. Perhaps the reason for the alarm." He licked his lips and ignored the bead of sweat that trickled from his hairline.

"You show signs of nerves," Tork announced. "I believe you may intend duplicity."

"I'm only nervous because of all the weapons pointed at me. Can't you convince your robots to stand outside while I work?"

He kept walking, hoping the android was desperate enough to get his handlers back to risk putting some faith in Casmir.

Tork's pale silver eyes watched him intently. Casmir felt bad for trying to dupe him, but he didn't know what else he could do. Like the android, the robots would have their own power supplies, so he couldn't cut *their* electricity. And he'd likely need a manual connection to the android to alter his programming. He hadn't seen a wireless network specifically for Tork, though it was possible one of the jumbles of numbers and letters represented him. It was also likely he was connected to the security network. *Someone* was giving those robots commands.

As Casmir slid open the electrical panel, Tork walked over to stand beside him. "I do not see anything that would indicate power fluctuations. There are no errors to the bridge currently. I have been running diagnostics and repairs on the minor damage we've received from the enemy ships."

"I'll just take a quick peek." Casmir whistled cheerfully—and nervously—as he pulled up the bridge diagram on the touch display inside.

Zee moved to stand close enough to Tork to react if he reached for Casmir. Several of the robots moved close to ensure they had a line of fire if Zee did anything to *their* leader.

"Casmir," Qin whispered tensely. "You're in the middle of—"

"Stop." Tork reached for his arm.

Zee snatched him around the waist and hurled him across the bridge.

"Down!" Qin and Asger shouted at the same time.

A barrage of fire opened up, and Casmir flattened himself to the deck.

Zee lunged at the closest robot, knocking it into a bulkhead. But the robot recovered and lunged back. Asger sprang behind two of them, wielding his pertundo like a logger. Casmir had no idea where Qin was. Red and orange DEW bolts flashed as they pounded into the deck, ceiling, and equipment, and he didn't dare lift his head.

Shouts, crashes, and thuds rang out over the buzz of weapons fire. An explosion ripped through the bridge. One of Qin's anti-tank rounds?

Casmir resisted the urge to hide behind something and curl up into a tiny ball. As good as his allies were, he feared they would need help to win this. He also feared Tork could call up more robots from the bowels of the ship.

Trying to make himself as small a target as possible, Casmir pushed himself into a crouch so he could reach the touch display. A bolt slammed into the panel door, blowing it off its hinges.

"Shit!" He ducked down, glancing back.

Zee slammed into the robot that had fired toward him. They went down in a tangle of arms and legs.

Across the bridge, Qin grappled with Tork.

Casmir rose up, knowing he had to try again. Without the android watching on, he let his fingers fly over the interface. He found a recently added unlabeled line that was in use. Hoping it led to the stealth generator, he did the computerized equivalent of switching off a circuit breaker in his cottage back home.

The indicators on the physical unit went dark as Asger was hurled over it, flying and crashing into a bulkhead. Nothing greater happened. Was it still humming and whirring? Casmir couldn't tell over the cacophony of the battle.

A bolt slammed into the wall near his head, and he dropped to his belly again.

Was there more he could do? Had what he had done even accomplished anything? What if that generator had backup power? Or what if the Kingdom ships weren't in a position to take advantage of the now-visible cargo ship?

"Need to get control of the robots," he muttered, using his chip to look for networks again.

A feminine cry of pain came from across the bridge. Tork had gained the upper hand—with help. He and two of his robots had Qin pinned to the deck.

Casmir grabbed the stunner off his belt, but it would be useless here. Why hadn't he asked Bonita to borrow a weapon with more power against robots and androids?

Qin grunted, trying to fling off her attackers, but they'd torn her weapon out of her grip and kept her down.

"Zee, help her!" Casmir cried.

But Zee had been mobbed by five robots with the same strength that he possessed. They blocked his attempts to obey orders. One fired a huge bolt of energy at his head, and it exploded. It overwhelmed Zee's surface tension, and his head and neck warped into indistinguishable pieces.

Casmir scurried behind a console, hoping it would provide cover enough to keep a stray shot from hitting him. He needed a minute of peace to work. He needed to gain access to the robots' network. Or to shut it down. If he knew where the damn router was, he might have been able to pull the plug, but it was probably down in engineering somewhere.

The ship lurched, hurling Casmir sideways, and the force of rapid acceleration pitched him against a bank of computers. The cargo ship had started evasive maneuvers.

"We're being hit by the warships' fire now!" Asger yelled as he sprang onto Tork's back, pulling him off Qin.

"No kidding!" an angry Qin yelled back.

She found the energy to throw off her remaining robot attackers. Asger spun about and hurled Tork across the bridge. The android slammed into the electric panel and tumbled down right behind Casmir.

His first instinct was to scurry away, knowing the android wouldn't be down for long, but he spotted a small panel ajar on the back of Tork's neck. Casmir fought to stay put against the myriad forces trying to throw him in different directions as he tore it open, hoping for an off button. All he saw were access ports with connectors he didn't have a match for. Wait, there was an ID code on a tiny plaque across the top. Casmir recognized it from his network search. Underneath it, a line held a bunch of symbols. The passcode? Was it possible the crew wouldn't have changed the factory settings?

As Casmir ordered his chip to try to make a connection, the ship lurched again. A snap and a pop came from the front of the bridge, and the acrid scent of something burning filled the air.

Even as Casmir linked to the android's network and tried the passcode, Tork turned his head, eyes locking onto him.

"Would you believe I'm still checking voltages?" Casmir blurted as a screen came up on his contact. Commands for Tork. He'd gotten in.

Tork's arm moved faster than a viper, and a hand wrapped around Casmir's neck. Before he started to squeeze, another attack from outside hit the ship. The deck heaved, throwing them both into the air. The android's head cracked against a railing, and his grip slipped.

Casmir jerked his neck out of reach as he surfed through the menu. Diagnostics, file downloads… power off. There!

Tork grabbed him and snatched for his neck again.

"Go, go, go," Casmir ordered as the system lagged.

He tried to knock away the android's arm, but Tork had strength superior to any human's. A hand like a vise latched onto his shoulder and squeezed. Casmir couldn't keep from screaming in pain.

But then the android stopped moving. His grip released, his limbs sagged, and he toppled sideways onto the deck.

Casmir lurched away, putting his back to the wall and bracing his legs against the deck. The fight continued to rage on the bridge—and outside. One of the Kingdom warships was flying straight toward them. The cargo ship lurched wildly, its automatic piloting system still engaged in evasive maneuvers.

"Asger," Casmir shouted over the thuds of punches connecting and the buzz of weapons firing. "Tell Ishii to stop attacking, that we've got control of the ship." A bolt slammed into the wall an inch above his head, and Casmir flung himself onto his belly again. "I mean that we *will* have control!"

"I tried," Asger's voice came back, muffled.

He was on the deck under a pile of attacking robots as Qin and Zee fought back to back several feet away. Detached robot limbs littered the deck, but the constructs fought on. There seemed to be more than before. Tork must have called up reinforcements.

"Comm system," Casmir blurted, lunging to his feet but staying low as he raced toward the front of the bridge.

He needed to figure out how to take control of the robots now that Tork was out of the picture, but if he didn't stop the warships from firing, they could be blown to pieces in seconds. He rose up just enough to access the comm panel and figure out how to open an outgoing channel on a burst broadcast.

"This is Dabrowski with Sir Asger. We disabled the cargo ship's stealth technology, as you can see, but we're on the bridge ourselves right now. Cease fire. Captain Ishii, please cease fire. We'll update you when we've gained control over the security system." A thunderous boom punctuated his last sentence.

Wonderful.

Hoping the warships would hear him and stop firing, Casmir sank behind cover again. He checked the networks, then attempted to connect to the security one. It had shown as locked before, and it still was. He tried the same passcode that had worked for Tork.

Access denied.

On a whim, he tried Tork's ID, the numbers and letters burned into his brain. Maybe he was always in charge of the robots.

He gained access, and he let out a whoop. Until nothing but ones and zeroes appeared on his display. Right, androids and robots wouldn't need a human-friendly interface to communicate.

He transmitted a zero for off, though it was probably vain to believe something so simple would work. Until it grew abruptly quiet on the bridge.

"They stopped attacking!" Qin yelled.

"They stopped doing anything." Asger sounded puzzled.

Casmir flopped onto his back and laughed, not caring that it had a hysterical edge to it. He managed to stop himself only because he was afraid his words wouldn't have been enough for Ishii and the other warship captains. He sat up and waved Asger toward the comm.

"Tell them we have control of the ship, please."

Asger eyed a robot standing in front of him, frozen in the middle of lunging at him. "Are you sure?"

"I think so. It's possible they'll reset themselves, but I got access to their network, so if I have some time, I can probably reprogram. And the human crew..." Casmir looked grimly at the pods. "Isn't going to wake up."

"What about the android?" Asger lowered his pertundo and walked to the console, peering down at Casmir.

Casmir waved at the deck where he'd left Tork. "He's off too. He'll be more complicated to reprogram. I'll just focus on the robots for now."

"Huh." Asger gazed down at him.

"The last time you looked at me for that long," Casmir said, "I got a little worried you were going to kiss me."

"Well, the helmets would preclude that."

"*Only* the helmets?"

Asger snorted, looked around at the immobile robots, and lowered his hand. "You're not what I expected, and yet... you kind of are."

Casmir accepted the hand and the help to his feet. "Care to explain that?"

He remembered Asger saying he was helping Casmir because the queen wanted him alive. He also remembered that Asger had paused before giving that answer, as if it hadn't been the first one that came to his mind. Was it possible he knew something more about Casmir?

Asger looked over at Qin. "Maybe later."

"Right," Casmir said.

The comm light flashed with an incoming message. Casmir waved for Asger to answer it, figuring Ishii would be more likely to listen to him.

"This is Sir Asger."

The ship had steadied, no longer accelerating wildly through its maneuvers. Casmir hoped that meant the warships had stopped firing.

"I want visual," Ishii's voice came over the comm. He sounded suspicious. "How the hell did you and Dabrowski get over there?"

"It's a longish story. Let me see about a visual."

While Asger poked around, the smoke from damaged computers hazing the air, Casmir stapled together enough binary to bring the robots, those intact enough to walk, over to stand behind him at the console. That ought to help convince Ishii that they had indeed taken control of the ship.

When the visual link came through, two faces appeared side by side on the display, replacing the visual of the warship. Captain Ishii and a beleaguered man in his fifties or sixties, also with captain's rank. Smoke filled the air behind that man, and his white hair stuck up in a dozen directions. Red emergency lighting flashed behind him, and someone in the background was helping someone else off the bridge. Maybe he was the captain of the ship that had been blockading the gate.

"We had a bit of a battle, Captain." Asger removed his helmet so they could see his face. "But we've come out on top and, barring unexpected surprises, have control of the ship. Apparently, it's useful to take a computer hacker along on combat missions."

"I'm a robotics engineer, and I didn't hack anything. I pulled some plugs." Casmir also removed his helmet, then promptly wished he hadn't because the unfiltered, smoky air assailed his lungs and he ended up coughing.

"Why are you surrounded by robots?" the second captain asked.

Asger looked behind him. "I believe that's Dabrowski's new army. Any minute, they're going to swear to live and die by his command."

Ishii scowled.

"I'm not sure this is the time for humor." Casmir worried jokes like that might be interpreted literally. He didn't need King Jager's intelligence people to hear rumors about a rogue engineer gathering a robot army. "Besides, didn't we decide knights don't make jokes?"

"You decided that. Based on my deadly weapon and my cloak, I believe."

"Have you checked for our stolen cargo?" Ishii asked.

"Not yet," Asger said. "We've only had control of the bridge for two minutes."

"Go check. I'll bring the *Osprey* over while Captain Hildebrand continues to blockade the gate."

"Lucky me," the other captain muttered, wiping his brow.

"Check for the cargo and report back within fifteen minutes," Ishii said.

The display switched back to a view of the warship as the comm ended.

"He still hasn't grasped that I'm not in his chain of command," Asger said.

"I think captains are just accustomed to giving orders and being obeyed."

"Maybe so. I'll see if the gate is here and all this was worth it." Asger patted him on the shoulder and turned to walk around the robots and toward the exit. He looked at but didn't say anything to Qin, who'd walked up to Casmir's other side. "Do whatever you need to do to make sure the android doesn't wake up and you retain control of those robots for now," he called back.

"You know I'm not in your chain of command, either, right?" Casmir asked.

"Knights are also accustomed to giving orders and being obeyed."

"That may be why people think they're humorless." Casmir lowered his voice and smiled at Qin. "And pretentious." He gripped her shoulder, though she wouldn't feel it through her armor. "Thank you so much for your help. That wasn't your fight."

"Was it yours?" she asked.

"Ah, technically, I don't think so. But there were robots, and I did volunteer myself to come over here, so…"

A new message scrolled down Casmir's display, and he held up a finger. It was Kim.

Casmir, I'm incredibly busy, but I wanted to let you know that I'm back up on the Machu Picchu, *and we're trying to figure out a solution to the pseudo radiation problem. I may have a lead, but it's too early to tell, and my health is deteriorating. Don't worry about me. I have more resources now to hopefully solve this, but I want you to stay away from any of those gate pieces. It's not just the wreck that emits this stuff that's deadly to us. Even a small gate piece could kill a crew—did* kill a crew.

"Uh," Casmir said, looking in the direction Asger had gone. *Kim, I'm on the cargo ship that we think was trying to steal the gate. We've gained control of it, but the gate… you said Rache is immune. Do you think I would be?*

He bit his lip, glad they could talk but annoyed by the time lag.

"What is it?" Qin whispered.

"I got a message from Kim. Hold on," he said as a reply filled his vision.

I think so, but unless I miss my guess, nobody else with you is going to have that immunity. You better get everyone else off that ship before it's too late. The more exposure they get, the faster they'll die.

Damn it, Kim. What is *this stuff?*

I think you may be right in that it's the ancient ship's security system. If you're not human enough, you get zapped with some homemade type of radiation we can't detect.

Not human enough? *What does that mean? You said Rache is immune. There's no way he's more human than you.*

I'll explain that later.

"I found the cargo hold," Asger said over the comm. "And more giant segments of the gate than I can count."

"Get out of there!" Casmir yelled. "Close the door. Bar it off. Get back up here. No, you need to get the hell off this ship now." He glanced at the pods full of dead people. "Damn it, why didn't I realize what must have happened to them earlier?"

Because he'd had a dozen robots pointing weapons at him, and contemplating *why* the people were dead hadn't been his highest priority...

"What?" Asger asked.

"The gate is what killed the crew. It's emitting some kind of radiation we can't detect. If Kim doesn't find a fix and if we can't get to her in time, we'll suffer the same fate as these astroshamans."

There was a long pause and the faint hiss of a door shutting.

Asger swore vehemently. "Everyone, get to the shuttle. We'll explain it to Ishii from there."

Casmir opened his mouth to agree, but another message came in from Kim.

I hate to give you more bad news, Casmir, but Rache dropped us off and took off to rendezvous with his ship, which has, I believe, been repaired enough to be dangerous again. He openly admitted he'll do whatever it takes to keep King Jager from gaining control of that gate.

Shit, I'm standing on the same ship as that gate right now.

There was a pause that went beyond what signal lag should have caused.

It's on the Osprey? Kim asked.

No. I took a small trip.

If you were here, I'd punch you.

It's possible I might deserve it. Casmir thought about saying that he'd only been trying to assist the Fleet so they would assist him in retrieving her, but it seemed like too long a story to explain now. *How long ago did Rache leave you?*

Uhm, eight hours? Ten?

"That means he could be here any minute." Casmir groaned.

CHAPTER 14

CASMIR CAUGHT UP WITH QIN AND ASGER IN the shuttle bay, trailed by Zee and ten robots from the bridge—those with legs and arms still mostly attached. Asger threw a startled glance at the small army but waved Casmir toward the open hatch of his craft. Qin was already inside. Good.

"You two go," Casmir said. "I have to stay here."

"What? You just said we all have to go. That we've already likely been afflicted."

"That is true. Take the shuttle back to the *Stellar Dragon*, make sure Captain Lopez runs the decon shower in the airlock, and then get back to the *Machu Picchu* in orbit around Skadi. I have faith that Kim is on to something by now, and she'll have a cure."

"Which you'll need as badly as the rest of us, right?" Asger asked.

Casmir hoped not. He wished Kim had gone into more detail on Rache's immunity.

"I got a message from Kim," Casmir said, trying to figure out a way to explain why he was the only one who could stay without revealing the secret he didn't want to have. He suspected his trustworthiness among the knights, the military, and the queen would plummet if people knew he was Rache's twin brother. "That's why I realized we needed to avoid the gate. But it's also how I know that Rache is on his way. And he'll do anything to keep our king from taking delivery of it."

Asger banged his fist on his armored thigh. "He's not working with those freaks, is he?"

Asger flung a hand upward. To indicate the dead people in the pods on the bridge? Casmir bristled a little at his willingness to label everyone who wasn't like him as a freak, but this wasn't the time to argue semantics.

"I actually don't know," Casmir said. "It could be possible. He's a mercenary, right? Meaning he'll work for the highest bidder? But he definitely has a grudge against Jager, so maybe it's just personal."

"Yeah, I know about his grudge." Asger shook his head in disgust.

"I'd ask you to enlighten me, but I'm not sure how the exposure to the gate works. It sounds like it's *something* like radiation, and I know radiation would have no trouble going through the decks of this ship. The sooner you get out of here, the better."

Casmir nodded to Qin, who'd appeared in the hatchway, no doubt wondering why they weren't already taking off. He wished he wasn't sending her off alone with Asger, but now that they had battled killer robots together, maybe they could survive a shuttle ride without springing for each other's throats.

"And what, you're going to stay here and sacrifice yourself to keep Rache from getting the gate by blowing up this ship? Don't tell me you think you can fly into battle against him and his hardened pirates. This ship may have good guns, but you disabled the android controlling them."

"I wasn't thinking of doing either of those things, actually. Especially not while I'm on board."

"What *are* you thinking of?"

Casmir hesitated, feeling he shouldn't admit that he hadn't gotten far yet with his plotting and scheming. His main thought was that he should reenable the stealth system so Rache couldn't find the ship or the gate.

"Look, Dabrowski." Asger stepped forward and gripped his shoulder. "*Casmir*. You and your new allies—uh, that one's arm is falling off— aren't a match for Rache. Let Ishii and the other captains handle it. There are three good warships out there. Rache only has one ship. It's state-of-the-art, yes, but so are those warships."

Casmir thought of the beleaguered captain who'd appeared on the comm. "How much damage did they take battling Tork and *this* ship?"

Asger winced. "I'm not sure yet."

"Rache's people have probably had time to get their ship back in top condition."

"You don't need to sacrifice yourself to keep him from getting the gate." Asger shook his shoulder gently—or maybe the act only seemed gentle through Casmir's suit. "I promised the queen I would try to keep you from getting killed. This wasn't what she had in mind at the time, I'll admit, but you're meant for greater things. I'm sure of it."

"Care to explain that?"

Asger hesitated, then tilted his helmet toward the hatchway. "If you hop in the shuttle and leave this mess for the military, I'll tell you what I know."

Oh, how Casmir wanted answers. Whatever answers Asger could provide.

The temptation was real, but... Casmir couldn't help but believe that Rache would get the gate if he walked away from this ship, and even though it didn't make a lot of sense, he felt some responsibility for Rache's actions. As if, because they shared DNA, it was his responsibility to stop him.

Maybe all Rache wanted was to keep Jager from getting the gate, but what if he wanted it for himself? To sell it to the highest bidder? Casmir didn't know if King Jager was the most honorable person in the Twelve Systems, but the Kingdom government was stable, and life on Odin came with a lot of freedom and opportunities. He wasn't convinced the man was evil. He definitely wasn't convinced that this technology would be better off in a pirate's hands.

"It's not my intention to sacrifice myself," Casmir promised. "Just to hide the gate somewhere so Rache can't find it."

"You need to just hand it to the Fleet."

"I'm willing to do that, but I'm concerned they might not be a match for Rache right now."

"Where are you going to hide it?"

"I don't know yet. I need to get the stealth generator back online." Casmir smiled and didn't mention that he hadn't the foggiest idea how that stealth technology worked or that he worried the ship had been damaged enough that simply fixing the electrical connection wouldn't get it working again. "I'll meet you at Skadi, at the *Machu Picchu*, as soon as I'm able. I promise."

"There aren't any other shuttles in this bay, Casmir. And if you bring the entire ship to Skadi, nobody's going to have a hard time finding it."

"I'll find a way to get there. I'm crafty. Really!" He gave them his most winning smile, more because he wanted them to leave the ship before they were exposed further than because he had any clue what he would do or how he would do it. "Now, you both need to go. Please. But thank you for everything on the bridge, for risking yourselves and keeping me alive. You were amazing. *Both* of you." Casmir met Qin's eyes and nodded to her. "Tell your captain that you need a raise. Or at least a new candle. A really big one."

"Casmir," Qin whispered, distress in her voice.

But she didn't try to stop him. She hopped out of the shuttle, gave him a crushing hug that made his bones creak, and then ran back inside.

"Stay safe, Dabrowski," Asger said, then also stepped through the hatchway, shaking his head as if he knew he'd never see Casmir again.

The hatch closed, and Casmir ran out of the shuttle bay so they could depressurize it and fly out. They *would* see him again. He wasn't sacrificing himself. He swore it.

Casmir doubted he had much time, but he couldn't resist running down to the cargo hold, his new robot friends clanking and clattering behind him, to take a look at the gate.

When he'd been back on the university campus, light years from System Lion's existing gate, he hadn't thought much about it, especially since it had been more than ten years since his class on astrodynamics, which he'd mostly taken because it had satisfied an elective and hadn't involved getting up before dawn. But now that he was out here, traveling between the planets, he found himself more curious than ever.

He stepped into a vast cargo hold—it had to occupy half of the massive ship—filled with great puzzle pieces, as his mind immediately identified them. The gate was so large that each section only curved slightly, but he could envision them fitting together to form a circle, one large enough for the largest ships to fly through. What he didn't know was how they communicated with each other once they were together and somehow created a wormhole in space, allowing nearly instantaneous travel between one star system and another, systems that weren't even that close to each other.

Nobody knew that. But if they had the opportunity to study these disassembled pieces, they might learn.

As he walked among them, peering at the ends and searching for seams or panels, Casmir had the urge to take one apart and see what was inside. To try to figure out how they worked. It was amazing that humanity had managed to keep anyone from doing that for centuries, collectively agreeing, when various systems agreed about nothing else, that the gates had to be guarded at all costs, that they couldn't risk breaking the network.

He reached out to run a hand along one of the pieces but drew back. His eye blinked a few times.

He couldn't see the glow he imagined of some highly radioactive piece of metal, but Kim's warning came to mind. She hadn't explained why Rache was immune—if she knew—and maybe he was foolish to be down here, assuming that he shared that immunity. She'd seemed to believe he would, but what if she was wrong, and it had to do with the various upgrades Rache had admitted to getting?

Casmir backed away from the gate, hoping he hadn't needlessly exposed himself. Though it probably didn't matter. As soon as he'd come aboard the ship, he'd exposed himself.

Kim, he composed a message as he headed to the bridge. *I'm sure you're busy, but I've visually confirmed that the gate is on this cargo ship I'm aboard. Some astroshamans were apparently trying to steal it and take it back to one of the systems where they have their monasteries. They died before I got here, presumably due to exposure.*

I have control of this ship for the moment, but I'm expecting both Rache and the Fleet to try to take it from me. Given what you've told me, I'm not sure I should let even the Fleet have it until someone has figured out a way to keep more people from dying. Let me know if you have any ideas about that, eh? If it's akin to radiation, would creating a magnetic field around the gate pieces work?

I sent Qin, Bonita, and a knight named Asger to find you on the research ship. Qin and Asger were exposed. I hope you can help them. I'm positive you wish you were back home right now, and I definitely wish you were somewhere safe instead of dealing with this, but I know you're the person to solve this problem, and I'm relieved you're on it.

Anyway, I won't distract you further while you're trying to fix people, but I hope you're safe. We need to figure out how to get back home. I doubt anyone else is feeding the squirrels in the tree out back. They might starve.

~Casmir

P.S. If it turns out you make it and I don't, please tell my parents that I love them. And make sure my collectible automata toys go to a worthy home. I'd give them to you, but I've noticed they don't delight you as much as they do me. That's very odd, but I forgive you for your flaws. Thank you, my good friend!

As Casmir sent the message, he was walking past the shuttle bay. He glanced through the hatch window to make sure Qin and Asger had taken off. Yes, the knight's craft was gone.

It was what Casmir had wanted, but he couldn't help but be aware that he was alone now, on a giant ship he didn't even know if he could fly.

Well, not entirely alone. He glanced back at Zee and his cadre of robots. A lot of them needed repairs, but they trooped along without complaint. It probably helped that only one of them could speak.

"What do you think of our new friends, Zee?" Casmir asked.

It was silly, since he knew the crusher had no feelings, but he couldn't help anthropomorphizing and thinking Zee might be jealous or worry he was being replaced.

"They are inferior models," Zee stated.

"So, I had better keep you?"

"I am necessary to protect and defend Kim Sato and Casmir Dabrowski."

"Yes, you are. And we better get that stealth generator back online to help with that."

He could worry about choosing a hiding spot for the cargo ship afterward.

As soon as he stepped onto the bridge, Casmir headed for the electrical panel, intending to return power to the stealth generator. But lights flashed on numerous other panels on the bridge, and a ship filled the forward display. His stomach churned. It was the *Fedallah*.

He could see one of the warships in the distance, still guarding the gate, and the two other warships had to be out there too. Hopefully, coming this way with railguns pointed at the *Fedallah.* Assuming the fleet *saw* the mercenary ship. Casmir knew from his experience at the refinery that the *Fedallah's* slydar hull plating made it almost invisible until it was within a few miles. Right now, it was almost up the cargo ship's nose.

He tapped furiously at the touch panel, reconnecting power to the stealth generator. An error message flashed. A connection had been damaged in the fight on the bridge.

"Not good." Could he even reach it without tearing out half of the consoles?

A flash of yellow came from the forward display. The *Fedallah* was firing.

Casmir vaulted a railing and flung himself into one of the helm positions. Shielding? Did this ship have any sort of shielding?

A missile slammed into a lower section of the hull near engineering, and a shudder racked the cargo ship. Casmir would have ended up on the deck, but Zee had followed him and pressed a hand down on his shoulder, keeping him from tumbling from his seat.

"Comm," Casmir whispered, lunging over to slap the panel.

He had to let Rache know he was here and hope that mattered to him. He didn't allow himself to consider that Rache might already know he was here and might not care. What if he was holding a grudge for how their last meeting had turned out? With the bioweapon blown up and his ship damaged from the explosives that had gone off in the refinery? Granted, those had been Rache's explosives, but Qin had ensured they detonated prematurely.

"Captain Rache," Casmir blurted.

He sent his broadcast wide, hoping the warships were paying attention and would realize the *Fedallah* was nearby, if they hadn't detected it yet. As he spoke, he found the controls for the cargo ship's shields and raised them.

A flashing diagram showed that he had numerous weapons online and available to him, should he wish to engage in a firefight with the *Fedallah.* Considering he was the entirety of the bridge crew—of *all* of the crew—that didn't seem smart. Tork may have been keeping the warships busy, but Casmir didn't have the processing power of an android.

"It's Casmir Dabrowski. It's been a few days since we chatted, but I'm hoping you remember me. Uhm, I'm over here on the cargo ship.

I've liberated it from its previous crew, and I'm deciding what to do with its cargo. I'd appreciate it if you not fire at me currently, as I haven't had a chance to take a thorough inventory yet. I thought you might be interested in this cargo, actually, so I'm a little surprised you're flinging missiles at it."

As he waited for a response, Casmir crawled to the stealth generator and opened a panel on the structure, hoping that broken connection was in a spot he could reach. He wished he'd been able to find schematics for the device during his earlier search. It was probably too top secret for that.

Rache's face appeared on the bridge's big forward display—technically, it was his mask and hood, his face hiding somewhere behind all that.

"I assume the pieces of the gate are largely indestructible," Rache said calmly, not sounding surprised to find Casmir on the vessel. "I was going to blow up the cargo ship and collect them."

"Fishing them out of wreckage sounds like a tedious project, especially considering a bunch of Kingdom warships are heading your way right now."

"Actually, they are engaged in repairs and don't seem to have noticed me yet, though I see you're transmitting your message to everyone within a light year who's listening, so I suppose that will change."

"Am I?" Casmir asked with as much innocence as he could muster. "Sorry about that. I'm brand new to this ship and still finding my way around spaceships in general. This isn't exactly my milieu."

"What are you planning, Dabrowski?"

Yes, what *was* he planning? To fix the damn stealth generator for starters.

"I'm open to suggestions. Do you want to barter for the cargo? The previous owners of this ship passed away, so I believe under the intergalactic salvage laws, it's mine to do with as I please." Technically, those laws did not apply in Kingdom space. Casmir was fairly certain anything found and not rightfully owned by someone belonged to the king by default.

"You killed the crew?"

It bothered Casmir that Rache didn't sound stunned. Did the man truly think he was capable of that?

"The *gate* killed the crew. I'm sure you know all about how that works by now. An android was in charge, and the ship's autopilot was battling the Kingdom warships and trying to get through the gate and back to its system."

Rache barked a short laugh. Casmir didn't think he'd heard the man laugh before. It wasn't a friendly or appealing sound.

"And all those Kingdom warships couldn't handle it? Pathetic. Let's talk terms of surrender."

"You wish to surrender to me?" Casmir asked. "I accept."

Apparently, the joke wasn't worth responding to, for Rache ignored it. "How many people do you have with you, Dabrowski?"

Alarms jangled in Casmir's brain. Did Rache want to know because he had changed his plans? Because he now intended to board the ship and take over the whole thing? That would definitely be easier than fishing hundreds of gate pieces out of space…

"I have whole armies of people with me. Knights, marines, snipers, bounty hunters who love pirate targets…"

"I'm a mercenary, not a pirate, and you're an abysmal liar."

The channel cut out, and Rache's face disappeared from the display. Unfortunately, the *Fedallah* was still there.

Casmir found a melted cable inside the stealth device. The good news was that he thought that was the only problem. The bad news was that he didn't have a replacement cable in his tool kit.

"Let's hope we can borrow an identical piece from somewhere else," Casmir grumbled, crawling to the scanner station. "Zee, let me know if that ship moves, please. Or if anything significant happens."

"I will." Zee faced the display, his head not moving.

"Also, can you see if you can figure out how to send a tight-beam communication to Captain Ishii's ship? The *Osprey*."

A beep came from the comm panel. The *Osprey* was contacting him.

"Never mind," Casmir said, then ran over to accept the incoming message. Why were all the stations on this bridge so far apart?

Captain Ishii's face appeared on the display.

"I hope you're here to tell me that you're on the way and plan to keep Captain Rache from blowing me up," Casmir said, heading off whatever Ishii had intended to open with. He wanted the warships to take care of Rache, but he feared they wouldn't be in position in time and that he had to come up with something on his own. "I tried to stall him, but I don't believe it worked."

"Where is he?" Ishii asked. "We intercepted your message."

Shuttle-bay doors opened on the side of the *Fedallah,* and Casmir grimaced and ran back to his work, not caring that Ishii wouldn't be able to see him.

"You didn't intercept it; I broadcasted it. And he's about two hundred meters in front of the nose of this ship. For now. It looks like he's launching a shuttle."

"*Shoot* him!" Ishii ordered. "I know that ship has weapons capability."

"Most of its capabilities are compromised right now. The bridge took a lot of damage when we were taking it over."

Irritation mixed with puzzlement on Ishii's face. Asger must not have kept him as up-to-date as Casmir had expected.

"I'm the only one here," Casmir said, glancing to make sure this was a tight-beam transmission, but with the *Fedallah* so close, he couldn't guarantee they wouldn't intercept messages. It might not matter. Rache had been certain Casmir was lying about having allies on board. "I have limited options. And no time to discuss them. Sorry, Sora." Casmir waved at Zee. "Turn that off, please."

He stuck his head back under the console and looked for—

"Ah ha, there you are, my match. What do you control? Weapons? Well, I wasn't going to start a war with anyone anyway." He grabbed a few tools and carefully disconnected the cable.

"The mercenary warship is moving off," Zee announced.

"It is?" Casmir jumped to his feet with his new cable in hand. Maybe Ishii and his allies had located the *Fedallah* and were swooping in to attack. He didn't know how they could miss it. However camouflaged it was, it ought to be blocking someone's view of the cargo vessel.

Casmir started to let out a whoop as the *Fedallah* navigated away, thrusters firing orange, but then he spotted a sleek combat shuttle heading for the cargo ship's airlocks.

He groaned. Rache must have sent his warship to deal with the Kingdom vessels, maybe even clear a way to the gate, while he brought a strike force over to capture *this* ship.

Casmir hurried to affix the cable. If he didn't figure out something clever, Rache would have the cargo ship, the gate, and *him* within minutes.

As he worked, he looked up the model and passenger capacity of the shuttle heading over. And groaned again. It could hold eighteen people, plus a pilot. Casmir had never learned how many men Rache commanded, but he was positive he could fill that many seats with elite fighters in the best combat armor and carrying the best weapons that money could buy. Not to mention most of them were cybernetically enhanced or genetically modded to be superior warriors.

With the cable plugged in, the stealth generator came back online. Casmir jumped up and manually toggled it on. An indicator flared to life, informing him that stealth mode had been activated.

But it didn't matter. Another indicator flashed on the docks and bays monitor on the other side of the bridge.

Rache's shuttle had docked. It was too late.

CHAPTER 15

KIM WATCHED THE ARTIFACT FLY OUT INTO SPACE through a porthole next to an airlock, not caring if anyone ever found it again. Someone somewhere had the entire gate—no apparently, *Casmir* had the entire gate. Or was at least in the same place where it was located. She hoped he wasn't with a lot of people—and that he truly did share Rache's immunity.

She headed back to her lab, walking the eerily quiet corridors of a research ship capable of housing a thousand people, crew and scientists. Including the quarantined people, there were fewer than forty aboard. She ought to be able to let them out now that the artifact was gone, but she would wait longer to make sure. So far, those people—and Rache—were the only ones who'd survived a close encounter with the ancient technology without being afflicted.

When she walked into her lab, the display for the computer monitoring the bacteria growth was flashing. Had another strain died swiftly and dramatically? Grimacing, she stepped up and scanned the results. Several more had died when exposed to the blood of people affected by the pseudo radiation, but one of the modified strains was doing well. More than well. It was thriving and multiplying quickly.

"Are you the answer, my little friends?" she murmured, sliding the dish under a microscope so she could look herself.

The tiny wriggly worm-like bacteria were indeed alive. Alive and thriving. She couldn't *see* what they were eating—the microscope wasn't good enough to view subatomic particles—but they were dividing every twenty minutes, so they had to be munching on something they found nourishing.

Kim grabbed a stack of empty dishes. It was time to make a lot more of them and hope this was the answer. Or at least part of it. She still needed to get a report from Angelico—he was the one inspecting the cryonics lab—on whether they could repair damaged cells here.

As she worked, a new message from Casmir came in. She kept working as the words scrolled along at her preferred reading speed. He was very vague on how he'd gained control of the gate—how did a robotics professor who couldn't float through zero-g without puking take over a spaceship?—but his suggestion that he would keep the Fleet from having it, for their own good, made her uneasy. She highly doubted the military would appreciate that. She could understand not wanting to let *Rache* get it, but… why was this Casmir's problem to deal with? He already had someone sending crushers after him, and he hadn't gotten to the root of *that* problem yet. If he continued along this trajectory, he would end up with the entire system pissed at him.

Yes, she replied, making herself hold the censure for later—if Rache showed up, he wouldn't have time to read a long diatribe. *A magnetic field might do the trick.*

When she read his postscript, her eyes teared, and she grew more frustrated at him for willingly getting himself into this mess. She definitely needed to punch him.

And you better survive, she added. *Otherwise, I'm giving your automata toys to the squirrels out back.*

There. If that didn't motivate him, nothing would.

She shook her head, wishing she'd found an opportunity to shoot Rache. Or drug him. She might have been able to slip something to him when she'd taken his blood. If she'd known he would leave her only to go harass Casmir, she definitely would have tried something.

A knock sounded at the door.

"Kim?" Dr. Sikou asked from the doorway. "Dr. Angelico and I have been studying the offerings in the cryonics lab, and it looks like there *is* equipment for reviving specimens. Hopefully, there's no need to freeze yourself first." She smiled slightly. "It does look like a complicated process, and we'll have to see if there's enough of the solution to do everyone here. Will you come take a look?"

"Yes."

As Kim followed Sikou into the corridor, she almost mentioned her new strain of bacteria, but she was hesitant to speak about it before she had proof that it worked. There were no lab rats to inoculate with her bacteria, so she would have to be her own test subject.

She told herself the bacteria shouldn't be that different from the proven efficacious-and-safe strain that had been in use for years, but she couldn't help thinking of the early days of medicine when scientists had tested things on themselves… to deleterious results.

Casmir ran to the cargo hold, ordering all of the ship's security robots to meet him there. He'd surfed the network and found a few more in storage compartments in lower decks, and he'd activated them. He wished there had been time to repair the ones that Qin and Asger had torn apart on the bridge, but he wasn't even sure he had time for this diversion.

It had been almost ten minutes since Rache's shuttle docked. Casmir had made sure the airlock hatch was secured, but the mercenaries would have tools to force their way in. How long would that take? Not long, he was sure.

He swung into the hold and did a quick count of the robots waiting for him there and the ones who'd followed him. Sixteen, the same as his network connection indicated. He would have felt better if they outnumbered the members of Rache's strike team, but he doubted that would have mattered. Though the robots looked intimidating, with their shiny large bodies and cannon-like arms, Qin and Asger had been able to fight off superior numbers, and he had little doubt Rache's men would be able to do the same. All he could hope was that he could perhaps surprise them or trick Rache somehow, but Rache didn't seem easy to trick. Casmir reminded himself that he was dealing with his twin, his twin who'd spent the last however many years of his life in space, making war on people *professionally*.

"Nothing to worry about, nope," he muttered, waving to the robots to hide among the gate pieces, even as he sent the more precise and necessary commands across the network.

Once they were out of sight—poised to strike, he told himself, not hiding—Casmir rushed back out. "Follow me, Zee."

"Are you going to put yourself in danger, Casmir Dabrowski?"

Casmir almost laughed. The crusher never asked questions and usually only spoke if he was given an order or asked a question. Did this mean he worried he wasn't going to be able to fulfill his mission?

"Unfortunately, yes," Casmir said, breathing heavily as he ran toward the shuttle bay. If Kim had been there, she would have berated him for not keeping up with the treadmill work. "But I'm going to try to talk to Rache first, so don't open up with an attack. I'm hoping I can... Well, I haven't figured it out yet. I'm hoping for inspiration, brilliance, and an opportunity that gives me an advantage. Is that too much to hope for?"

"Yes," Zee said in his typical monotone.

"I see I should have programmed you with more optimism."

Casmir skidded to a stop at the shuttle-bay door, pausing to catch his breath and collect himself. Sweat ran down the side of his face. He peeked through the Glasnax window. The bay was empty, but he'd expected that. Rache was coming in through one of the three airlocks at the end. A blue light indicated which one had a shuttle hooked up to it.

Casmir walked into the bay. Should he put his helmet up? Or was there even a point? With it, he wore a self-contained suit that could take more of a beating than simple flesh. But it wasn't the equivalent of combat armor. If the mercs unloaded their weapons on him all at once, they would perforate his galaxy suit—and his organs—in seconds. Casmir didn't even have a weapon that would be effective against them.

He snorted at the stunner still holstered to his suit's utility belt. Again, there seemed little point in having it. He removed it and stuffed it in his tool satchel.

The less he looked like a threat, the less likely they would be to shoot him. He hoped. He still wasn't sure how angry Rache was with him over the refinery incident. As far as Casmir had heard, Rache's voice came in two tones: deadpan and icy. So far, he'd mostly been deadpan with Casmir, but Casmir had a feeling Rache could shoot people with his mood never escalating to ice.

A warning bleated, informing him of a rupture in the outer hatch. Casmir hoped his seizure medication had kicked in. He was pleased he hadn't collapsed on the bridge during the fight, but this almost seemed worse. There was too much time to think.

Afraid he would think himself into a panic attack, Casmir strode to the airlock hatch and overrode the lock. It swung open, revealing a man in combat armor with a blow torch in the middle of cutting through the lock.

"Greetings," Casmir said cheerfully while spreading his open hands—the blow torch had already swung in his direction, along with the weapons of the five men crammed in the airlock chamber behind him. "Welcome to my newly acquired cargo vessel. Which one of you strapping fellows is Captain Rache? I'm ready to start negotiations for my cargo whenever he is." He raised his eyebrows toward the man in the middle, the only person under six feet tall and precisely Casmir's height. "Or do you want a tour first? The bridge is a little bunged up, and there are a bunch of creepy dead people strapped into pods, but other than that, it's a pretty nice ship."

"Fan out," Rache ordered.

The men strode out, weapons at the ready, and Casmir stepped back lest he be trampled. One of the men pawed him over, grabbed his satchel, and opened it.

"That's a little rude," Casmir said. "Do you do that with women's purses too?"

"Only if they're on the ship we're commandeering for ourselves," Rache answered, striding out. His weapon—one of them—found Zee right away and pointed steadily at his chest. "Is this the same robot that we keep utterly destroying?" He glanced at Casmir.

"Perhaps not *utterly*."

"I should have you make me some."

"Well, we can put that on the negotiations table, but I'll warn you that I doubt this ship or yours would have the raw materials I need."

"Negotiations. Right. What are you even *doing* here, Dabrowski?"

"That's a long story."

One of the hulking men shut the hatch, and the airlock cycled behind him. More of Rache's men coming in, no doubt.

It occurred to Casmir that if he'd wanted to have a shot at overpowering Rache, he should have had his robots stationed in here, ready to spring into the airlock chamber and take the first group by surprise.

"What course did you set this ship on?" Rache asked. "It started moving right after we latched on."

"Did it? Huh."

Casmir hadn't set it on any particular course, just in the general direction of Skadi Moon. Mostly, he'd wanted to move it, now that the stealth technology was engaged, so Rache's warship wouldn't easily find it again, just in case Casmir somehow managed to defeat the strike team and keep Rache from taking it over. An admittedly idealistic hope.

Rache's rifle swung toward Casmir's chest. "Quit playing stupid with me, Dabrowski. I *know* what your IQ is."

"You do? That's kind of odd, don't you think? Unless you're a fan of mine. Did you see my videos on the net? About some of my team's recent projects? The one with the fire-breathing robot got a lot of play. Especially popular with visitors aged ten to fourteen. The university is thinking of adding it to their portal to help recruit students into their science and engineering program." Casmir could hear how quickly he was talking—babbling—and feel sweat running down the back of his neck.

Stop *panicking*, he told himself, and did his best to smile affably at the men fanned out around Rache. He doubted he had a shot at winning any of them over to his side, but he held the hope that they would hesitate to fire at someone who seemed harmless and goofy.

The man who'd been searching his satchel handed it back sans the stunner. Casmir was somewhat bemused because at least three of the tools in there would be more dangerous to someone in combat armor. But it wasn't as if the men would give him the ten minutes he would need to drill, burn, or pry his way into their tortoise shells.

The hatch opened, and more mercenaries filed out. More weapons pointed at Casmir and Zee. The hatch cycled again, and Casmir grimaced inwardly. It seemed Rache had brought along the full passenger complement of men. All to deal with Casmir? He must have thought Casmir had some allies. Which he *did* have. Just not of the human variety.

It irked him, on the mercenaries' behalf, that Rache was willing to expose so many of his men to the gate's deadly radiation. Did they know they were on a death mission?

"Go secure the bridge, Sergeant, Lieutenant," Rache told two of his men, then waved for four others to follow them. "Turn it toward the gate, but don't get too close yet. Let the *Fedallah* deal with the Kingdom ships. It was convenient to find them already damaged."

Casmir refrained from commenting. He'd used the access he'd gained from the android to put a passcode on the navigation system, but since he'd only had seconds to do it, he wasn't confident it would keep Rache's men out for long. Or at all.

"Dabrowski, you offered a tour. I'm eager to see the cargo hold." Rache put a hand on Casmir's upper back and pointed toward the door. "And for the record, I'm commandeering your salvaged ship and its cargo. There will be no negotiations."

Casmir knew that hand could go easily to the back of his neck and that with his cybernetic implants, Rache could break it without much effort. Why had he opted not to wear the helmet? So he'd look unthreatening? As if he'd needed a lack of a helmet to achieve that. He was a bump on the sidewalk to these men. For the most part. Zee strode up to Casmir's other side.

"Are you threatened, Casmir Dabrowski?" Zee's vaguely human face turned toward Rache. "Shall I use force to remove this human?"

Casmir couldn't see Rache's face through his helmet and the mask he wore, but he heard a faint snort.

Rache wasn't worried, not with his men marching behind him. The ten that remained after he'd sent that group to the bridge. Casmir wondered if his robots had any chance of defeating Rache in the cargo hold. And if he attempted to defeat him and lost, would Rache shift Casmir from the annoying-twerp category to the dastardly enemy category? Someone to be shot on sight the next time they met?

Casmir still wasn't sure Rache wouldn't shoot him *this* time. Once he'd secured the gate and the ship, what need would he have for him? Casmir feared he might only be alive now because Rache wasn't yet sure if there were any booby traps about that would require a robotics geek to deactivate. Unfortunately, Casmir hadn't had time to lay booby traps.

"No, Zee," Casmir said. "Thank you, but Rache and I aren't confirmed enemies at this point. There's even the chance that we could become friends." He tried his affable smile on Rache, but he felt stupid smiling at someone wearing a black mask. "Do come with us to the cargo hold, though, Zee. The mercenaries may need you to move heavy things."

"We can move our own heavy things," the closest man behind them said.

"Where are you going to take the gate?" Casmir asked Rache as they walked into the corridor. He was genuinely curious, but he also figured that the more he learned, the more opportunity he might find to escape his current predicament.

"Out of this system," Rache said.

"And then? What will you do? Sell it? Keep it? Will you warn people that exposure to it can kill them within days?" Casmir pointed his thumb over his shoulder. "Did you warn your team that they were going to die?"

"Quiet, Dabrowski." As anticipated, Rache's hand moved up to the back of his neck for a warning squeeze. Somehow, it was at once more intimate and more terrifying than a weapon simply poking him in the back. "Does your mouth get you in trouble as much as I suspect it does?"

"It hasn't been a completely innocuous body part in my past, but you do make me nervous, so I babble." Casmir had hoped that Rache's men would scream and run away when they learned about their fate. Unfortunately, they hadn't reacted. They continued to march down the corridor after their leader. Maybe Casmir had been too subtle.

"Uh huh." Rache lowered his hand. "We don't need to be enemies, you know."

"Are you sure? You're commandeering my ship and my cargo. Being enemies seems right."

"*Your* ship and *your* cargo. How long have you even had it?"

"I acquired it roughly ten minutes before you showed up."

"So it has deep and sentimental value for you."

"It's more that I'm concerned about what you plan to do with it," Casmir said, struggling to fight down rising panic as they turned down the corridor that led to the cargo hold. He hadn't come up with a brilliant plan yet. Once they were inside, he would have to decide if he wanted to activate the robots and start a fight he couldn't win... or let Rache have his way. "Or who you plan to sell it to," he added.

"Anyone but Jager," Rache growled.

"That's unspecific enough to worry me."

"It's not a *weapon* that could be used to destroy people."

Aside from the fact that everyone who came in contact with it was dying...

"But it's potentially access to the rest of the galaxy," Casmir said. "Eventually. Once the scientists figure it out. That's opportunity and power. If you didn't agree, you wouldn't care if the king got it."

Rache stopped and looked at him, and the ten men and Zee also stopped. The entrance to the cargo hold was less than twenty-five meters away.

"Wait here," Rache told his men, then waved for Casmir to continue on with him.

At least he wasn't guiding Casmir by the scruff of the neck this time. Zee followed close on their heels. Rache glanced back but must have decided the crusher would be indifferent to whatever tête-à-tête they had. Casmir let himself feel a smidgen of hope when Rache turned his back on his men. What was he about to tell Casmir that he didn't want them to overhear?

"I was serious earlier when I said I could use a squad of those robots." Rache waved at Zee.

Casmir bit back a sarcastic comment. If Rache was about to make a concession or an offer, he had better keep his mouth shut, lest he irritate the man.

"I have a couple of good engineers, but I could always use more. I'm sure, even if it's not your area of expertise now, you could pick up ship systems easily enough."

It slowly occurred to him where Rache was going.

"Are you offering me a *job*?" Casmir asked.

Rache spread his hand. "And answers to questions you may have. I don't know everything, since I didn't even know you existed a month ago, but I think I know more about you than you do."

Casmir rocked back. The idea of a job working as a mercenary—a pirate and enemy of the Kingdom—was far more horrifying than it was appealing. But information. He *craved* that.

A couple of months ago, he would have said he'd long ago come to terms with not knowing who his real parents were or how he had come to be in foster care, and he would have meant it, but now? Now that someone wanted to kill him, either for who he was or something he might do the in future? Now he wanted to know. He *ached* to know. And it sounded like Rache could tell him.

But to say yes to him was to say goodbye to his job, his friends, his adoptive parents, and his life back home. If he sided with a criminal, an enemy to the king, he would never be able to walk freely on Odin again. And he would be choosing to act against a king he didn't even know beyond the sound bites that went out to the media. The problem was that, as far as he believed, Jager wasn't an ass. His government was stable, people had freedom to come and go as they wished. Only his stance on genetic engineering was restrictive to someone who loved science, but it wasn't as if Jager had put those policies in place. They had existed for centuries, the Kingdom's answer to some of the crazy and dangerous things that had happened elsewhere in the Twelve Systems.

"Dabrowski," Rache said, then softened his voice and switched to, "Casmir. I know it's not a simple decision to make, but if you're considering it, I need to know soon." He gazed at the door. "And I need to know if any booby traps are going to go off when I walk into that cargo hold."

Casmir realized the offer might be in earnest, but it was prompted by concern. Did Rache believe he had something up his sleeve? More than he truly did? Casmir felt honored to be considered such a clever and dangerous adversary, even if it seemed wholly unwarranted. Maybe Rache was basing his assumptions on himself, believing *he* would have put together a booby trap. Unfortunately, Casmir hadn't had time to do more than gather his robots.

"And if I decline the job offer?" Casmir asked.

"You're not even going to ask about salary and benefits?" Rache asked dryly.

"Do mercenaries get benefits? Paid vacation? A retirement plan?"

"Of course. We're not heathens. Though few survive long enough to retire."

"That shouldn't be part of your recruitment pitch."

"I'm an honest man."

"Are you?" Casmir squinted at him, wishing he could see Rache's face. All he had was his memory of what Rache looked like under the hood. He still didn't know why his genetic twin bothered to wear it. As far as Casmir knew, he—they—didn't look like anyone. "What were you going to do with the bioweapon?"

"Exactly what I did to it. Blow it up with the refinery. Admittedly, my ship wasn't supposed to be *attached* to the refinery when that happened." His tone grew a touch frosty.

"You paid fifty thousand crowns so you could blow it up and not get any use of it? You couldn't know at the time that Captain Lopez would return that money." Casmir realized he had only her word that she had done that. "She did, didn't she?"

"Yes, and your bounty also. Look, I'm sure you believe I'm a heinous villain, but I have my reasons for acting against Jager. God knows someone has to keep his schemes for retaking the Twelve Systems from finding root. I'm not…" Rache brought his open hand to his face and closed his fist. Tightly. "I wouldn't want to see a horrific weapon like that used on civilians. Kingdom or not. I have a hard time forgiving ignorance in people who ignore what's going on beyond the neighborhood they live in, but I wouldn't want them to die as pawns in some war."

Casmir hated to admit that *he'd* barely paid attention to what happened off campus and out of his narrow field of passion and expertise. He still didn't know much about what was going on in the systems beyond their gate, what truths were and weren't being conveyed by the media.

"You know he's using your crushers, right?" Rache asked.

Casmir gripped the wall. "What? Jager is?"

"In other systems, yes. I was offered a job by Stribog Station in System Augeas. To get rid of them and some Kingdom infiltrators."

Casmir stared at him. Was he telling the truth? That Jager was using the crushers against people in other systems?

"I didn't know, no." Casmir decided he would search the news for himself rather than taking Rache's word for it.

But what if Rache was telling the truth? He supposed, deep down, he'd always known it was a possibility that the military would use them for offense and not just defense, but he'd been told… He closed his eyes. Maybe he'd been naive to believe anything he'd been told.

"So you bought the bioweapon to get rid of it?" Casmir asked, turning the conversation back to that, not wanting to deal with his own mistakes, not until he'd researched Rache's claims and knew for certain that self-flagellation was in order.

"I bought it to get rid of it," Rache said. "Yes. And I put the bounty on your head so someone would bring you to my ship and get you away from whoever is trying to kill you."

Was it true? Was any of this true?

Casmir would like to believe that Rache wasn't pure evil, but he couldn't help but feel Rache was playing him, trying to win him over just as *he* might try to win someone else over. Because he thought Casmir had set some booby trap that might endanger his men.

"I don't suppose you know *that* information. Who's trying to kill me."

"Not that, no. What—" Rache lifted a finger and paused.

Receiving some communication from his ship? The thought reminded Casmir that Ishii and his colleagues were fighting Rache's big warship right now. As soon as the outcome of that battle was determined, Rache would be done chatting and would force the issue. One way or another.

Rache lowered his hand. "I need you to make a decision. Whether you're with me or against me. I can forgive the refinery—you were a prisoner doing your best to escape, and I would've done the same thing. But if you try to get me killed again, we're done."

Casmir closed his eyes. Logically, he knew it would be smart to play along with Rache, to save his ass today, even if he meant to escape at the first chance, but his sense of honor wouldn't let him.

"I cannot forgive *you*," he said slowly, his eyes focused on the wall past Rache's shoulder, "for knowingly screwing over my best friend by exposing her to that radiation. And for doing it to all of *them*." Casmir flung a hand toward the armored men waiting patiently—brainlessly— for their boss to finish. "You want to know what the end result is? Go up to the bridge and look at the people who died because they wanted to take this gate home. I'm sorry that King Jager did something to piss you off, and that maybe it ruined your life, but that doesn't give you the right to throw other people's lives away."

Casmir lifted his chin and made himself look into Rache's eyes—or where they would be if he could see them. He wished he could tear the mask off and force Rache to look back at him. But maybe this was better. Maybe it would be too eerie to have his own eyes looking back at him.

Several long seconds passed. Rache was still holding that rifle, and Casmir still didn't have his helmet up. If the man wanted to shoot him… he was fast enough to do it before Casmir could don the protection.

Rache grabbed Casmir by the front of the suit and pushed him against the wall opposite the door. He waved for his men to come over.

"Check the cargo hold. Make sure there aren't any booby traps and that the gate is in there." Rache tilted his helmet. "Lieutenant, you have the bridge secured yet? Report."

"Working on it, sir. Everything is locked down with passcodes. Dao Hu is trying to hack his way in."

"Understood. I'll be up shortly with someone who will tell you the passcodes." Rache stared at Casmir, who couldn't do much while he was pinned to the wall. He didn't even have his borrowed stunner anymore, not that it would have done any good against the fully armored Rache.

Casmir watched helplessly as the mercenaries stalked into the cargo hold. His chip was still logged in to the robots' network. Should he order them to attack? What would he be starting if he did? Or what would he be *ending*?

Rache was staring at him, not his men. Contemplating killing him? Or torturing him for the passcode to the ship's navigation computer?

"Uh, sir?" came an uncertain query from the cargo hold.

"What?" Rache grabbed Casmir's arm, his grip painful even through the protective layers of the galaxy suit, and pushed him into the cargo hold.

As they walked in, the door slid shut behind them, and the lights went out.

CHAPTER 16

YAS WOKE GROGGY AND CONFUSED TO THE SOUND of voices.

"…can't just stay in here and *die*."

"Breaking out of here isn't going to keep that from happening."

"At least we'd die on our feet."

"No, you'd die collapsed in a corridor, marinating in your own piss."

"I'm not going to piss myself as I die."

"You sure? I don't know about you, but I don't have the energy to pull my dick out of my pants right now."

"If you don't have your suit's piss sucker hooked up, that's your own fault."

"They took our armor off, you idiot."

"Oh, right. Shit. Where is it?"

Yas blinked slowly, gradually identifying the speakers as Corporals Gonzales and Chains. How fortunate that he was going to die in the company of such cultured and erudite individuals.

He touched his chest and found that he was indeed in nothing more than the wrinkled long-sleeved shirt and underwear he'd worn under his borrowed combat armor. The thin material lacked temperature-regulating capabilities, and the hard deck was cool under his back. He vaguely remembered people who hadn't identified themselves promising treatment and then, as he lost consciousness, dragging him onto a hover gurney. And into this unremarkable room. Better than being shoved out an airlock, he supposed.

"Doc." Corporal Chains shook his shoulder.

Yas groaned.

"If we can get out of here, can you fix us up? I feel like shit. I don't wanna die like this. Why couldn't Rache have taken us into battle somewhere if we had to die? This is godawful."

Yas tried to focus on the speaker and what he was saying, but his brain wasn't working at optimum.

"Doc?" Another shake.

"Sorry," Yas rasped. "If I could do anything, I would have. I'm sick too. Trust me. I—"

A soft hiss sounded, and the door opened. Chains lurched to his feet and whirled toward it.

"Back up," a woman said—Kim Sato. She still wore her galaxy suit, but without a helmet this time, and a dark braid of hair hung over her shoulder.

She stepped in, a rifle pointed at Chains's chest. Another man, the one who'd helped the female doctor knock them out, eased in beside her, a rifle also in hand. He didn't look like he knew how to use it. She did. Maybe she was simply better at faking it—Yas couldn't imagine that a bacteriologist spent a lot of time at the shooting range.

"I'm in need of lab rats," Kim said, "and you five are all I've got. Besides myself and my colleagues."

"You got another *cure*?" Chains growled. "Your people knocked us out last time. *That* one did." He thrust an accusing finger at her companion. He crouched, as if he might spring out the door.

Kim's eyes narrowed as her finger tightened on the trigger. Chains wasn't wearing any armor, and at that range, it wouldn't take an expert in marksmanship to hit him in the chest.

"I told them to," Kim said. "You killed Kingdom marines the last time you visited this ship, so we had to get you out of your armor and locked up. But here's the deal: Rache said he'd get me some decent coffee if I managed to save your lives, so I'm extremely motivated."

Her buddy glanced at her in surprise.

Yas thought it sounded like a joke, but it was hard to tell. She was deadpan.

"I've created a strain of bacteria that can eat the pseudo radiation swimming through your bloodstream right now. You need to get rid of it before your body can heal. Dr. Sikou is working on that part of the equation upstairs in the cryonics lab. This is Step One."

Yas pushed himself into a sitting position. "You honestly found an answer?"

He would have been inclined to trust her without question, but he shared Chains's feeling of betrayal from their interaction with the other doctors.

Kim nodded. "A way to slow down and maybe completely counteract the effects of the attack, yes."

"Attack?"

"Defensive measures may be the more accurate term. I'm not sure yet. Our engineers are going to have to build a special meter to even be able to see and measure this new type of radiation. If any archaeologists truly want to study that gate, they're going to have to do that first. Or find scientists who are the descendants of some centuries-old humans who were never inoculated against the Great Plague."

"Er, I think I missed something." Yas looked past Chains and Gonzalez to where Jess lay curled on her side, one of her legs twitching. She'd vomited while Yas had been out, and his fingers twitched in sympathy. The assassin, Chaplain, was behind her and either sleeping or unconscious. Hopefully not dead.

"I usually do," Gonzalez muttered, sitting against the wall and looking less inclined than Chains to jump up and cause trouble.

Yas frowned at Jess. "Will you check her?" he asked Kim. "Or let me do it? Vomiting hasn't typically been a symptom, has it?"

Kim shook her head. "Of typical acute radiation sickness, yes, but I haven't observed it so far with this."

Yas looked around, but he'd been too ill to worry about taking his medical kit off the shuttle, so he had nothing, not even a diagnostic scanner.

Chains shifted, maybe thinking of attacking again.

Kim jerked her rifle. "Go stand over there," she told him. "If you try anything, I will shoot you. Rache didn't stipulate that you *all* had to survive for me to get my coffee. He'd probably be happy even if all he got back was his doctor and engineer."

"What, combat specialists are disposable?" Chains glowered, but he backed away, moving past Yas and folding his arms over his chest as he leaned against a wall in the corner of the room.

"Combat specialists who kill Kingdom marines are," Kim said coolly.

He curled his lip but didn't object further.

"There's coffee in the mess hall two levels up," the man with her murmured.

"Coffee or coffee *bulbs*?" Kim tilted her head for him to go check on Jess. "They are not synonymous."

"Uh, coffee in little boxes that you can heat up."

"That's primitive. I can't believe people willingly live in space."

Jess groaned, and Yas willed them to stop the banter and help her. But the man also didn't have a medical kit with him. Was he even a doctor?

"Dr. Peshlakai." Kim slipped her hand into her pocket while keeping an eye on Chains. "I've already injected myself—about a half hour ago—so you would be lab rat Number Two. If you're willing." She withdrew a jet injector and five vials.

"That's the new bacteria you made?" Yas held out his open hands, not trusting his legs to hold him if he attempted to stand.

"Yes. Inject yourself and any of your people who are willing. I think it's the only way you'll survive. We all got exposed to a lot more of the pseudo radiation down at the wreck site than the crew did here when the archaeology team brought back a piece of the gate. And none of them made it, except for those who had some warning and quarantined themselves before the gate piece arrived."

"Everyone on the ship should have done that."

"I agree." Kim walked over and laid the injector and vials on Yas's palm while continuing to keep the rifle pointed at Chains.

Yas held up a hand toward Chains, just in case he still had notions of escape in mind. They could escape *after* they were better.

"When will the Kingdom ships be here?" Gonzalez asked.

Kim looked at him, her brow creasing.

"Someone must be on the way by now," he said. "It's been, what, three days since we kidnapped you?"

"Maybe so," Kim said, "but there's a lot of craziness happening at the gate. Rache and all those warships headed that way."

"Still, your Fleet isn't going to forget about a ship full of scientists in trouble for long." Gonzales exchanged a long look with Chains, who nodded slightly.

"The Fleet is busy right now." Kim backed to the doorway, where she could easily keep both of them in sight. "You should rest your bodies. It'll take time for the bacteria to multiply, and that's only Step One, as I said. Dr. Sikou is working on a way to reverse the internal damage."

"Cryonics treatment *should* work," Yas said. "I know the anti-aging spas use something based off that technology. A lot of their stuff is hokum, but that obviously works to revive frozen corpses and turn back time for them. We're not even frozen, so it should be easier." Yas smiled, feeling encouraged. He hadn't considered cryonics treatment, but it made sense now that she'd brought it up, especially if her bacteria scoured any lingering radiation out of the body.

"So I'm hoping," Kim said.

Jess moaned again, her eyes squeezed tightly closed.

The healer in Yas wanted to go over and comfort her—to *do* something for her. If only he had the strength.

"Her pulse is fast," the man said, "dilated pupils, tremor. These aren't symptoms of the radiation."

Yas almost slapped himself in the forehead as realization struck. "Damn it."

The doctor looked toward him.

"I don't suppose you have any trylochanix?" Yas asked. "I suspect she has an addiction, and I want to help her switch to something else, but this isn't the best time for her to have to deal with withdrawal symptoms. On top of everything else."

"You give your patients trylochanix?" the man asked, frowning deeply, his eyes full of judgment.

Yas clenched his jaw. "Their previous doctor did, or she got it herself. I don't know. I didn't sign up for this damn job. I was coerced by threat of death."

"Rache has an interesting method of recruiting people," Kim told her colleague.

"Not everybody can be won over by coffee," Yas said. "Will you find her something? Please?"

The male doctor shook his head, but Kim said, "I'll see what's in the sickbay cabinets."

"Thank you," Yas said.

Jess could wean herself off the drug later, when she wasn't dealing with another health crisis.

They backed out of the room, and a thunk sounded as a heavy lock was thrown.

Yas injected himself, then inoculated Chains, Gonzalez, and Chaplain without asking if they agreed to being lab rats. If the alternative was death, what did it matter?

Lastly, he pulled himself to Jess's side on his hands and knees. "I'm sorry, Chief." He rested a hand on her shoulder, then touched her cheek, where sweat glistened on her dark skin. "I'm sure you're miserable."

"You're not miserable?" Gonzalez asked.

"Probably not as miserable as Jess—Chief Khonsari."

"I wouldn't bet on it," Gonzalez muttered.

Yas used the last vial on Jess, hoping the bacteria wouldn't make her feel any worse as they worked.

She groaned but didn't open her eyes or otherwise respond. Yas leaned against the wall, hoping Kim would be able to find some of the medication. And wondering if he would be able to talk Jess into weaning herself off it after this.

If they survived and if they didn't all end up in a Fleet prison somewhere. Yas assumed that would be his fate, the same as the other mercenaries, if the military showed up. His fate might even be worse. What if he was extradited back to Tiamat Station, where the authorities were *still* in the mood to kill him rather than give him a fair trial?

Something slammed into Rache, knocking him away from Casmir.

In the darkness that had fallen over the cargo hold, Casmir had no idea what had happened, but he welcomed his chance to escape and scrambled farther away from Rache. Weapons fired. What the hell? He hadn't ordered the robots to attack yet.

A crimson bolt struck the wall inches above his head. Casmir dove for the hulking segments of the gate, for their protective cover. He tapped his chest controls, and his helmet unfurled and *clicked* into place. It gave him a semblance of night vision, and he glimpsed Rache's armored men whirling and trying to find a target. A dark figure pushed away from Rache, sprang to the top of one of the gate pieces, and ran out of sight, chased by energy bolts. A cloak flapped behind him, one bolt scouring a hole through it.

Casmir shook his head. He didn't understand what he was doing here, but unless some other knight had sneaked aboard, it had to be Asger. And all of Rache's men gave chase.

Attack! Casmir silently ordered the robots through his interface with their network. *The men in black combat armor,* he added, hoping they could differentiate between Rache's mercenaries and him and Asger.

He scooted back into a narrow aisle between long gate pieces stacked two high and crouched down as the robots streamed out, firing at the armored men. A cacophony of noise rang from the walls, and Casmir winced at the assault on his ears. But better than an assault on his body.

Zee stood behind him, ready to defend him. Even though it felt cowardly, Casmir kept himself behind cover. There was nothing he could do against those men. He had to let his suborned robots fight his battle for him. Which was easier than he could have hoped—they had been programmed to defend the ship, and they did, attacking the mercenaries with more coordination than Casmir could have managed if he'd been manipulating them one by one.

The fight raged out in the open, between the stacks of gate pieces and the door. The mercenaries, accustomed to their armor protecting them, weren't quick to duck for cover. Casmir had no idea where Asger had gone. He also had no idea where Rache had gone, and that worried him. Would his twin see this as a betrayal, the very booby trap he'd suspected, and take the opportunity to kill Casmir?

The robots crashed into the men, a tide of machinery slamming to the deck. Unfortunately, the mercenaries crashed back. Casmir winced as one of his new allies was hurled against a wall so hard that one of its limbs flew off.

Nearby, a crunch sounded, and someone screamed.

"It's a knight!" a man shouted. "He's got a halberd."

"Comms only," someone barked, which Casmir took to be an order not to shout anything else, to communicate quietly over their helmet speakers.

The doors opened, and the mercenaries Rache had sent to the bridge flooded in, joining their comrades.

Casmir cursed under his breath. Even with Asger helping, the odds were against their side.

Something clattered across the deck and skidded toward him. The stunner. He almost laughed. The mercenary who'd snatched it from his tool satchel must not have had a secure place to put it, and it had fallen out of some pocket or pouch in the fight.

Casmir grabbed it. Unfortunately, there was still nobody he could use it effectively on.

He backed farther down the aisle between lengths of gate pieces stacked atop each other and pulled up a schematic for the ship. Was there anything built into the hold that he could use? The lights were still off—he assumed Asger had done that to create confusion and surprise—but with his helmet on, he had night vision, and it was clear the mercenaries did too. Maybe he could key into the mainframe from here and do something that would make more of a difference. Like stopping the ship's spin? Would suddenly having to fight in zero gravity convey an advantage to his side? No, it would change the situation but affect both sides equally.

There was an environmental-controls access panel in the back of the room. Not sure yet how he would use it, Casmir turned, slipped past Zee, and jogged toward it. Once again, he hoped inspiration would come along the way.

As the access panel came into view, a thunderous scrape sounded above Casmir and to the right. He skittered to the left, his shoulder bumping against the stacked gate pieces. The top gate piece on the right shifted off the pile and toward him.

He squawked and sprinted for the end of the aisle. That thing had to weigh tons. It would crush him.

It fell before he reached the end, and he flattened himself against the other stack, praying the aisle was wider than it looked.

It wasn't, and the piece blocked out the light as it fell, but it halted an inch from smashing onto his helmet. Zee had dropped into a low squat, his arms overhead, holding up the gate.

"Escape, Casmir Dabrowski," Zee ordered.

Casmir gave him a thumbs-up and sprinted out of the shadow of the massive slab. He dove as he exited the aisle, certain that had been a trap meant to kill him or drive him from hiding—or simply occupy Zee.

He was right. Rache was waiting.

He swung a rifle butt at Casmir's head, but he hadn't anticipated the dive. Casmir flew under the swing. There wasn't room to roll or stop himself in a competent manner. He slammed into the back wall of the cargo hold. His suit and helmet insulated him somewhat, but it still took him a split second before he could think to jump to his feet and get out of the way. A split second too long.

Rache gripped him from behind, grabbed the top of his helmet, and supposedly impervious Glasnax crunched in Casmir's ears. He threw an elbow backward, wishing he'd spent more time sparring with Kim. Even if he had connected—he didn't—it wouldn't have mattered, not with his assailant in armor.

Rache broke his helmet and ripped it back, exposing Casmir's face and neck. Terror coursed through his veins as Rache spun him around, slamming his back against the wall. He'd missed his opportunity, said he wouldn't work with Rache, and now Rache—his twin brother—was going to kill him.

Rache ripped the stunner from Casmir's grip and pressed the cool muzzle of a DEW-Tek pistol against his temple. Casmir begged his brain to stay calm, as he doubted Rache would bother keeping him alive again if he had a seizure in his arms. At least he hadn't strobed some light in Casmir's eyes. No, he wanted something.

"What's the passcode for navigation?" Rache demanded, the cacophony of the battle raging on the other side of the cargo hold almost drowning out his words.

Was Asger still in the fray? Dare Casmir hope the knight could somehow help his robots win the day? Was there any point in delaying giving in? Would Rache kill him as soon as he *did* give in?

Casmir licked his lips, tasting the sweat on them. "It's long. Numbers, letters, symbols. Would you like to get out a piece of paper and a pen?"

"Just say it, you ass. I've got a—"

Rache broke off, jammed the stunner into his armor's utility belt, and spun around as a shadow dove toward him. Asger.

The knight's halberd swung at Rache's head, but Rache sprang to the side. The ends of the gate pieces hemmed him in, but he contorted and leaped with uncanny agility, avoiding the weapon and Asger.

Casmir scurried sideways along the wall to get out of their way. Rache glanced at him, keeping tabs on him no doubt, but was forced to deal with this new threat. Asger was almost a foot taller and bigger of arm and broader of shoulder, but whatever implants Rache had, they let him move faster than any human being should.

He was a match for Asger, not simply avoiding him and dodging the swipes and stabs from the deadly pertundo, but rushing in and driving Asger backward as he fired a stream of bolts at Asger's chest plate. The energy attacks bounced off, but Rache came in behind them, lunging and grappling with the knight.

The stunner slipped from his utility belt and clattered to the deck. Neither man noticed. Asger heaved his foe away, but Rache sprang back in, launching a side kick that caught Asger in the hip.

The force spun the knight, and Rache grabbed him from behind, smashing him into the wall, much as he'd done Casmir.

Where was Zee? If Casmir could get both of his allies fighting Rache…

That gate piece was still in the air, still being kept from crashing down. Casmir scooted back to peer down the aisle, ready to order Zee to release it and come help.

Zee was indeed still holding it aloft, now with one hand, but two mercenaries faced him. They fired rifles at his torso. Most of the energy bolts were deflected, but Zee's mercurial facade had numerous dents in it. He was too busy holding up the gate to focus on repairing himself. More than that, he was blocking those mercenaries from getting through and attacking Casmir. Was that why he was standing there like a boulder?

"Zee," Casmir called softly, hoping his crusher would hear but the mercenaries wouldn't. "Scoot back here. If you drop it, and you're fast enough, they'll be flattened."

Rache punched Asger with the power of a mechanical battering ram, and Asger flew through the air right in front of Casmir. Asger's hand banged against one of the gate ends, and his halberd clattered to the deck.

Casmir sucked in his belly and pressed his back to the wall as Rache blurred past, throwing himself after his foe. Too late, he wished he'd stuck out his foot to impede Rache, but with the power and momentum those two were employing in their battle, his leg might have been ripped off.

Asger. Casmir risked sending a chip-to-chip message, hoping it wouldn't distract his ally at a crucial moment. *Back him up to the end of the aisle here. Right in front of me. Zee will help.*

Before Asger could reply or react, Zee sprang out of the aisle.

He no longer held up the gate piece, and it clattered down hard enough to make the deck shake. The shouts of men trapped under it echoed through the chamber. Casmir hoped they were still alive, protected by their armor, but also that they were out of the fight. He didn't ever want to be responsible for people's deaths, and he'd already given Rache enough reasons to detest him.

When Rache glanced back at the dropped gate piece and the appearance of Zee, Asger had the opportunity to spring to his feet. He snatched up his halberd and swung it at the back of Rache's head.

Either through instinct or a helmet camera, Rache saw the blow coming and ducked—almost.

Zee lunged toward him and grabbed his arms, arresting his movement. The halberd sliced through the top of Rache's helmet, lightning flaring as it sheared off a piece.

Casmir sucked in a scared breath. From his position, he couldn't tell how much had been sheared off—and if part of Rache's skull had gone along with it.

Zee, still gripping Rache by the arms, lifted him several inches off the deck, as if to hold him so Asger could strike again.

Rache coiled his legs into a tight ball, then shifted in Zee's grip and pounded his heels into his captor's chest. Even the strong crusher couldn't keep from reacting to the force. Zee stumbled back, one hand slipping from Rache's arm.

Asger readied his halberd for another swing and rushed in. Somehow, Rache twisted in the air while his other arm was still stuck in Zee's grip, and he kicked backward, catching Asger in the chest. Asger staggered back, but he set his jaw with determination and kept his footing. He lowered his weapon to use it like a lance, to ram it through Rache's spine.

Casmir, his back to the wall as this unfolded in front of him, realized that as good as Rache was, he wasn't going to come out on top, not unless more of his men figured out where he was and got back to help him. Judging by the buzz of fire and the battle shouts from the other side of the hold, they were still busy with the robots.

Rache twisted in the air again, almost evading Asger's attempt to ram the long point of his halberd straight through him. The weapon clipped the side of Rache's armor, and white lightning branched from its tip, engulfing him.

Rache screamed in pain, startling Casmir. Then he realized why. His helmet had been breached, so he wasn't fully protected any longer.

That ought to mean…

Casmir lunged away from the wall, grabbed the stunner off the deck, and fired at Rache's head. He didn't have the right angle to shoot into the hole in the helmet, but the nimbus must have been enough to catch him. Rache went limp in Zee's grip.

Asger had stepped back to ready himself for another attack, and he roared in glee and lowered the tip of his halberd for another stab.

"Wait!" Casmir lunged forward, raising his hands.

Thank his imperturbable ancestors, Asger paused.

"*What?*" he demanded.

"Drop him, please, Zee." Casmir stepped between Asger and Rache, not trusting Asger's battle fury to not get the best of him—or simply his desire to see the infamous pirate dead at his feet. "He's stunned," Casmir added for Asger's sake.

Zee released Rache, and he flopped lifelessly to the deck, his armor clunking down hard. Casmir peered through his faceplate to make sure he truly was stunned, but his mask was still on, hiding his eyes. Casmir had to trust that Rache wouldn't be lying on the deck in front of enemies if he was conscious.

"Sounds like an excellent time to finish him off," Asger said.

"Isn't there some knight-chivalry thing about not beating up on helpless opponents?" Casmir asked.

"Chivalry means I open doors for ladies. It doesn't mean I let heinous enemies of the crown survive to harass—to *slay*—our people another day." Asger loomed above Casmir, his grip tight on the shaft of his halberd. Would he simply pick up Casmir and set him aside so he could finish off their enemy?

Casmir waved Zee forward. "I need you two to help the robots with the rest of the mercenaries. I'm not convinced our side is winning. I'll keep an eye on Rache." Casmir waved the stunner.

"Or," Asger said, "we could kill him now and then go defeat the mercenaries, who will be like headless chickens with their leader dead."

"You're not killing him." Casmir, realizing he had no right to give orders to a knight, groped for a way to convince him. "I have a plan. Please, Asger. I'll explain it as soon as we're sure we have the ship secured. I want the mercs knocked out and stripped out of their armor." He looked at Zee.

The crusher nodded, sprang atop the nearest stack of gate pieces, and strode toward the front of the hold.

Asger scowled, but all he said was, "Don't take your eyes off him, and don't hesitate to shoot him again."

"I won't. Thank you." As Asger strode away, Casmir added, "And thank you for disobeying my wishes and staying behind to help."

Asger waved his halberd but didn't look back.

Casmir looked down at the brother he'd never known about, dozens of thoughts and feelings tangling up in his brain. The idea of killing Rache, or letting one of his allies kill him, repulsed him. As he'd just admitted, he didn't want anybody to be killed because of him, but the thought of ending someone who had the exact same DNA as he did was even more unappealing.

The problem was that Rache would keep coming after Casmir as long as he had the gate, the gate that Rache had been willing to sacrifice so many people to get. To keep *Jager* from getting it, he said. Casmir had no idea if that was the truth. He had no trouble believing that Rache hated Jager, but what of his own personal ambitions? Maybe he dreamed of having power over and controlling more than a mercenary ship, and he saw the gate as a way to do that.

The obvious solution was to hand the gate over to Captain Ishii and the Kingdom military officers, ideally in a way that Rache would believe he'd had no choice. That ought to keep him from fantasizing about avenging himself on Casmir. Which he might after this. After having Casmir get the best of him—or at least escape his clutches—two times.

Though Casmir had to wonder if his ability to execute those escapes represented a similar ambivalence from Rache. After all, Rache had admitted he'd posted that bounty and had Casmir brought to him out of curiosity. Maybe deep down, he didn't want to kill Casmir either.

Unfortunately, depending on what Casmir did next, that might change. And Casmir regretted that.

He'd been raised as an only child, and he'd occasionally wondered what it would be like to have siblings. He hadn't imagined a twin, but more an older brother who might have been young enough to chum around with but old enough and big enough to protect him from bullies at school. Someone who would have been a friend, even if Casmir was a big doofus and they had nothing in common, because that was what blood meant, wasn't it? An automatic tie. His parents were wonderful, but he'd often felt alone as a boy and longed for more ties with others of his age.

"What did you long for as a child, I wonder?" Casmir murmured. "And what did you have? More than I did? Less?" It was hard to imagine someone with Rache's bitterness having grown up in a normal loving family. Something had to have shaped him into a killer.

Casmir crouched beside him, careful to keep his stunner ready, and fumbled for access to remove the rest of Rache's helmet and check to see if there had been a head injury. The helmet broke in two, the Glasnax having lost its semi-fluid folding ability. Casmir pushed the pieces to the sides. He was tempted to take off Rache's mask so he could tell when he woke up and his eyes were open, but then he would have to explain to Asger why there were two identical faces looking at him.

Unless Asger already knew? He knew *something*.

And so did Rache. If he'd had the medical resources, Casmir would have been tempted to try Ishii's truth-telling drugs on him. Though it was possible Rache had the same food and drug allergies Casmir had. Maybe. That seemed a deficiency of the immune system, something that might have been fixed when Rache was gene-cleaned as a baby, or something his subsequent genetic and cybernetic tinkering might have addressed.

A wrenching sound came from the front of the cargo hold, and Casmir jumped. It had grown silent save for that noise.

"Asger?" Casmir checked the network to get a status report on the robots. Only three of his machine allies remained upright and intact. The others were damaged, many missing limbs, and some were so broken that they no longer registered on the network.

"I'm prying mercenaries out of their armor," Asger called back. "While your crusher stomps on them to keep them from moving. For the record, this isn't the approved use of a knight's mighty pertundo."

"No? Perhaps if you sent me the schematics that explain how exactly that blade pierces combat armor, I could come up with a more appropriate tool for the job."

"You'd have to talk to Weaponssmith Ariyoshi in the castle. He's the keeper of that secret."

"If you can get me into the castle, I'll certainly accept the invitation."

Another wrenching sound was his only response. Too bad. A few months ago, Casmir had never dreamed of going to the castle or cared much about talking to the king or anyone in government, but now that he had this gate, he felt obligated to make sure it didn't fall into dubious hands. He found he wanted to know more about what the king and the Senate were up to. He feared he might regret it if he handed the gate over to the military without knowing more about why they wanted it.

He *already* regretted helping to invent the crushers. He thought again of Rache's words about them being used on people in another system and shook his head.

"I need time to think. And to research that incident." Casmir rose to his feet, a plan percolating through his mind. It was one that would most surely get him into trouble—*more* trouble—but maybe he could make things turn out for the best in the end. Maybe he could even leverage the gate to force government leaders to work harder to get along with each other. "Zee, will you come back here, please? I need a hand."

Casmir searched the schematics he still had up for the ship and located two emergency escape pods that could be launched. They were more akin to lifeboats than shuttles and wouldn't get the occupants very far. But Casmir needed Rache's shuttle for his plan. He would leave it somewhere the mercenaries could find it later and hope, perhaps vainly, that Rache wouldn't hold a grudge for all of this.

Zee strode into view, and Casmir pointed at Rache. "Lift him, please. He and all of his men are going into the escape pods."

Wordlessly, Zee hoisted Rache over his head. Casmir followed with the stunner in case he woke up. Sometime very soon, he needed to figure out the last part of his plan, how he was going to hide this ship without anyone seeing where. That was going to be hard with Asger standing at his side, Asger who was loyal to the king and could tell Jager everything he knew.

CHAPTER 17

KIM DIDN'T WANT TO GIVE IN TO SLEEP, but she finally collapsed on a cot in the lab, unable to continue to function. She had lost all track of time, but she'd barely slept—mostly by dozing off while standing up— since Rache had kidnapped her. No, since she'd volunteered to leave the *Stellar Dragon.* Three days ago? No wonder she was exhausted.

Despite that, she dozed fitfully, waking often with a start and glancing at the computers she'd left running, their displays illuminating the dim room. They were monitoring the multiplication of her bacteria. She kept dreaming that they ran out of food and died or that someone opened an airlock and all her work was blown through the corridors of the ship and out into space.

More than once, she dropped her hand to the deck next to the cot, making sure the rifle was still there. She and Angelico had left the mercenaries locked in that room, but something kept niggling at her weary subconscious. A certainty that they still represented a threat. She'd given them the bacteria, and they might start to feel better soon, if only nominally better until the other treatments were implemented. But good enough that they might be able to conjure up a plan, a way to escape. And she doubted they could accomplish that without hurting people as they fled. They certainly hadn't managed to kidnap *her* without doing that.

But no, they were locked in that room, and she'd made sure they didn't have any weapons or keys or—

Her eyes flew open as if someone had dumped a bucket of ice water on her face. They didn't *need* keys. She remembered Rache's muscled chest and forearms. *Enhanced* muscles. Idiot, she'd forgotten. Half of those mercenaries had some cybernetic enhancements or another. That meant—

A faint rustling sounded in the corridor outside. Kim lay on her back on the cot, but she eased off it and grabbed her rifle.

She slipped into the nearest corner where she wasn't visible from the threshold and further hid behind lab coats hanging on hooks. Soft seconds passed in the dim room, the only light a green digital counter on the computer display, updating the amount of bacteria in the dishes.

Maybe she hadn't heard anything. Or maybe one of the doctors was up and working.

Someone silently stepped into the doorway, the brighter light of the corridor sending a shadow across the deck. Kim didn't think it was Angelico or Sikou. There shouldn't have been anyone else out of quarantine—or that locked room.

She lifted the rifle, pressing the butt into the hollow of her shoulder. Most of her familiarity with firearms came from learning how to disarm someone carrying a prop version, but she'd taken enough of her brother's kyudo classes to be practiced at hitting a target. She was confident that if she could do it with a bow, she could do it with a rifle.

Her brother's voice floated through her mind, and she could see him out behind the dojo, sun shining on his short black hair as he taught, sharing one of his favorite quotations from an ancient Earth sensei. "When shooting, sometimes we will hit the target but miss the self."

Another time, she would have happily pondered the philosophical connotations of the line, but now, she willed her mind to empty, to push away the homesickness that plucked at her soul.

The figure stepped into the room, large, broad, and muscled. And armed.

The mercenary must have roamed the ship until he'd found some weapons.

Kim's finger tightened on the trigger, but she hesitated to fire, to use deadly force. She wished she'd found a stunner among the fallen weapons. She lowered her aim to the big man's thigh.

He looked around, and she held her breath, waiting. He'd broken out of his room and armed himself, so she was inclined to mistrust him, but what if he'd come looking for medicine or just wanted to speak with her for some reason?

A few days ago, she would have shot first and asked questions later, but uncertainty turned her to a statue. This was one of Rache's men, and that made him... she wasn't sure. Still an enemy, but she'd implied she would try to help his people, not kill them. And he'd promised a favor if she succeeded.

But they'd killed Kingdom marines. If she sided with them, she sided by default against her government.

His gaze lingered on the cot. She was fairly certain this was Corporal Chains. He didn't seem to see her. The men hadn't found their armor, so he was relying only on his eyes. Eyes that didn't have a night-vision enhancement, or he surely would have picked her out among the coats.

He must have decided the lab was empty because he walked across it to the counter. He reached toward the petri dishes. To *steal* one?

"Stop, and drop your weapon," Kim demanded. She meant for the words to come out with calm authority but heard the alarm in them and winced.

He whirled toward her, his weapon rising instead of lowering. She fired at her target—his thigh—and dropped into a low crouch. He returned fire, a crimson bolt streaking into the wall above her head. Shards of paneling flew, raining down on her.

She fired again, not worrying about aiming for a nonlethal target this time, then lunged behind the cot.

He grunted—with pain? She couldn't tell, but he swung his rifle toward her again.

The cot was flimsy and didn't provide proper cover. She kicked it across the room at him, then fired again. This time, she saw her bolt catch him in the shoulder.

Instead of continuing to fire from the open, he sprinted out the door, limping slightly but still running fast. Too fast. She fired again, but her bolt only slammed into the jamb. He was already gone.

Kim lunged to her feet, leaped over the cot, and paused to check the dishes before pursuing him. Two were missing. She had more, but those had been farthest along and had grown the most of the bacteria she needed to inoculate the quarantine crew—and anyone else who came in contact with the ancient technology.

She growled and rushed for the doorway but made herself halt on the threshold, envisioning men waiting in the corridor, ready to shoot.

But her quick glance revealed that it was empty. Thundering footsteps rang out in the distance. The corporal.

She ran after him. Unless Rache had shown back up with his shuttles, the mercenaries didn't have anywhere to go. Or did they? There were shuttles in the bay here. She remembered from her stultifying perusal of the ship's camera footage.

She ran in that direction and made it to a bank of lifts, not in time to see the mercenary run into one, but an indicator showed it descending to the lower decks. To the shuttle bay.

A few blood droplets spattered the deck in front of the doors. She'd hurt him. That might make him more likely to hurt her back.

Too bad. She was *not* going to let him steal half her work, work that the people here needed.

Kim gritted her teeth and slammed a button for another lift to come, then flung herself into it. It descended with tedious slowness, and she waited behind cover as the doors opened, again afraid the mercenaries would be lying in wait to stop pursuit.

More blood droplets dotted the deck, a trail of them, but nobody waited. She raced for the shuttle bay even as she wondered if she should let the man go. Let all of them go. If he hadn't stolen half of her bacteria, she wouldn't be chasing him. Why did the mercenaries even want the dishes? She'd already given them each a dose. It was possible they would need more, but they ought to multiply in their bodies without need of more shots.

But did they know that? She hadn't told them.

When she reached the bay door, it was locked. She peered through a porthole in time to see one mercenary help another through an open hatch and into a shuttle. Dr. Peshlakai and Chief Khonsari, her arm slung around his shoulders, stumbled toward the compact vessel with the corporal trying to urge them along more quickly.

Kim stepped back, tempted to fire at the control pad by the door, but she slapped her palm to the reader, hoping to get lucky. Surprisingly, the door hissed open. Sikou must have added their team to the ship's security database.

The corporal in the rear spun toward her, and she fired preemptively this time. Nobody had a stunner. These lunatics would kill her if she got in their way.

Her bolt slammed into his leg. Just as he returned fire, Yas knocked his arm aside.

"Get in the shuttle," he ordered. "Fire it up."

The mercenary hesitated, glancing from Yas to Kim.

"Do it, Corporal," Jess whispered, her dark skin pale, though she looked better than she had.

Kim had brought her that medication. Had it been a mistake?

"You're not leaving with my bacteria," Kim said, noticing that Yas held the containers.

Had he been the one to send the mercenary for them? Or had the corporal simply thought they needed the bacteria?

"You don't need more doses, and you're not giving that *man* samples of my work," Kim said.

Yas licked his lips. "He was going after the people who took the gate."

"That means more of our people will have been exposed by now," Jess said.

"Because he's an *asshole*," Kim said, frustration welling inside of her.

She didn't want people to die when she had something that could save them, but damn it, they could come here if they wanted to be healed. Shouldn't they have to turn themselves in to be treated? And to accept the consequences of the lives they'd chosen? They *deserved* to be locked in prison cells.

The corporal was watching Kim, his body a statue, his weapon pointed toward the deck at her feet, not at her chest. Abruptly, he shifted it, and she almost fired at him. But she wasn't his target. He fired at a spot high on the wall above the door. The shuttle bay security camera. His aim was accurate, and the small dome on the wall melted.

Kim scowled. What was *that* supposed to change? Did they think she would let them go as long as there were no witnesses?

"I can see why you would think that," Jess said slowly. "He's not the most lovable man, but he helped me out, and he saved Dr. Peshlakai's life."

"Yeah, I heard about that winning bargain. We call that indentured servitude in the Kingdom."

"It's better than being dead. And asking for something in trade seems fair when you're putting your life at risk and getting yourself marked a criminal in a habitat."

Yas's lips thinned, but he didn't shake his head in disagreement.

"I won't argue that he's a good man or that he doesn't have a chip the size of the Great Wall of Andovia on his shoulder, but *we're* just soldiers." Jess waved at the corporal and at herself. "Are you going to punish us for that? For following our captain's orders?"

"A lot of evil has been done throughout history by soldiers who were just following orders," Kim said.

"And what about scientists working for totalitarian regimes?"

"The Star Kingdom is not a totalitarian regime," Kim snapped, annoyed that they were standing at gunpoint and having this conversation. Another time, she would have willingly debated the various political structures in the Twelve Systems, but she was exhausted and tired of this whole situation. "The king can't pass any laws without majority approval from the Senate, and citizens of the Kingdom are free to come and go as they please, so long as they obey the bioengineering mandates. I don't claim to know what's going on in the rest of the systems right now, but I'm sure it's not anything simple or propagated by one man. And for the record, I work for a private corporation with headquarters in three different systems. We make sure anyone who wants our work has access to it. It's not even expensive, not like something out of Sayona Station or the Sun Asteroids Habitats."

Jess slumped against Yas and sighed with weariness.

At first, Kim thought she was being theatrical, but she remembered Jess was dealing with even more than the radiation sickness, and she felt bad for bristling and spewing defensive words.

"We're not bad people," Jess whispered. "Sometimes, the universe just gets screwed up, and you end up losing everything. Everyone."

Her eyes were so bleak and haunted. And Kim couldn't muster the energy to argue further.

She lowered her rifle. "Just take it, and get out of here."

Yas murmured something to the corporal, and he slung his rifle over his shoulder and took Jess, guiding her into the shuttle. Leaving Yas facing Kim, no weapons in his hands, only the stolen petri dishes.

It crossed her mind that she could probably wrestle him to the deck and take them, but a wave of weariness washed over her, and she only shook her head. She didn't agree with anything Rache was doing, but Jess's point that Rache's soldiers were just following orders and didn't deserve to die from this poison rang in her mind. Kim didn't think *she* was wrong, but she didn't think Jess was entirely wrong either. One probably had to get shit on a lot in life before ending up soldiering on some mercenary ship, and Jess likely wasn't the only one for whom it had been a job of last resort.

"Thank you, Scholar Sato," Yas said quietly.

She bowed and tried not to make the gesture grudging. Yas wasn't who she was angry with.

Rache's masked face floated through her mind, and she silently growled at it, willing it to go away. But her brain wasn't in the mood to comply. She blamed her weariness. Sometime soon, she hoped to sleep for a full day and night. Or three.

The shuttle engines rumbled to life, but the hatch was still open, and Yas was still looking at her.

"You're still here," Kim observed.

"Yes." Yas looked to the open hatch, then back to her. "I have no love for Rache, even though Jess is right. He saved my life, but as you pointed out, demanded five years in exchange for it. Five years of serving as a doctor to people who make a habit of slaying other people."

"So don't go back."

"I am tempted." He looked from the shuttle to her again, his gaze wistful. "But I did give my word, however desperate I was at that moment, and even though my life has fallen apart, I can't bring myself to go back on it. When everything else is lost, honor may still remain, eh? Someone long dead said that, I believe."

"Yes, Dr. Kensington Sage. But he was writing about how cultures of honor often develop in regions without central authority, which leads to increased brutality and homicide rates due to a tendency to answer insults and transgressions with violence. His quote is almost always used out of context."

Yas chuckled. "I believe quotations are frequently uttered based on the needs of the speaker rather than the intent of the source. For myself... I believe I will do as Jess suggested."

Kim had no idea what that was, but Yas nodded, as if he'd made a decision.

"Rache will probably never thank you for saving the lives of his men, but I will thank you. For them and for myself."

"You won't be in the clear from the bacteria alone." She waved at the dishes. "You'll have to take everyone who was exposed to a cryonics lab and get the cellular damage reversed. Otherwise, you'll all have significantly reduced lifespans."

"I understand. I will make sure Rache knows." Yas lifted a hand in parting and climbed into the shuttle.

Kim shuffled back to her lab, wondering when her colleagues would figure out that the mercenaries had escaped. And wondering what she would say.

Casmir exhaled a sigh of relief when the two escape pods shot away from the cargo ship. He'd tranquilized Rache and his men before having the robots dump them inside, so they shouldn't wake up for a couple of hours. He hoped that would be far too late for them to find him. The cargo ship had been underway for a while, but he'd changed the course again, and he would do so one more time once he knew Asger wasn't paying attention.

For now, Casmir sat on the bridge with tools purloined from engineering, and he was repairing some of the least damaged robots while Zee stood guard over him. He expected Asger any moment and had a medical kit waiting nearby, his stomach twisting and knotting as he prepared to lie to a man who'd risked his life to help him.

More than that. Asger must have believed he was giving up his life when he'd chosen to stay, further exposing himself. It was only a matter of time before the effects of the gate touched him—and Casmir still wasn't positive they wouldn't touch *him*, that he would share Rache's unprecedented immunity. He was sure Rache's men didn't, and, knowing he was eventually going to rendezvous with Kim in Skadi Moon's orbit, he'd felt bad about booting the mercenaries from the ship. But if she found a cure, Rache could negotiate with her himself on his men's behalf. He owed her, and he could damn well grovel, if that was what Kim wanted. And if Rache was willing to do so on his people's behalf.

The door slid open, and Asger walked up to where Casmir sat cross-legged on the deck between the captain's seat and the navigation station, disassembled robots all around him.

"Are you reconstructing your army?" Asger sank into the command chair with a weary groan. He was still wearing his dented and charred combat armor, but he'd removed the helmet, and his long hair hung limply about his shoulders. He let his head flop back against the seat.

"Just repairing a few of the less broken ones."

Asger grunted. "You've talked to Ishii, right?"

"No, he hasn't commed me."

Actually, the comm light had been flashing when Casmir had first walked onto the bridge. It had been Ishii. And Casmir hadn't answered or commed back. He hadn't even looked at the message.

"Really? He messaged me personally earlier, asking for an update. I was busy fighting at the time. Now, he's not answering. He and the other captains must still be busy dealing with Rache's cursed warship. Hopefully, once Rache wakes up and comms the *Fedallah* to pick him up, it'll break off. Or, even better, the warships could just defeat it. That would be nice. They've got the mercs outnumbered. Even if they were damaged fighting this astroshaman ship, they should be able to take down the *Fedallah*. Especially considering Rache wasn't on the bridge for the battle."

The fact that Asger could communicate so easily with Ishii was another reason Casmir had to relocate the ship without his knowledge. Easier said than done.

"Yes. And since Rache didn't get the cargo—" Casmir waved in the direction of the hold, "—he won't have a reason to keep fighting to reach the gate. With luck, he'll give up for now and disappear back into the ether to lick his wounds."

"I hope he *has* some wounds." Asger rotated his shoulder, grimaced, and gripped it. "I also hope to never face him in battle again. He *had* to have had some knight training at some point. He knew exactly how to fight someone with a pertundo."

"He does have that Kingdom accent." Casmir smiled, though mostly, he added another piece to the puzzle that was Rache.

"Yes… Have we reached the point yet where you're going to explain to me why you didn't let me get rid of the Kingdom's most hated enemy?"

Casmir had promised to explain, even though he hadn't been sure then how he would, and he wasn't sure now. "Not yet. First, it's time for some medical treatment."

He pushed himself to his feet and headed for the medical kit, willing his hand to be steady as he reached for the jet injector he had prepared. He glanced toward the doorway to make sure Zee was where he'd left him, in case Asger twigged to this and fought him. Yes, the crusher loomed by the door, watching attentively.

"I just need to get back to Odin and spend a couple of days in a regeneration tank," Asger murmured, his eyes closed.

"Unfortunately, that's not all you'll need." Casmir stopped in front of him. "I appreciate you staying aboard to help me—I'm not exaggerating when I say that even with all those robots, Rache and his mercs would have come out on top if you hadn't jumped in—but there was a reason I wanted you to go."

"The disease from the gate."

Not a disease, it sounded like, but Casmir nodded.

"Which you were willing to expose yourself to in order to stop Rache from getting the gate," Asger said.

Guilt stomped all over Casmir's soul. It was possible he'd exposed himself, but he'd definitely believed he might be immune. However, he couldn't explain that without explaining his link to Rache.

"I couldn't let you die doing something heroic—this wasn't even your battle—while I ran off with my tail between my legs. That's why I told the—that woman—to leave without me. She wanted to stay too." Asger smiled slightly. "You seem to inspire loyalty in people who don't know you that well."

"That goes away once they know me better and find my quirks annoying instead of charming."

Asger snorted, but then his gaze strayed to the jet injector. "Are you going to test my blood to see if I have it?"

"I'm just assuming you do since everybody gets it. I spoke to my medical researcher friend, Kim, the one Rache kidnapped to start working on a cure, and we're going to have to go meet up with her on that research ship if we want solid treatment. But this is supposed to slow down the rate of the cellular damage." Casmir lifted the injector and tried to look honest and sincere. He'd looked up the name of a drug that was used in radiation treatment, and he was ready if Asger asked.

"Did you already dose yourself?" was what Asger asked.

"After I verified the gate was in the hold, yes." Lies, lies, lies. Why did it bother him so much to lie? He'd never been great at it, but something about this seemed particularly heinous. As if lying to a knight was the equivalent of lying to a rabbi. "I guess we'll find out how much it's been helping when we reach the research ship."

"We need to hand over the gate to Ishii and the other captains first," Asger said, "but that mercenary shuttle should have enough juice to get us back to Skadi."

Casmir nodded. "Of course. That will be perfect. Ready?"

"Yes." Asger tilted his head and pushed his hair back to reveal the side of his neck.

Casmir grimaced, though it was what he'd come to expect from people wandering around in battle gear. Knight liquid armor wasn't as bulky as typical combat armor, but it was probably just as tedious to remove.

He pressed the injector to the side of Asger's neck, appreciating the show of trust but also hating that he was betraying it. Yes, only for a short period of time, and only because he wasn't sure handing the gate to Jager was the right thing to do, but who was he to make that decision? As Asger had pointed out, this wasn't even his battle. It was chance that had brought him this way, a suggestion that the military would help him recover Kim if he helped them.

But she had recovered herself—he would have to ask her for the details on that—and he... had searched the network for news of that station attack Rache had brought up. And found it. The crushers hadn't been mentioned specifically, but he'd found a video clip with two of them stalking through the corridors, chasing down what had looked like the local police.

It mortified him to think that his king might be secretly making war on other nations. Or, more likely, picking on small stations in an attempt to bully them into joining his side. Casmir had always hated bullies, and if King Jager now fell into that category...

"You sure you've got the right drug?" Asger smirked at the long delay.

"Yes. Sorry." Casmir blushed and pressed the button, eliciting a soft hiss as the injector delivered the measured dose of tranquilizer. "I'm not that experienced at giving people shots."

He started to back away, but Asger gripped his arm.

Fresh fear chilled Casmir's blood. Had Asger already sensed the betrayal?

"I helped you because the queen assigned me to protect you," Asger said, meeting his eyes, "and because I thought you might be the man to beat Rache. I was glad to be right, glad you made good on your word and came and helped keep him from getting the gate. And kept the shamans—their robots—from getting it out of our system. You're crafty. I thought, if I was guessing right, you would be. That you *had* to be."

Casmir felt like a heel since Asger was praising him and he was in the middle of betraying him, but he was bewildered and intensely curious about where this was going.

"Oh?" he prompted. "Why is that?"

"Just something I overheard the queen say." Asger smiled blearily and yawned.

Casmir's heart sank. Was the tranquilizer kicking in already? He would have waited to deliver it if he'd known Asger planned to divulge deep secrets.

"What did she say?" Casmir asked. "Does she—do you know where I came from?"

The comm panel flashed again—Ishii wanting to ask where the gate and the cargo ship had gone, no doubt. Casmir shifted his position so Asger wouldn't see it.

"Just a hunch," Asger mumbled sleepily. He yawned again, and this time, his eyes closed.

"Asger." Casmir patted the side of his head. "You can take a nap in a minute, but can you *please* explain your hunch to me first?"

Asger's head lolled to the side, and the even breathing of sleep overtook him.

Casmir groaned and stepped back. He told himself that the tranquilizer would wear off in eight hours, and he could ask Asger to explain then. *If* Asger was still talking to him. Unfortunately, he didn't know if that would be the case.

CHAPTER 18

T HE STOLEN MERCENARY SHUTTLE WAS JETTING AWAY FROM Modi Moon, one of Saga's many natural satellites, when a faint groan came from the rear row of seats. Casmir dimmed the navigation display and wiped everything that would have shown their route and where they'd come from off the control console.

That sound signified Asger waking up, and Casmir worried about how he would react once he recovered from a drug-induced hangover and figured out what was going on. Casmir had tranquilized him again when the first round had worn off, realizing he needed more time to hide the cargo ship. He'd been in the middle of programming navigation instructions into its navigation system and a routine for it to follow for the next two years, if need be. At that point, it would run out of fuel, and its orbit would decay, but he thought he could resolve the gate situation, one way or another, before then.

Now, they were hours away from the stealthed cargo ship, flying in Rache's shuttle, which thankfully had an excellent auto-piloting system. A good thing, because Casmir had almost crashed twice getting it out of the cargo ship's bay. He wasn't sure, however, if the autopilot would be able to dock with the *Machu Picchu.* Casmir hoped Asger would handle it, since it seemed like the kind of thing that would require excellent depth perception.

Asger groaned again.

Casmir walked slowly to his spot on the bank of seats, his magnetic boots required now that they were back on a small craft without spin gravity. He'd harnessed Asger into the seats as well as he could, but he'd wondered if locking the powerful knight in the lav—the small bullet-shaped shuttle didn't have a brig—would have been wiser, at least until he promised cooperation, or a lack of antagonistic behavior. But he suspected Asger had the power to break down a lav hatch.

Casmir risked sitting next to him as his eyes opened, bewildered at first as they focused on him. They stayed bewildered as he lifted his head and glanced around.

"Are we in Rache's shuttle?" Asger asked.

"Yes. Since Qin went back to the *Dragon* with yours, it was the only option."

"What happened to the cargo ship?" Asger's brow furrowed as his gaze locked on to Casmir again. His eyes slowly narrowed into a suspicious squint. "That injection you gave me… It wasn't for radiation, was it?"

"No, but I have had time to talk to Kim, and she's optimistic that she can help you when we get to the *Machu Picchu*. Help *us*." Casmir didn't know how to test his own blood for signs of cellular damage, so he still didn't know if he was immune or not. He didn't think he had any symptoms, but he also didn't know how long they took to show up.

Sweat dampened Asger's brow, and his skin had felt hot when Casmir checked him earlier, but he didn't know if that was a side-effect of being tranquilized twice or a sign that his body was deteriorating.

"You knocked me out," Asger said. "Why?"

He didn't sound angry—yet—but maybe because he was trying to figure out what was going on. The anger might come, and Casmir lamented that. He'd never dreamed of having a knight for an ally—for a protector—and he fully acknowledged that Asger had saved his butt.

"It's mostly luck rather than a premeditated plan that I ended up with the cargo ship and with the gate," Casmir said, "but the more I thought about it, the more I realized I wanted to talk to somebody, a neutral third party if possible, before handing it over to the military. To King *Jager*." Casmir assumed they were one and the same. The military served the king. Jager might not know everything they did, but Casmir suspected he'd heard about the gate and given orders to retrieve it. He also suspected that when those crushers had been sent in to subdue that station… he'd known about it. "I've always considered myself a loyal subject," Casmir added as he watched Asger's eyes cloud over, "and it's not my intention to do anything that could harm Odin or the Kingdom, but I'm not sure yet that I believe King Jager is the ideal keeper for the greatest technology our people have ever known."

"That's not your decision to make. You just admitted that it was nothing but luck that put you on that ship."

"Maybe not *nothing* but luck," Casmir murmured.

"You're a *math* teacher. You don't get to pass judgment on the king or decide if he's good enough for something you essentially stole."

"No, the astroshamans stole it. I—we—recovered it. I just haven't decided yet when and to whom I'm going to turn it in. I *will* turn it in. Gates aren't my field of study, so it's of limited interest to me. You know, as a math teacher."

"Where's the ship?"

"Somewhere safe."

"You *hid* it?" Asger tried to lurch upright, but the seat straps caught him. He snarled and unbuckled them, so he could sit up.

Casmir made himself stay in place, fighting the urge to skitter back. "I'd already re-engaged the stealth generator so Rache's people couldn't find it again. After I sent them off in their escape pods, I put it on a different course. One I'll share as soon as I've talked to a few people."

"What people? What neutral third party could you possibly have in mind?" Asger gripped the seat to keep himself from floating off it—or maybe to keep himself from throttling Casmir.

Kim, for starters, Casmir thought. He wanted to get her opinion, but also… "If it's possible to repair her body and her chip wasn't too damaged, Professor Erin Kelsey-Sato."

Asger gave him a blank look.

"A loaded droid and one of the archaeologists who was down there and found the gate. Since her body isn't human anymore, she's probably the only person left alive from that team. I'd like to hear her thoughts as one of the scientists who was presumably involved in discovering it."

"Scientists? Scientists serve the Kingdom." Asger scowled at him. "Like knights. And math teachers. They don't judge the king."

Casmir smiled sadly. "It's robotics."

Asger groaned and dropped his face into his hands.

For a moment, Casmir wanted nothing more than to turn the gate over to Asger and go home, back to his old, comfortable life. Back to being respected by his peers and working on projects he loved. Back to being roommates with Kim and debating over the grocery list rather than having their lives threatened at every turn.

But even if that was an option, could he do it? Could he ignore the rest of humanity now that he knew Jager was using his crushers on other systems and that war might come to Odin one day?

"Dabrowski," Asger started, sounding like he was trying but failing to be patient.

"I understand your frustration and that you've sworn an oath to the king. And you're correct. I don't have any right to do this, but I feel strongly about it, that maybe it's worth my career, if not my life, to make sure I don't make a mistake—*another* mistake—that could affect the lives of people throughout the systems. I *am* sorry I blindsided you. You don't deserve that, but I knew you'd be loyal to the king—and rightfully so. I wasn't sure you would allow yourself to contemplate morality if it might go against his wishes."

"I *always* contemplate the morality of my actions," Asger said stiffly.

"Good. I'm glad. But I think it's better this way. You don't have to contemplate anything. You were unconscious, and you don't know where the gate ship is, so when the king asks, you can't be found at fault."

"I can be found at fault for not strangling you."

"Ah. Yes, I suppose that could be problematic, although…" Casmir cleared his throat and pointed to where Zee stood by a wall, along with the ten security robots that had been in good enough condition to bring along.

"Are you suggesting that your robots will stop me if I attempt to strangle you?"

"Zee will. I'm not sure about the others yet. I haven't had time to teach them about how delightful and worthy of protection I am."

Asger flopped back against the seat, looking more frazzled and irritated than delighted. "I took a chance in helping you get off Ishii's ship. There will be repercussions, especially now. If you'd saved the day and handed the gate over to the military, maybe my actions would have been overlooked." He looked at the porthole.

"I didn't *not* save the day," Casmir offered. "We kept Rache from flying to another system and handing the gate over to someone else."

"There's not going to be any proof of that, especially if the mercenaries ended up getting away."

"If you get kicked out of the knights, you can come work for me. As a teacher's assistant. The cafeteria food isn't bad, and there's a nice gym on campus. You can fall back on your bodybuilding career."

"*You* aren't going to be able to step foot back on Odin. If the Black Stars terrorists don't get you, the king will have knights waiting to wring your neck until you share the location of the gate." Asger shook his head. "You should talk to *him*, not some archaeologist."

Casmir hesitated. He hadn't considered that as an option. If it was possible, would it be worth it? He definitely wanted to talk to Kim's mother, but... how better to gauge Jager's plans and motivations than by speaking directly with him? *If* Jager would be honest with him. That was a big if, though. Who was he, in the eyes of the Kingdom, but a *math* teacher?

"Do you think you could get me a meeting with him?" Casmir asked.

"Probably."

"Do you think he would actually speak to me instead of sending me down to some dungeon to be interrogated?" Casmir had never been inside the castle, but it supposedly dated back to the arrival of the original colony ships, and it had been quarried from the local limestone. He was positive an old stone castle had to have a dungeon.

"Probably... not," Asger admitted.

"Given how my last encounter with truth drugs went, I'm not eager to volunteer for interrogation again."

Asger sighed and reached into his cloak. He patted around before pulling his book out of some inner pocket, the corner burned off as if an energy bolt had blasted it. It probably had.

Casmir watched as he leaned forward, his elbows on his knees, and studied the book. Did that mean the conversation was over? Asger was looking at the cover, not opening it to read. *Either/Or.* Søren Kierkegaard.

Casmir tried to dredge the name from his memory. Some Old Earth philosopher? Kim would know, he was certain.

"You may not believe it," Asger said, rubbing his thumb along the spine, "but I contemplate ethics and morality a lot, and how I can navigate between my loyalty to the crown and what's the right thing to do as a human being. Sometimes they're the same, and sometimes I'm not certain they are."

"Of course." Casmir nodded, encouraged by this thoughtfulness—and the fact that Asger wasn't trying to strangle him. "Why wouldn't I believe that?"

"Because I'm a bodybuilder on posters and cards and calendars. I think there's even a puzzle." Asger waved a dismissive hand. "I don't pay that much attention. My agent just sends me my cut."

"So pretty people with muscles can't contemplate ethics?"

"Not according to most people." He snorted. "Only the queen…" His gaze grew less focused as he trailed off.

Casmir raised his eyebrows, waiting.

After a moment, Asger looked at him. "If I could get you an audience with *her*, would you go? I think… I think she wouldn't throw you in the dungeon."

"Ah, so there *is* a dungeon. I knew it."

"Of course. What kind of castle doesn't have a dungeon?" Asger smiled but fleetingly. He kept watching Casmir, his eyes intent.

"I'm not sure about the logistics of getting in to see the queen without the king finding out and throwing me in that dungeon, but I will trust you if you're willing to set it up." Casmir admitted that there probably wasn't anyone in the universe that he wanted to speak with more than the queen right now. She seemed to know who he was, and he wagered she knew more about him than Rache did. Would she tell him? That was the question. He would have to do his best to charm her.

"You have my word," Asger said. "I'll take you to see her, and I'll do my best to keep you from getting captured prematurely by anyone else."

"Will flex-cuffs be involved?"

"If that crusher wasn't looming over there, you'd already be cuffed and locked in the lavatory."

"That's where I was thinking of locking *you*. I noticed the lack of a brig."

Asger snorted softly. He was still watching and waiting for an answer. A confirmation.

Casmir had a feeling Asger hoped he would hand the location of the gate over to the queen once he met her, but he hadn't made him promise to do so. That was a relief. Casmir wanted the queen to be someone good whom he could trust, and he even hoped to find that Jager hadn't known about the crushers and wasn't behind these encroachments by the Kingdom into other systems, but he didn't want to walk into a meeting feeling obligated to hand over the gate, lest he learn something… unappealing.

He just hoped he wasn't being naive in believing Asger could get him in to see the queen without castle security finding out and arresting him.

Even if he was being naive, didn't he have to take this chance? Not only to learn more about the king and queen and their motives, but to learn about himself? About who he really was and where he'd come from?

Casmir nodded. "Excellent, then it's decided. We get all fixed up—I hope—on the *Machu Picchu*, and then it's back to Odin to speak with the queen. While dodging terrorists who still want me dead for some reason. I wonder if I could get an audience with *them*. Then we could chat about our differences."

Asger laughed. "You would do that, wouldn't you?"

"My odds are generally better in a chat than in a gunfight."

Asger looked to the robots. "I don't know about that."

"It does help if large hulking metal constructs are willing to stand in the way of the bullets."

"Or knights?"

"You do hulk well."

"I know. Two of the calendar photos involve that."

Casmir thought about asking if nudity had been involved but decided he didn't want to know.

The comm beeped, and Casmir maneuvered back to the pilot's seat. His first feeling was dread, expecting it to be Captain Ishii. Even though they weren't near the gate anymore, Rache's shuttle lacked the slydar-covered hull of the *Fedallah*, so if the warships were looking for other ships in the system, it was feasible they would find it. Would they assume Rache's men piloted it, rather than a rogue roboticist?

But the familiar *Stellar Dragon* identification popped up, so Casmir answered.

"This is Laser Lopez, hoping the robot whisperer is alive and aboard that shuttle, over."

Casmir wondered how she had guessed that he was in charge instead of Rache's people. Maybe it was a simple hope? He glanced at the collection of robots lined up in the passenger area.

"I think that term applies to taming animals, Captain Laser. The Robot Programmer would be more apt."

"If you've ever had eight automated vacuums try to slurp up your socks as you're putting them on, you would agree that robots are more akin to animals than computers."

"It's possible the vacuums need a calibration."

"*Possible*? It's a certainty. Are you coming back on board?"

Casmir brought up the scanner display, checking to see if the *Dragon* was nearby.

The answer was yes. They were also on their way to the *Machu Picchu*.

Casmir looked over his shoulder, but Asger had flopped back onto the seats, perhaps still feeling the effects of the tranquilizers—or the early effects of the illness.

"I'm without a pilot at the moment," Casmir said, "so maybe we better meet at the *Machu Picchu*. Qin should see Kim, to have her blood checked."

"So I understand," Bonita said, grimness replacing the humor in her voice.

He regretted that. He much preferred humor. How many people had died or would die because of the gate? The radiation threat was another good reason to keep it hidden a while longer. Maybe Kim would be able to advise on a good way to protect the next research crew from it.

"We'll meet you there," Bonita added. Then her tone turned dry again. "Though you're going to have to dock that shuttle eventually. Unless you're planning to spacewalk to the research ship."

"I'm hoping my pilot will feel better by then. Otherwise, someone will have to put out a ball on a stick for me."

"We'll figure something out. Glad to hear you're alive. Viggo was worried about you."

"I appreciate the sentiment."

CHAPTER 19

KIM WAS EXHAUSTED BY THE TIME THE *STELLAR DRAGON* and one of Rache's shuttles docked. A shuttle that Casmir had stolen after somehow defeating Rache. Apparently, a squad of robots had been involved. She'd only shaken her head in bemusement when she'd read his version of events.

Rache was a wrecking ball who'd managed to smash into both their lives this week. Kim had a feeling she would have to use her favor, should he see fit to redeem it, to keep her best friend alive. She had no trouble imagining Rache's icy rage, perhaps less over the loss of the shuttle and more over his defeat at Casmir's hands. It was unfortunate that the Kingdom Fleet didn't owe her any favors, because Casmir had to have irked that Captain Ishii too.

Whatever had truly happened out there, she was glad Casmir had survived. She had been as worried for him as she had been for herself, and she jogged out of her lab to greet him.

Casmir rounded a bend on the way to sickbay, grinning and waving enthusiastically when he spotted her. Zee strode around the bend right on his heels, which Kim expected by now, but the rest of the robots, each a hulking dark gray construct with a cannon-like left arm, startled her. She'd assumed he had left them behind on the other ship.

He broke into a run, arms spreading wide, but he paused before he pounced on her with a hug. "I know we've agreed that touching is wholly unnecessary in a platonic relationship, but since these are extenuating circumstances, will you—"

Kim stepped forward and hugged him. *We've agreed*, he'd said, but she knew he was a hugger and only abstained out of respect for her boundaries. Which she appreciated—more so than ever after enduring the handsy Dr. Angelico—but they'd both looked death in its ugly slavering maw this week. Hugs seemed appropriate.

"Excellent," Casmir said, squeezing her and thumping her on the back. "I'm so glad you're all right." He stepped back while leaving a hand on her shoulder and squinting into her eyes. "You *are* all right… right?"

"I'm fine now."

"*Now?*" His eyebrows rose.

Worried she had insinuated that Rache had been worse than he had been, she clarified. "Now that the bacteria have consumed the pseudo radiation in my body. The kidnapping itself was largely a non-event for me, other than getting me exposed to more of it more quickly. But I've undergone the cryogenic revival, and my cellular function is improving. With luck, I'll be back to my biological age soon. Or even younger."

Casmir grinned and released her, seeming relieved and also to accept her words at face value. "Don't let it make you too young. You know how hard it is to be treated seriously in academia if you don't have a few gray hairs."

"True." Kim waved him toward sickbay. "Let me take a blood sample and see if you're immune or if you need treatment. And then, if you don't mind—"

"I'll look at your mother's damage and see if I can repair it."

She nodded with relief. "Thank you."

"I actually want to talk to her and get her opinion on who should and shouldn't be involved in researching the gate, so I'm crossing my fingers for more reasons than one. I have… Well, it's a long story. But it won't be safe for me to stay here for long. Captain Ishii will be back for his doctors soon, and I don't want to be here when he arrives. Do you want to return to Odin with me? I've decided I must confront my enemies there—I'm hoping it'll help that Asger was able to give me a name of the organization. He also says he can get me an audience with the queen, ideally one where I'm not thrown into the castle dungeon and interrogated at any point."

"Confronting enemies and an audience with the queen. Oh good. I was worried our lives would get back to normal and how tedious that would be."

"I sense sarcasm from you."

"You do have that gift for reading people." Kim eyed what had gone from one crusher to a total of eleven robots as his troop followed them into sickbay. "Are you keeping all of those?"

"Possibly for now. It's good to have allies."

"I imagine so."

"My new human ally should be along soon—Asger—and I can introduce you. And Qin will be coming for treatment too. They probably won't come together, since they tried to kill each other when they were on the same ship, but they were both exposed to the gate. Especially Asger. He was in the cargo hold, fighting Rache's men with me, close enough to the gate to lick it."

Kim pulled Casmir into the lab she'd claimed as her own and drew a blood sample. While she analyzed it, he poked his head into the other labs and also the now-empty quarantine chamber.

"The people who were in there were safe, you said?" Casmir asked. "Because of a magnetic field someone threw together?"

"It's possible there's another explanation, but that seems a plausible one. Glasnax alone wasn't enough to protect anyone."

"I'll keep that in mind in case I find myself in the position to advise people on the gate."

"Where *is* the gate?" she asked.

He'd been extremely vague on that.

"Safely hidden." Casmir winked.

Kim checked the microscope and also the results that came up on the computer display, then turned around, folded her arms over her chest, and leaned against the counter. "You're fine, Casmir."

"Naturally." He wriggled his eyebrows at her. "But am I immune?"

"Just like Rache, yes."

His amused expression turned to one of distaste.

"I'm sorry. I know you don't want to be compared to him, but in this case, it's a good thing." Kim waved toward the slide.

"Right. You implied that you figured out *why* we're immune."

"Well, I've come up with a hypothesis. To make gains at proving it, I'd have to test more people who weren't genetically altered to grant immunity to the Great Plague, and I don't even know where I'd look for qualifying subjects. That disease spread faster than the speed of light through the Twelve Systems, and those who weren't altered *died*, so to find people alive who don't now have that induced mutation in their mitochondria…" She spread a hand. "Regardless, I believe that, as you suggested, our pseudo radiation wasn't naturally occurring but was man—or machine—made. And that it was employed as a defensive attack against anyone who tried to take the gate who wasn't human. But humans today are a little different than they were thousands of years ago when that ship left Earth—assuming we learn the gates did indeed come from there."

Casmir nodded. "We're still without proof of alien intelligence in the galaxy, so that's a reasonable assumption."

"It's not that humans have experienced that many generations or evolved significantly in a mere two thousand years, but we have adapted to our new environments, in some cases even drawing from them. There have been substantial changes of the types and amounts of bacteria within us, for example, but since you and Rache are immune, I suspect it was the change we chose to give to our mitochondria in order to survive the plague virus that altered our humanity, at least in the eyes of that ancient technology. My guess is that whoever—or whatever—programmed the security system realized it would be faster to read the DNA base pairs in our mitochondria than to sequence the entire human genome. How it does that without taking blood samples, I don't know, but if they had the technology to build the gates, they were presumably more advanced across the board than we are now. And then, if the security system didn't get the precise match it wanted, it would assume a non-human being was trying to make off with the gate and attack. I don't know how mutations would have been handled. Maybe a certain number of them were factored in, but the changes we made for the plague were simply too much."

"The alteration didn't intrinsically change anything about what it means to be human, though, right?"

"No. We actually have a lot of genes that you can tinker with without fundamentally changing how our brains work." Kim thought of Qin and wondered if she would represent any challenges insofar as her bacteria were concerned. She would have to make sure to start her on the treatment right away so she could monitor her here in these state-of-the-art labs rather than on the *Dragon* or whatever craft Casmir planned to take back to Odin. "If this security system is something integrated into all of the gates, it's a good thing that none of our ancestors ever tried to disassemble one and take it home."

Casmir dropped his chin in his hand. "This is all interesting, and it makes me wonder if our Earth ancestors believed there *is* intelligent alien life somewhere in the galaxy, but being the self-absorbed person I am, I can't help but wonder how Rache and I avoided having this alteration."

Kim gazed at him, wondering if she should share her hypothesis on that, or if he would find the connotations disturbing. It wasn't as if she could truly know, and she might distress him for no reason. Or he might take it in stride. For a Kingdom man, he was fairly enlightened. He'd never found the circumstances of *her* birth that alarming.

"You know?" Casmir was watching her face. "Do you think we were... made in a lab, or something?"

"From a DNA sample more than two hundred years old, yes. From before the Great Plague. Rache knows. He more or less confirmed that he's from, ah, old stock, I guess you would say."

"*Who?*" He stared at her, his brow furrowed. "Some old dead guy from Earth? One of the first colonists, or something?"

"Rache didn't say."

"Kim... I." Casmir rubbed his face—hard. "I don't even know what to say. That's mashugana. Who would intentionally create someone like *me* more than once?" He waved at his own body, probably indicating the various medical issues he had. "Even if it seemed like a good idea to make a—a—robot whisperer, as Laser called me, then why fix Rache after he was born and not me?" He started pacing, hands jerking in frustration. "What, was I the byproduct? An extra to keep around just in case? I wouldn't even be good for spare parts. Who wants a brain prone to seizures?"

Kim lifted placating hands, wishing she hadn't said anything. Maybe she had misunderstood Rache. Maybe she was wrong about it all.

"Easy, Casmir, or I'm going to have to get you a paper bag to breathe into." She stepped in front of him to stop his pacing and patted him on the shoulder, wishing she weren't so clumsy at comforting people.

"We're in a sickbay full of advanced laboratories and medical equipment, and you're offering me a paper bag?"

"You want a sedative?"

"Maybe a few shots of vodka." Casmir looked around for somewhere to sit, but he eschewed her cot and sank down on the deck against the wall. "Sir Asger said the queen sent Sir Friedrich, the knight who was killed by the crushers in the parking garage, to warn me to get off the world, and that she later sent *him* to protect me. From some terrorists called the Black Stars who want me dead because of something I might do in the future. That's *his* hypothesis. I thought he was wrong, that it must have to do with the crushers, but he seemed doubtful."

"Did you get a chance to talk to Rache?"

Casmir snorted. "Not about his home life and where he came from, like you suggested. He was busy threatening me and making demands." Casmir hesitated. "He actually did offer to tell me things about myself... if I agreed to come work for him."

Kim stared at him. "As a mercenary?"

"I guess. I think he was impressed by how many times he'd utterly defeated Zee, only to have him keep showing up. He wanted me to make him a crusher army of his own. Of course, I couldn't say anything but no, especially when he'd just kidnapped *you*, but a part of me wishes there had been a way to play along, if only for a while... Long enough to find out what he knows."

"I have a feeling that would have been a Faustian deal that you would have regretted."

"Oh, I have no doubt." Casmir leaned his head back against the wall.

"You don't need him. I think the answers are back on Odin. You said you're getting an audience with the queen?"

"Sir Asger said he would try to set something up. I... hope I can trust him. I did tranquilize him. Twice."

"You left that out of the messages you sent me."

"Did I? Huh."

Kim shook her head slowly. She hoped Casmir wasn't going home to a trap. Especially when she planned to return with him.

"The queen has the answers," Casmir murmured. "She must. She's the one who set all of this in motion. I just have to convince her to tell me. Without being shot or thrown into a dungeon along the way. That's doable, right?"

His eyes had an uncharacteristically bleak cast when they met hers.

"I hope so, Casmir," Kim murmured. "I hope so."

Kim wanted to stand and look over Casmir's shoulder while he reassembled her mother's droid body and attempted to fix her damaged circuitry and chips, but maybe it was better that there were more treatments to give and two new people who needed the bacteria injection. She'd been told that the *Machu Picchu's* scanners had picked up Captain Ishii's warship leaving the gate and heading their way, so neither of them had time for distractions.

"Are you sure this will work with my body?" Qin asked, clasping and unclasping her hands, as Kim prepared a dose. "And not kill me? You may not have noticed, but I'm not entirely human." She held up one of her clawed fingers.

"It didn't escape my notice. I've run a few tests from the blood sample you gave me earlier, and I think you'll be fine." Kim smiled, though she felt leery at injecting her new strain directly into people— there should have been *years* of testing first—but when the alternative was letting someone die… she had little choice. "The original bacteria was tested on rats, cats, and dogs without ill effects, and this new change just slightly adapts its preferred energy source."

"Good." Qin nodded, but she continued to pace back and forth, her six-foot-plus frame making the lab seem cramped.

Kim thought it might be good to distract her. "Are you and the captain leaving the system next? Or sticking around?"

"I'm not sure yet. Casmir gave the captain some sort of schematic patent… *thing*, and she's afraid the only place she can sell it is Odin. Or maybe that's the only place Casmir has the connections to get someone to buy it. I'm a little fuzzy on what exactly their deal was."

"Well, we're planning to head that way soon. Before the Fleet comes back here to retrieve its doctors. I think Casmir's knight offered to give us a ride back to Odin, but I'm not sure we can trust he won't deliver Casmir to the Kingdom Guard as soon as we land. Do you think Captain Lopez would be willing to transport us? If you're going that way anyway?" Kim pressed the jet injector to Qin's lightly furred arm.

"Casmir's *knight* tried to kill me the first day we met."

"Sir Asger?"

"He called me a freak and blamed me for something someone else did. Someone who looked like me, I guess." Her lip curled. "He just assumed it was me, that I'd been there. He labeled me an enemy before I'd even said a word."

"Ah." Kim decided she should have left negotiating for transportation to Casmir. She also decided she shouldn't refer to the knight as Casmir's, not if Qin loathed him. "I'm sorry."

"I hope his balls wither up and fall in the toilet and get flushed out into space where they're sucked into a black hole."

"That sounds unpleasant."

"*Good.*"

Kim set the jet injector aside. "Your next stop needs to be the cryonics lab, two levels up. Dr. Sikou will be waiting for you." She hoped Sir Asger had already finished up so Qin wouldn't run into him. He was in too weakened a state to risk losing his manhood to a black hole. "I'm going to check on Casmir's progress with my mother, but comm me if you feel strange. You shouldn't, but take a nap after the treatment. It's tiring for the body to rejuvenate itself."

"All right. Kim…?"

Kim paused in the doorway. "Yes?"

"Do you think there are any friendlier knights on Odin? Or are they all… jerks?"

"Uh." Kim had no idea how to give advice on romance—she wasn't even sure if that was what this was about. "I'm sure you can find someone who thinks you're wonderful. I don't know if he will be a knight. You might want to cast a wider net."

And look beyond Odin, Kim thought silently—and sadly.

"I guess," Qin said. "Thanks."

Kim found Casmir in a laboratory near engineering, her mother's droid body on a work table, already reassembled with wires running to an open access panel. Toolboxes and meters sprawled across the counters, and he had a schematic up on one display while he ran tests, sure fingers shifting competently from one tool and task to the next, almost eerily efficient. As she watched—he didn't seem to notice her arrival—he performed repairs on a memory chip with the easy precision of a surgeon.

She couldn't guess whose DNA he might have been cloned from, but she had an easier time imagining the scenario than he did. He was gifted at his profession, and if anything, the medical issues had probably helped keep him humble all of his life. Rache could use some of that humbleness.

After Casmir slipped the repaired chip back into the droid head, he touched something just inside the access panel. Her mother sat up abruptly, eyes opening.

Casmir breathed a soft "Ha!" and stepped back.

Kim gripped the doorjamb.

Would her mother retain her memory? Or had it all been wiped? If it had… Kim had no idea if she had a backup in some storage center on Odin. They'd had so few conversations since she'd reached adulthood. Kim barely knew anything about her mother or what she'd been doing for the last ten years. It had been a mistake on her part to get so wrapped up in her work that she didn't take the time to communicate. Even if her mother was the same way. Kim should have made the effort.

"Ms. Erin Kelsey-Sato," Casmir said. "Do you remember anything?"

Kim's mother looked up at him. "You are Casmir Dabrowski. You've visited my apartment in Zamek three times, and you've never been able to remember to use a coaster. I had to clean sticky rings off my coffee table."

Casmir's eyebrows drifted upward, but then he grinned. He noticed Kim standing in the doorway and waved her in.

"Your mother remembers me," he reported.

"Fondly, I see."

"Accurately, anyway." His brow creased, and he looked a little embarrassed. "I get intimidated and nervous sometimes meeting notable people, and I forget my manners."

"You leave drink rings on the coffee table at our house too. That grape fizzop stains."

"Oh? I'll work on that." Casmir smiled and backed away to pack up some tools.

Kim took a deep breath, feeling nervous herself as she came around the table to face the only mother she'd ever known in the only body she'd ever known. She'd seen photographs of her mother as a human, pale-skinned and blue-eyed, and had often struggled to find herself in that face. She'd always thought she looked a lot more like her darker-skinned and darker-eyed half-brothers, but her father had often noted that they were similar in other ways.

"I'm glad you're in working order, Mother." Kim winced at how formally her words came out, but they'd always been formal with each other, and she didn't know how to be anything else. "We're on the *Machu Picchu*. We found you outside on Skadi Moon next to the wreck that had held the gate. It was gone by the time we got there."

Kim wasn't sure why she was including herself in the *we* of Rache and his people. As if they had been a cheerful team working together. It was easier, she supposed, not to explain the story of how she'd been kidnapped by pirates. Besides, it seemed a failing to have allowed that to happen, and she was reluctant to admit to it.

"Outside?"

"Buried in snow drifts. In pieces."

"Yes…" Her mother looked to the schematic on the display, a schematic of *her* body. "I suppose I'm not surprised that those miscreant astroshamans tore me to pieces. They've all the power of androids, all the manners of animals. The others—my team—got away before they showed up and headed up to the ship to comm the military and show a piece of the gate to the crew up here. Did they make it, do you know? I tried to delay the astroshamans, to keep them from going after the others, but I had no weapons or the inclination to use them. I suppose they're the ones who got the gate." She tilted her head. "What are you doing here, Kim?"

"It's a long story," she said, finding herself echoing Casmir's earlier words.

When she looked up and met his eyes, he raised his brows and pointed toward the doorway, silently asking if he should leave.

Kim shook her head. They didn't have much time, and Casmir had mentioned wanting to ask her mother some questions.

"I'm afraid… We don't believe the rest of your team made it," Kim said. "Also some of the crew here passed on. Some of the scientists successfully quarantined themselves and can likely answer any more questions you have."

"I see." Her voice sounded more android than human, devoid of emotion, but Kim had been called a robot more than once in her life, so she didn't know how much of this was an effect of her mother's droid body and how much was just… how they were.

"I'll explain everything I know as soon as I get a chance," Kim said, "but Casmir has a few questions for you. He's the one with the gate. Sort of. I gather he's hidden it and wants advice on what to do next."

Kim nodded at Casmir, inviting him to take over.

"*Hidden* it?" Her mother's droid did not have eyebrows in the human sense, but she could make an impressively surprised face.

"Yes. I didn't want the mercenary Rache to have it, but I also wasn't certain I should just hand it over to the Fleet, and ultimately the king." Casmir came forward and, speaking animatedly and with a lot of hand gestures, relayed the story in his rambling style.

Kim would have been more succinct and used fewer adjectives to describe Rache's dastardliness.

"So, I'm basically wondering what the best course of action is going forward," Casmir said. "I'm afraid I've put myself, and maybe also Kim, in some danger, which would not have been my first choice, but the Kingdom is using some of my prior work to hurt inhabitants of other systems, and I'm a little gun-shy about trusting Jager's military right now."

Kim wondered if Rache had told him about the crushers attacking that station. She hoped Casmir had looked that up and confirmed it for himself.

"The simplest thing to do, and the easiest thing for your career and welfare, would be to hand it over to the military," Kim's mother said.

Casmir nodded. "Yes. Is that what you think I should do?"

"I can't tell you what you should do, but I will admit that I would have been uneasy putting such powerful technology into King Jager's hands. I've been around, in one form or another, since before he took the throne, and I've seen the changes over the last thirty years, the evidence of his ambition. I've traveled to many other systems for my work, and I've heard stories from the denizens there of knights and Kingdom agents quietly going about, taking advantage of the existing discontent out there. I do believe he wants to see the Twelve Systems reunited and back under Kingdom rule, and he wants that to happen in his lifetime. I don't believe he's inherently evil, but he is definitely ambitious and manipulative."

"And am I overblowing the potential importance of discovering this new gate?" Casmir asked. "Could it tip the scales as much as I fear? I know Captain Rache was desperate to make sure that Jager doesn't get it, but he's hardly an unbiased party."

"Rache the pirate? I can imagine." Kim's mother rose on the table and flexed her knees and articulated her arms and rotated her shoulders. Testing her body?

She swished her tail in a circle while looking over her shoulder and nodded, as if pleased it was still there. Not for the first time, Kim wondered what had possessed her mother to choose an animal droid instead of an android body.

"I don't think you're blowing anything out of proportion," her mother said. "With the gate—and the promise that it could be reverse-engineered, replicated, and the gate network extended—that would definitely give King Jager more to build on, as far as establishing his platform and his case with the other governments of the systems. Join the Kingdom, and we'll colonize the entire galaxy—and reap the benefits of its resources."

Casmir appeared morose at the answer. Kim wished her mother had told him to hand over the gate. She had no doubt that the moral concerns were real, but it wasn't their place to judge the king or risk themselves over vagaries. She'd endured enough risks and enough adventures in the past weeks. She wanted her old life back and to return to the work she enjoyed. She wanted to go home.

"Thank you, Ms. Kelsey-Sato. I'm going to—"

Kim's mother held up a hand. "You've already told me more about your plans than you probably should have. If the military shows up here and starts questioning everyone, it would be better for you if nobody knows where you are headed and what your goals are."

"A consideration, to be certain, but I'd think you would be immune to truth drugs." Casmir smiled.

"Unfortunately, I'm not immune to being deactivated and having some overly smart programmer poking around in my head."

Had that happened with the astroshamans? Had they downloaded everything she knew about the gate before tearing her into pieces and hurling her out the hatch? Kim grimaced in sympathy. Even if her mother could no longer feel pain, that couldn't have been a pleasant experience.

"We could add some layers of security to your brain emulator," Casmir offered.

She considered him thoughtfully while fiddling with her tail. "I actually wouldn't mind that. How much time do you have?"

"Enough," he said firmly.

Kim thought of the approaching warships but said nothing.

"Good," her mother said. "I accept your offer."

Casmir nodded and went to work again. Kim's mother spoke to him, asking questions about software, automated security updates, and hardwiring failsafes. Casmir answered with knowledge and enthusiasm that seemed to satisfy her. The robot whisperer, indeed.

Kim stepped out into the corridor, disappointed that she hadn't gotten to catch up more with her mother—and that her mother didn't seem to mind—but telling herself there would be another time.

Casmir had to get off the ship before the military showed up, lest he truly be thrown into a brig cell this time and tortured until he revealed the gate's location. And she… She wasn't sure how much danger she was in now, but she couldn't imagine leaving Casmir to fend for himself. She would help him defeat those terrorists, or at least figure out how to get them off his back.

As she walked back to her lab, she wondered if Yas and Jess and the other mercenaries would rendezvous with Rache and find treatment in time. If they survived, Rache should concede that he owed her a favor. It might have to be simply asking the man not to avenge himself on Casmir, but she hoped she could help Casmir find out whose DNA imprinted his cells.

THE END

The adventure continues in Book 3, *Hero Code*.

Made in the USA
Middletown, DE
22 June 2020